Through the Needle's Eye

Through the Needle's Eye is a moving novel about one child's need for love in a hardscrabble world. Young Jessie tells much of her story herself, and her voice is both gritty and poetic. Linda Bledsoe's novel is an exceptional debut by a very talented writer.

—Ron Rash, *New York Times* bestselling
author of *Serena* and *Above the Waterfall*

Linda Bledsoe's *Through the Needle's Eye* goes deeper into the genre of Appalachian noir fiction than anything I've read to date. One could even say that this book challenges Cormac McCarthy's dark corner of the genre. Told from the perspective of a young girl, this book reads more like memoir than fiction and goes deeper into the human experience and psyche. If this novel by such a talented and honest writer doesn't send chills up your spine yet touch your heart then nothing will. If there were an Oscar for historical literary fiction, Bledsoe and her characters would all be going home as winners.

—Thomas Rain Crowe, author of *Zoro's Field:
My Life in the Appalachian Woods*

Linda Bledsoe portrays her exquisite sight as she peers "through the needle's eye" with Southern Appalachian authentic observations spoken with dialect—constantly stitching together Jessie's mesmerizing journey. A page-turner immediately enfolding you, Bledsoe completes her tapestry documenting "just like it was." This historic preservation of Southern Appalachian culture is imperative.

—Shirley Sparr, Southern Appalachian
off-the-grid homesteader

This novel is not for the faint of heart. Linda Bledsoe has given us an unflinching look at how poverty can ravage a family. Yet I kept being reminded of James Still's *River of Earth* during the telling. A powerful read.

—Wayne Caldwell, author of *Cataloochee*

UNIVERSITY

MERCER UNIVERSITY PRESS

Endowed by

TOM WATSON BROWN
and
THE WATSON-BROWN FOUNDATION, INC.

Through the Needle's Eye

LINDA BLEDSOE

MERCER UNIVERSITY PRESS

Macon, Georgia

1979–2019

40 Years of Publishing Excellence

Through the Needle's Eye is a work of fiction. Names, characters, and incidents are either the products of the author's imagination or used in a fictitious manner. Any resemblance to actual persons, living or dead, or to actual events is completely coincidental.

MUP/ P581

© 2019 by Mercer University Press
Published by Mercer University Press
1501 Mercer University Drive
Macon, Georgia 31207

9 8 7 6 5 4 3 2 1

Books published by Mercer University Press are printed on acid-free paper that meets the requirements of the American National Standard for Information Sciences—Permanence of Paper for Printed Library Materials.

Printed and bound in the United States. .

This book is set in AdobeGaramondPro.

ISBN   978-0-88146-703-1
Cataloging-in-Publication Data is available from the Library of Congress

There is no agony like bearing an untold story within.

—Maya Angelo

Dedication

I dedicate these words back to the Father of Lights, who breathed them onto these pages. May all who read these words be bathed in love and hope and feel what I experience as a peculiar supernatural illumination. I call all readers to become filled with their destiny, to know that the impossible may become possible and find assurance that, through the needle's eye, the potential is there to surge unto magnificent stars. I believe freedom and healing are for everyone, and if they watch and listen, a ray of light during the darkest hour of need will come.

I dedicate this novel to wounded children everywhere. One incident of abusive exploitation is enough for any human to endure. Some agonize over countless terrors, including physical abuse, mental cruelty, and neglect. Some endure outright abandonment and murder. These cruelties most often originate from the hands of family members.

I marvel how we, in such a progressive era, can brilliantly wage great world wars, build massive skyscrapers that withstand earthquakes, and propel human beings into boundless skies and yet, as a society, we barely dare to protect our little ones—a task animals do far better in some cases.

I also devote these pages to "adult children" who have survived horrible denigration. I hope these words will strike a gentle chord so that perhaps you will leave behind a different kind of legacy. Reversing familial patterns and healing one's own wound is a tremendous step toward a better life.

—Linda Bledsoe

Through the Needle's Eye

1

My Scar

My family huddled like dense shadows in the dingy, crowded room. Some sat in ladder-back chairs, others perched on thick coarse chair arms, but mostly they leaned wall-side, whispering in hums. The women clumped together, wadded on one side, ears straining for trouble. A lofty, soot-ridden woodstove stood center-room like an armless black iron-woman. Her red round belly pushed and belched heat onto us, flavored with pine, oak, and hickory. Hotness scorched my clothes brown when I warmed too close. I'd turn front-to-back and back-to-front so as not to burn. Red-cheeked, in awe, I watched her magnificent sweltering glow sprinkle dust mites through the air as I picked at them while warming.

A smoky cigarette stench laid heavy in cloudy swirls above our heads as stifled hocks coughed and sputtered sporadically, throats cleared. Stinky men huddled about telling nasty jokes while spitting tobacco slime into the stovetop's burner. Papa Harkus hunched onto the wall so as not to fall, a loaded whiskey bottle pushing outward from his grimy back pant's pocket during this special holiday visit with my cousins.

"Mama," Deb whined. "He ain't lettin' me have my turn again."

"Now Barney, y'all go on ahead and give Deb and Jessie tha' tricycle. Santa done brung it for Deb. You have your own Santa, Barney. Y'all hear me," Aunt Lizzie said.

"Mama, he ain't listenin'," she whined again.

Aunt Lizzie walked over, full-of-hateful, and grabbed the boy by his arm, jerking him plum off the toy. He staggered angrily, kicking wood ash into the air. Deb, with gouging elbows, shoved him behind us. Then she climbed on her tricycle and circled the room around the heater.

Speechless and excited, I waited for my turn, clapping my hands and then scrunching my dress hem into cottony dents.

Aunt Lizzie helped me onto the shiny red tricycle. Deb placed my feet on the pedals, showed me how to turn the handlebars to go in different directions. After a few jerky starts, off I went like the rest. Laughter and squeals bubbled out of me all over the place. Deb's Santa had made me happy. The parents mumbled as my laughter bounced off the walls, hurting their ears. I rode on squealing.

Then something terrible happened. The handlebars slipped from my hands. My lower leg landed smack against the heater. Skin stuck onto red iron. My screeches turned to silence.

And then out of nothingness, "My leg, my leg. My leg. It hurts. It hurts so bad." Cries spewed from me. My ears grated as iron scraped iron—a man lifted a hotplate from the stove's head and spat. Spittle sizzled, sputtered off the top, steaming with smoke as it wiggled toward the dingy ceiling, slithering and sliding like snakes. My ears grated again as another sputtered hock fried.

No one unstuck me. I was glued iron to skin. I jerked my leg away. It was mottled purple, a shriveled-up skin splotch—coffee-cup size circle. I cringed, searching for Mama, groaning and grunting hoggishly for her.

"Mama, I need ya. I need ya, Mama, so bad I need ya," I begged. My hands fished for her, but nothing came back, just air. She couldn't come. Her face went to the wall.

"Look, Mama. Look what the mean red tricycle did to me," I shrieked. Mama couldn't look.

A single light bulb dangled from the beaded-board ceiling in the room's middle. Light shimmered, pushing miniature gray dogs everywhere. Puppies looked down on me, saw my awful pain, and abandoned me. But Mama's face was nowhere. It was gone. I was seeking Mama's face but it was hidden from me. Everything around me went cold silent.

Jokes stopped, unfinished. One about a bumblebee in a man's shirt. But bumblebees ain't funny. Blended wood and beer scents, mingled with whiskey and human flesh, wafted into my nostrils. My stomach sickened, guts quivered. Retching, I vomited on the iron-woman. My body chattered, shivered and shook. I was upside down, my legs tangled amongst the tricycle wheels, looking like pretzels.

2

Then filthy words ejected through the air, like spears, stabbing and blaming me. Daddy's voice rose high, cussing God. Like he was gonna kill God and Jesus. Like he was gonna beat them with his fist. Tiny grates of the stove burner lifting came to me from faraway spits.

"Mama, please come and make it quit. Help me, Mama. Help me, Mama." My hand curled to bring her close. Mama couldn't see or hear. She couldn't come. Daddy wouldn't let her. He was on top of her.

Her face was caved in, twisted. Her eyes were gone. On her knees, her hair, a knot in his hands. I had no help. Then Daddy came to get me. He did help me. Lifted me up. Took me home with Mama's hair. Then, he beat Mama some more, just cause.

Next morning, Mama borrowed some butter for the deep wound. A neighbor came with the butter. The nice lady said, "Mamie, she needs to see a doctor. Its third degree, easy for infection to set in." She wanted to help me. Her eyes said so.

Daddy declared nastily, "Ain't no doctor fit to be had."

"I wanna go to the 'doc-tor,'" I begged, to help the woman help me. But I wasn't yet four years old. My voice couldn't go nowhere. The raw foul splotch didn't hurt. Daddy said so.

Time passed. Days and nights traveled by. Springtime was coming; the air felt stiff and brittle as we waited for something better. My leg was wrapped with moist, smelly rags, coiled and tied over a splay of dabbed-on lard, the festered place well hidden.

Weeks later, I stood littler, in the cousin's shabby tricycle room. Not wanting to be there ever again. Standing sick-stomached with my weepy rag leg. The iron-woman's face staring me down—stout and haughty. Gawking at me. Her bloody plump belly, poked out like Mama's.

I loathed her—the black iron-woman.

Distanced, I gaped shakily at her, in horror, as familiar stale air scratched and choked my throat. Fear packed into my chest like a heavy sack to be carried. Ears muffed, I backed into a dark corner, invisible. A plastic lopsided grin hid my real face, covering my blended fear and hate.

The people acted as if my leg didn't hurt none and never had. The room mumbled as smoke hung low in beer-ish swags. Daddy said something about "a bee in his shirt." Bony men laughed as if they'd never heard it. Gaunt women stood wall-propped—gazing wordless. They snickered like it was funny.

Papa Harkus hocked and spat into the heater's burner. Sizzles squeaked out, giggling at me. My hands cuffed my ears tighter. Sounds lingered like low-honking geese. With me, squatted alone, cornered. Not burning no more and never did.

2

Granny Isabelle and Me

Some people said Granny Isabelle raised me. She taught me about gardening and life. "A needle ain't worth a hill of beans 'thout no eye," she said, "and no thread in the eye, can't nothing be sewed up."

I whispered, "Can a needle sew me up when I ain't nothing much left but bitty pieces? Even if I'm all gashed up inside?"

She spoke wisely. "Some things a body can't fix. But some stuff ya can ya own self. The good difference is knowing what can an' can't be helped. Knowing what ya can or can't do 'thout making things worse off. Then let the rest go."

I studied on my own self getting sewed on, rolling her words over, as she rambled on.

"A needle with its eye full of strong blue cotton can sew 'bout nigh anything, even you, I s'pose. But I hope to God it won't never happen, me having to sew you up an' all. Ya my own little angel." With that, she patted a scrawny, veined hand on my stringy head for a bit. And then her dull eyes fastened to the ground as she hoed faster, it nearing suppertime.

She tooled the red clay and said, "I know you ain't but five years old, but I gotta drum a lotta stuff in that there head afore the flesh side of ya wins out—even if I have to pack it in sideways. I'm gonna keep going at it as long as there's breath in my old worn body."

It probably won't be too long, I thought to myself in the midst of her chatter, cause she's already too old to live right now anyway. Her back all humped from slaving so hard. I wondered what might happen if there weren't nobody left for me, like some kin had spoken of so many times, my ears hearing their whispers.

Granny Isabelle constantly preached about one thing or another, teaching me with slow, long words and short, grunting promises. As if alive, the hoe clicked and chomped; her words clunked out, matching her digs like a song.

I yearned for the teaching more than her pouncing preachy words. They were the ones that came hitting me square in the face, squeezing on my sinful heart. Repenting me, like Preacher Smith did at the Baptist church.

That preacher man only wanted to keep me from busting hell wide open. But Granny Isabelle hoped to save me from them wolves roaming in the world. Wolves that looked like people, she said. They were just waiting to come and rip me into pieces any time now.

Ain't many times Granny Isabelle was without no words 'less she was worn out, dead tired to the world. Even then, there was times she spoke out into the air not knowing it, sitting there lifeless after supper. Chair rocking, squeaking like a mouse. Me talking back to nothing but two eye slits and some soft purring sounds.

But out in the cornfields she'd gab on, wagging them skinny fingers to the north and south, then east and west. Tugging on her crumpled paper-bag hat every once in a while to get a point across. Solid on her feet like a mountain goat, she'd preach.

Acting like we was gonna go on some faraway journey where we ain't never been. Getting there with no way of going. Not knowing where we were going in the first place. Us just putting one foot in front of the other—doing a wee step at a time.

Granny Isabelle prattled on in the garden, chopping what didn't need no more chopping. Half of me listening, the other half not. Her chats went way over my own thoughts that tried to bring some sense inside me as I sat playing in dirt clots after she passed through hacking furrows, hoe locked tight in her calloused hands.

Mud all up under me, I worked up a grimy wet wad from the mason jar of water I done poured, making a red pie for her and myself by breaking up some earthy blobs with gooey baitworms pulled into pieces. Curiously, fingering the fat squished-up ones, I probed some unmeshed worms back together again like they were puzzles.

I'd gulp the fresh sweet soil scents into my nostrils like water as hope climbed inside my heart. I wanted in the worst way to be like Granny Isabelle someday, paper hat and all.

Out of nowhere, she'd speak way too loud, like I couldn't hear nothing.

"Life's that way. Like them clomps of dirt ya playing with. Folks always trying to stick shattered bits of their souls together. Trying to fix things that can't be fixed by man's hands. Most times after somebody or their own sorry selves done ripped things wide open. Lord Jesus can fix 'em, though."

I shook my head in agreement as I shooed some nasty black crows, throwing dusty dirt clots at them, leaving dirt crumbs behind at my feet. Granny Isabelle would smack her dry lips, making mine thirsty too.

"Its human nature I guess. Making a mess outta things, not caring 'til it's over an' done. Always wantin' what they don't have or never worked for. Honing in on somebody else's wife and such. Like that sorry James, son of mine I ain't claiming, and the awful things he puts Mamie through."

As for myself, I only knew what I saw—Daddy was mad a lot and hit Mama. For sure I didn't yet know the depth of her suffering, but I still sat there mud-faced, nodding at Granny Isabelle like I knew exactly. Like I got plenty of her same sense. I watched her looking to the sky, crinkly eyes hand-sheltered, checking the time of day. Her green eyes blinked at mine in between falling words.

Granny Isabelle said she ain't got long to teach on me. To learn me some things about life and such that I gotta know in case she ain't around. I wasn't worried none too much, though, cause she was always there for me.

I was thinking Jesus'd never be so mean as to take my Granny Isabelle from me, too. Me not handling things none too well with all my crying spells without no Mama or Daddy most times, since they had left me behind with Granny as they went on their merry way once again. Her being all I got in the world to lean on. Tears clotting my eyelashes as my sorrows and loneliness filled my chest like a water trough.

Sweat dripped from Granny Isabelle's craggy brow as mud splats from pie making leaked atop my freckles, dragging down my face. She stopped to wipe the brownish smudges from my cheeks, whistling soft through her toothless mouth, "Now, now little chile. Don't ya go lookin' sad again." But I was sad. Although my parents had been gone for six months by Granny's guess, it seemed so long ago and I was missing them again.

Her briny touch brought us together, making it seem like a good day then, with me grinning up at her. Me and her standing in the tall straw grass beside the hand-plowed rows—us both looking far off to the hills with a heartfelt hankering for something better, not knowing for sure what.

She stooped, reached down by the garden wayside, and picked up a rough, faded corn husk that was shed off its shoot some year or years back. Crumpled and curled up on the ends, it'd laid beneath my feet, crunching as if wanting to live again. To breathe once more but couldn't. All willpower left out. Kind of like my insides felt.

Granny Isabelle saw the meaning in it too. "Like this here blade of corn now dead an' gone," she said. "We too will wilt an' pass on. Wanting to breathe once more, but no drive left to live."

Still looking off, I forgot the corn stalk, thinking more on my stomach full-of-empty. My mind gone far from her words. Her way off from me but still alongside.

"Do ya still have some of them biscuits left over in the stovetop?" I could see them as I spoke.

"Sure, I do."

"Can I have one with a little sugar sprinkled on it?"

"Ya sure can. But I got me some more things to say first." Granny Isabelle took hold of my head and turned it sidelong into hers. Looking at me straight on.

"An ear of corn still tastes mighty good. Even 'thout no teeth. A little sweetness and goodness can come outta most anything if ya keep gnawing at it."

I looked at her dumbstruck. And then I thought on chicken bones, and me sucking the meat off where there wasn't none much but gristle. And I thought I knew exactly what she meant, but might not. Cause of her being a prophet speaking in riddles sometimes.

Then I asked, "Why do some people like us work so hard an' have nothing much to show for it? And others have everything good, even ice cream?" I didn't understand those who had and ones who didn't. Mostly cause we were the ones who didn't.

She said back in a quiet way, "Some of us have to go the tough way. It's what's done been give to us. We play the cards we are given. If we try hard 'nough and long 'nough, some answers will come. We jus' keep working hard and walking on the right path. Dig. Plant. Water. Weed. Pick. Save. Keep them ornery bugs outta ya patch."

I nodded yes at bugs, cause it was what I was doing right then.

"Keep on trying even when it ain't nothing left inside. Like tastin' that sweet corn 'thout no teeth. Keep gnawing. Good things come to those who try. Not those who wait for things to get done by somebody else's blood, sweat, an' tears. We gotta keep going."

I looked on her hard. Me talking in my head about bugs and worms. Me knowing about sweat and tears already and not near half-grown, staring blankly at my scarred-up leg. Wishing it not to be so horrid. Missing my mama and daddy, even if my ugly leg hung on me.

I was wanting to see my beat-up Mama just for a bit. Hankering to see that baby girl she done pushed out sometime back, like Daddy's scrawny letter done said. Them being way off from me now. Them loving on that baby and not me. Me knowing I'm way too much trouble for them to carry along.

"One day, Jessie, ya gonna be on the 'have side.' Jus' ya watch an' see what I'm telling. Ya got my big thumbs, meaning we are too strong-willed to sit still. To live a life of nothing. No good to nobody. Not even our own selves."

What made sense to me was not to wait so long for my sugar biscuit, like I was having to do. I spied the house, wanting to see Smokey and give him a bone, but plain knowing there weren't none to give him.

Then Granny Isabelle spluttered some more, "One little grain of corn can make a whole row. A row of kernels can make a cornfield that'll spread like a thousand stars in the midnight sky. You'll have a dab of money an' more than a plenty of seeds to plant the next year."

I looked away, thinking on our dark beautiful sky, when it'd come without no moon. "Like a thousand stars?" I whispered.

"Yes, but one little seed won't be nothing if nobody bothers to dig a hole an' pack a little dirt up next to it. Ya gotta dig ya own holes, chile. Cause it's what has been give to ya.

"Ya already stronger than most women folks are. Heck, some can't even make a biscuit. But my Jessie sure can. Do ya know what I'm saying? We gotta have faith in what we plant. Seeing things that ain't there yet. Faith is what calls out good things. It's what makes water spout from rocks."

I nodded my head yes, blowing a dandelion puff, while my mind was stuck on garden kernels with nothing sprouting. Nothing at all. Like it happens sometimes when rain doesn't come and the bloodshot ground cracks curled edges. With the sun beating down strong and heavy on Granny Isabelle's seeded field, sprouting nothing but her words.

Sometimes, I'd tiptoe through the jagged-edged earthy tiles, trying not to break my Granny Isabelle's humped back like I'd heard many times. If I stepped on a crack it'd break Mama's back, but I was afraid the superstition would affect my Granny's poor back too. Knowing nature had broken it long ago, before the land dried up. Knowing full well them kernels done been planted for nothing. No faith inside me then or now.

I savored up Granny Isabelle's words for another time, chomping on my wet hair ends. I planned, when my mind wasn't aching and my stomach wasn't starving half-to-death, to think on them things some more later on.

"Work hard in other folks' garden if ya have too. Toil in ya own if the Lord's done blessed ya like He did me afta my son John went away to the other side. Good things come from hard work. Might not right away, but it'll come soon 'nough. That's a promise I make to ya from the Lord above."

"Stars in the sky," I sighed, wishing to know what she was saying.

"See them rows I done chopped." She yelped out, sounding like Smokey when his tail was stomped.

"Yeah." Not wanting to listen no more.

"See how one row goes that way, while another goes yonder?" she asked, knobby fingers pointed like a crooked fork.

My head nodded yes some more. Waiting for another dose.

"Well, little chile, someday not far off ya gonna come to a split road in life. Ya gonna hafta choose one, cause ya can't do both. Ya gonna hafta direct ya own feet to the right path for ya own sake. Don't never let nobody else pick your way. Don't never let nobody trod on ya back like it's a road. It's what the Word of God done said. Never. Not never. Do ya hear me, little one?"

"Yeah," I said, shaking my head severely, having stood all I could. Acting as if I had some understanding. But didn't.

"There's good an' evil all round us. Don't never let darkness blot out that burstin' light inside of ya. Be your own self. Don't change who ya are for nobody else. Do what needs changing for ya own self. Ya can do almost anything, if ya got the gumption to reach for the stars and push through the needle's eye."

10

With head shaking, hair flinging off to the side, soppy locks blobbing my face with bouncy slaps, I pondered things—gnawing on my mawkish hair ends to ease my edginess—thinking on how to help Granny Isabelle get some peace in her heart over my sorry lot in life.

Our minds met. Unified, we sauntered on to the house, me munching hairs and her preaching glory. Me and Granny Isabelle. I couldn't be one place and her at another. We just stuck together most times, my hand laid up in hers, walking side-by-side. Me stepping on her moon-ish shadow and her on mine, along the way in our thoughts.

She said we were just alike—me and her—all the while, us standing quiet in the cornfield as the orange sun melted down. To sleep a distant somewhere—way beyond some ripe meadows—pulling a quilt of muted purple, red, and yellow over its glowing giant head. Together, we watched another day drift into soft, still nothingness.

She rattled some pans, warmed up the greasy gravy, fried fatback, and cold biscuits. We sat tabled, one facing the other, gazing out of the kitchen window. Stars shooting down from heaven by the handfuls. Me wishing ever so hard on each one as Granny Isabelle murmured a weary food prayer into the air. It hanging for a while, like a balloon. Me listening to silence.

Exhausted, she washed our gravy dishes and I dried them. I sloshed the gray dishwater clumps into the yard from the pan, for a few chickens that wasn't roosted yet. Then, seemingly not tired no more, Granny Isabelle stooped and rubbed a sweet feeling over my face with a wet rag in her hands, as love tears welled up in her eyes.

Me, full of her warm earthy odors, tucked into bed alongside her icy feet. Me fighting not to sleep now, but to talk some more about life things, like corn kernels and such. Her purring, not talking much.

Me loving my Granny Isabelle and them stars full of fire, shooting down at us from God's hand. Her sugar biscuits and never-ending holy words. Her teaching, teaching, and teaching. Me knowing I got the best Granny Isabelle in the whole wide world. Me sleeping, sleeping, and sleeping.

3

Isabelle

Earth Mother

Isabelle, this little woman—earth mother—born with hoe in hand. Born with soil in her blood. Birthed to chew Virginia's hard clay into pieces—always tasting the musky earth through her nostrils. She carried dust in the seams of her tattered stockings and worn shoes as she picked her way through the soil.

Isabelle believed in miracles: good things would come if she asked, trusted in a power greater than her own self, and did her part. Alone, she inched through the earth's crusty cap, laboring faithfully—like the Word had taught her. She blessed her own handiwork in the Lord's name, through the blood of Jesus, believing in His power as she spoke.

She'd talked to Him, like a friend, many a time in the blistering cornfields. Sometimes in the cool of the day, after all of her sweat and strength was spent, her eyes would wander to the green hills just beyond the holler—a place of rest, wishing for more. Wishing for better.

Quietness called her name. Often she slipped off to a corner where the four winds met and sat for short spells to dream, pray, and think on things. Deep things. She'd quench her thirst from a hidden icy spring and splash water on her saline-laden face. Ah, refreshing coolness was beyond delicious.

Isabelle worked the neighbor's gardens for money. Afterwards she'd seek rest where three large boulders stacked, one heaped on the other. She named it Three Rocks for the trinity. Three Rocks came to be like Jacob's altar—for thanksgiving and asking. She'd plead her cases before the Judge, the Lord God, and beg Him for help and hope.

Then one day she was especially drawn to Three Rocks. She had come to her wit's end. Regardless of how hard she worked, her circumstances remained the same. She'd come to the end of herself and needed a higher power to strengthen her. Her body was sapped at near fifty years old. She had no support. Her sons and spouse were drunks. That particular day was heavy with sweat and thirst. The rolled-up paper-bag hat hadn't given her head much relief from the boiling sun. Her pitiful body ached for water, her bones for rest.

Worn and tired with painful hands and legs she came seeking. Thirsting for more, like the lady at the well. She knew there had to be more than just settling for crumbs in life. A time comes when a body can't keep thinking something is what it ain't. She came to that thought down in the holler on a visit where the four winds blew.

Isabelle realized her empty life and fell to her knees, forehead propped against her clasped hands, forefingers pointing like a steeple on her brow. From the rock's breast she thanked the creator for all He'd done for her. Then she trailed her prayer by asking for a favor. More selfish this time than usual.

"Don't hold it agin' me for my husband's an' son's sins. I don't mean to be ungrateful or greedy in any kinda way. But I say to you now—I ain't had no speck of peace since them boys been born. Since I done been with Harkus. Him an' them sons of mine drinkin' likker all time. It ain't been much but hell. I don't want to be ungrateful, I do thank ya for taking Harkus, Ed, and James all to Canada to work in tobacco when ya do. I get a little peace then. But they jus' drink all the money up.

"Onliest way for me to ever have anything is ifn' ya give it to me. Rudy and my girl Lizzie seem okay, but the other two, James and Ed, are...well, I won't even say it, cause you know all my thoughts already.

"The onliest one I got any speck of hope for is John, my baby boy, but he's still a little thing, littler than a gnat. Who knows what'll come of him as he grows to be a man. He seems to have some love in his heart an' he talks 'bout ya all the time.

"If it be your will, Dearest Father, please give me this little piece of land as my own for hoeing. Lord Jesus, I want a tiny place to call my own. I done saved a bit workin' everybody else's land. Maybe 'nough to get my hand on a acre with a tad of help from you. So if ya get a mind to help me, do it jus' cause ya love me. I know I'm your chile an' my name's all 'scribed in the palm of ya hand.

"I'd be so happy to have my own little house with a kitchen window so I can see the stars at suppertime. An' a garden. Maybe, I could

13

sell food to the stores like ole man Mayes does. Jus' send me a sign an' I thank ya ahead for what ya gonna do for me. I won't tell ya my name again, cause ya know that already, too; ever since before I came through the womb of my blind mammie. I thank ya again in Jesus name. Amen."

Isabelle toiled on, wearing perspiration on her forehead and a parched tongue like clothing. Paying attention to nothing but the ground and little John as he grew. She chopped and chopped, dawn until dusk, from dust to dust, row to row, finding peace in the Word of God and in John, her favorite son.

4

Mama's New Baby

I don't know what brought it on, but Mama, Daddy, and Ginny (Mama's new baby) came piling up on Granny Isabelle and me. On a whim they drove up, they said. Just like, on a whim, I'd often been left behind with Granny Isabelle or taken along with them. But this time was different. They brought me a sister to play with, they happily stated. She could walk and even say a few words, they bragged.

I didn't know how to feel. I didn't want Ginny around, and yet I did. When they first drove up, my heart beat hard and fast when I saw her. I hated her and loved her in the same moment. She was my sister. She had a head of yellow curls and the bluest eyes. Her small hands fit into mine easily as we were sent outside to play in the yard without nothing much to do except kick rocks, play in anthills with pine straws, and call up doodlebugs from sandy tunnels. Sometimes we'd chase hens to see which one's wings flapped the loudest.

My best fun thing was calling up some doodlebugs. Dusty little bugs buried beneath dirty funnels, living there, doing nothing much but hiding from me. Waiting on their house to be burned down as Ginny squatted, watching alongside.

5

Pilot Knob

My Uncle Ed, Daddy's rich brother, and his family had come to visit us
for a spell—his kin was headed to the mountains for some family time.
Somehow, Daddy took up the notion for us all to have the same closeness, like them. Me knowing it wasn't never gonna happen, but a little
hopefulness filled me nevertheless.

I'd begun thinking I had done had enough of my cousins, and I'd
be better off just with chickens, ants, doodlebugs, and such. But I ain't
got no say cause I ain't big as a gnat. I get led around to places I don't
wanna go, and I hafta kiss ugly old faces, just cause they're Daddy's
blood.

A family trip—I'm thinking—had some other motive with Daddy
involved. Daddy hated Uncle Ed on account of my uncle's new Cadillac,
but Daddy acted different to his face, rubbing on that shiny car, his face
full of crooked grins.

We all loaded up for a picnic in the mountains. Now, I hadn't never seen a picnic nor been on a family trip, nor even heard talk of such
before; so I felt kinda uneasy doing what I ain't never done. Daddy and
my rich uncle piled two families, plus Granny Isabelle and Papa Harkus,
into the cars and we took off, no food or drinks to be seen, except whiskey.

Daddy had several bottles of likker wrapped up in paper bags,
screwed and scrunched at the top. Him not caring that I saw what I had
no business seeing, cramming them thick pokes into the car trunk,
smiles pasted all on his face, teeth un-gritted. My stomach was already
wadding into a close-fitting knot over something that hadn't happened
yet. Kids like me could sense when things wasn't right.

We wound through some scary high-climbing roads on to the Blue
Ridge Parkway. Granny Isabelle said it was it sure was "purty." Me, half

sick to my stomach, bile rolling like water slopping around in a bucket, saw no beauty anywhere.

I was dry heaving, set to retch, my hand holding it back for a while. Then, involuntarily, I gagged to get the stomach lumps out. Daddy started cussing God about no puking in his car with me puking anyway. We stopped none too late, at a spot with plank tables full of splinters. Some rested while others stretched their legs.

Still there came no mention of food or water before the hike started. My family sat bunched on one table end while Uncle Ed's folks sat on another. Them not talking much to each other across the way. Me thinking it sure wasn't no fun yet.

The men popped the trunk, pulled out Daddy's brown paper bags, and walked off to the woods to pee together, laughing full of happiness. They would come on back hugging one another's shoulders, much better off than before peeing. Those of us left behind was not the least bit glad.

My uncle wanted a Polaroid picture of Papa Harkus and Granny Isabelle sitting together on a great rock. Stinking of puke, I smiled, hankering to be in it too, sticking my head under Granny Isabelle's arm. I was pushed off to the side by them rotten cousins I didn't hardly know, making me mad again, before we got started on any family closeness of our own.

A narrow path with a sign stuck out of the ground pointed toward a trail into sightlessness. I studied on the letters and couldn't find their meaning.

I said, "Why is that there sign poking out like a finger?"

Cousin boy number one said, "It says, 'Come on stupid.'" I stuck out my tongue at him for his meanness and shrugged air off my shoulders, thinking they wasn't no fun.

I squatted down low, farted on his shoe top long and loud, pushing a special stink up to his nose with my unfolded hands like a fan. Me sitting there laughing, then running away, more excited to move on up the hillside, as he punched at my head.

We stood, resting still, waiting restless. Some of us leaned on trees, others hunkered down like ducks. I chewed on tree twigs, planning what to do next to cousin number one. I traced my fingers on the sign letters as I craved to eat, thinking Uncle Ed had brought a load of food in his trunk that I hadn't seen yet.

That's when we started lining up, one behind the other to go up the mountain. Uncle Ed was the leader cause he was the smartest and biggest—already I'd done seen madness cross Daddy's face cause he was number three in line and not one. Never knowing about my daddy, I could plainly see him in a fit, throwing a rock against Uncle Ed's big head without thinking on it none too much.

We lined up man-woman, man-woman, and man-woman, and then us kids trailed like stair-steps. Me and Ginny was last cause we were the littlest. Ginny being the least. Being last ain't never easy, especially left behind, me dragging on a load like Ginny and her backing off from me.

As I tugged on Ginny's hand moving up the trail, I said to my know-it-all cousins from Tennessee, "Are we on Pilot Mountain yet? And what's a picnic?"

Cousin boy number two said, "You're too stupid to believe. How can you even be alive? You don't even know what a picnic is." They all laughed hard some more. I stuck out my tongue at all of them as they tossed looks around. I searched their faces for more mocking, wanting to throw a rock, but I didn't for the moment, not wanting to hit cousin number three, who was a girl like myself, named Dorothy, and who smiled at me some of the time.

Better than the rest, Dorothy explained it to me. "A picnic is where we spread quilts on the ground and eat lots of food." Hunger reminded me of meal times with not much but leftovers, especially since Daddy had done heaped his burdens on us. Plus his fighting at the table didn't help none, wadding our stomachs up like a balls of twine.

I replied, "What are ya talking 'bout? All our quilts are still on the bed." Belly deep, they sniveled and hooted at me again, calling me stupid. Cousin number one laid down on the ground, kicking his fat legs in the air an' snorting 'til he cried.

Then the hateful cousin number two said, "Let me enlighten you. We usually have things like potato salad, fried chicken, and watermelon. Afterwards, we have seed-spitting fights."

I gazed outward through my squished-up eye, like Daddy looks at me when I might tell a lie. I studied on what I was told, reading their better-than-me faces for a grain of truth. My eye shrunk to a squeaky slit, showing them I had some witchy powers that would tell me if they were speaking a dog-face lie.

I said, matter-of-factly, "Well, I'm for spitting stuff on others, so it suits me jus' fine." The mean one rolled his eyes and had no more to say, while I thought on where that watermelon was. The men snuck away into the bushes to pee some more.

"Where's that picnic gonna be?" I asked everybody, looking face to face, wanting some answers. Not a word came, just a few shrill laughs and harsh stares shot out to shut me up.

Then I said, "They better lay that quilt down soon, cause my stomach's done drawed plum up to my backbone." I obsessed over fried chicken legs, potato salad, and such things. My mouth was watering for potatoes mashed up with pickles, something I had never heard of, but loving pickles any which way they come.

Every once in a while the men pulled off the trail together beyond the mountain laurel and rhododendron bushes to pee some more, coming back red-faced, like God's glory's was shining on them, them more satisfied with life. My pitiful legs—everything ached, my head throbbed, my stomach growled, and my lips had dried like a potsherd.

The rocks kept going up high beyond imagination and I couldn't see the top. With most steps, I was still asking about where that picnic was. By now, most of us kids were acting like mad hornets. We went about swatting one another with tree branches, sticks, rocks or whatever, cause we couldn't slap the big people leading us on to nowhere.

On top of my weakness from starvation, fear came stalking, as my shoes slid on acorns and pine needles. My sister's arm was apt to get pulled off, I thought, as I tugged on it; or maybe she'd fall off the cliff to die where the tiny houses lived, looking no bigger than mice and I'd be blamed for it all.

Then it happened. I lost control. We went belly-sliding, barely stopping before going over the mountainside. Us both screaming for help as we slipped away through gooseberry bushes, slick mushrooms, and dead leaves and brambles.

Daddy skidded down clumsily, a cigarette clenched between his teeth, mad at me, with the devil red in his eyes. Smoke streams curled into my nose like serpents as he jerked on my arms, lifting me onto his wobbly shoulders. Mama grabbed Ginny, hugging her she walked on, while I teeter-tottered on Daddy, swaying like a hung man dangling from a tree limb in the breezes.

19

Whiskey odor and smoke wafted into my nose as he staggered on the trail of what seemed to be no return. I screamed in spells, panic-stricken, dying a hundred times while the cousins and all goggled stupidly.

Toted perched high, everybody below looked like pop-beads yoked together. Daddy's wobbles widened as he snuck swigs from a coat-pocketed amber bottle.

Daddy showed off, doing some be-bops, hops, and jigs with twirls. I would screech, grabbing air to hold onto. My hysterical heart pounded like a runaway train. Utter terror and a hollow stomach brought on more puking.

Uncle Ed kidded Daddy about his puniness. By the terrible finger-nail gouges, I could feel Daddy's fury scrape into my legs. He plunked me down and hatefully jerked my arms as I pulled to run. Grabbing, he clamped my arm and pushed me toward the mountaintop guardrail. My head twisted fruitlessly as he shoved it; gripping it, he forced me to look downward. The vast green valley below glowered up at me.

Daddy, I'd reckoned, wanted to kill me. Maybe he'd throw me over Pilot Mountain. I'd die in the worst way, splattered into pieces in front of everyone. Maybe then they'd all be happy, picking up my broken parts. I imagined it in my mind's eye.

I yanked, feverishly twisting my hands and blood-filled fingers, letting out screams of terror and desperately trying to get away from him as Mama hugged Ginny safely into her bosom, a place I wanted desperately to be.

"Mama, help me. Mama, please help me," I pled, my arms searching for her embrace. "He's gonna throw me over the hill to the little houses. I don't wanna die. Please. Please help me, Mama." Tears tore down my face. She looked on with pity, but her arms were already full.

Granny Isabelle, breathless, scrambled over rocks and feebly said, "James, let me take hold of her for a while. Mamie's arms are full. You jus' rest a bit."

Without being told, I knew I was headed for a beating. I knew by the looks in his eyes. I knew lots, like who to trust or not to.

He dropped my hand. Eagerly, I unraveled my fingers and slid them into Granny Isabelle's wrinkled hand that fit perfect, like a warm soft mitten. Simple and sweet, we walked together without any slips down the mountain, cause I had no heavy load pulling against me.

6

Isabelle
John the Baptist

Isabelle sat on Pilot Knob's big gray boulder beside of her husband as the camera clicked, picture pushing out like a baby being born. Sweet and sour memories of her dead son John mentally gushed as if it had happened yesterday. She wondered how different it would be if John had been leading them on the nature walk. He loved nature so much.

Being the baby, John was special. She recalled silently how love had bloomed in her multi-stretched belly as she'd read scriptures to her unborn. She had named him after John the Baptist.

From the beginning, he had delighted her soul. He cuddled, goo-goo'd, drooled, and clutched her neck with his tiny fingers. She relished being his safe haven, the one he looked up to.

His small, sparkling eyes lit up every time he heard her voice or caught a glimpse of her. Intuitively, even as an infant, he knew who to reach toward and who to pull away from. His mother noticed an unreasonable wisdom in this child, unlike the others.

John loved people spiritually. Even those dark souls, like his brothers. He wanted to show them life's beauty. Discernment was imperative when he dealt with them. He tried to teach them about goodness, and to be giving, and to abstain from evil things like promiscuity and drunkenness, but it fell on deaf ears. Isabelle told him to be shrewd as a serpent and gentle as a dove, like Jesus had advised.

"Even evil ones have a soul that can be saved," he'd tell her. He believed, but she doubted. Only on this point did they differ.

John came out of the womb knowing the Lord, hungry for His Word and truth. He pondered the meaning of Bible stories, heaven, people, hell, life and death. And then concluded that something better was on the other side.

21

During his childhood, he followed Isabelle everywhere, strolling with her side by side, hand in hand. At times in silence. Always, there was a sense of belonging to one another and to something higher and greater than themselves. Especially at the end of the day, the time was the sweetest as they pondered the dark skies and shooting stars together.

When he was two years old, he ran up to a big rock, wrapped his little arms around it, and declared, "Oh, big rock, I love you."

Why would a little child love even a hard, weatherworn stone? Isabelle had chuckled to herself about this and tucked it away.

Isabelle kept a close eye on him when he was a youngster. She taught him to recognize and avoid danger, and how to survive in Virginia's thick musky woods. But mishaps were unavoidable with his passionate curiosity about life.

When he was three years old, his sister Lizzie came running with him in arms, screaming for help. Attached to his great toe was a dangerous, dangling copperhead. Isabelle snatched its shifty head, clasped the clamped jaws, as she wretched and wrung its pointed, bulging face. A face with murderous eyes and hobnail fangs was detached from his toe and hurled skyward. Isabelle's vehement eyes set like flint as she cradled her son and bulleted off like lightning to get a ride, the pitiful clan at her heels.

The neighbor's vehicle was impelled toward town. With John cradled in her lap, Isabelle hurriedly tied her shoestring around his toe base. Snatching Papa Harkus's pocketknife, she vented two red dots, and sucked the carved "X." Resolute to beat death, she withdrew blond putrid bitterness, spitting cyclically through the open window. Then, she plucked her husband's chewing tobacco from his mouth, and lathered it over the spot to remove more venom. John's throbbing, teacup-sized toe brought demonic wails, then the poison relented his pale body into sweat and limpness.

Gathering her son's flaccid human lump into her skirts, she dashed for the doctor's office door before the car stopped. The doctor rushed forward, scowled over wire-rimmed glasses, and ordered through his pursed lips for the family to go away while he injected anti-venom and tried to save the boy.

The nurse obeyed him and whispered, "Will the poor child make it?"

The physician saddened. "Not likely. Not likely at all." Hours passed. Isabelle's stiff, tenacious prayers winged heavenward.

Haggard, the doctor eventually shuffled, scuff-shoed, into the waiting room where the clan hovered and said, "Thirty more minutes, you would have lost him. Sure as God lives, you woulda lost that child."

Isabelle convulsed in tears of relief, and Lizzie laughed like clanging cymbals as Papa Harkus stifled a tear through his alcoholic haze, still not twigging the situation's gravity.

"No kid his age is supposed to survive such a bite; especially a snake that grips on like that one. That serpent must have been straight from the pits of hell." Baffled, the doctor pulled on a wet Pall Mall butt, blew off a blue smoke ring, and shook his disbelieving head. He turned his tired back and ambled off to see another patient.

The trio tailed the nurse down the narrow dim hall, with Isabelle praising Jesus as the door opened. John glanced up grinning and said, "I want my mama."

After the viper bite, Isabelle had a propensity to worry even more over her son, especially if he strayed too far from her line of vision or out of her ear range. Hawkish, she lingered over him. John's outdoor fascinations included anything in springs, rocks, creek beds, and cracks. He liked to rummage around in places he shouldn't, and danger was always nearby.

Long poisonous copperheads, fat toxic moccasins, and deadly timber rattlesnakes were known to sunbathe frequently on the smooth boulders where he liked to play.

Once, on a porch post, he found the drilled-out home of a carpenter bee. He stuck his finger inside, then yanked it out screaming.

Knowing that recluse and black widow spiders loved shoes, Isabelle would stick her fingers inside his shoe tips and finagle them searching, rathering herself and not her beloved be bitten.

Engorged striped hornets swayed in gray corrugated hives on porch corners or tree branches, awaiting intruders. Hundreds of malicious creatures conspicuously drifted overhead, ready for attack.

Like guardian soldiers, they watched for John's make-believe jabbing stick swords and swatting slingshot rocks. John called them "buzzies." Seemingly fearless, head sporting a rolled-up paper bag hat like his mama's, he'd spread his arms like wings, mimicking their blub-

23

bery hums from his lips and occupying himself for hours. He was a smart boy.

Once Isabelle was telling him a bedtime story about the three bears.

"Stop, stop, stop," he said as his little hands blocked the space between them. All of a sudden, he hurdled from the bed running.

He promptly returned with the scuffed-up testament she had given him. He scaled the bed up to her, released the bound pages of miniature words, and ran a tiny finger left to right, line by line, courting the manuscript as if he knew exactly what it said. Mysterious silent black words appeared to have spoken to him.

His mother tried again to speak of the three bears, but respectfully, John muted all conversation with a tiny obstructive hand gesture, the other hand's finger still gliding, as if on braille.

Isabelle felt a strong, peculiar sense of reverence fill the room. When his finger finished reading, her son placed the testament onto his heart space and nuzzled down, sleeping in complete peace. Amazed, she pondered.

When John was five years old, while gardening, he peered up at Isabelle out of the blue and said, "You know, Mama, I was sent here to love you." He grinned sweetly, then bent down as his hands continued piddling with invasive garden weeds.

Such sweet hands, she thought. She'd felt the softness of his hand as it took hold of hers during their walks and talks, smelled his clean hair after a bath, and relished his childish giggles as he pulled a toy behind. Astounded, she tucked his words into her spirit and waited.

Could it be that we humans lived before being born here? Could it be we come to earth from another place for a reason: a task or a specific purpose? If so, what is my duty, my calling? Isabelle wondered, perplexed that somehow John had spoken from a place unknown to her.

Joy and delight filled her soul when John would hug her neck. Adoringly, his small body would melt into hers, heart beating on heart. Affection from John was the only real love she had ever known, and it was delicious. He was so unlike Isabelle's other sons and Lizzie, who resisted her hugs. Even at birth, they pulled and yanked on her womb as if to rip it out. Worse still, each infant would stiffly jerk away, refusing to breastfeed. Always fighting against her. John was different.

He'd show up with a torn-wing butterfly on his fingertip or a tattered kitten tucked underneath his armpit and say, "See Mama, we can fix him if we jus' try." Her small boy was bigger than life itself. "See Mama. See what I found. Can we keep it forever?"

She'd answer, "But forever is a long, long time."

"But Mama," he'd reply, "love don't go away. No matter what. It's forever and ever." Then he'd stretch his arms out, as far as he could, to show her.

He crayoned happiness. In her treasure box there were drawings of skinny stick people holding hands, happy smiling hearts, bold home-made kites, and beautiful butterflies. Big brawny suns, multicolored rainbows, and fluffy white clouds in blue skies. Life easily flowed out of him through his art, and on into her heart.

Isabelle's daily mantra was "Thank you, Father, for this loving creature you have so blessed me with."

John grew into a fine-looking preacher man, a good catch for any woman. He didn't want just any female. He wanted the one God had in store for him. His life lay ahead of him with promise and hope.

7

Home

We went to Pilot Knob to get the family together, but as always, every good intention ended in a drunken disaster. Night came swiftly after we got home. Granny Isabelle hurriedly went off to the kitchen, scraping on pans and dinging on pots and bowls. Scents of warmed-up pintos and pone bread stretched into my nose. I rushed to the kitchen, not noticing much else.

Then some mighty shouts blasted and familiar mousy screaks bleeped from the dark outdoors. Peering from the window's edge through the shimmering porch light, I saw Mama all laid out onto the ground, her body rolled up, worming a hand-covered, big belly. Daddy was cussing, kicking her head with his boot like it was a rock.

His stinking words reeked of filth. My guts shook, no longer hungry. Granny Isabelle searched mine and Ginny's eyes, pushing us ahead of her skirt out of the kitchen. Like an unusually strong woman, she physically wrenched the frizzy couch arm and drove the whole thing dead-center of the small room, stouter than I had ever guessed of her.

"Get ya'selves behind the couch. Be quick." She shoved us. Worm-like we curled into balls, like Mama looked in the front yard. Our cousins had long left us behind for family time at their original destination. We were all alone.

"Now get on in there and stay. Don't sneeze, peep, or make a whimper. Not 'til I come back an' get ya. Ev'n if he comes in here mad as fire, don't make a sound." She was frantic, her top lip quivering and her flour-covered nose sniffling as if to cry.

"Granny Isabelle," I said, "I done caused him to half kill Mama. All cause of them little houses. I jus' knowed he was going to throw me down an' make like I tripped or something. He's gonna kill Mama. We gotta stop him."

"Lordy chile, I think ya might be right somehow. He ain't got no soul. But then was then, an' now is now."

26

"We gotta help her." I begged Granny Isabelle with my eyes and heart.

"She can't be helped. He'll kill her an' y'all too if y'all go out there. So stay tight 'hind this couch and don't breathe no more than y'all haft to."

"We gotta breathe a little," I whined helplessly as my sister and I huddled together as one. I snuffed my nose to show her what I meant. Vinegar odors crawled from the kitchen into my nostrils.

Sliced cucumbers smothered in liquid amber, sprinkled with salt and pepper, along with a saucer of skinned green onions off to the side. Nothing better than beans, onions, and cucumbers. My mouth watered for brine. Hunger grew again.

"If'n y'all make sounds an' he catches on, he ain't beyond killin' me for hiding y'all, and 'en kill y'all jus' cause. Lord, Jesus God, please 'tect these little chillens of yours. Please dear Jesus keep 'em safe when I can't do nothing." She shoved the horse-hair sofa back to the wall, squeezing Ginny and me together, full of shakes and shivers. My sick stomach flooded full of worry and fear, food urges dwindling again.

Crude cusses stomped the porch, walking heavy, through Granny Isabelle's screen door. Her oven door screeched shut like nothing was going on.

"Ya got them kids in here," he probed, as the lawyer in him pried for truth.

"I thought they was with ya outside. Out there playing with lightning bugs or somethin'. Jessie done come in for a little jar to put 'em in an' left on out. Y'all 'bout ready to eat a little somethin'," she asked, pretending.

"Eat hell. I wanna get my hands on that kid. I wanna teach her who is an' ain't boss 'round here." His words got bigger, cussing God high to the ceiling like he did. Probably remembering my poor beat Mama on the ground, wanting to get at her some more, I imagined.

Footsteps stumbled toward our hiding space. They sounded giant-like, ant-crushing. That's when Ginny peed herself with me petting her head like a hurt kitten, shushing with my fingers and no sound.

Things got knocked over on the way to get at us through the kitchen. Sounds hollered, like a chair slammed against the wall. A table jounced, a dish smashed. Probably Granny Isabelle's white porcelain candy bowl she bought at the dime store the other day. She loved the little curved legs. "I ain't never seen one with legs a'fore," she'd said, looking on it longingly, grinning over it. "Guess it'll cost me a bunch of onions. But some things are jus' worth it."

Gigantic boots hoofed through the small dim sitting room where Papa Harkus's bed sat tight against the wall. We heard them move towards Granny's bedroom where a sofa also sat, and then we saw a light sliver at the doorway. He studied the room. God-like legs squatted down at Granny Isabelle's bed, searching unhurried. Our breaths stopped.

Granny Isabelle stood behind him, sipping air through her nose in tiny whistles. "Why don't y'all come on in the kitchen an' eat a bite. Ain't nobody had a morsel of nothin' much all day. Them chillens probably outside playin' an' will be back in soon. Y'all got to be hungry."

I peeked from the couch edge as she motioned for him and shook a dusty dishrag my way, flour spraying. I pulled back, now soaked from my own pee and Ginny's. Like Ginny, I needed to be stroked like a kitten in these times, but knew I never would be cause I was the oldest.

Daddy trudged to the kitchen, looking famished from beating Mama and hunting us. He ate his fill and then laid on Papa Harkus's old bed, springs creaking, until he passed out. Extra darkness soaked the yard as eerie clouds covered the moon while Papa Harkus's 'whoops' wafted from the distant woods.

Granny Isabelle fetched us from behind the couch. She rag-washed our hands and gave us pone bread to eat, then pulled some dry clothes over our heads and sneaked us into her bed.

"Guess I'll go try and find Mamie. If he wakes, get under the bed." She looked for Mama a while, but, not wanting to leave us long, she came on back in and slid between the sheets so that Daddy had to come through her first to get hold of us.

"Lord, Jesus God, have mercy," Granny Isabelle whispered with a weary sigh. We slept scrunched up tight, worrying over our maybe dead Mama but too worn out even to hunt for her.

Morning came just like all mornings. Cautiously, we wiped sleep from our eyes with fisted hands. Soft murmurs flowed from the kitchen and the smell of biscuits baking permeated the air. We crept toward Granny Isabelle's voice, pushing past Daddy still lying in bed sleeping. Mama sat at the table nursing two swollen black eyes under a wet rag and sipping gingerly on a cup of coffee through torn lips, acting as if nothing terrible had happened.

8

Isabelle
The Copper

Officer Newsome and two ambulance workers had recovered John's mangled body and twisted car pieces from the train's undercarriage. Newsome had brought Isabelle to the place where John was killed at her insistence. He held her frail hand as he placed a worn-out testament and a tiny, bent silver cross necklace into it. He folded her fingers around them for her. She couldn't take hold of them.

In puffs, his breath vapored out into the cool, dark night as he advised compassionately, "You have to go on with your life somehow." Resigned, she nodded in agreement, staggering backwards on her spindly legs. Weakened, she sank onto the damp ground beyond the tracks, mumbling incoherently. She seemed to have aged many years in those moments.

"Ma'am?" Newsome asked.

Agitated, she slurred, "I said I will. I done it many a time afore."

Torn, she struggled within over what had come on her. Her tired, quivering hands unwillingly clutched her son's relics. Isabelle didn't want things; she wanted her child, his love.

Memories of John's childhood were aroused as images of the little presents and pictures stored in a box underneath her bed blossomed into her mind. What good were these lifeless, dusty trinkets from the past? It was John's love that gave her the will to live.

His delight for life and nature, his smiles and giggles, flooded from her memory closet like moths. As if she'd lifted the top of an old chest, recollections, like knives, grabbed and jabbed at her heart. She soaked up images and mused on his once-upon-a-time littleness in swoops.

John had grown to be a fine man. He cut timber for money and preached. He was looking for a woman to share his life with but lived with Isabelle for the time being. She looked guiltily into death's haunt-

29

ing face. "I caused it all." She fiddled and fumbled with the half-peeled gold "Mother" pin stuck to her bloused breast, gifted from John last year.

With glassy eyes and a dry mouth, she bawled at the policeman. "It's my fault. All my fault. I sent him to the store for a can of 'vaporated milk. I was gonna make us a pie. He loves choclit, you know. I had them black walnuts an' was gonna add them to it. He loves black walnuts nigh as good as anything."

Louder, she exclaimed, "Mister, did I tell ya he jus' loves choclit too?"

Dazed, he replied, "Sure did, ma'am."

Winded, she paused and inhaled the crisp air. "It took me four hours to crack them nuts. They so hard to break with a hammer, but a rock ain't no bit better." Her spastic head jerked up as she brushed a black widow's web from her cheek, not caring if she was bitten.

She stuck a bruised finger with half a nail into the cop's face. He scanned it skeptically, shuffled his feet, and then slid a step backward, spitting snuff juice.

"See," she said, "I 'bout smashed it off. No sirree. I weren't gonna let them nuts get the best of me, so I just kept on whoppin' an' hittin' at 'em. Look what happened." She presented the finger again, then latched it into her parched mouth and sucked some lingering pain off. "Tears come in my eyes cause the hurtin' was so bad, but I had to keep on crackin' 'em, cause my John loves them so good. Did I tell ya how much he loves choclit? Ain't never seen a man love choclit like he does."

The tall man squirmed.

"Now, hickory nuts is 'bout bad as them black walnuts. But walnuts is the worse in the world to crack I ever did see. They awful messy too. Awful messy. Jus' look at my hands, all smudged with black stains. An' they won't come clean for a month or so, no matter how much I wash on 'em." She prattled on.

The man heard a ruffle in the frantic, growing darkness. Officer Newsome's ears halted as he peered toward the treetop. Rough wings fluttered, stifled, stopped. Overhead, a hoot owl had landed on a giant oak tree branch. Wings fanned and flicked. Bird claws clinched around some splotchy bark. Perched, the owl watched with giant, solemn eyes and then stared knowingly at the man beneath.

Three fervent hoots hovered overhead as if to warn the forest. Forlorn sounds magnified each cry. Tree frogs, crickets, distant dog barks, bobcat calls, and winding wind breezes seemed to gather around as if to help lift the grief-stricken woman's head. Nearby poplars seemed to bend and bow low to monitor her sorrow.

A floating leaf tapped Isabelle's shoulder as if to awaken her from a spell. Two whip-poor-wills echoed from a nearby field and seemingly signaled for help for Isabelle. As if encouraged, the stars of heaven sought to shine a drop of light upon Isabelle's horrible curse, but they flickered harshly and then dimmed, withering into no light.

"I bet you didn't know a squirrel can crack one in its tiny jaws, 'thout a speck of trouble whatsoever," she babbled as the man groped mentally for a response.

He lifted an eyebrow inquisitively. "No ma'am. I didn't."

"Do you know how hard it is to pick meat out of them cracked shells?"

He shook his head.

"Well, I do." She glared angrily at him for being ignorant. "I take me a bobby pin, not one of them big ones but a small, strong one, pull off the little rubber tip. Like this 'un." She pulled one from a hair roll at the base of her leathery creased neck. Silver tangles fell around her face, witch-like. "Then I poke it into the meat jus' so. Real slow."

Her gnarled fingers trembled, demonstrating. "Like this, stick it in the biggest part and pull out real easy." She showed him again using a dried acorn.

Detached, he gazed, steadied himself, looked nearby at the wreck site and quaffed some weary mouthfuls of air, like whiskey. He hunched over, rendered throat foam onto the crunching granite gravel, kicking a boot tip at some displaced clumps of fescue grass wedged between two rocks. One chunk flipped sideways with a thud near a broken-down barbwire fence line. Some distant cows mooed, signaling it wouldn't be long before they would escape. Cows were always looking for a way out. When they got outside of a fence, they frolicked and kicked their heels in abandonment as if released from prison, a beautiful sight to behold.

Suddenly, Isabelle's wretched screams shredded the air, jabbing Officer Newsome's thoughts, slicing them like a knife. His guts fretted as his eyes lurched toward the woman.

31

"No, this can't be," she squalled. "Never can this be. He's a preacher, you understand, Mr. Policeman. I gave him this testament when he was three." She pulled it out from under her shirt top, showed him, viciously shaking it in mid-air. "He's been reading ever since, even when he didn't know what the words said." The man looked at her, disbelieving.

"He did," she insisted, daring him to think otherwise. "Sometimes a person jus' got a gift from the Lord, an' they can see things others can't. My John can." She rested her words and groped a lungful of air.

"I guess so," he said. He gritted his teeth, sucking on a frayed toothpick edge.

She dribbled out more words. "I'm tellin' ya', he could read 'thout no learnin' when it came to the Word. Three years an' he could read it good as me." She shoved the other unhurt forefinger onto his broad chest, impressing a point with the nub. Restless and unnerved by the jab, he coughed, moving backwards automatically. Hateful silence squatted between them, as if a person.

Mute, he tossed the chewed toothpick with a flick and pulled out a piece of gum, peeled the wrapper, and rolled it into his mouth. He chewed, wallowing the spongy wad over his tongue and against his jaw, salivating.

Rocks shifted under his feet. Lonely, a whip-poor-will sung out again as its estranged mate echoed from somewhere down the road. Tree to tree, it seemed as if sadness was being tossed like a ball by nature's creatures.

Confusion clouded Isabelle's mind. "This ain't the way it's 'posed to end. I ain't 'pose to bury my own kid." She grabbed the officer's coat sleeve and held on vise-like. He stiffened. The little woman writhed like a pretzel.

Defensively, he concurred, "I know ma'am. I know."

"He's named after John the Baptist, you know. He's baptized more than anybody—more than any preacher I ever heard of—do ya hear me, mister," her voice screeched, reminding him of a cat. "Peter's Creek ain't never had so many people dipped clean afore."

The officer chomped his gum like a cow chewing cud.

She droned on. "When he dips 'em in, they stay that way. Ain't no fallin' back for his sheep. Not like some other preachers 'round the state

32

of Virginny haulin' 'bout them big tents like a circus sideshow or some-thin'." She drew a prideful breath.

"Yes ma'am," he replied.

"Things done got plum out of hand with them 'vangelists, doin' preachin' for money and not a bit for God's glory and kingdom. With their slicked-back hair, big smiles full of clickin' an' clackin' fake white teeth, them shiny tie-up shoes with little brass tips on the ends, and fancy dry-cleaned two-piece suits. I heard now they be passin' water buckets for plates, an' sellin' miracles an' the Holy Ghost."

Interested, he leaned toward her, snorting.

She peered angrily from the slits of her eyes. "Now, ya know your-self it jus' ain't right. They gonna be held 'countable in the worst kind of way. They all gonna burn in flames of hell for fleecin' God's flock."

He gazed at her, sniffing in agreement.

"God got the sheep part right," she smarted. "People'll follow jus' 'bout anything, jus' cause they told something or their ears itch. They think they can buy their way into heaven's gate with money or good deeds."

"You right about that too, ma'am," he responded, getting involved in her conversation.

"To hear 'em tell it, they's better than other folks in the kingdom cause they be a deacon or be the sister who prays or shouts the loudes', or gets to be the plate-passer or bake the best coconut cake for the cake walk. They jus' wanna be seen by all the church folks like they're better than the rest."

The policeman's forehead beaded sweat. He wiggled and chuckled softly, then acknowledged agreement. "I see it in church all time," he said. "One woman in my church, plays the organ, raising her arms all in the air, like she's on fire or something. She's got a nerve to look down her nose on me because I'm a copper."

Isabelle's miffed face approved.

"I admit I say a few bad words now and again, take a few drags of a cigarette, dip a little snuff, and drink a beer if I have a mind. But look what I gotta put up with. That woman's got herself out messing with South Pick's deacon from down the holler. See, I know all kinds of stuff 'bout people; most people thinks it's all hid. I just don't go gossiping all over the place. You sure got a point there, ma'am." He spoke emphati-cally, lost in her topic.

"I sure do got a point," she cackled, way too loud. "Like Sister Agnes. She be the only woman deacon in the big church. Course I ain't never been there. She says she works harder than any man. What folks don't know is when she goes 'round doing the Lord's work, she baits pitiful helpless souls, snatching pieces of folks' lives, and spreads it around like soft butter on a hot biscuit."

He looked off at the noiseless wreckage again, agreeing with a hidden belch.

"She brags 'bout every kid she feeds a meal to or puts a pitiful rag on its body. If she does it, everybody sure 'nough gonna' know 'bout it. They don't even catch on 'bout the braggin' cause she does it all sly-like, in the name of the Lord. But she don't fool me none. I see right through it all when she comes around me." Her tongue licked out of her dry, puckered mouth.

"She doesn't know who her husband's out foolin' with; but everybody else sure does," Newsome added, knowing who Isabelle was talking about. How many Agneses live in this small town? Not hard to figure. Plus, he'd caught her old man parked at Belmont's overlook, in different borrowed cars, more than once.

Newsome pulled out a yellow-splotched handkerchief, blew his nose. "She doesn't know half what he's been up to. Doesn't want to know. Just pretends all is well, casting a blind eye to it all."

"He sure 'nough got that big church preacher fooled," Isabelle huffed. "That black-headed heifer's done been in Agnes's own house with him all alone, time and agin. While Sister Agnes be about helping the homeless. And he's got a gall to come to the cake-walk throwin' hundred dollar bills 'round for a pecan pie, not much bigger than my own hand. It's what's goin' 'round anyways. 'Thout his dollars he'd be nothing to nobody in that church. Nothin' I tell ya. Much less a Sunday school teacher and big-shot city leader. He'd be nothin'." She puffed.

He adjusted his black holster, checking the gun's safety.

"She's 'bout as bad as he is, showin' off and braggin' all time 'bout all they got. If 'n it comes right down to it, not a dab of cool water would she put on a dry tongue, 'thout 'spectin' somethin' back. A body'd jus' haft to thirst plum half to death."

"You got that right," Newsome said.

"The good book says to give a drink of water when it's needed and a blessin' is sure to come. Sister Agnes abandoned her own best friend

Shirley for nigh two years." Isabelle's eyes glued onto a skirt button. She fiddled at it, flinching when it raked the wounded finger.

"You okay, ma'am?"

"It don't hurt none much," she moaned sadly and continued. "Shirley jus' needed a little 'couragement to get through the dark times. You think she got any from the good sister Agnes? No sirree. Nary a bit. The good and righteous sister jus' be off doin' the Lord's work an' tellin' all 'bout it. 'Stead of helpin' somebody who helped her for years on end, she went 'bout like nothin' was goin' on while Shirley 'bout grieved herself nigh to death. But she sure got through it 'thout no help from Sister Agnes. Thanks be to God. Leastways, it's what I heard."

The officer stretched and yawned.

"She be jus' as bad as them shiny-shoe preachers out for money. An' she don't know them scriptures. She jus' knows 'nough to hark it out, making herself look good to poor old ign'rant souls," she added.

"The church is full of them, if you ask me," the copper sneered. "Ones like her has just about ruin' the house of God, bragging on their hoity-toity selves."

"Sure 'nough do. They don't have gumption to study the Word an' see what really is and ain't. Jus' want somebody to cook it all up, poke it in their mouths an' chew it for them. Guess to swallow it too, I reckon. I guess, then, they want somebody to wipe their sorry stupid asses. For God's sake, don't make 'em do a little work for their own salvation or care enough about their own kids to do a little extra for deliverance. It ain't gonna happen."

Fatigued, time lingering, Newsome barely grunted.

The words kept spilling and splattering. "I see'd it way too many times over the years. Some people there ain't no hope for. They jus' want to be led along like blind sheep and never work for nothing. So I just say, let the blind lead the blind, fall into the ditch, an' go straight to hell. See if that helps 'em do any better. See what they think 'bout things then. Course my John, he don't see things like I do. He thinks there's hope for 'bout anybody. We jus' don't see eye to eye on it." She hesitated.

Tears overwhelmed her eyes. She stopped and blew her slimy nose on the bottom of her torn skirt fringe. An unnerving thick quietness hovered, covering them like a shroud.

35

She gathered herself. "Some of 'em preachers ain't nary one of 'em worth a nickel, 'cept that man in Buffalo. I send him a bit of money here an' there, cause I know he is for real. But them others, they in it for the money an' it's all for show."

Silence returned, sitting stony, leaning heavy against Isabelle like a weighty body. Her chest ached, pulled and throbbed with each heartbeat. She shrank, shriveled, and breathed into the naked void.

The cop glanced at the old woman's pasty face, now full of gravest sorrow.

She wavered. "What my son John washes into salvation, not a one turns back to the old ways of living." In restless waves, she stood up and sat down, finding no comfort in either position.

"But some people you can't help," he gaffed. "No matter what you do, they go right back to the pig's trough to wallow."

"Yeah, like a dog goes back to its vomit. Now his brothers, 'cept Rudy, they a different story; they so full of the devil and his works, can't nobody help 'em. You can smell the evil spirit in 'em coming into a room afore they get there. I'm tellin' you, they ain't no sheep, but they ain't no hypocrites, neither."

Momentarily she decided that at least some good was in them. "Their legs run 'em to evil, an' seeks it out. They's meaner than any copperhead, moccasin, or rattlesnake. It ain't beyond 'em to steal every dime ya got. Even mine, their poor old mama's onion money."

The big man shrugged his broad shoulders. Clearing out the hollow of his throat, he offered, "I know what you're saying, ma'am. Excuse me, ma'am, but some people just plain mean as hell." His legs squatted down alongside of her.

"And they'll gouge one 'nother for a dime," she kept spouting, "if they want somethin' bad enough. John tried his best. Nobody can help them vipers. They straight from the loins of their sorry-ass father," the woman raged, sputtered and gagged in disgust, forgetting the whit of goodness mentioned before about them not being hypocrites.

The tired policeman stood and backed away as she arose and her hand attacked his shirt sleeve like a saber-tooth dog. He squirmed, shivered, tugging his extremity.

"Can I take you home or something, ma'am? I'm powerful sorry." He pulled harder. "I...I, I just gotta go. It's awful late, we been here

36

about all night, and the other shift's coming on, and the truth is, I need to pee."

The round icy moon dangled and glowed akin to a lamp in a stone-cold sky. Like an ancient man, it crawled, creeping slowly. Thousands of stars became lusterless while the great light sneaked westward, snail-like, making room for Isabelle's sad ending and sad beginning.

"I wish I could help you, but I gotta get back to the station," he explained shamefully. Her anguish rubbed all over him as his impotence settled within him like grimy soot.

She tagged onto him a few more seconds, grappled, then respectfully let go as she slumped onto her bruised knees. Grieved to the pulpy quick. Mercilessly weighed down, back to front, top to bottom—as she muttered and uttered guttural, unrecognizable wails—with the necklace and manuscript buried tight into her hollowed-out chest cavity. Tears and silky snot soaked the dirt-grimed skirt, leaving wide ringlets on her garment hem, much like pond ripples after a thrown-in pebble.

The big man backed off softly, fading ghost-like into the unrooted night shadows. Slinking behind a cluster of locust trees, he fumbled, unzipped his fly, snagging flesh. He fussed and fumed and then squirted out little streams of relief through an engorged prostate.

The wind shimmied, bringing a barrage of cries to his ears. He heard her agony, then, ignoring it as best as he could, he turned his back and walked toward his car.

Isabelle spied the copper's silhouette, hooked onto the moon's frosty bottom, bobbing. "He turned thirty-three last week," she shouted at the disappearing man. "His life's all snuffed out, you tell me. You're a lying, devil. It can't be. You jus' trying to drive me plum crazy. Why you doing it? Why ya tellin' me all of them lies?"

Her squalls gyrated into the shadows as distance grew between them. From the night's palpable, dark agony, the man moved slowly, shriveling into a dot, then nothingness.

Then he halted, turned slightly as if to go back, but thought better of it. Another piece of gum gusted out of his mouth as he reached a helpless hand toward his head and removed his stiff cap. Split fingernails gnawed at a bald spot. He tucked a sliver of gray hair over the crusted, empty space. It didn't itch, more habit than anything, scratching what didn't need scratching, just because.

Digging into his dried, slightly blood-stained shirt pocket, he pulled out a scrunched-up pack of Pall Malls and tapped it against his hand, jarring a cigarette loose so that it poked out farther than the rest. He struck a blue-tip match, fire cindered, and it lit. Crackling happily, the red-flowered tobacco tip glowed as he took a hearty drag. God, it tasted so good. "No quitting," he mused, wondering how anything this good could be so bad.

"Ain't nobody can help her. Nobody. She's beyond it," he murmured hopelessly. He walked on, bent a stocky frame into the vehicle, and cranked the starter. A switch flipped. A whiny female dispatcher came to life: "ten sixty-two in progress," the static, spit-infested device transmitted.

"Ten-seventeen responding." Red lights whirled. He raced to leave the old woman behind in her salty puddles and dust.

Earlier that night, a focused, furtive light beam had come through the darkness from nowhere, like a great searching eye. It pointed straight as a sharp dagger seeking prey. Swarms of screeches had bellowed from the train's black navel. Greasy rails screamed like dancing demons, warbling underneath. Paralyzed, like an animal with its foot hung up in the grips of a steel trap, bursting with fear and distress, writhing and waiting for death's call, John was. Then John was no more.

9

Isabelle
Afterwards

Officer Newsome left Isabelle rooted at the awful spot of John's death. In the darkness, time gulped and swallowed. Isabelle's knees crinkled and crunched on the cold fallen autumn leaves. Acorn hulls cupped gouges into her numb, rubbery legs as obscurity hugged her. She rubbed her lower extremities, urging them, though dead, to rise.

Talking to the wind, she lifted herself. "I'll do what I gotta do by myself, like I always have and always will. People don't stand by a person when they need 'em. Not even your own kids. 'Specially mine. But I'll get by." Parched air traveled, rasping like sandpaper through her throat, tracheal membranes as tight as a double-tied shoestring. "Somehow, I will, if a mind to."

A wild rosebush reached out and seized her arm, miniscule thorns digging flesh. She jerked, increasing the pain. A vision of Jesus's face birthed.

She'd seen it before. That awful vision. Huge thorns clawed his head, flesh ripped open to the skull. His mouth parched, face purple-splotched, pockmarked from pulled beard. Mouth full of anguish and dreadful dryness, lips ruptured wide open like river canyons. "He's thirsty, too weak to moan, I bet. He looks more a car-hit mangled dog than human. How can he still be alive?" Isabelle whispered.

She whimpered, leaving some prickly briars embedded, stinging. The left-behind woman marveled at the surfacing bloody spots, one behind the other, like tiny stepping stones.

"Why God, why not me. I ain't no good for nothin' now. Ya done took my only reason for livin'." And then Jesus dissolved.

Isabelle fisted the sky. "Why him? Why not one of them others who live to hurt and do wicked? Why not one of them? Why?" She staggered and struggled in guilt and shame. She hollered, dickering with God, "I'll trade you any of them for him. Take me, why don't ya?"

Dejectedly, she stared down at her hands. "What will I ever do with an old worn-out testament an' a tarnished cross? They can't take hold of my neck, or tell me they love me, or help me dig weeds from my flower beds. They not my John." She raised her eyes and screamed louder, "They not my John, I tell you."

Into her gnarly orange sweater pocket she fumbled the tokens, her small numb feet trailing homeward. The hoot owl fluttered, flitted, twisted his fierce head, glanced shoulder-wise and called. His heavy wings swished the air into slices as he flapped upward. A windy current carried him high as the winding muddy Dan River flowed on.

With each step, Isabelle relived images, flashes, remnants of her son's bedraggled body, the copper's already hardened bloody shirt, and John's shattered vehicle. "I shoulda' paid 'tention to them vultures when they landed all 'round the house the other day," she chided herself hatefully. As if she could have prevented the catastrophe.

Flocked in hordes, the black turkey vultures had landed in the trees, on the roof, under the work shelter, combing the ground. So many she couldn't count their ugly, mocking faces.

Not to say the fowlish horde didn't disturb her, but she had things to do. Like hauling water and firewood in, and cooking, and gathering dried clothes off the barbwire fence. She should've said words of faith but instead just let it go. Nothing but bitter regrets taunted her. How could her only light be wiped out in the blink of an eye? She begged God, and the guardian angels, or whoever would listen, as her body trudged onward one step at a time, the sun beginning to uncover herself.

She rehearsed the steps in her mind. Newsome had told her he'd find her boys and send them to her home. He knew about their favorite beer joined where brawls often occurred and Rudy hung out with that Fanny woman. Isabelle would talk to Lizzie later, when she finished her third-shift job at the laundry house.

One step at a time.

"John's gone, he's dead, the lawman said it to me," she announced early that morning, sitting in her own living room. Relief flickered across her sons' faces. Suspicious, she wondered if they'd done something to the gas pedal or brakes. Did they shed his innocent blood? Their own brother's blood. Even brothers in the Bible killed their kin. Family members kill relations. It happens.

Why not now, in these ages? Clan members against members. Betrayals, broken trusts, abandonments, murders, and sheddings of innocent blood. Why not now? Isabelle speculated as she looked on Ed, James, and Rudy—her remaining sons.

Jealousy can do that. It makes people do terrible things to other people and even animals. Perhaps, if she had not shown John so much attention, he'd still be with her. What if she had only taken more stock in his brothers when they came around? Maybe she should have given them her onion money. If she had done this or that, would her John be alive? She figured he just might.

Death stalks, snatches and steals life. His black veil happily settles itself, smothering everything good, leaving only weeping and gnashing behind.

Ghoulish, it pops out of nowhere, choking necks like a heavy millstone. The anguished soul gurgles, haggles, and writhes with futile groans. Distressed moans turn into unknown languages babbling, with no meaning found in the deepest, darkest abyss of human agony.

Days passed into weeks, then months. With one foot barely in front of the other, Isabelle moved hypnotically. Memorized pictures of John, plastered mindfully and set in stone, troubled her.

She had not touched the Word since her son died. She just didn't care anymore. Three months, four, then five passed. Lethargy and sleeplessness consumed her.

Time wore on until one day came and night creeped up and settled upon her like a comforter. Though drained, she was drawn toward her Bible, like a "flibbie," a small moth, to flames. Wooden floorboards creaked underneath the old rocker as it scraped sparingly. Light rays splayed from the noble kerosene lamp as the dull globe sat steady beside her sad chair.

Lonely, she watched glows wobble, wave, and weave patterns of soft flickers. Fading shadows on the wall danced like mischievous imps, then slid away into the unknown world.

Scripture opened itself on her lap. A soft, supernatural breath leafed through the Bible's thin, fragile, fettered pages. Singularly, they flipped and flopped and deliberately spread open. Spiritually prodded, she read from Isaiah 59:

> Therefore is justice far from us, nor does righteousness overtake us; we look for light, but there is darkness! For brightness, but we walk in blackness! We grope for the wall like the blind, and we grope as if we had no eyes; we stumble at noonday as at twilight, we are as dead men in desolate places. We all growl like bears, and moan sadly like doves. We look for justice, but there is none; for salvation, but it is far from us. ...for truth is fallen in the street and equity cannot enter. So truth fails, and he who departs from evil makes himself a prey.

Like her dead boy did. Maybe he made himself a prey. Her finger drew lines beneath the words. Her eyes wrinkled. Wincing, she whispered, "For truth is fallen in the street and equity cannot enter. So truth fails, and he who departs from evil makes himself a prey."

Was John a prey because he separated himself from evil? Was she right to wonder if his own brothers may have destroyed him because of jealousy? Was John trying to tell her something? Was Jesus?

Isabelle had given some of her boys godly names, thinking it would magically help their destiny. She had never dreamed her own seed could be so wicked. Some were dark souls, she knew this. John's brothers were wife-beaters, whoremongers, and alcoholics. They'd just as soon shoot or stab a person as look at them.

They were the epitome of depravity. They survived to inflict any and all kinds of pain on others. John thought his kin could be saved, but she knew better. She knew better long before John was ever born.

She had told herself to quit deceiving herself and see people for who they really were. Just because they came out of her womb didn't mean they were good. It was a cold, hard lesson for any parent to learn. Admitting their own seed were born losers, users, liars, thieves, killers, and just plain evil. Wishing to God that the others had never been born.

A wolf is a wolf, plain and simple, she reasoned. It can turn against anybody, tearing its own mama to shreds if it has a mind to. Wolves take everything a body works for, as if it's their own, and would leave behind a penniless mama to die with nothing.

Scripture nudged again:

For your hands are defiled with blood, and your fingers with iniquity; your lips have spoken lies, your tongue has muttered perversity, no one calls for justice, nor does any plead for truth.

They trust in empty words and speak lies; they conceive evil and bring forth iniquity.

They hatch vipers' eggs and weave the spider's web; he who eats of their eggs dies; and from that which is crushed, a viper breaks out.

Their works are iniquity, acts of violence are in their hands.

Their feet run to evil, and they make haste to shed innocent blood: their thoughts are works of iniquity; wasting and destruction are in their paths. The way of peace they have not known, and there is no justice in their ways; they have made themselves crooked paths; whoever takes that way shall not know peace.

Aside from giving her some affirmation of the depth of evil in the world, the verses gave little comfort. In death's cold cavern Isabelle existed. Truth unveiled itself. Hateful haunts troubled her spirit, tormenting her wits with questions. Queries flooded about goodness, death, justice, sorrow, pain and suffering. Hope wearied itself out of her dull eyes.

The pit of bereavement carried her storm-tossed body and mind through more unwanted weeks and months. She labored with life, welcoming death. But dying evaded her. Her toxemic spirit groped, groveled, and prayed for the powers that be to take her from this misery.

Sleeplessness overcame her. Again, one peculiar night, Isabelle slid the poor book from the dusty dresser top. It opened to a dog-eared page at Isaiah 49. John had marked the passage. She kissed the wise pages hungrily as if to ingest him. To make him live in her as he had once lived in her womb.

The Lord has called me from the womb, from the matrix of my mother he had made mention of my name and he has made my mouth like a sharp sword; in the shadow of his hand he has hidden me, and made me a polished shaft; in his quiver he has hidden me.

The room stood still. Neck hairs bristled as a cool peculiar presence arrived without form. She knew not if evil or good had come for her.

She clutched the silver cross to her withered bosom and wept with gratitude for either.

Like figments, John's childhood images came alive: like the time he suffered a skinned knee, and the time he stumped his big toe so badly the toenail was severed, and the time his first tooth detached after it had dangled for days on end, and he wouldn't let her touch it.

She recalled his little tear-drenched face as it was many times during childhood. John was there. "I'll fix your boo-boos," she said. Then Isabelle reached up and dried his tears as if he was there.

Torrential tears poured from her own eyes. She fell on her knees and lamented profoundly, with gut-wrenching sobs. Afterwards, sleepless, she crawled back into bed.

"Mama," Isabelle whispered. "Mama, I need you. I can't do this." She curled her fingers but nothing was there. Just air. In the blackness sound came. Seemingly, fingernails tapped on glass. Tap, tap, tap.

"Mama." Taps continued and a voice called. "It's me. It's John. Mama, let it go. It doesn't matter what they did to me. The evil they did will come on them. Let it go and smile again. I'll be with you in the garden every morning. Just look for me. Now smile. I'll see you briefly."

Her hand slapped her cheek. Was she going crazy? She felt foolish. Longingly, a dove cooed wooing her.

"Doves don't coo at night," she whispered. The tuts persisted. Raising herself up from the stacked pillows, she scooted off the bed and shuffled her feet toward the sound.

She peeled a dowdy window curtain from the window's edge to see if she could spot where the bird's voice emanated. Yet she saw nothing. Can the dead to come back into the world of the living? Her John was gone to the other side, but his presence was there. Now she could rest reassured.

He'd always be with her. She knew her son had been sent to love her from the beginning and now at the ending. From out there, he came back to fix her broken heart. Love crossed infinity. "I'll be fine now, John, don't worry ya'self 'bout me no more. I'll miss ya but I'll smile someday, maybe. But I'll never know love like I have with you. My precious chile."

As the days continued to pass, odd thoughts skipped through Isabelle's mind. She remembered the pint-size clothes she had made for John as she lovingly swaddled the precious book and silver treasures in a delicate white handkerchief, cotton cornered with embroidered purple and pink flowers: a birthday gift from him.

She knotted twine around the bundle to keep the trinkets contained, then placed it under her feather pillow, heart twisting, hot tears staining the tufted ticking. Helpless, she let him go. And then, there at a time of prodigious sorrow when there should have been no peace, there was ephemeral serenity.

After the dove's visit, she began to search nightly underneath the plump feather pillow, gently caressing the bits and pieces in the handkerchief, much as she had done John's hair locks when he was a tot. "Good night, son," she said. "I'll always love ya. I'll see ya on the other side."

Seemingly, eons had passed. But John's memories always came when least expected, tramping through her mind like troops, uninvited, like on the ill-fated trip to Pilot Knob with her family.

After sitting for a photo with her husband Harkus, wishing he had it in him to be a better man, Isabelle raised herself from the knob's dusty boulder. She brushed her skirt tail with brisk hand waves and wiped resurgent, silent tears from her eyes.

Later that night, as she and the little ones endured yet another tirade of fear and terror from her son James, she clung tightly to John's memory and ached for him. Some memories were as real as yesterday. John's life. His death. Her poignant agony. Nothing would take it away completely. Nothing. How she wished he were here with them now. Maybe his love and compassion would temper his brother's drunken anger. She couldn't for the life of her understand why her beautiful angel son was taken from her.

It was the cards she was given, though, and she'd do the best she could with what she had. She would.

10

Me and the Scaldings

Mama had another kid. A boy called Danny. Me and Granny Isabelle weren't happy when I had to take off and go live with my parents again. They needed me to take care of the young'uns. It was all I was good for. Daddy blamed me when anything went wrong. Sometimes I had to scrunch up into a ball to save my own self. There weren't no help when Granny Isabelle wasn't around.

I huddled, head packed tight between my knees, hands wrapped around my head, fingers spread like a wide fork to cover it. Shrunken little, like a no-see-um, unable to push backwards no more. My feelings sapped. Empty inside, I prayed for somebody to save me. Maybe Granny Isabelle or Jesus. Maybe God.

Scalds covered my slapped, soaking face. My cheeks ached from where he knocked me sideways. Piggish giggles came. Jerks and snubs. I craved to die. I sat jittering like baby Danny. Strong salty tears filled my chattering mouth to choke me, but didn't.

Exhausted, crumpled, and confused. Puddled, huddled in the darkest corner, empty like a shadow, I lay. He was God, more powerful than anyone on earth, bigger and stronger than the other God in heaven. Daddy was.

"Please stop," I whispered like my mouth had a dry rag in it. My racked voice long gone. "Please stop. Don't hurt me no more, Daddy." Me not yet knowing what I'd done wrong, sitting alone, befuddled.

A big man's noise roared, jeered and sneered from the rafters. My daddy turned into an awful man. Even his voice changed as if demonic.

"You think I don't know what ya do every minute." He cussed God, spewing filthy words, cutting me inside. I peeped out through my swollen eyelids, hunting his voice.

I was a squashed gnat. Nobody could see me. I sat in the wet, warm place. It felt good, the warm wet did. Painless. Nothing could hurt me now.

46

I retched forward, swayed back, rocking and rocking—seated in tepid golden puddles—and studied the salty amber pool, tasted it, drew doodles with my fingertips. The leg welts burned, feeling good.

Me, Ginny, and Danny always peed on ourselves. Sometimes, even Mama did. It couldn't be helped. After we done said we wouldn't soak our britches, we still did. But words didn't mean nothing. Not nothing.

Shamefully wadded, like a rolled-up wooly worm, I hovered, shivered and shook all bruised, belittled and hated—alone, seated in my ripped, urine-soaked clothes, speechless, teeth chattering as I waited for more.

Way off I heard a door shut tight. Spit happened somewhere. Daddy left. Danny and Ginny's eyes followed mine. I knew them again. Pity oozed from their fuzzy faces. Squatted, like inchworms, they wiggled to get closer—to rub my damaged parts—but I pushed them off and away like dead flies.

"I don't want nobody close," I spit through clenched teeth. "He ain't never gonna die no matter how bad we pray."

Mama woke from the floor where she'd been smashed, hurt even worse this time. She weren't supposed to be hit cause she couldn't bear no more pain. She said her wrinkles came from weariness, not worry over us young'uns. She was lying, I could tell, cause her eyes went to the wall with fibbing. But I just let things be.

Nobody much cared for us. I was just a little kid and I knew that. The wet black spell of another night had been spent, and darkness dragged into the misty morning as if nothing awful had happened, and we went on breathing. Nothing more, nothing less.

11

Peace Comes Hard

Seems we were always moving in and outta somewhere. Daddy took a notion to go again, leaving us behind with Granny Isabelle. Leaving us kids tangled in knots, not knowing which end was up. Headed back to where we came from before to Granny Isabelle's little house. Part of me glad, part of me hurting, being left behind yet again. Half of me wanting to go while the other half wanted to stay. Coming and going at the same time was the way we lived.

Granny Isabelle came dragging her broken hoe behind her the day we were put outta the car.

"What happened to ya hoe?" I asked.

"It jus' gave out I 'pose. It jus' happens sometimes. Like us, I guess, when we get used too much 'til we jus' break in two. Anyhow, I gotta burn the wood outta this thing and take the split part out and put a new handle in. Let the others play in the dirt and you come on to the kitchen and I'll fix you a little sugar biscuit and you can sit with me for a spell."

Ginny and Danny took off to chase chickens for a while. She rambled around the room, stoking the kitchen stove fire, placing the old hoe remnant in sideways as the coals danced into a slow jittery flame. She commenced to fixing my sugar biscuit, crumbs scattering across the table, eyeing me sideways simultaneously. Home-churned butter smeared across the flaky edges as sugar was applied to the moist bready bed. My mouth watered.

"What's that little head of yours hanging so low for this time?" Granny pried inconspicuously.

"Nothin'."

We sat at her small cluttered table as she rested after pouring some cow milk into my glass. I watched the yellowish thick cream float to the top and dipped my finger into it, sticking the milky end into my mouth eagerly.

"For a chile's head to hang that low, somethin' must be hindering the good thoughts somewhere."

My mouth chewed thoughtfully on my milky finger, me not wanting to hurt her feelings. Not that I wanted to be with Mama and Daddy; it was more about being left behind than anything else.

"It ain't about being here with ya," I finally said. "cause all I really want to do is be here. Ya the only one who cares for me, Granny Isabelle. I'm jus' a kid, but I see it. Anyway, why they jus' pull up and go off and leave me behind, I jus' don't know. They my mama and daddy. Ain't they s'pose to take care of me somehow?"

Granny Isabelle leaned forward toward me, twisting her half-full glass sympathetically and wordlessly. "Have ya seen that pack of baby birds out there in the birdhouse we built some years back?"

I shook my head, wondering what birds had to do with me being left behind.

"That batch of little barn swallows has a mama and daddy bird that hovers over them day and night and come what may. They must grow awful tired of fetching worms and such, chewing 'em up and spitting food into them kids' mouths. It is never-ending work waiting 'til them kid birds can fly on their own and take care of their own selves. But they do what they have to 'til that happens. Then the babies can take care of their own selves. They have to."

Looking at her, interested in her story cause she was always a good storyteller, I felt perplexed over the tale's relationship to my dilemma. It must have shown up on my face.

"The other day I heard the worst racket ever coming from the far side of the sky on the other side of the porch there." She pointed outward. "Birds come from every direction. Birds of all colors, big and small, and in between. They came zooming in like war planes. It took me a few minutes to see what was going on at first. I had to get my bearings with all the commotion happening. It was a terrible racket in the air. Wings flapping, zooming in and out, squalls and shrieks filling the sky. Then, I heard some crows screaming to high heaven. Caw, caw, and caw they went. Caw, caw, and caw they went some more. Do ya know what happened?"

"Nope."

"Them crows was trying to steal the little swallow's eggs and babies. That's what happened. All them birds from kingdom come came to rescue some family they didn't even know. They jus' knew from the bird calls that them crows was going to destroy somebody's little babies."

I thought on it a while, licking the milk off my lips, not wanting to waste a drop. "But Granny Isabelle, what's that got to do with my hung head?"

"It's got a lot. Some mamas and daddies ain't worth a plugged nickel or they jus' don't know how to care 'bout nobody but their own selves. They don't build nests and feed their own little babies and they sure don't fight the big bad crows off of 'em. But Jessie, some people jus' can't love nothing if they tried. It ain't in 'em. We'd all be better off if we was jus' birds. Then we might know how to take care of what we bring into the world."

I looked on her face, studying her words. "Then it ain't me that's the reason for their not lovin' me and them leavin' me behind all time. It's cause they can't love nobody." I said it back to her slowly, fidgeting with my crumbs and milk drops, still not quite getting the gist of her lesson but getting a smidgen of it to be built on later—wishing so much to be a bird learning to fly from wings of love.

She raised up, wiped the table, rinsed the rag out, and poured water to the stove fire.

"I think this here hoe is ready for a new handle." She grinned as steam spewed from the fire. "Now, let's fix a biscuit for the rest with a little glass of milk."

Often, afternoon summer thunderstorms came to Granny Isabelle's house, shaking it like a baby rattle. Into our chests came the thunder, thumping like a drum as furious, frenetic noises clanged and banged, bouncing like sky cymbals, loud enough to rupture eardrums.

Us kids would run and sit in the middle floor 'til the rumbles passed on by. Granny Isabelle would rear back in her rocking chair, open the Holy Bible, and pray for lightning not to strike us. Other times she'd just fall to sleep, right in the middle of a windy rage. I'd sit at her feet, staring at her dirty skirt ruffles, dappled with red splotchy mud stains, making animal shapes from them like I did the clouds sometimes.

Once, a fierce storm came on us, as we had ridden "horses," old tobacco sticks, giddy-upping in the yard. Our tranquil sky colored tar-paper black, then puked into pasty red and green hazes, like an old bruise. Quiet hovered stagnant overhead. Windy squalls, not of the ordinary kind, came belching from the still silence. A long arm like a tea-pot spout came slurping, reaching out to suck on us.

"Holy Jesus," Granny Isabelle bellowed. The screen door banged and clanged as she rolled out of the house onto the warped, paint-peeled porch. Waving scrawny arms, elbows bent atop her head, she motioned mightily for the mean clouds to come closer. Yearning, stooping forward onto its frayed edges like a captain going down with his ship. Resolute she stood, peering upward, a withered hand covering her old eyes, watching for the gale's obedience.

Granny Isabelle meowed, like a cat with its tail being pulled, "Jesus, Lord of lords, is a comin'. Gabriel's a blowin' his horn. Pay 'tention little chillens." Her screeches gyrated and blended into the harsh, windy wet howls set against us. I don't think Gabriel paid her no attention, cause the clouds spoke louder than any man. She'd been waiting for this day: "The Day of the Lord's Return."

Black clouds billowed and trundled. Frantically, Granny Isabelle screamed for the Lord to come. Her bony fingers shook as they crooked toward the heavens. I wasn't thinking Jesus had heard her; the wind knocked her down. I, myself, just wanted Him and Gabriel to leave us alone.

In an instant, Mrs. Red, my favorite hen, half-plucked already, squawked toward a bitsy blue-sky spot. Granny Isabelle's orphan cats hung, without clothespins, electrified, on a barbwire clothesline. A neighbor's chipped red bricks sailed like bullets and then stood steady as a rail, before our faces, before swirling away again.

"Finally," she said, "He's comin' an' all's gonna be alright." Wind and water pried her face, spreading old skin like a wax doll. Mockingly, ours stretched taut like Granny Isabelle's as we gazed at one another's plastic faces.

"What if we look like this forever?" Most pitifully I cried, cringing. No one else said a word as thunderous booms bantered, dueling. Explosions roared. The porch quivered and quavered, jiggled and wiggled my feet.

Like magnets, windy torrents snatched Granny Isabelle's hairpins. Her gray hair was usually rolled like a snake at the base of her tough, sun-creased neck. Small black bobby pins flew like spears, spun beyond, probing blankets of tree leaves, acorns, and tree trunks or whatever. Her old energized tresses unfurled, snapping, jerking outward. Witch-like, the crazy curls straightened, peaked and pointed into mysterious directions, like sharp shoots on a thorn bush.

Crone-like, Granny Isabelle stood in a soaked cotton dress plastered into every crevice of her waterlogged body. Akin to Humpty Dumpty, her potbelly poked out over two twiggy toothpick legs. Then the wide runners ripped into the nylons, making ungodly railroad tracks.Seamed stocking tops, earlier twirled into knots beneath her knobby knees, fell slackened.

Baby, spindly legs with bent doorknob knees, wagged about in thick-sole black tie-up dusty red shoes. Hunks of yesterday's porch-scraped mud, from nasty shoes, vortexed, whirling into nowhere.

Perplexed, petrified, and terrified over Granny Isabelle's unusual war dance, we observed, feet hopping and much screeching over nothing visible. We scooted and scuttled on shifting mud puddles like oil on water, as our drenched bodies lifted off porch boards sporadically.

Windy arms yanked our clothes, exposing our raw nakedness as shame crawled onto us; disgrace gloated over our glaring private parts. Tiny things nibbled at our legs like fleas, but not really fleas; rather, little rocks were chewing us.

"What if Gabriel takes us away, far away?" I yowled, not knowing who he was in the first place. The littler ones wailed into the wind with me, their sounds going nowhere with mine as our voices were pushed and poked back down into our throats. Choking, I gasped, studying on Granny Isabelle's wild eyes, flagging thin hair, and flailing arms. I recalled something.

Papa Harkus and his stinking dog, Smokey, remained in the woods where the wind wanted to go. Now, I didn't care none for Papa Harkus or Smokey, but I reasoned nobody ought to go to the other side, drunk and all.

So I shrieked loudly to wake Granny Isabelle outta of her spell, "What 'bout Papa Harkus?"

She screamed back, "If'n he ain't got sense to get out of the storm, then he can go straight to hell."

So I yelled some more louder than she did, "What about Smokey?" cause we all knew he didn't have no sense enough either to get outta the rain.

She blared back, "That dog can go where ya Papa goes for all I care. They's two of a kind an' hell'll be happy to get 'em. Far as I am 'cerned, they can stay here left behind for the great tribulation. They both done tribulated me 'nough in this old world, so to hell with 'em. Ain't no way in heaven I'll clean up their sorry mess after what they done put me through."

Enough said, she turned from me as lightning baptized her face into evil shimmers. The blustery weather raged as Granny Isabelle talked to invisible sky people.

By then, I knew Granny Isabelle wasn't in her right mind, her wanting somebody in hellfire. So I prayed out loud for her to come back to her senses. Zippers of blasting light banged the thunder, booming, booming, and booming. Swords of zigzagged brightness hit the porch yard, licking it like great tongues, dancing, cracking like whips on a mule, but worse.

The yellow neon jags split in half two gigantic oak trees, quick like a big hot knife on butter. A massive maple tree uprooted, akin to a pulled rotten molar, and then it spun into the roaring funnel.

Everything shook, jiggled, jangled, and juggled. Panic seized us like choking hands, urging us inside the house. Passing through the kitchen door, I spied in the cracked, soap-smudged mirror an evil stain set on my face. A gray, dragon-shaped watermark dripped from my forehead.

"I done been struck with the mark-of-the-beast. Gabriel must have brought it on me," I wailed. Granny Isabelle had preached on that wicked mark. "Surely, I'm going to hell," I caterwauled.

Was this fierce storm about my bad words? My chattering teeth prayed piercingly. "I done caused it all," I said, feeling bad about myself and what I'd brought on everybody.

Grabbing Granny Isabelle's hem, I yanked it, confessing, but she was somewhere else, eyes glazed. Pulling more, I told her, "I been saying the 's' word an' I asked for forgiveness. I'll never say it nor even think it again." Speechless, with fixed eyes she gazed back.

It was just as well. The more I promised not to think the bad word, the more it came to my mouth, blubbering over again with some more fresh cuss words sailing midair. My flesh not letting go, sending me to hellfire with the demons.

Later that night, regretful for swearing, I wept about everything: I cried over the "s" word and worse cusses, Granny Isabelle's skinny elbowed arms, her toothpick legs and knobby knees, her train-track stockings and her embarrassment of being left behind by Jesus. I cried over how she had to work hard like the ants do, toting big back burdens, cutting gardens with nothing but a hoe, to keep us fed and have Dr. Peppers for our birthdays.

I sniveled grossly over her useless hallelujah jigs, our shameful nakedness, and Gabriel who came to rescue us but never did. Still, he'd marked me for my evil ways and showed the world my wretched heart.

I sobbed hysterically about my Granny Isabelle's heart boo-boos, her inside-out hurts. About her night tears over paths leading to nowhere like mine. I wept about the crying spells of me and my siblings as we sobbed into pillows at night, the trails they left behind on our dirty faces, knowing nobody saw or cared how much we hurt, except Granny Isabelle. And knowing we'd have to go away from her and be with my folks sometime later broke my heart.

"Maybe it weren't time yet. You know. Time for Jesus to come," I told her. Unfixed, she just carried on and cried along with me. I wiped her tears with a dishrag, it smelling of clabbered milk and old flour from biscuit-making. I wiped just the same.

"It don't matter no more," she whispered.

"It'll get better." Rattled over her weakness, I spoke lies, like she did to me when she said our hurts wouldn't last forever, without no mama and daddy. But they did hurt. They were packed inside and just didn't show out.

"Maybe Gabriel didn't see us this time. Maybe the wind was too loud or it was rainin' way too much. Our plastic faces an' twisted smiles coulda scared him plum off," I explained to her simply.

I gave her lots of reasons to help her get over it. She just bawled on. I gave her my dried up tumble bug that I'd kept hid in her lost snuff can, but it didn't help none neither. Even so, a bit later, Ginny, Danny, and me was a little happy cause the bad mark had washed off me and our flesh faces came back.

The storm passed, giving Papa Harkus and Smokey time to repent. They showed up dripping, with Papa Harkus only half-drunk. I was upset at the angel for putting a devil mark on me instead of Papa Harkus and his sorry dog, Papa Harkus being from the pits of hell to start with, like Granny Isabelle had said. Smokey stood stinking, soaked to the bone like Papa Harkus.

Granny Isabelle said, "Ain't nothin' smells worse in the whole world, 'cept a drunk an' a wet dog with mange."

54

I watched her think over whether to open the door or not. Her hand holding the knob steady. Never before had she reasoned so long. As they passed through, dripping, stinking to high heaven, I believed she was right as rain. Nothing stunk worse than them two. Me wondering why she turned that doorknob and let the worthless things back in.

After the bad storm calmed, darkness and moisture brought thousands of fireflies. A time came to sit encircled around my Granny Isabelle's worn-out knees, resting, rocker creaking, and reading about Jesus, though her heart wasn't in it, I could tell. Bible or memory, I knew not, cause she quoted scripture awake and asleep. I could see her madness at Jesus and Papa Harkus, but she pressed on for our sakes.

Her nose wrinkled beneath her scratched, bent, wire-rimmed eyeglasses, like the weight was far too heavy for her saggy skin. A kerosene lantern flickered spirit shadows against the walls, dancing like Indians without whoops, as we listened to the Word once more.

Gospel's okay, but mostly we watched wraith-like beings float around, pondering their realness. Granny Isabelle's head bobbed as the bulky book slid easy down toward her knees. Awake, we three watched on for it to fall, slamming the floor. But it never did.

Sleeping, Papa Harkus farted long and loud, but he didn't know it, an odor worse than himself. Smokey even. Granny Isabelle's head jerked up; startled, she grabbed her nose and the Bible's edge, before it fell. She shook her head, disgusted over Papa Harkus's stench, but she was grinning a little with us anyway.

Giggling way too much for what had happened, hands went over our mouths to hold the laughs in, but it didn't help none; afore long we kids were rolling, squalling, and laughing in the floor like stuck hogs.

Granny Isabelle settled us and forced another Jesus story down our throats about a man named Job with too many troubles and lots of reasons for being mad at God. We talked it over a bit and then let it be.

Then life gentled down, shifted into a slow, soft, sweet time. A moment just for the four of us. A space after the storm had passed, where quiet was absolutely motionless; the fireflies glittered through dull window panes as gray kerosene wall apparitions gobbled at each other, and Granny Isabelle's washboard nose drooped as her Bible story seeds were replanted.

Right there, right then, in this little crooked circle, peace was in a spot where it should've never been. It just was. For a moment, all was still, quiet, and well with our world.

12

Smokey and Me

Sometimes Smokey gets to the feeding bowl when nothing much is left in it to slop on. But for some reason he stays awful fat. Maybe cause all he does is eat, lick, scratch, and sleep. Granny Isabelle says most probably he's got a "tyroid" problem, but I don't know about that. All I know is he's mighty heavy and maybe it's why them nineteen cats is starving to death.

Smokey knows I don't like him cause he's Papa Harkus's old dog. When we're outside, I poke his thick lazy tail with a stick and watch him raise his sleepy eyes to look me over. And then half his top lip raises up into a "u" shape to snip on my arm with his broken-off tooth. But he ain't never done me no harm yet.

He stinks like old soured wet rags, and flocks of fleas jump from his back with a raking of his hind leg. Most times them fleas hang on, sucking all his blood and making runny scabs in his grubby fur.

Granny Isabelle declared, "Fleas, ticks, flies, yellow jackets, hornets, rats an' bats an' Aunt Fanny ain't got no purpose whatsoever in life, 'cept to torment the life an' hell outta somebody." I wrinkled my forehead at her, squinting against the sun. She pronounced, "Some things a body can't do nothing 'bout. But some ya can. I wouldn't mind taking some tar and feathers to Aunt Fanny's fat tail." I giggled, picturing her wide waddling behind, feathered like a hen's butt. Then, holding the kerosene jug, Granny Isabelle laughed wild, unlike my real grandma.

Not taking kindly to Smokey's fleas and ticks, she took hold of the oily jug and greased his sores before he got a chance to take off. He couldn't get too far from her anyways; when her head set on something, there weren't no going anywhere. Plus, he couldn't run for nothing cause of all that flab, I supposed.

As she rubbed, she held tight to his ears and I held his thick tail, nearly pulling it off. Afterwards, he took off running down the holler. Faster than any lightning streak, madder than any hornet, way back off

57

into the woods, like a bat outta hell. Granny Isabelle laughed again, unlike herself.

So I guessed he could run if he had a mind to. Smokey could. Sometimes he'd stay away for days. Granny Isabelle retorted, "He's probably off sulking somewhere, but he'll be on when he's good and ready. Now you quit worrying so bad over that mangy hound, Jessie."

It was hard for me to believe he could run so fast on them short stubby legs, worn-out toes, and cracked-up toenails. But like Granny Isabelle said, days later, he loafed on home, huffing weak and outta breath, half-dead. With his tail slipped between his legs and dry tongue hanging out in need of something, he looked at us sleepy-eyed. Mostly, he came on home full of whining over his greased-up self and all hungry for Granny Isabelle's leftover gravy and biscuits.

Sometimes, I got to feeling terribly sorry for Smokey cause the kerosene didn't help him none and he came back, often worse off than when he left on out—flea-packed, fur all caked and stuck together full of oil and dirt and blackberry thorns.

He didn't do nothing but work on them fleas, mope around, and wait for Papa Harkus to come back from wherever he'd headed off to. I tried to tell Smokey 'bout how life was. "Papa Harkus'll come back when he wants to. But I ain't caring none if he never does, so long as I live. I swear to God and heaven above. Why you want him back I'll never know."

He didn't pay me no mind, just scuffed another ear part raw and acted like he was deaf or something. Granny Isabelle said, "Them ear mites can do that to a dog an' his is full of 'em." So I was thinking maybe he read my lips for the most part, to hear what I had to say to him.

Like Granny Isabelle's old friend, Mrs. Mayes—the one with the earhorn who lived down the road a far piece—the one I liked so much. She made us a good strawberry shortcake when we walked there for a visit or for my Granny Isabelle to hoe for a little money.

Granny Isabelle hoed the old woman's garden cause she couldn't do nothing worthwhile for her own self. I just settled down in the dirt and started calling doodlebugs up from the ground. Chanting at the top of my voice, spraying saliva over the hole, "Doodlebug, doodlebug, ya house is on fire. Come an' get some water." I said it a thousand times, spit-words flinging into the holed-out funnel. Getting plum happy to see a dust-covered bug scrounge on up to the sandy top for me to blow on. I played, picking at it with a twig 'til I couldn't do it no more.

Finally, Granny laid the old hoe down as the day ended and we moved on up the road to cook supper. My mouth watering as I thought on the old woman's strawberries and shortcake, not wanting gravy one more time.

We reached home, my legs full of aching, Smokey's tail wagging. But I knew it wasn't us he cared about, cause of that tongue leaking out-ta his mouth full of drool. Me and him took up where we left off earlier in the day, about his useless papa.

I looked at Smokey through the sides of my eyes to see if anything I said done sunk into his skull. He just rolled over onto his back with his four legs stuck up in the air, scraping on rocks, roots, dirt wads, or about anything he could get hold of. Scratching, scratching, and scratching.

I said to him, "Ya jus' plain hopeless, Smokey. Everything I done tried to teach you goes in one ear and outta the other."

He moaned and cried with the itching and went to more grinding, and then he rolled his eyes on me for a little while, soon forgetting I was there, and he got focused on his wretched body, howling some, almost whooping like Papa Harkus, but not drunk on whiskey.

"I wish so bad you'd be like them other people's dogs an' learn to stand on hind legs or at least fetch me a stick." Then he started licking in places he hadn't got no business, like he didn't care for what I said.

"You ain't good for nothing 'cept clawing your own self plumb to death," I said, plain out disgusted for his stupidity.

Then he looked pitiful at me like he didn't want me to think on him as senseless. So I threw a stick out on the rocky path.

I said, "Now go fetch me a stick like a good dog." He wouldn't do nothing. I shook my head, clean tired of fooling with him cause I knew he still hadn't learnt one thing.

"You jus' plain dumb 'thout no understanding. Ya jus' mope around looking for a drunk man."

For a while Smokey and me went on without no more words to be said between us after his awful scratching spells, and I moved on to my other thoughts. I lay back to the ground, watching clouds sift whiteness like Granny Isabelle's flour did for biscuit making.

I chewed on a wild field straw, going over things in my mind. Things like how glad I was to have them cats and even Smokey around sometimes when Papa Harkus was off drinking and Mama and Daddy had come and then took off again with Danny and Ginny. Thinking on doodlebugs and my poor drained Granny Isabelle and her wore-out garden hoe, still laying in the field waiting on us to return the next morning.

Wanting that good gravy she was working on inside the house, as biscuit scents reached my nose for tasting. Almost forgetting all about them red juicy strawberries and that sad lady with the horn stuck up in her ear. I would only whisper into it, playing a trick on her, just to get her say, "Heeeh?"

So then Smokey looked more pitiful and pathetic like he knew what I done said about his papa being a no-good drunk and himself being so stupid. I felt a smidgen of sorrowfulness for him and looked off to think on life some more. And when I did that, I felt more than a smidgen of sorrowfulness for my own sad self.

13

Life at Granny Isabelle's

Granny Isabelle said we were almost orphans, but we still had her. I was near seven years old. I showed my age on my fingers, proudly, as if it meant something special. I showed four fingers for Ginny and two for Danny. I helped look after my little sister and little brother ever since they were born. Danny thought I was his mama cause I watched over him so much.

We stayed with Granny Isabelle now, just a few miles from Aunt Lizzie's house. Papa Harkus and Granny Isabelle were old. Real old. I didn't think much about Mama and Daddy anymore since they came and went so often. It was like a dream—things didn't seem real, like they never were and never would be. Papa Harkus didn't seem real either. He hardly ever had anything to do with us and often was hidden away in the back woods.

He was tall with slouchy shoulders, his thin face whiskered, smudged with chewing tobacco or snuff spit. Brown crusty stuff held on to his chin cracks like glue. I hadn't never seen his eyes, wasn't sure if he had any for that matter.

Neighbor families had big homes with inside toilets. Our toilet was a stinking little room over a hole outside, loaded with granddaddy long-leg spiders. They held to the ceiling upside down, staring at us as we gawked at them. Thankfully, they never fell on my head.

Onct, a great big one fell on Danny and scared him plum to death. He almost fell into the deep dark hole to never be seen no more. Granny Isabelle said they weren't poison, but even if they were, their mouths was too little to bite on us. I still studied on them as I sat on the cold, hard, shit-smudged seat under my butt. So did Danny. He was the most scared, cause of what happened to him, so I held his hand whenever he went.

"The carved-out hole's way too big for me, and 'specially Danny, cause he's a itty-bitty thing," I explained, but they didn't listen none.

I asked Granny Isabelle, "Why can't we have a littler hole jus' for us?"

She said, "Cause its jus' the way things is."

So I let it be, but I didn't hafta like it none.

I said, "I get real 'fraid that if I fall in, no one'll know or find me." I thought to myself how awful to be lost forever in a world of shit. Dirty words were always lurking on my lips, but I figured it was okay as long as they didn't come out of my mouth.

"You can speak bad things into bein'," Granny Isabelle said. She knew the gospel through. I got to where I didn't even whisper the "s" word. But I thought it. I thought it a lot.

One day, I declared that I hated toilets, especially at night. I hated toilets and nasty stinks that reeked through the crusty hole. I hated the hard, turdy smudges scratching my hind-end. Worst of all, I hated, hated, hated big-eyed, long-legged granddaddy spiders.

"If I fall into the toilet hole, who'd carry the water?" I begged to know.

Granny Isabelle just looked at me. I had to carry water a far piece, from a neighbor's house for us all. The beat-up bucket hung on a spout as I'd pump. Tired out, I dangled on the handle in the air like a rag doll, cause I wasn't none too big myself.

Water toting was hard for a little kid like I was then. It was cold and heavy and sloshed in my shoes with each step. My feet slid sideways when I walked, especially on a hill.

Sometimes I fell and had to go back and do it all over again. Half of the water would be gone by the time I got home, but I still did my best. We all drank from the red-dirt-tinged, metallic-dipper in little gulps, to be sparing.

"It ain't fair for me to be so sparin' cause I do all the totin'," I told them.

Granny Isabelle said, "Ain't nothin' much fair 'bout this life."

"Why I hafta do everythin', all of the time?" I argued.

"Cause you the oldes'," I heard back. I hated being the oldest.

I did get weary of carrying hate on my insides. There were lots of things I couldn't stand: hard biscuits, tiny water gulps when I was thirsty, thunderstorms, slick water-sloshed shoes, red dirt that stuck to my shoes after a storm, floor sweeping, dishwashing, water-toting, big toilet holes, and granddaddy longlegs.

Mostly, I couldn't stand my lazy, drunk, good-for-nothing Papa Harkus and his dog Smokey. Even more, I despised my most-of-the-time-gone-away-mean-Daddy. Not wanting him close but wanting him at the same time. Yearning for something I didn't have, and didn't want it if I did have it.

"Why can't Papa Harkus do nothin' once in a blue moon?" I questioned loudly, cause his laziness disgusted me. I got no look nor answer from Granny Isabelle.

Papa Harkus just laid around in old brown dirty pants, scuffed-up boots, and drooled-on shirts. A felt hat hid his eyes from us, if he even had them, since never had we seen them, not onct.

I said to Danny, "Should we see a person's eyeballs?" And then I answered myself, "I think so."

"Why don't he look at us none?" Ginny asked.

"Maybe they's glass ones, like Aunt Lizzie has," I said. Lizzie had a lopsided brown eye. Danny and Ginny stared hard, disbelieving.

"Onct she even took it out an' showed me." I demonstrated, my fingers twisting at my eyeball.

Danny shrugged. Ginny gaped.

When Papa Harkus was not in the woods drunk, he scrunched in his little bed tight against the wall. It had a squish-squashed, torn-up, striped cotton mattress, all dirtied by his boots and Smokey's muddy, floppy tail. Everything was filthy about the two of them. I loathed Papa Harkus's shoes cause of all the muddiness.

He laid out hollering and whooping in the woods, drunk as a coon, with his fat ugly dog. Aunt Lizzie said he got the whoops from his Indian daddy—a horse-riding medicine man from way back who sold moonshine, mostly. Papa Harkus couldn't help it, Lizzie said.

He wasn't all bad, she said, cause he loved Smokey more than anything in the wide world. More than Lizzie, and she was his own blood. I thought it, but didn't say I wished I was Smokey. Wished Papa Harkus loved me like he loved Smokey. I craved something from him down deep inside.

Often a bottle, in a brown paper sack, stuck out of his back pants pocket. It poked into his coat and made his butt look lopsided. One day Papa Harkus was sick with something in his stomach. My Aunt Lizzie said it was cause he drank too much whiskey. As she took pity on him, I studied her face, then the whole of her.

Her full body didn't amount to much, being short as she was. But it was rounded out big, like a puffed-up bullfrog with them eyes bulging in different directions. No neck worth mentioning.

She sat half-squatted on the chair, overflowing, huffing words, blowing spit bubbles, with both knees looking outward, just like her eyes. Sat like she was waiting for a fly to cross her path so she could slurp it up on her tongue's end. But a merciful strange-looking aunt she was, just the same.

Aunt Lizzie said likker made Papa Harkus act stupid in the poplar woods. But I was thinking it was all 'bout his name, him hocking up spit stuff all time.

I explained to her, "If my name was Harkus, I'd hide in them woods, drinking likker an' whooping all the time too. His mama musta hated him something awful bad to name him somethin' like snot. But with him hocking spit all time, it sure does suit him."

She said back, "Ya Granny Isabelle was named after a queen or somethin'."

I smiled, getting happy inside over the queen thing, thinking I was gonna watch over Granny Isabelle more than usual.

"But she's always tired. When she sits, she sleeps," I told my pitiful, toad-looking aunt.

Aunt Lizzie said, "She jus' got too much burdens to bear." I think on it, biting on my lower lip, guilty cause I was one of her heaviest burdens. Aunt Lizzie never said it outright, but I knew she meant my siblings and I added extra hardship on Granny Isabelle.

Granny generally settled down in her rocking chair at the day's end. I stared until she dozed, her eyes shutting down until they were slits. Her mouth stayed lined up, prunish, toothless. She smiled fine through her eyes when they opened, though. Little puffs slipped out of her lips when she breathed. I would sneak up real close into her face and smell the whiffs. I liked the musky smell of her breath.

When Granny Isabelle was awake, she worked hard in her kitchen feeding us. Her biscuits were the best thing ever. Before she got started, she would pinch brown powdery stuff from a little round silver can with D-E-N-T-A-L written on it. Quickly, she poked some under her lower lip, then hid the tiny tin in the kitchen cupboard, over the wood cookstove that held our leftover biscuits. She thought I didn't see. Onct I sneaked a dab and then I puked.

She made "angel biscuits" using the washed-out tin boxes. She called us her angels. I loved the small tins with lids and the way they fit together perfectly to hide things in like bugs and such, and her soft warm "angel biscuits." I didn't care much for the cold, hard crusts though. Sometimes we got a little sugar on the end of a biscuit. It was so good.

Onct, I cut myself on the lip and jaw with the snuff box. Granny Isabelle made a big fuss over it, but it healed up okay, just a little moon-shape chin scar is all.

Granny was the best storyteller on earth. One night she told us of a time when a great storm came. Wind shook the house, and rain and beads of ice beat all her corn down to worthless. She avowed to have seen great big balls of fire hit inside the house and dance on the floor, then leave out the wall without a sign of ever being there. I didn't believe her much until she swore on the Word. After that, every time a storm came, I just ran to Granny Isabelle.

She said we wasn't to fear, that we had protection if we spoke the Word. Onct a storm came on my birthday. When the calm came, she found a bottle of Dr. Pepper and some cantaloupe. We divided it for my party. Right there in the middle of the floor, with the kerosene lamp flickering shadows everywhere, we sprinkled salt on the juicy orange slices and had a picnic just for me, cause I was so special.

"It ain't much," she said, but she acted like it was her prized possession, and most probably, it was. Cantaloupe and Dr. Pepper weren't my favorite. Still, I wanted more just cause.

Granny Isabelle said, "Things is what it is."

I took her to mean there weren't no more birthday treats to be had. She always found a way to make things special anyhow. Even my birthday, after a bad storm.

14

Granny's Garden

Each year Granny Isabelle hoed a garden for us. Each row was dug, planted, watered, picked, and plucked by her alone. At night she talked about the Little Red Hen who did all the work and then ate all the food cause nobody helped her. I did my best part for a biscuit. She would can food for winter, and then she would beg a ride to sell leftover onions at Flannigan's Food Store.

"I bought a bedroom suit with more an' a few dimes," she bragged to us. Prideful, she stood like a scarecrow in the grassless, hard red clay yard. Seemed she was always dressed in dirty stockings, dusty black shoes, and a crumpled paper sack hat stuck on her head. It was rolled up on the edges to keep the sun off her eyes. Most times sweat balls rolled down her hot brow and her tongue clicked against a dry mouth, chicken-like, for want of some cold water. Ancient callused hands gripped her treasured hoe as she gathered some thoughts of wisdom to spout off to us.

"You chillens listen to what I'm a tellin' y'all." She paused her work with a daring stare.

We glanced up, me swishing dry dirt with the straw broom she made me. She took the paper poke hat off and wiped her forehead with a dusty rag. We each got a head nip from her cap as it swished against the air, yanking our attention on her.

"If y'all work hard with what ya have, y'all can make something outta ya life. I don't want y'all chillens livin' like this. Now, each one of ya gotta promise me to do better."

We nodded our heads yes but became slack on listening cause we heard it afore. Looking down, we kept playing with our rocks in the red dirt. Me sweeping and the other two gathering pebbles.

Nothing came easy to our Granny Isabelle and us. I was just a little kid, but I saw how she struggled so hard and how life really was. I knew we weren't as good as other people, but I wasn't too worried, knowing she bought that bedroom suit with a few bunches of onions.

Tall corn rows reached out high over our heads. Dark green blades pushed skyward, like Granny Isabelle's arms did when she shouted, "Hallelujah to the Lord." Of late, I'd been crying a lot cause I couldn't be a kid. Other times, I'd sneak off and hide, quiet and still, in the corn rows with made-up friends to play with.

I liked to hear wind rustling against the sharp corn blades, making funny noises like paper crushing. I made-believe the swooshing came from fairies' wings. I pretended they had come to help me with all the work, so I could be a young'un for a while.

I played hide-n-seek in the corn with my fairies. I dug at little round grainy ant houses with a straw to see what was inside. Just ants was all. Ants and more ants, running up and down their tunnel, in and out toting heavy loads on their backs.

They worked nonstop like Granny Isabelle. It came to me I might be part ant, cause I carried loads bigger than myself, my shoulders humped over from weariness and not knowing who I was for sure, me looking more like Granny Isabelle with every passing day.

I tore off a piece of tough corn blade, squatted down, placed it just so between my two big thumbs, and blew a whistle through it. Granny Isabelle always said I got my big thumbs from her. She said it meant I got a strong self-will. To this day, I still don't know what it means for sure, but she was happy for me cause I took after her.

If I was in the hiding mood in the corn rows, I didn't whistle. I just played with anthills.

Black tumble bugs were fun, too. I flipped them with a little stick, watched them kick at nothing for the longest time. Then, I felt sorry and turned them over again onto their scissor-like feet. They would get mad and walk away—pouting—cause it was all the spunk they had left in them.

Little green inchworms hung by threads so tiny I could hardly see them. They rumpled their tiny slender bodies into loops and measured air. Sometimes, they measured my finger. It was fun.

On my back between rows, I watched silver planes hum far away in the sky. I wished to be one. I pretended to be a miniature silver needle sewing up patches of blue and white puffs, weaving a quilt in heaven. It seemed easy, so soft and easy to be high up looking down.

But for some reason my little bits of peace got tied together like a ball of twine, and everything came right back to Granny Isabelle's onions. The day had fizzled down and fatigue had set into me and Granny Isabelle. Out in the side yard sat mountains of onions to wash with toted well water. The water filled buckets and bowls all around our feet. I had half-dragged the water from the neighbor's pump to the mounds that rested before us.

I helped her slosh the onions as clean as we could, freeing them from the sticky red clay. But that was just the beginning of our task. Peeling was the next step. After batches and batches had been washed, I plopped myself in the middle, doing what had to be done with Granny by my side. Try after try, I failed miserably. Detaching the outer layer was the hardest thing for me to learn. Frustration and saline-oniony tears poured profusely down my cheeks in defeat.

"I just can't do it right. Can ya show me how to peel the onions, Granny Isabelle?"

She slid closer, her humped back sitting by my side, her bird-like eyes glancing at me as she began softly wiping my face with her red-stained dress hem, careful not to get dirt grains in my eyes.

"I think ya can do it, chile. I think ya trying to do it the hard way. Let me show you a different way how to."

She gently lifted an onion by its green tails and shook it, easily smacking it against her hand; most of the dry clayish clots effortlessly fell to the ground. Then she sloshed its head in the pail, snapping it slightly against the container's edge. She laid the wet onion in the grass blades, settling water off of it, and then did another, and another, and another. Doing each one the same way. "See? One dries while the other onion waits for its step, and so on."

I nodded, amazed at how she had made something difficult appear simple. Now I knew to spank each onion a little first, then slosh, then shed the outer skin layer. Wet clots were so much harder to remove.

"So what else is hard for ya, Jessie?"

"The worst part of all is pulling that outside skin down and not gouging fingernail holes deep in it, messing up your whole onion so you have to throw it away. Can ya show me how to peel the onion?"

"I will. Sometimes it takes a while to do it the right way. First ya gotta shake the dry clots off, then swish it in water, let it dry a spell, then peel it. There is a time to do each step jus' like there is a season for everythin' under the sun. We try not to scar it up so bad an' make it useless."

She picked one up and, with one hand holding the roots, she used the other to glide the skin off, like shedding a glove off a hand.

"That's how you do it, sweet chile. No need making jobs worse than what they is. Let's jus' be glad we ain't crackin' black walnuts to sell." She laughed impulsively.

As Granny Isabelle would sometimes recall, years back, black walnuts had been part of her great grief, but here she was laughing full of love and being loved. A little one by her side that God had sent down just to love her. Love made her smile and laugh out loud again. It was like she always said: "a season for everything."

15

Pillow Tears

Sometimes, I thought on us being orphans, left to find our own way. About Granny Isabelle working her gardens for a dime. Her angel biscuits full of love. Us being her angels. And me sewing up clouds to make something beautiful for Jesus. That was when I felt most peaceful inside.

I came to understand that we were okay for a little while. I didn't know why Daddy wanted us with him and Mama sometimes. But he would take a wild notion and just come hauling us away, then back again when he was through with us. He hated me the most. I could tell. Mean stares came from his eyes, despising me. I was just a kid, but I knew about eyes. My broken heart was awful sore, and I wasn't worth nothing much and didn't know who I was to begin with. I cried a lot for want of my Granny Isabelle when I wasn't with her.

My pillow tears came cause Daddy was bigger than God, larger than the whole-wide world. Words like shit-head, whore, and bitch named me and thundered into my ears. "Get your damn ass outta here; I don't want to look at your ugly face no more." "You are crazier than hell." "Shut the hell up, stupid." My daddy's cruel words worked inside me cause I wasn't worth a damn nickel.

I took the tar-like loathing in on myself, tucking it deep inside my heart pocket—like a twisted, locked box, a damaged something without keys. Couldn't nobody get inside of me. Not even my own self.

Mostly, I put my hopelessness where nobody would see. Like a window, depending on which side I looked through. People didn't know the inside out, just the outside in. I could see the same bare pain in Mama's eyes. I just tried not to pay attention to hers. I couldn't live no more if I studied her miseries.

At the end of the day darkness came. All by myself, I was. Even with people's snores all around. That was when nobody saw me crying and bad stuff got stuck in my chest, like a knife gouged in rock. Memories and screams cried out in the silence without me saying words, smothering me in some bottomless darkness.

Even at Granny Isabelle's, pillow tears came from my deep shame, I suppose. They seeped inside and played tricks on my beat-up heart. They were special tears of a dreadful loneliness. There weren't no words for them. They left dirty trails down my cheeks. In the morning, when the sun came out, nobody paid attention to them. Tears were more common than not.

I would awake with a deep throbbing inside, my chest aching, breaths hurting. Bunches of tears and clear snot came, then hiccups. Where they came from, I had no inkling, except that being left behind as useless and worthless made me feel shameful over everything I did that didn't suit someone else.

Stringy drips made ringed blotches on my Granny Isabelle's silky feather cushions—ringed brown markings—and how clear turned to brown I didn't know neither. I despised what my crying did to her pretty striped cases with the tatted edges. I apologized to her for making such messes on what she worked hard for. She would say back, "Jus' let it be."

Sometimes, I rubbed the lovely cushion embroidery between my fingers. It comforted me, where she let me rest my head. Some nights I buried my face deep into the pillow, pushing deep and deeper. I held it, dug down, trying to suffocate. Thinking maybe I'd go away to the other side with smothering—being nice and easy—or I'd go be with Jesus and He would rub on me like He did the lambs in Granny Isabelle's wall picture. My head fought against me, as it pulled away from the pillow, breathing. I couldn't do nothing right.

One night, after returning to stay with Granny Isabelle from being away with my parents, I suffocated into my pillow again but failed. Thinking afterward, I'll go to Mayes River beyond the tall poplar woods, where Papa Harkus whoops, and follow the green mossy trail to the rocky place and sink down in the cavernous water on a warm day. I'll let the cool water wash me away in swirls. Far away; then I'll quit breathing.

16

Jesus and Me

A dream so real came one night after Daddy had whipped me at Granny Isabelle's when she was gardening. That night, I visited that man who lived in Granny Isabelle's lamb picture. He was so happy to see me. He had the prettiest blue eyes I ever saw. He grabbed me, picking me up like I was light as a feather, and He swung me in circles.

He toted me all over the place, bragging to everybody about how I was His little girl. He said I was smart as a whip. I swelled full of happiness. He told them I even had His eyes. I thought it couldn't be true cause they stayed in his own head.

We played like kids. He threw me upward into puffy clouds for the longest time. As long as I wanted, we played on. I giggled all the way down through white softness, legs and arms flailing, to get back into His arms only to be tossed again.

"Have you had a sufficiency?" He asked.

"A what?"

"Are you ready to try something else?" His hearty laughter rang out like bells through the air. He led me to a most beautiful yellow swing, hanging on long ropes from nothingness. A gorgeous red heart was painted in the middle. How did He know I loved to swing more than anything? How did He know that hearts were my favorite of all things?

I swung upwards as if into forever, it seemed. My legs wriggled in wondrous excitement and happiness. Happily I returned to Him again for another push into oblivion. He sang, "How would you like to go so high, high into the sky, my child?" It was the best day of my life.

After we played until I was exhausted, He cuddled me close, touching His soft gentle fingers over the hot red marks my daddy had left, leaving cool calmness instead. I snuggled deep into Him like a baby kitten. His fingers were the most gentle I'd ever felt. Something came to me I'd never known before. Love so deep and kind.

The love feeling went down deep where my hurts stayed, making my heart hungry for more. He petted my head, singing another song. "Hush little baby, don't you cry, Mama's gonna buy you a mockingbird, if that mockingbird don't sing, Mama's gonna buy you a diamond ring. If that diamond ring don't shine…uhmmm, uhmmm, uhmmm."

I sobbed. Shame and worthlessness poured out of me like pee in the corner, when my daddy would beat me so bad.

"Nobody helps me," I told Jesus between hiccups. He flinched as if He knew what I meant.

"Can you keep a secret?"

"What do you think?" He winked.

"Can we be best friends forever?" I asked Him.

"Better yet, I'll be your good Father and your best friend," He responded.

"Promise not to tell," I said. We hooked pinkies, joined together and pulled. Instantly I trusted Him. "My daddy beats an' cusses us awful. I'm so afraid he'll kill us all. He scalds our faces an' legs. And Mama, she ain't no help. She ain't worth a hill of beans to help. He scalds her worse cause she's a big whore."

"I know he does. He chooses the evil life." His voice was kind. He rubbed circles on my back for a while where the welts lived.

"Can he be comin' over here and hurt me again?" I scrunched closer to Him.

"No way. The abyss is too wide. Way too wide and deep." He turned my face to His with a gentle hand and peered into my eyes, holding the look.

"What's a 'byss'?" I asked.

He explained 'bout the dark, deep, and wide pit between good and bad people. "Your Daddy can't cross it," He said.

"He can't?" I asked.

"Nobody crosses unless I say so. When I draw the line, I draw it. See, nobody has my key but me." He pulled out an ancient gold key from under a huge round stone. Rainbows shimmered everywhere from its glow.

Amazed, I replied, "Where'd ya get it?"

He chuckled. "It wasn't easy. In fact, it was the worst kind of hard it's ever been. But that's all in the past."

73

Then I cried over my poor bad Daddy and crushed, fish-face Mama.

Jesus shushed me and said, "Peace be still, little one." He petted me.

"My daddy won't let me sit in his lap. He says I'm too big. But he ain't never held me. It don't make no sense cause I ain't bigger than a flea," I expressed.

"Well, you can sit in mine. I think I can hold you." He smiled and tossed me up. His teeth sparkled sheer whiteness.

I nestled deep into Him and rested my head on His big shoulder. It felt strong and safe.

"Jesus, I don't think nobody loves me down there. I can't do nothing right."

"Oh, what about Granny Isabelle?" He paused.

"You know her too?"

"Yes, I know her."

"Yeah, she loves me. But I can't stay where love is all time. I feel little and dirty and awful stupid at Daddy's. He says I can't pour shit outta a boot an' I don't think I can neither."

Jesus laughed at me. "You probably ought to try not to say words like your Daddy does."

I grinned back.

"You've got nothing to be ashamed of, little angel." He nuzzled me closer.

And then He carried me around for days—toting me like I was a little baby or something—as if I couldn't walk a lick for my own self. Other times, without a word, He'd scoop me up in a warm blanket and hold me so close, rocking me in a special chair.

"I ain't never been rocked afore. Not to recall no how. For the most part I rock them other kids." I spoke maturely.

I laid my head down on His chest, listening, His heartbeat drumming easy into my ear. Restful, I fell asleep, dreaming in my dream. Jesus had something in his hands. It was a silver needle with bright, beautiful, crimson red thread. He was sewing a little round something up.

I said, "Jesus, whatcha doin'?"

He answered, "Sewing."

"Whatcha sewing? A strawberry?" I asked.

"No, sweetie, it's a precious little broken heart."

I watched him sew perfect stitches, as if He'd done millions. In wonderment I asked, "Whose heart is it, Jesus?"

He smiled back, "Yours, honey. My sweet little Jessie." Warmth came cause He called my name.

"But Jesus," I said, "it looks awful tore up. I don't think it can be fixed cause it's all in pieces." My finger pointed out what a bloody mess it was.

A sad look gentled his face. "Some hearts are ripped even worse than yours, little one."

"I don't think so, Jesus. Mine's awful bad off."

"It is," He agreed.

"It don't hurt none?" I asked Him in awe. He sewed on.

"My little darling lamb. I promise. You won't feel a thing. It'll be like new. I'll even make the memories that tore it to pieces go away someday," He whispered.

Unafraid, I watched Him fix me. Tenderly, He held the bloody mess in His hands. After the last stitch, He rubbed on some ointment and whispered special words.

"What's that, Jesus?" I asked.

"Balm of Gilead," He replied.

After He perfected it, it fluttered into my heart space all by itself, like a butterfly.

We sat quietly as He curled my hair around His fingers.

He said, "You're my precious little princess."

I felt good inside with my new heart. So I rested a while and forgot the scaldings, until my brother and sister came to mind. I wanted Him to bring them to this side so they could be real kids with me. I wanted Him to love on them like He did me. I asked, "Can you go get them?"

Amused, He explained, "In a little while. Let me take care of one child at a time. I just have so many fingers to work with."

I laughed too loud. He let me. I snickered a while with my forefinger in my mouth, where my front tooth was missing. He let me.

"Can't you jus' magic my teeth back?" I asked.

"I have my priorities," He retorted. I started to ask, "what's priorities," then saved it for later.

"I guess you can't do no magic or nothin' then," I said.

He poofed a patch of glistening angels into the clouds. They danced like my fairies in the corn patch, all singing happy tunes.

"How's that for magic?" He chuckled.

I beamed. "It'll hafta do."

I studied on His big hands as my small fingers curled around His. Excitedly, I discovered a new thing. My finger sported a sparkling silver ring.

"Where'd this come from?" I asked.

He laughed loud. "I was wondering when you'd notice. All little boys and girls get one when I finish mending their broken hearts. It's so you'll never forget what I've done when you go back."

"You mean I have to go back." My heart sank as we walked beside a clear stream of water. Pure warm water gurgled and rolled over my bare feet. Goldfish kissed my toes and spat waterspouts at my face. I laughed as they waggled.

He smiled down at me. I felt happy cause I finally had my good Father.

"It's hard living on earth," I said.

"I know," He agreed.

"Can't I jus' stay with you?" I whined.

"Somebody has to be there, or darkness will take over." Then He sprinkled me with something like red dust.

"What's that?" I asked.

"My blood," He answered.

"Blood!" I screeched like a train stopping on tracks.

"Yes, mine. I know how cruel it is down there. You will get through. Watch. It turns colors as it covers you with courage and strength."

A refreshing warm white glow flowed over me from head to toe.

"I will give you strength to go through anything. Just stay in the light. Your Daddy's a bad person, real bad. But Jessie, he has a soul. He needs to know me. Just pray. You can't do anything else for him. The rest is totally up to him."

A happy-faced man named John breezed by us. He interrupted my visit and told me a short story. A train had run over him years ago. He was frisky and full of glory. He asked me to tell Granny Isabelle he was waiting for her and that he loved her. To tell her that I was sent to love her in his stead until they came back together some glad day. Then he meandered away laughing happily.

76

Suddenly, I was tired. Jesus piddled with my hair some more, making curls.

I questioned, "Do you still pray, Jesus?"

"Of course I do, to our Father, the Ancient of Days. We want pain and death to end on earth and it will. I promise you that. It will end." He stroked my hair some more. I rested.

Morning lit up the room. Un-smothered, I awakened atop the hollowed-out, punched-in pillow, telling Granny Isabelle about me planning to go down to Mayes River and drown. I told of the dream while Ginny and Danny slept on their floor pallets. I told her about my new Father, Jesus, who loved me. About the strawberry heart and the painless needle sewing on it; about the yellow swing with a red heart in the middle that hung from nowhere and swung into nowhere; about how He called me Jessie and toted me around like a baby; and about the silver ring I wore cause I was His sewed-up child. How He'd stitched up millions of hearts just like mine. Then I remembered the floating man called John and told what he said as best as I recalled.

Granny's eyes glistened and she cried long and hard. Glad not sad tears. We hugged, releasing softness from hard inside places. Then she lit out to make a swing for me on the big oak tree. Now I sing to the others about going high into the sky. So high.

Daddy whipped little Danny today. It was his turn. To the core it hurt, and nobody helped him. Not even me. I just tried to be like Jesus and rub the pains away real gentle. I smoothed his sweaty face, parted his hair to the side. His curls slipped like soft ribbons through my fingers as I sang that sweet Jesus song, "Hush little baby, don't you cry, Mama's gonna buy you a mockingbird, and if that mockingbird don't sing...uhmmm, uhmmm, uhmmm."

17

The Field Trip

We were back with Mama and Daddy, and Daddy had talked Granny and Papa into living with us. One Saturday I told my siblings, "Ain't no school today for me, and it's gonna be the best day ever. Y'all jus' wait and see." Their faces were covered in grins as they held hands and danced in the room's middle. Making up some words to Mama's hums about "Standin' on the Promises."

The night before, Daddy had taken off to Canada, looking for to-bacco work. Bricklaying had fizzled out. Mama said he was gonna bring back a bunch of money and get us some new furniture, maybe put a new linoleum rug down and a real sink in the kitchen. I pretended her light-heartedness. Mama wiped some old cornbread crumbs from the table, fetched a broom, and swept the dickens outta the floor—just humming nonstop, "Standin' on the Promises"—just cleaning, cleaning, and cleaning. Humming, humming, and humming.

Granny Isabelle was off hoeing dirt clots in Mama's garden while Papa Harkus stood at the yard edge, his coattail pushed up, hiding what was. He was spying on us, looking under his old sweat-stained hat brim, hunched over with stinking Smokey alongside.

"Y'all kids come on here and get some of this here soup to take with y'all," Mama excitedly called out. I took hold of the quart jar, lid screwed on tight, grabbing spoons and coffee cups all at once.

"Y'all best not get into no trouble," Papa yelled hatefully behind us.

I carried the warm, moist jar tucked under the wing of my right armpit, feeling kinda like it was full of good luck.

"We know," I said back to him, not hateful, but glaring full of meanness, cause he couldn't see my insides.

We moved toward the distant wooded field. Top-heavy pines swayed and sheltered the meadow's edge, shaking long brown needles about our feet. The sharp sprigs jiggled into our shoes, sticking like bob-by pins. I delighted in nature's wonderful quietness.

We tramped a telling trail of bent weeds as we wound through the meadow's blanket of dull, once yellow-face daisies. Sweet passion fruit bowed downward under the heaviness of the ripe green bulbs, while Queen Anne's lace perched upward, watching us with white grainy eyes.

Content, I bent and gently snapped the luscious fruits from its vine and poked them into my tattered sweater pockets, traipsing along.

Danny touched my hand and attached, yanking. "Jessie, why don't Santa ever bring us things like pop guns and such?" he asked. His hand was tiny in mine, though he had turned four. Ginny skipped on, pretending not to care or listen, but doing both just the same.

Danny added, "You know Billy has pop guns and a holster. I jus' don't understand nothin' cause he's mean as hell most time." His eyes searched my face for answers. I scolded him with my eyes, cause he knew not to say hell. His eyes looked down at his feet, saddened for a brief minute.

"So, let's pray to Jesus for some help. Maybe He'll help Santa find us somehow."

Ginny repeated Granny Isabelle's Bible, saying, "His eyes go over the whole earth to help his children."

Danny resisted pragmatically. "Eyes don't go over the whole earth."

"Hold hands, let's just close our eyes real tight, see it in our minds and make it happen," I urged. Joined to one another, we circled, our eyes scrunched tight, our faces lifted skyward. Acting like Granny Isabelle. "Today we come for some help, in any way you see fit, Lord Jesus. Please protect us an' our Mama and watch over our Granny Isabelle and do what you want with Papa Harkus an' Daddy," I prayed. They nodded.

Ginny liked what I said and said aloud, "Amen." Then Danny echoed. We all giggled. "Just maybe things'll get better with Daddy working away," Ginny said, looking doubtful.

"It is always better with him gone. Hold hands, let's just close our eyes real tight, see it in our mind's eye and make it happen," I said. "Maybe now you'll get a holster and a cowboy hat and Ginny'll get a little doll with a milk bottle. We got to believe it though. Remember what Granny Isabelle says 'bout changing things, speaking things into being. We did jus' that."

Hesitantly, they considered my words, Ginny mumbling, "Daddy don't never change."

I said, "Oh, yeah, it's true. It really, really is." Danny's cheeks reddened, covering his little copper freckles, and Ginny gleefully hopped and skipped. "We gotta keep lookin' for good in things. We jus' gotta," I lectured.

Then I changed the subject. "I spy something orange."

Danny blinked, squinting toward the pointed direction.

"I ain't seein' nothin'," he whined.

"I do spy somethin' orange," I repeated. They became happy cause they loved "I Spy." Now, I wasn't much for playing it, but I did for them what I wanted when I was little. They both bounced up and down, hunting orange. Danny's joyful eyes wrinkled smaller to see.

Ginny begged, "Give us a little hint, Jessie." Tugging my arm, looking for the hue.

"I done give you a hint, it's orange and over there." I pointed again. "It's little and round," I added.

"Is it that bush over there?" She giggled, still leaping.

"Yep, you're right as rain," I told her. She glistened with pride; Danny pouted. I rushed headlong, almost tripping over a gnarled tree root that resembled an octopus.

The deceptive persimmon tree was loaded orange. I lifted Danny, dangling him, to get his own. Together we gnawed down on the fruit and then spewed out bitterness. "Ugh!" We sputtered and spat. "They ain't ready to eat yet but will be in a few weeks," I said matter-of-factly. "We'll come back and get Granny Isabelle a batch to make us a pie. By then it'll be good an' sweet." We moved onward.

Velvety red cardinals swooned over our heads and succulent green grasshoppers flicked from long autumn grasses, scurrying, drawing arches as they hopped kangaroo-like. We scampered freely through the brushy field toward our secret hideaway.

A distant large red-headed woodpecker broke the silence. He hacked and hammered in the tall oak tree just above our heads: rat-a-tat-tat, rat-a-tat-tat, rat-a-tat-tat. I halted to show where the bird sat, and they quietly returned a knowing nod.

"Do y'all know why he doesn't get headaches from rapping?"

"Nope," they replied in unison.

"My teacher said they have fat, long tongues that wrap clean around their brains and become a cushion. They don't feel much at all." Ginny and Danny stared at me in amazement.

We kept going until we reached our spot. "We jus' make play outta nothing," I told them. "It could be a stick, a string, a can, or a rock." We plopped down, contented.

We squatted, sprawling our legs outward on some rotted tree stumps to scoff down our meal. Fallen logs lay scattered, smelling like Granny Isabelle's garden after she dug a fresh hole. The black soil reeked earthiness. We sniffed moist leaves for a while, doing nothing else.

Our feet pocked and punched into bug-packed mulch, insects like coppery winged roaches and soft brown wooly-worms with yellow stripes thrived there. Wooly worms would ball up and curl together foot-to-head with the touch of a straw or finger, wadding for the longest time.

Sometimes like a wooly worm, I curled myself together, when things got so bad with Daddy. Mama wadded up too when Daddy beat her head. We all did.

"What do they eat?" Ginny asked.

"I don't know, maybe jus' ants or something smaller than them," I said.

"Granny Isabelle says they eat leaves," Danny piped up.

I poured the soupy vegetables into the chipped, handle-less coffee cups. We smelled the vapor together. The steam reeked of onions, beans, tomatoes, and carrots, all from Granny Isabelle's garden. Our breaths puffed, cooling it, and then we slurped, wiping red dribbled streaks from our chins with arm sleeves. We kept chomping.

In our haven, hordes of wiry crickets sprang into action from no-where. Pine needles slid and scrunched under our shoes as earth scooted sideways. Nature's perfume let go as footprints created little brown shoe tracks where we wiggled, jamming our feet.

Quietness broke off and away from the world's prattle, as we three sought pleasure in the simplest of things: dining together in our hidea-way.

"This sure would be good with a few crackers," I said.

Danny belched louder than Ginny, puffing his chest out. Together they snorted laughter. Ginny chimed in, "A glass of milk'd be good too."

When she said it, I was wishing for some too. Danny had a big red ring around his mouth. If we had milk at home, he would always get a milk ring. The same held true with soup.

"Danny looks like a monkey. Danny looks like a monkey," Ginny sang. We laughed, but then quit because his nose wrinkled up, meaning he was ready to cry. And he wasn't one to be joked on.

The sweet hearty sun felt silky as we basked, warming us like a true friend. Through golden leaves her light patinaed our cheeks with splotches. I scooted backwards, close to a big tree trunk scratching between my shoulder blades, like a snake getting dead skin off. The oak felt strong and solid as I leaned into it and let the snappish fall air and light love on me.

I breathed, my nose whistling. Firm sweater bulges reminded me of dessert. Hand cupped, I fondled the greenish, fruity eggs, then pulled them into jagged pieces. My mouth watered as the sweet juicy pomegranate-like kernels wallowed and slid across my tongue. Life paused for a short spell. We, like a pile of full-bellied kittens, lingered, bathing in splotches of soft sunlight.

Huge trees shaded the playhouse. Long limbs stretched out like big arms with lumpy muscles. Our house was built of scrounged-up rocks, green moss, and sticks. We pretended to protect it with stick swords and guns like Daddy had under his bed.

We made rock bean soup with water, pine needles for green beans, and mudpie biscuits. Ginny and Danny acted like babies as I spanked them, here and there, to teach them a lesson or two. I couldn't take but so much whining and baby stuff until boredom set in on me.

A grand idea came to me as we sat wishing for a jump rope or swing like the one Granny had made for me at her house. I pulled a tree branch down and straddled it like a horse. Bouncing, I demonstrated, exaggerating the fun. Saying, "Gitty up, old Ned."

"Jessie, let me do it; let me be next," Danny squealed several times as I saddled him up for a turn.

"Now, y'all gotta be awful careful and hold on tight as sin," I asserted.

He held tighter to the horse's neck, and I sent him into the sky.

"I ain't gonna let ya fall," I called upwards.

Then Ginny wanted her turn. Timeless, we played on as I sang the song, "How would you like to go high into the blue sky, way, way high, way, way high in a swing?" Just like my Jesus dream of sometime back.

Danny was beside himself, throwing his feet out like a chicken does in a squawk. His eyes glittering.

"Looka here. Look at me. I'm Roy Rogers riding my own pony," he yelled.

I explained how we had to make our own toys since we didn't have any. Pride filled my chest from my belly, then covered my heart. I was so happy. It felt good to do something fun and fine to make the littler ones laugh out loud. My own importance shined in their admiring eyes.

As the day tired and the sun curtsied in the sky, it dipped, dappling red clouds, puffing and purring out orange and purple and yellow pastels overhead.

Our spirits dampened, realizing daylight had withered. A gut-gnawing dread came creeping into our consciousness. Night's darkness often brought evil to our door. Daddy was gone off. Papa Harkus, the guardian, spied distantly, his crooked dirty finger, like a hook, drawing us to him through the thick air back home. No one knew how long he'd been watching.

In our make-believe hideaway, slivers of hope had come. It was where we could giggle and laugh. We never wanted to leave our prized moments behind and return to the dingy rental house. It was of course even more cramped now that Granny and Papa had moved in with us. Daddy had brought them there to babysit and to keep the family together. I thought about how Granny Isabelle had left everything she'd worked for to do his bidding, and now there they were—father and son drunkards piled together in that shack Daddy had rented. There, prohibitive curtain-drawn windows disallowed sunshine. It was a crude, emotionless place that reeked of piss puddles, tobacco spit jars, cigarette smoke, and burnt wood ashes. Harsh, hard chairs were for sitting. The floor was a breeding ground for roaming stink bugs, kink-legged cockroaches, and restless weaving spiders.

Speechless, as if dead, we'd often sat heavy-shouldered, chest-aching, craving to know the why of things. Things like where do baby kittens come from or why do boys and girls have different pee holes. Shamefully, unanswered questions hung speechless.

"I sure hope Mama has some more of that soup for tomorrow," Danny said. He continued, as we packed up our playthings, "I sure do like that tree horse. I didn't get one bit scared." He bragged with his chest protruded, matching his words. Danny, looking much like Tom, our proud red and green rooster. Each morning the bird strutted and crowed effervescently, screeching time like an alarm clock.

We gathered dishes and retraced our steps homeward. A mocking-bird cranked up blabbers, jabbers, tweets, and rapid squeaks—mincing bird languages from the tipsy-top of a mulberry tree as we passed. Bossy blue jays swooped and, not wanting the likes of strays around, busied themselves plucking fine rusty fur from an orange alley cat's head.

A few gray squirrels created havoc, snatching rich acorns and hiding their treasures in some small, self-made ground caverns. Our laughter frightened them into leaved nests, tucked high into crooked forks of black walnut trees.

We staved off gloom by playing games of "London Bridges Falling Down" and "Ring around the Roses." We all fell down and wallowed in the knee-high grass. Itching from the tall blades, we finger-nailed splotchy letters on our skin to make life more interesting.

Ginny, trouble-faced, said, "What's poor white trash?"

I replied, "Garbage, I think."

Her blue eyes cornered a knowing look.

"Then why do school kids point and laugh at me when they say it?"

I spit, then I swallowed, knowing the meaning but not wanting to explain—not wanting her to ache inside as I did.

18

What We Were

We were different from others. Maybe a lot like stray cats being different from happy, loved cats. We begged for morsels of attention and leftover love, like vagrants. A world of plenty surrounded us, yet we had nothing. Lack and loneliness oozed from our insides like pus-filled sores. We dwelt on our need. Hating those who had, and despising ourselves for what we didn't. We were poor white trash, thirsting for what other kids had.

A floor-centered woodstove heated the house during winter. With sock-covered hands, Mama would dig old tree stumps from the frozen earth to burn. We pulled together to get wood. We had to so as not to freeze. Daddy was usually gone away during times of our greatest need.

Water, with the dancing wiggle tails of mosquito larvae, came from a distant spring. In summertime, we thirstily drank the wigglers too, being that or nothing. It was the way it was.

Our bellies growled, gassy from weeks of re-cooked pintos, lard-fried potatoes, fried fatback, and greasy cornmeal gravy. Sometimes, there was no food; the wall ate it if Daddy was angry.

Jagged and dirty fingernails. Greasy, snarled, snagged hair with bugs on occasion, sore-laden scalps from nit-picking, like monkeys we were. Granny Isabelle's kerosene treatments helped but stunk us to high heaven, disallowing school visits.

I'd pick my crooked teeth with broom straws and show my sister and brother how to clean their front teeth with soda- or salt-dipped rags. Sometimes our clothes, too loose or crack-tight, stunk of number one or two, from a night gone by of Daddy's hell-raising, leaving us too tired to clean ourselves for school the following day.

We walked funny, feet aching, raw-toed, heels blistered from tight or loose shoes sent from Aunt Lizzie's kids. Though we were happy hunting through her paper bags, I longed for pretty hair bows, lace-topped socks, and fitting patent-leather shoes. Those bags of used things, ripped and worn, were still way better than what we had.

Worse than public bean farts and head lice, for me, was begging for free school lunches. A fat, fault-finding, forehead net-creased, wide-nose, horse-looking woman challenged me daily.

"When's your mama gonna to sign them forms I sent with you?" Bug-eyed behind the counter, she'd look me over, lice hopping through my hair like jack rabbits, me rubbing their scabbed raw itches, conjuring an answer. Words squirming wordless, face blotching crimson, neck scorching upwards, I'd reached to claw some more scalp crusts.

Other women looked on pitifully, scooping large dollops of creamed corn, mashed potatoes, and fish sticks, flopping and thumping abundant doses onto our hard plastic plates and sliding them onto the rectangular brown trays. Horse face fumed about my unreturned papers loud enough for the whole cafeteria to hear. A fear-stricken, mousey la-dy, with two missing top teeth, seized money from some rich kids and then punched our welfare tickets with holes, eavesdropping on the sly. She mentioned to me that we'd better not miss another day of school or that battle-axe would have the truant officers after Daddy again.

Humiliated, avoiding eye contact with horse face, I'd shrug my shoulders ignorantly. "I asked Mama all time. She jus' won't." Mad at horse face for what she'd always put me through. "She just won't do it," I would stutter.

"Bet you haven't even give them to her," she'd growl back.

"She jus' won't is all I know." Then, whispering to her, "Daddy said Mama ain't signing no papers so the government can get hold of him."

She sneered. "I bet he did."

Agonizing, I would grit my teeth sideways, then chew my soppy hair ends as shame slapped my face like a hand. Fear knotted my guts each day as I hoped she would forget to ask me the next day, but she never did. Not once did horse face forget.

We'd sit with other ticket-kids, not speaking. I was blamed for the paper forms never showing up, so I detested cafeteria time but not the food. Each tomorrow would be another day of interrogation, and I'd burrow through it.

We headed toward the hovel at the end of a dirt road, where nobody visits. Our rental shack—filled with want and brokenness, cracked and ruined things, often without water or electricity or a toilet even.

We couldn't wait to tell Mama about our fun hideaway. Like a proud mama duck, I led with Ginny and Danny trailing behind, zigzagging to the right and left when I did, lined up together like a rope with knots in it.

A yellow jacket buzzed around my feet. I stomped and squashed the life from it just because. To hurt something smaller than myself made me feel tall and strong.

Happy over the tree horse, yet full of hatred for yellow jackets and other things, I wondered how a person could be full of two feelings at once. Then I thought on fun things to do the next day as we headed back. My heart was prideful of my inventive expertise.

19

Was Daddy Back Again?

Could it be? It must be. We saw it at the same time. That car. The familiar rusty front fenders with a broken headlight, staring at us like a snake's face. Daddy was back. He didn't go nowhere much in a day's time. I looked at my duck kids—white faced. My stomach churned, groaned and gnawed, overcome with sickness.

"Damn him. Damn him to hell," I said. "I'm sorry. I shouldn't cuss."

Whining, Ginny said, "He's 'posed to be gone for a long time."

"Yeah," Danny said. "Wonder what's done happened now. Maybe that old car ain't worth a damn." I stared at him to let him know that cussing wasn't right. What he said. What I said.

"Mama said he was leaving. But she ain't one to know much 'bout what he does an' don't do." Breathless, I wheezed.

Ginny looked pitiful. "Oh, no, Oh no."

Reality hit Danny. "Does it mean we ain't gonna play none tomorrow?" Tears balled up in his eyes and wet his long auburn eyelashes. I shook his hand to reassure him.

Forcing steps, I pushed my legs, feet feeling like heavy cinder blocks. My numb hand motioned them to follow closely.

"Come on now," I said maturely. They trudged like slugs on a salt path—steps slackened down.

The sullen door piped open. Mama's face said it all. It had happened. Everything lay still and lifeless. My eyes telescoped the hollow, deathlike room. Mama sat stiff-faced. Vacant, murky brown eyes stared through us. Mama's left eye was puffed out, swollen, red, blue-black, and watery like a giant blackberry. Red oozed from her bulbous fish-lip.

I unstuck my eyes from her face. She wasn't humming anymore. Other things, like broken chairs, lay about, and feelings like odors wafted into the room. Pig snort sounds came from somewhere. Should we run and hide or stay? I wanted to run, but I knew we'd done stepped into it and there wasn't no going back. Trapped. Bee-line, I hurried to fetch a dishrag to dab Mama's pathetic twisted face, my legs barely holding me up.

Daddy must have gotten mad over the soup, I reasoned. He did that sometimes, if he was looking for beans and he got soup, or the other way around. I wondered why Mama couldn't straighten up and do right. She was continually in trouble.

She constantly was scalded the most, but it didn't matter none. Every time she was hit we died inside. My heart withered into little black pieces every time she was beaten. She was too weak to help her own self, much less us.

Maybe he caught her humming. He hated gospels when he wasn't saved. I wished she wouldn't hum so much when he left, in case he walked in on her. It was easy to get caught humming or singing or laughing.

When he got saved, he would let her sing. He preached God and Jesus, iniquities and hell. It was hard to tell when he was and wasn't saved. But that day, I knew he wasn't.

"What?" I panicked. "What's wrong, Mama?" She kept looking at the floor like I wasn't there. "What happened?" Nobody spoke. Like a waterless jug, I filled up with awful dread and needed to pee.

My eyes slid sideways. The table propped up on three and was hung over with a broken leg. Confusion stormed my chest, heart pounding like a restless train, thumping over tracks.

The thick air cramped cold and quivered under my sweaty armpits. Sweat's voice reached out, choking me and grabbing my hands and seeping into wall cracks. It appeared that everything dripped red and bloody, wet, even the ceiling.

Silence lunged and stopped, and then I heard the strange pig snorts, like a hog being butchered. Yelps hit windowpanes, pings bounced and shattered into my ears.

The broken table appeared to be praying to God. A begging table was so hilarious. My eyes scanned further. Dishes were smashed to smithereens into pointed, dingy glass hunks.

Granny Isabelle's pan-fried pone bread lay like clumps of plump fish bait, floored. Half-fried fatback pieces curled up together in a room corner. The left or right corner I know not which. Pinto beans jammed onto walls like chubby bugs; gooey, they slid downward with juicy paths following behind. I sniggered hysterically some more over the praying table.

As gruel touched the floor, hog snuffles croaked louder. Mad grunts exploded. Granny Isabelle edged herself closer to us kids. But couldn't nobody come between the hate Daddy had for us. Nothing. Not even my old wearied-out Granny Isabelle. In panic, Granny's face tunneled into my view.

Daddy's hatred circled like a spirit, then it pried and poured inside of me like poison mist. Just kill me and get it over. I wanted to die.

His eyes glazed over, set fixed, strangely inhuman. Deep, dark, stone-cold like steel, eyes hating me. Mama said Daddy didn't despise us cause we were his flesh and blood. With all my might I wanted to believe her. Right then, I knew she was a liar. Her lies left me empty like a tin can with holes in it, unable to hold water.

The room stabbed at me like a ton of icy spears. My hands and feet felt like pins and needles. The hateful air pushed against my body, winding me tight like a spring ready to break any second and fling my body parts to shreds.

Everything went to hell—before an eye could bat, feeling, as if we might all blow up into kingdom come—much like Granny Isabelle's cornbread thrown against the wall. Uncertainty, like a big hand, grabbed and squeezed my chest, bulging my eyes. I considered faces, one after the other: Mama, Granny Isabelle, Papa Harkus, Daddy, and Ginny and Danny.

Everything slowed way down. What was happening? I turned to read Ginny and Danny's eye thoughts. My eyes pled with theirs.

"Do y'all know what's going on?" my eyes asked them. Their eyes read mine and shrugged helplessness back on me. Their small clutched hands knitted together like a short chain.

Danny peed his britches. A big apple stain outlined his crotch. Urine dribbled onto his shoe tops and caused them to squeak while he jittered and wrung his hands. His legs shook and his teeth clicked against each other. Soft, yet earsplitting. I wanted to hold him but couldn't.

Shaking, Ginny slunk backwards into a corner, like a shadow hovering alone. She grunted like a hurt puppy. I wanted to pat her whines away but couldn't.

Bewilderment spread itself, sliding slick over the room. Terror loudly rattled around unclaimed spaces. It rambled like a big round ball with rocks in it, bouncing off walls and ceilings, and rolling over the linoleum. I stared at the floors, thinking Mama had done scrubbed them for nothing again.

Then I studied on Papa Harkus, reading his eyes. Nothing was there. He stood near the sooty black cook stove spitting. Juicy snuff clots popped from his scrunched-up beardy mouth into the round burner hole. He missed, spit sputtered and burned away as whistling steam. Reaching a finger up, he pinched a nostril and blew. Papa Harkus watched his trophy, a nasty green glob, sizzle on some fiery embers.

My stomach sickened as I recalled how we'd gratefully eaten sliced-up salty potatoes (tater chips) cooked on the stovetop the night before. I looked into his liquored eyes as spooky trick-or-treat shadows crossed his face from the dangling light bulb. We stood and waited, holding on.

20

Quiet and Still

"It don't hurt none," Mama mouthed. I read her lips, like I do people's eyes. Daddy threw a cane chair against the wall with a cracking thud, bringing us to life with jerks. The round wooden rungs splintered, flying like darts. We jumped, like scattering scared rabbits, all eyes switching to him in one stroke.

A broken stick jabbed Mama's leg, cutting deep a jagged gap, sticking. She bent and pulled it out like nothing. Blood trickled to her ankle from the gash. Her mouth looked up, moving hushed, "It don't hurt none." Her hand wiped the sticky red as she sat back up for more.

"You little shit-head," Daddy's purple-raged face screamed. We were all shit-heads. It was hard to figure who had wronged him this time. I went to guessing, getting nowhere for the moment. Shit-head boomeranged then landed on me.

His loathing gored my guts like screws tightening, squeezing my stomach into a walnut size. Oh dear God, it was my turn. I dry heaved as cusses hammered through wall cracks like spikes.

"Did ya take them kids out there on a limb, like ya Papa says?" he bellowed. Anger rattled the room, grumbled in other places. Papa Harkus scraped the stovetop with a smoldering stick sliver, getting leftover snot off. I glanced at his eyes; like icy balls they slid toward me. He spat.

Quiet and still—then a whooping cough came out as Papa Harkus's rubbing stick scooted and scraped. My giggles bubbled. Daddy's rage worsened. But when the rusty beans slid down and the stupid table prayed out loud, I couldn't stop. I became the broken table, mocking chortles at myself. The table begged Jesus.

"Dear God," I said, "I'm sorry we played. I didn't mean no harm. I'm so scared. Please save me." The rage came from the table. Out of nowhere came the biggest hate ever. It rose up like a coffee pot boiling over on the stovetop inside me. Enormous hate for Papa Harkus and

Daddy. Hate held my hand. I liked him. I wanted Papa Harkus to drop dead and die right then. Right that very minute. Die, you son-of-a-bitch, I said to him with my eyes. I wanted Daddy dead too. But he would never die. He was eternal God Almighty.

Then "it" happened real fast.

The belt jerked, unlooping briskly.

I counted, "Onetwothreefourfive," soft without breaths. Flinching, humped, heaped like a balled-up paper bag I withered small, crushed.

The black whip zipped, slicing, swishing the air. Unbreakable. Strong. Screaming, my eyes begged for mercy. I did it, God. Daddy God couldn't see my eyes and he had no mercy. Things moved like lightning.

His stood with whale-like mouth, gritted teeth, eyes set, glaring and glazed. He was high up. I'm low, little like a no-see-um. I looked upwards at the being's eyes, from slumping knees. Plump, some knees went onto the wooden floor. Onetwoonetwo. Two knees. Three knees. No two knees.

"I didn't mean to laugh. Honest to God, Daddy. It just came out." My eyes were full and hot. Salt dribbled into my mouth. Slams and knocks. Something was kicked. Something hit hard. Something shoved. Something twisted. I couldn't see, but I heard sounds. Stove scrapes happened to the left, a familiar hock-spit. My ears ringing, singing, ringing, singing.

"You little bitching whore. I'm gonna teach you a lesson you ain't never gonna forget the rest of your sorry-ass life." A massive fist pushed up, taunting God. "Woe to ye workers of iniquity." He preached, cussing God with "F" words. Too many to count. Too many times to count. Too many times to count.

I said, "London bridges all fall down, all fall down." "The 'F' word, the 'F' word, the 'F' word." Then, I preached like Daddy, "Woe to ye workers of iniquity." I whispered into my lap as if it was a bowl. "Daddy, please don't. Daddy, please stop. Please, please don't beat me no more," I pleaded, grabbing air as if a tree branch to hold on to.

I wasn't ashamed to beg him. We all did it. We said we wouldn't, but we did. "We are weak but he is strong. We are weak but he is strong. We are weak but he is strong." Just like church folks. Like Granny Isabelle had taught me. But it wasn't for Jesus, it was for Daddy God. God wasn't in heaven. Daddy God rolled the leather strap around four fingers. Onetwothreefour.

"Onetwothreefour," real fast without a breath I spoke. Then I said it some more, without the belt-rolling.

Daddy God is so big. Bigger than any man in the whole, wide world. Bigger than Jesus, bigger than any God. My daddy is so big. My sides, back, and legs, bruised and crushed. But dead. Not a bit did they feel. Just like my scarred-up leg. It never hurt either, not once. It never did. "Beat on, you son-of-a-bitch," I whispered into my damp cloth bowl, my hands folded, perched like broken bird wings within. Bird in a bowl. I laughed. "Beat on. It don't hurt no more, you son-of-a-bitch. Beat on some more."

My daddy couldn't help it. He couldn't quit beating when he started. Something took him over. He wasn't even real. He left his eyes. Mama and Granny Isabelle helped me, and I spoke without words. Mama's skull twisted to the wall, her fish-lip gulping for air.

Granny Isabelle stepped close. A thick, hairy hand shoved her. Backwards, she tripped over my pulled-off shoes. I counted some more. She fell up to ten. Her frazzled head slammed the corner cabinet, leaving a chunk of bloody flesh on it, hairs sticking out of the hunk. She laid still, slippery drool smearing her chin like soapy bubbled water.

"I caused Granny Isabelle to get killed." Soundless worry slipped from my dry mouth. "Nobody cares. Nobody does. No wonder no one loves me. Not Daddy God. Not Jesus. Dreams don't mean nothing. Dreams don't mean nothing. Dreams don't mean nothing."

Daddy scooted Granny Isabelle's old raggedy body outta his way. The living belt ate slivers from my skin. It chewed like dogs chew bones. Granny Isabelle woke up and crawled off to save herself.

Empty, shameful, I, a worthless nothing, crawling, worming. I struggled to hurry, to bury, to worry myself into a knot, a spot where nobody else would be. A place where I'd be invisible. My striped legs pushing hard, urging me backwards. Sliced burning welts covered me. Lashes coming heavy. I was stained.

I scrunched littler and littler, huddled head between my knees, hands and arms wrapped around me like a bandage. Saving myself. "Dear Jesus, save me," I prayed to Him, bowed down. But He didn't hear me.

It didn't matter what Granny Isabelle said about them men in the fiery furnace. About three men thrown in, but four was seen walking. Tonight it was just me. So I pitied myself being all alone walking in a furnace and hurting so bad. But it couldn't be helped. He wouldn't stop until there wasn't nothin' left. I reached, clutching more air, but nothing was there. Clutching, clutching, clutching.

Darkness fizzled into weary morning. Each one of us, dissolved into worthless wasted puddles. Spent, unable to hurry, but trying regardless. Trying to ready ourselves for the school bus. I staggered, disoriented with a belly bloated full of emptiness. Long sleeves, long dress, leave hair down. Don't look at people's faces, they don't care if we have faces or eyes. Look down. Don't speak. Bubble walk down to the last bus seat. Squish tight to the far corner like a no-see-um. Don't speak a word, I said. Hovering, waiting for shoddier things.

Rising up last, like a shadow longing for a body to latch on to. Behind swishing, crinkling skirts, shiny shoes, starched shirts. Following the good kids. Trailing them like a sheep. Hating hair braids and ponytails with bows. Girls with lavish lunch pails, frolicking and liking each other. Full of chatter and giggles. Me, hating everybody at once. Myself most of all.

Inching sloth-like into my scratched desk. Rested, quiet. Ceaseless peeing in the seat. Puddles in streams behind me. My palm rapped hard by the red-face teacher, her ruler a hammer. Spit on her lower lip. Her teeth gritted. Her whale mouth clinched. But it didn't hurt. It was nothing. I'd been through a lot worse than her ruler. Than a hammer even.

She was mad over the pee but I liked it. I stared down, eyes glued to the golden amber watercourse puddling behind my chair, wishing most to pull my finger through it. To taste it. To write "Onetwothree." Others giggled. They pointed. But I didn't see the kids. I loved my puddle. "It's my puddle," I wanted to scream at them. Wished I could draw in it with a finger. I tried. The teacher wouldn't let me. So I went on like nothing bad ever happened.

21

Foster Friends

Kids don't have much say about things most times. They are just stuck with what's put on them. That's the way it was for us. Nothing was good at the house we moved to on Barto Place. It was new to us but much like the other places we lived, other than Granny's. But Barto Place was evil. Dark, lonely, cold, with no one to turn to.

I'd take the kids to play at a nearby park. We passed by churches, but a smaller one off in the distance lit up, and wanted me. Sparkling windowpanes bounced light and soft songs reeked out, leading me to its red door. A tall steeple, pointed like a needle into the air, seemed to promise something good. Up, up, up and away beyond Barto Place.

"Ya'll wait here. I'll be back in a minute or so."

"Jessie, where ya goin'?" Danny moaned, tired from playing so hard on the merry-go-round.

"Jus' gonna check something out," I said. "Don't y'all get near the road, an' stay where I leave ya." I looked hard at them, but not meaning my hardness.

My face fixed as a woman's sweet voice caught on to me, sounding like Mama's way back. She'd be scrubbing, cleaning, sweeping, and singing. Full of hope for a better life. Thinking Daddy was gonna make money in Canada. Money for us to start over again.

My eyes searched. My ears strained, hungry. "Standing, Standing, Standing on the Promises of God." Their holy words fell on me like a soothing rain, loving me gently. Stroking my head with warmth. Hugging and rocking me. I felt as if I had bathed in a warm summer rain or sipped on cool water, my thirst quenched. But the church people's songs didn't match Mama's. Theirs were real. Not Mama's.

A man's deep voice led into another hymn: "Oh Why Not Tonight, Oh Why Not Tonight? Wilt Thou Be Saved." Feelings stirred my chest. On the step, under the steeple, I knelt there sinking, sinking, and sinking. Tears gushed onto the concrete porch. Everything coming undone inside me. Unmeshed—meshing. Listless, I laid down weak and empty. Just me, in that moment, puddled on the steps of God.

Slumped into a heap of nothingness when a set of black, shiny shoes with pant legs appeared. Then pretty, turquois high heels under a dress hem stood still beside him. His face had the gentlest gleaming eyes I ever saw. His golden tooth sparkled in sunlight and made a circle curl around my finger.

The blonde, curly-haired woman had twinkling teeth like pearls and a big bosom. Stooping to me, she patted my head, moving wet twisted hair sprigs to the side. I felt as if I was finally home.

"Oh, what a beautiful child. I'm gonna get me some chinny, chin, chin." She smiled, lifted my face, and studied my eyes. I glanced over at Ginny, Mama's pretty one. But the woman's eyes never left me. Thinking surely it wasn't me she meant. Ain't nobody ever said I was pretty. Much less beautiful. But she rubbed my cheek. Petted this and that. Pulled me into her lap. Snuggled me into her soft breast pillows and rocked me into safety singing, "Jesus Loves Me."

Then, like a dream it ended, a whiff. Ginny and Danny came, wanting some of what I had gotten. Arms stuck out like my faraway cousin's stuffed bear. Their eyes asked for something, not speaking but wanting. Hungry. Waiting. Wanting.

The man lifted them up sort of bear-like into his big chest, one on each arm, while the woman coddled me. We sat on the steps together, me feeling something I'd never felt before. Love, the kind in my Jesus dream, when Jesus toted me around for days as if I couldn't walk nowhere by my own self. Then the lady un-lapped me when she thought I'd had enough. But I wasn't near full, needing more.

"I have just the thing for you kids. I'll be right back." She smiled and went inside. Me not wanting her to ever leave me. Not for any reason big or little. My hand holding out, touching air only, nothing else, thinking she'd never come back. The man's face glowed light, touching my dullness and fear of losing what I'd found. His light touched Ginny and Danny also as we waited.

The woman returned with a bag full of things. Presents, she said. Three little books with tiny writing, testaments, she said.

"Just read John. Read it to them out loud," she said, pointing at me. "It's the one about love." I tried to decipher the words but couldn't. "And look what else I have for you little ones." She opened my hand and slipped a tiny silver ring on my finger. Then Ginny got one. And Danny got a toy gun that popped loud when he snapped it.

The man took off to his car and came back with a holster from a box of toys and strapped it onto Danny's hip. Danny shouted and danced, happy that at last his wish had come true. I remembered the time we'd prayed in the field. Our prayer was answered for Danny. He had his toy gun.

"What I've wanted my whole life," he squealed.

They laughed, delighted. Petting our heads and hugging. Hugging and petting us. Ginny and I couldn't believe little silver rings were on our fingers, never having any before. I recalled my dream of the ring Jesus gave me.

"Where do y'all live?" they asked.

"Yonder over that hill."

"Where have y'all been?" the man asked.

"To the park," we respond.

"Are you going on home now?"

"Yeah," I said, my voice sounding letdown.

The kind woman said, "Why don't y'all come here Sunday. We're going to have an Easter egg hunt. Right here under these big trees. With lemonade, prizes, and a whole lot of fun."

I was thinking there weren't no way in hell somebody could keep me from it. Then I hugged on them and thanked them for our gifts. I wondered how to hide our things from Daddy.

Peering back while walking on, I said, "We will."

The spotless, shiny-faced man looked happy. "By the way, we're Mr. and Mrs. Foster."

"And we're Jessie, Ginny, and Danny," I hollered back. "He's Danny." I pointed, giggling.

Off we went, knowing we had something good to come back to. We had never been to an Easter egg hunt like that one. Only like the one with Granny Isabelle, with boiled eggs, salt, and pepper that we ate long before the hunt.

22

Chasing Rabbits

Saturday was a day full of Daddy showing out and Mama being head-pulled through the house and over the rocky backyard first thing in the morning. Something about lady Red Cheeks next door. Daddy and Red Cheeks would drink likker together. Mama finally took off to see what they were up to. About what we'd been telling her since the woman's old man left off driving his tractor trailer.

That woman, Red Cheeks, laid up, crying on the sofa, full of beer and likker, smoking cigarettes, playing country records on her brown phonograph, sitting far off in the corner. She was crying one minute, laughing the next. Her old man usually came home honking his big horn, blowing black smoke all over the place, making her happy for a bit. At least, for a while. The time came when Daddy started going over to cheer her up from missing her man so bad. Daddy was right over there in the midst of it all when her old man was away, but he ran out when Red Cheeks's old man rolled home.

Mama got something stuck in her head about Red Cheeks and Daddy. I was thinking who gave a tinker's damn cause I sure didn't care if she took him off our hands. But Mama couldn't see things that way. Loving him so much, I guess.

So she took off to the neighbor's house, coming back after we were in bed, puking her guts out right outside my bedroom window in the backyard. Curiously, I watched through the window cracks, as two talking shadows followed Mama, helping her up two front steps into the house while she was gagging her guts out.

Daddy said, "It's okay to be sick the first time."

"It won't be so bad next time." Red Cheeks snickered, binding together with Daddy's arms. Mama's feet stumbled as she fell on the bed crossways, legs hanging, shoes dangling, toes touching the floor.

Daddy and Red Cheeks went on back to what they were doing over at her house. Me peeking, Mama laid dropped off the bed, moaning

99

over nothing hurting. Me testing her forehead for fever, asking what was wrong. Her saying nothing. Nothing. Me thinking on how we didn't even have her now. What we never had anyway. Not a dab of anybody to lean on, since she was gonna be a drunk like Daddy. Even if she never spoke much, we knew she was somewhere around, settled down, ghost-like.

Granny Isabelle always told us, "Once ya start the drinking it ain't no way off the stuff." Me wondering, since I done got a taste from Granny Isabelle's doctoring formula, if I was on my way like the rest. Straight to hell in a handbasket, with no hope.

Sunday came slow, dragging behind Saturday night, full of sunshine. The sun knocking at my window and some birds chirping to get me up. Waking me to go see the lemonade stand and egg hunt for prizes.

The three of us washed from the gray porcelain pan, cleaning our ears and faces using the same wet rag. Trying hard to rub shine on us, like the godly ones, but couldn't. Me knowing we had a long way to go yet to be saved into shining. We dried off, pulled on some cleaner clothes than we wore the day before.

Me, standing with the cold doorknob cupped in my hand, twisting and pulling for the life of me. Me, mad at Daddy for being part of two laughing shadows that aided Mama's walk. Her still groaning with a terrible headache. Legs still hanging off the mattress. Me, hating Daddy's sorry self in the worst way for taking what we never had in the first place. Our Mama.

Daddy said, "Now jus' where the hell do y'all think ya going?" More hatefully spoken than other times cause of his own headache. Him thumb-rubbing his temple, smoke curling from his nostrils like baby snakes.

I said, "To the park. We gonna get outta y'all's way for a while, an' these here kids gonna ride the merry-go-round." Me, telling Daddy the park was the best place for us to be while his head hurt so bad. Not saying "church," but "park" cause Daddy wasn't one bit saved that day and Mama wasn't far behind him. Me knowing what I was doing. Me thinking, ain't nobody gonna keep me from them eggs and shiny-faced people. Ain't no way in hell nor kingdom come.

I knew Mama was getting low down like him and on her way to hell. Knowing Daddy was responsible for her wayward ways too. Me, hell-bent, squint-eyed, studying on his face to a dare. Letting him know there wasn't no keeping me stuck here.

Wanting to raise cane like he did. Wanting to kick over some kitchen chairs and throw some dishes against the wall. After all I'd been through with Mama's puking at my windowsill, watching him and Red Cheeks hug and kiss on each other.

He said, "Y'all go on now." Holding his head, fingers shaking, grabbing another BC Powder and another cup of strong, black coffee with a splash of likker and looking some happier to be rid of us.

Church bound, we scurried through the wooded path, arriving barely in time to see some good folks sitting on wooden pews. Other kids we didn't know wiggled restless, like us wanting to hunt eggs before hearing the Word. Guitar people singing "Oh, Why Not Tonight" a hundred times too many.

Finally, the Word and songs being over, we headed on out to the front yard under the big oak trees with limbs poking like dingy arthritic fingers, clawing air, dropping broken twigs around us.

Sweet pine scents breezed in two directions at once, behind and in front of my flapping skirt and playing under it. Me feeling good below, warm wind flowing in and out, touching hidden places, like a secret door was opened somewhere to tingle my covered, shameful places.

Mr. Foster, preacher and egg-hider, stood arms wide-opened outward, helping us cheat above the rest—his fingers pointing wildly like some mad man. Him laughing, happier than us over some few lost eggs.

Spying and pointing first to the left, then to the right with his once whole finger—now a half, chopped-off stub from some lawnmower problem—screaming for us to go here and there. In leaf piles, beside rocks, and in grassy clumps he yelled. Colored eggs tucked in tree branches and all over the place littered the grounds. He lifted us high, getting what we couldn't get before the others grabbed them.

These people of God were way too happy to be real. Ain't no way people could be that joyful. Mrs. Foster doting on me like in my dream when Jesus did. On and on she went about how pretty I was. Rubbing my hair, pushing good thoughts into my hard head, all around my ears, like Granny Isabelle did. Me feeling. Me listening. Me feeling sweetness come inside me, like I might just be a wee bit beautiful in some way or another.

The best time of my whole life ended that day. I won a huge chocolate bunny in a big pink box with see-through paper. I was anxious to eat it and save it at the same time to nibble on. But left only the nose and a leg in the end for Mama. Ginny and Danny won jars of jelly beans and soft yellow marshmallow bunnies with brown eyes. It was a wonderful thing being saved by God and having lemonade and candy bunnies to live for.

And me, being squashed up onto Mrs. Foster's breast pillows all day with her telling me how sweet I was. Me thinking, it ain't so. Her saying it was so anyway. Her loving my freckles most of all—rubbing them with her painted fingertips, like an eraser—me liking my face speckles now. Me not ever wanting to go home, but having to go anyway.

23

Busted

Sundays came and went after that. Me still loving church, even without the candy. Keeping our secret from Daddy for the longest was hard. Nobody noticed us coming back from park playing, half cleaned up. Nobody noticed or cared.

Then, Daddy caught me reading the testament. Not reading good, not understanding thus and thou, but studying it nonetheless. Trying to get a touch of holiness and a face glow through the words somehow.

Me saying to Daddy, "I was only doing what Granny Isabelle done taught me. Going to church. Trying to be good." Daddy looking through scrunched-up eyes, slatted for truth-telling. Me telling only some parts that fit.

Me, still going to church come hell or high water. Me getting dipped under the creek water by some strong hands to save me— washing the bad parts away. I supposed between him and Granny and Preacher Smith, it seemed I'd run to the altar too much for my awful sins. Preacher Foster saying once was enough to be saved and baptized. Me not taking his word for it. Me, happy, going on in life with a pint-size hope.

My parents not a part of my different life. Things going pretty good, getting loved and petted by other people down the road, under the steeple. People being glad to see us walk through the church door. Feeling wanted. Feeling liked. Not ever wanting them to know where I came from. Nor know how and where I lived. Wanting to keep this special life to myself forever. A place I could feel valued.

Then awful happened. For us the day was normal. We got off the school bus. Nobody was home. Nothing outta the ordinary, but no note or nothing from Mama. Me feeling wound up, cause Daddy might be trying to kill her again, but not saying my thoughts to the others.

Ginny ate burnt toast and drank cold coffee with her feet propped up, watching television. Danny played with two armless toy soldiers. I was washing oatmeal bowls from the morning meal. Scraping, scraping, and scraping, being a mama with no help.

Clunky shuffling with hard knocks came on the door. Bam, bam, bam. Who could it be? Nobody ever came to see us. I turned the knob and looked up to see the ones who loved on us from church. Faces full of shine. Mouths full of teeth talking. The preacher's gold tooth sparkling from his top lip.

Not forewarned. Shaken. Wordless. Heart full of hollow, sinking down, down, and down. There stood my big Foster friends. I wouldn't share them with this awful family. How did they know where we lived? I winced. They couldn't be here. They just couldn't be here.

Words beyond my ears, talking from tin cans. Arms weighed down with puffed paper bags. Saltine crackers toppling out. Bread leaning over. Bananas poking from the side like spider legs. Full. Loaded down. To and from the car they came and went. No, don't. Don't bring that stuff here. You don't belong here. I don't live here. Not here. Me not wanting anything but them. But not here. Not in this dreadful place.

Them happy. Me not. I stood ashamed. Humiliated. Dripping sadness to the core over the crossed line. Them knowing who I really was and where I lived from then on. My secret shouted. Hope destroyed.

"Thank you," I said. Not meaning it. Not meaning a word of it. Not wanting bananas or crackers or butter for Ginny's burnt toast.

Never going back to the warm, white church with a pointy steeple, red door, and Jesus. Not another step did I make on the concrete porch, where I had poured my soul's agony out to strangers. Me, not ever again to be coddled or burrow my head into Mrs. Foster's chest pillows.

Me thinking for sure, only bad things last forever. Wishing Daddy to be dead. Then not. Knowing he'd made Mama call my Foster friends and take from them what he had no business. Taking from us kids what he had no claim to. The only good we'd ever had, now gone in the blink of an eye.

Me left alone, aching inside and out, undone, withered and lost all over again, back to where I started before knowing the good people. Knowing I could never face them again. Shame burning my face and bursting my heart. Them knowing we were hungry and so poor. Humiliation covered me like a soppy wet coat.

No way would I ever go back to church and face them. Now that the Fosters knew exactly who I was, where I lived, I could not pretend anymore. My secret was exposed. I was pure white trash. With them I had pretended to be more than that. Now they knew the whole truth about me.

Nothing worse than finding something good, losing it, and going back to the way life was before. A cruelty beyond empty and dark.

24

Christmas

Christmas wasn't no different from any other times. Weren't no such thing as a holiday to us. I wasn't telling my brother no more lies about Santa neither. No reindeer, sled and all. He kept hoping against all hope he might get something good to play with. But it wasn't never gonna happen.

I'd done planned in my head how to bring truth to him, so as not to hurt him so badly. It oughta help him see what was and what wasn't for real. I figured there weren't no use wasting time, wishing for something that wasn't never gonna be. It was the way I'd come to see things.

"Jessie, ya think he's comin' this time?" Danny asked.

"We ain't got no tree," I said back, as if that was reason enough.

"He could still come an' see us. Looks to me like us bein' good an' all, ought to be 'nough to bring him 'round sometimes." His voice let down.

"Well, I don't know it for sure, but the tree might have somethin' to do with things being the way they are. Them lights bring on the reindeer, ya know," I said, building up for the truth.

"But I been askin' for a pony for years, since I been five. Do you 'member Billy Joe? He had one way back yonder when we was little."

My head agreed, thinking harder on how to let him down easy. Now, being older, that make-believe stuff just couldn't go on hurting a little boy.

He wrung his hands like he needed to do something. Some tears blinked back, cause he was tenderhearted, and sad for his own lack and the injustice of things.

"Now you ain't gonna go crying on me again," I said, my heart lurching over his pain. I knew things wasn't right for him. Me neither. No more Fosters for me, since they'd found out who we really were. After that I was too ashamed to be around them. I was disgraced. They begged me to return with Ginny and Danny, but my pride wouldn't let me. No way. I would just have to do things on my own again.

Danny wet the bed and cried over nothing much most times, even without Daddy's rages. "No, I ain't crying," he said.

"You know its all 'bout givin' to each other, not what we get from a fat man in a red suit."

He slightly nodded his head.

"I ain't never seen Santa. Not a reindeer, and not a sled. Not even a sled track. Have you?"

"No, I ain't neither." He glared at me all the same.

"I know you got excited over them Baby Ruths and a few oranges an' walnuts fallin' on the floor from the chimney. All that ruckus going on the housetop. But it was jus' Daddy half-drunk outta his head. It weren't no Santa an' no reindeer."

"How ya know it were Daddy?" Danny asked.

"Cause he was cussin' like a devil from hell, when he 'bout fell and broke his foolish neck. You mean you didn't hear no cussin'?" I asked. "Plus all that mud knotted up in his hair with a bloody splotch on top his head. That's how I know for sure. I don't know what gets into Daddy sometimes. But anything's better than last night, when all hell breaks out." I shivered with memories. "Don't you think maybe one of us woulda seen some sign of Santa after all these years?" I asked him, plain and clear.

"I ain't sure. An' I ain't seen no blood in his hair," he barked hatefully.

"Ain't you never noticed when we write our list and leave a sugar biscuit out for Santa to eat, he never touches them? They still the same the next morning. One time I even dog-eared an' folded my note up with the top just so, to see if he even looked it over. Do you know it was jus' the same when we got up the next morning? I figured maybe he forgot, so I did it again the next year, an' will this one. The very same thing happened."

Danny looked at me nervous, seeming surprised that I'd be testing Santa Claus for authenticity.

"I ain't believing what I want things to be no more," I went on. "I believe what I see and know. Like them notes I left. Ain't you never wondered why Santa gives all them pretty presents for sorry-ass kids an' not us while we are being so good?" Things appeared to be sinking into Danny's brain.

"Yeah. That no count thievin' Billy Joe gets everythin'. If goodness brings them Santa gifts to kids, then he woulda got nothin'. Nothin' at all." He paused, thinking. "Plus all them lies he's done told his mama to get store-bought stuff outta her. He ain't nothin' but a thievin' liar. Ain't no real Santa gonna stand for that."

"So if our Mama an' Daddy don't have no money for nothin' an' Billy Joe's does, an' we don't get no Santa stuff an' he does, then who do you think Santa is?" I just said it plain and simple.

"I think Santa didn't read them notes cause he didn't see 'em," he stated emphatically.

It was then that I quit talking to the wall, cause little Danny wasn't ready for the truth.

Real Christmas was thrown in our face every which way we turned. We'd walk from school or to the store for a loaf of bread and see all that goodness in others kids' lives. We coveted the round green wreaths with big red bows, the big trees full of twinkling lights and pretty ornaments and tinsel. Other people's beauty sparkled through large picture windows to remind us of what we didn't have. The beautiful decorations seemed to poke fun at us, like tongues sticking from houses, as we ambled homeward from running errands.

Other people's specialness made our emptiness worsen as days ticked off the calendar for Santa's trip. For the most part, I'd just try to walk on by, not looking. But other folks' good stuff seemed to catch my eyes regardless, and grave wanting followed me. It would poke at my heart like a person prodding my chest with a hateful stick.

At last, part of me died when Christmas day came. I just didn't want to have feelings. I never knew what it was supposed to feel like to have a good holiday. We awakened to find a few scrounged-up things laid out for us. Still no tree was to be seen. Mama had gotten what she could for us. Lack laid in her eyes like a hollow grave. I felt no sympathy for her efforts that day, just a sick emptiness inside regarding Ginny, Danny, and my own self.

So I rubbed the hard doll's face and flipped her harsh eyelids up once or twice with my flicking fingers, caring for nothing except the tetherball I did not get. Deserting my cold stiff toy, more so despising it,

108

I walked away. Danny was excited over his squirt gun and a few little soldier men with arms, and Ginny tittered over her rag doll while I felt disgust.

I took hold of Ginny and Danny's hands, covered them with socks, and headed outside to make my own tetherball. I gathered a rag and old rope from the closet and headed toward a tree. Hardness had covered the ground; worn-out snow splotched the frozen red mud. The slick, steep hill and cold rocks folded around our shoes as we scooted sideways to throw the roped ball over a tree limb.

I finally suspended the old gray rag ball from a tree branch and we spent the day hitting, hitting, and hitting. I had my tetherball, nothing near like the one at school, but sufficient. Nothing else mattered as we waited for another school day to come, forgetting Christmas that never was except another day being ugly like all the rest.

25

Things Weren't Fair

Holidays always brought on Daddy's wrath. Christmas being the worst. Things would start out usual and then, before we knew it, something terrible would come about without a warning.

"Jessica, go on an' take them young'uns to the park for a while." Mama called me Jessica when she wanted me to pay attention. "Y'all can play on the merry-go-round an' have a little picnic." Mama stumbled slightly over the straw broom as she scuttled mouse-like, stuffing a splotched greasy paper bag with leftover bits of fried pork rinds. She rolled three peanut butter biscuits into some rutted waxed paper. "For God's sake don't be getting hurt. Y'all know how ya Daddy gets crazy when one of y'all gets tore or scratched up."

I said to her, "I don't know that he cares so much 'bout us getting hurt. We get beat up all the time by his hands. His harm's worse than ever falling off the merry-go-round—what he does to us some people wouldn't do to a dog, much less to their own kids. If you ask me he don't love us an' he never has."

She shushed me in front of the others. "You ought to be ashamed, saying stuff like that. Y'all know ya Daddy loves you. Sure as rain, he does. Y'all are his own blood an' bones."

"Right," I smarted.

Unashamed, I found her words didn't torment me as usual. I took hold of the oil-stained paper poke and we left to go play, hand in hand. The others felt happy over Mama's little talk about us being loved by Daddy. I just wanted to be a normal kid with normal parents.

I hankered to run free at the park with the bigger kids. Play Red Rover, King of the Mountain, or fly kites. Feeling haggard at nine years old, I did what I had to.

My shoulders slumped as we gathered, sitting on a rock to eat. We gnawed the gluey biscuits down, swiped bread bits off our clothes for bluebirds, and wiped brown nutty smears from our chins with the crumpled bag. Somewhat happier, with our bellies relieved, we lingered on that great stone. Slobbering over salty pork rinds, we pondered Santas and Easter bunnies that never visited us.

Funny how everyday leftover food tasted better at the park. I lifted Danny to gurgle down spurts of bubbling fountain water. He didn't look like much for his age, but he was growing heavier with each boost.

Unrelenting words needled my soul—"never let hurt come to them kids, and if ya do, I'll beat ya within an inch of ya life and you'll be wishing to die." Daddy's words. I watched over them as best as I could in hopes they didn't get killed or harmed.

People would say, "Jessica, hold ya shoulders up."

I'd say back, "I can't. They are too heavy." But I wanted to scream, "Hold up your own shoulders. If y'all did all I have to do, you'd be slumped down, with a Daddy like mine."

My feelings mixed up over Ginny, but not Danny. She played sick, never helping with chores, not lifting a finger. Every day, I scraped hardened oatmeal from morning dishes after I got off the school bus.

I soaked, washed, and dried them by myself, while she hid off watching television, her feet propped up. She wouldn't eat beans, fried potatoes, biscuits or gravy like the rest of us. Only toast and coffee. We never got coffee. Only her. Mama treated her like a princess, more special than us, but she said she didn't. Just like she said Daddy really did love us.

She sneaked Ginny store-bought things, like thick oatmeal cookies, potato chips, and dill pickles. Watching Ginny lick on the white cookie icing while we stood to the side looking on made me envious. I was tasting what I couldn't have, feeling much like yearning over other folks' beautiful Christmas displays.

Why did I think Ginny was treated better if she wasn't? Mama's words would swell inside of me, making me unsure if my feelings were real. My reality became more distorted. Her words and my feelings never matched up. Was I making stuff up?

Daddy's treatment felt like hate. Ginny wasn't treated better, but we never got cookies or wasn't even allowed to sop her salty potato chip bowl. But the leftover pickle juice, we got some of that, cause she just wanted pickles. Was real not real? Maybe it was like the fairies in Granny Isabelle's cornfield. I thought they were actual, but Granny Isabelle said it was all in my head back then. I missed her sort of since she'd returned to her little house where I played with doodlebugs.

"It ain't fair," I declared to Mama.

She said, "Nothing's fair. Ginny's small an' weakly. She's puny an' needs to eat anything I can get in her without her puking everything up."

At times I hated Mama and Ginny's relationship. They seemed to be tied together in a knot. I felt without value, the same as when some school girls whispered and pointed fingers at me. Ginny was lavished with big round creamy cookies and dill pickles, while Danny and me had nothing. I determined that someday I'd have all the pickles, cookies, and chips I wanted.

Anger raged up in me toward Ginny. I wanted to hurt her. Once, I knocked her head hard with a hairbrush and didn't give a hoot about her crying jag. She wouldn't let me even taste the white cookie cream. The more tears the better, I thought. Cry on, little bitch, I said to her. I didn't regret the brush whack or the bitch word.

Yet I felt a twisted sadness and protectiveness for her. How could I have two feelings mixed together? Later, I felt bad over the head lump that rose up, thinking nobody else better hit her head or they'd answer to me.

I acted grown-up and strong on the outside. On the other hand, I felt sad and confused, weak and helpless on the inside—so wishing to be like Ginny—oh, to be treated special just once by Mama. Maybe to get my head rubbed a little or a smile from her for all my hard work. Maybe half a cookie for me and Danny to divide. But all the wishing in the world never made it happen.

26

Mama the Whore

As the sun rolled to the west, we trudged homeward, talk-less, tired-out, and hungry again, but relieved from our getaway time at the park. For a while, we'd pushed aside our bad reality with play time.

Stepping underneath the front yard's big oak tree, an eerie foreboding came smothering me, like a cold, wet heavyweight blanket. Tripping over roots, with great trepidation we moved forward, acorn crunches exploding like bombs beneath our shoes.

Clueless to my alarm, Danny shoe-toed the acorns, splaying red dust wildly into the air. Hesitating, my uneasiness grew into a massive choke-hold. Danny's feet and giggles froze midair as I snatched his arm.

Fingers hunted my lips, shushing. I stepped up onto the retched dilapidated porch, eavesdropping by the shut screen door for sounds. Cusses bubbled, rumbled, and groaned from the house's innards, resembling a nearing train bumping on ruts. My guts ballooned into jittery convulsions as realization hit me.

The doorknob, covered with my hand's sweat, faintly clicked. My heart raced. My mouth dried up. My body weakened, fading away as my knees buckled. The metal lock clunked and whacked, releasing.

Screeeech, the green door whined. Screen was now ripped down the side that wasn't there before. Time crawled like ants. Mama's red-blotched face noticed us, her silent bloody dribbles spoke through her busted, broken lip. Now muddle-headed, confusion overwhelmed me. Everything was okay when we left—nobody seemed mad or bad then— but I should have known it didn't matter if things were okay or not.

I whispered, "I should've never left."

Mama mimed my whispers vacantly. Her swollen eyes searched mine, warning me.

Danny instantly peed. Puddles rippled outward, settling around his feet. Ginny grew white-faced, blue-lipped, seemingly famished of playground happiness. A state near hysteria shackled my legs as my heart thumped violently. Reduced and terrified. I considered how could we keep going through this agony? Deciding quickly it would be better to be dead.

I grabbed Daddy's stinking, sand-laden work sock from the floor and offered it to Mama's face as I patted her bloody drops. Mad at me for dabbing, Daddy thrusted my body against the beaded-board wall. Stumbling over a chair, my head knocked the doorframe with a dull thud. Mellowed, I lounged in the sweetest layer of forgetfulness, blank without sight or sound. And then, arousing into awareness, I wanted death fiercely.

"You lying, whoring bitch." Yellow-painted, wooden number 2 pencil flakes flew off in shards, and drifted to the floor. He sadistically knifed the leaded end as a pink eraser glared at me from the other end. Daddy's face was pinched and screwed up, full of purpose, needing to get to the bottom of things. His teeth gritted.

Mama was seated on a kitchen chair staring time-less, space-less. The few dishes we had lay strewn in fragments. A crimped-up torn brown paper bag piece laid on the table underneath her right hand. Her fingers constricted it as if it might magically fly away.

"Ya done been with 'em all. Whoring 'round day an' night," he yelled. "You better go ahead and tell me them names. You worthless whoring piece of shit." He squalled curses at God.

Her stretched hair hung in blood-matted twists. Mama's tearless pale face waited as her sunken eyes stared out of a window. She sat convicted and judged without proof of innocence.

Danny pissed some more, amber rippling onto his feet and mine. Ginny with hands shaking, backed outside and leeched onto the big tree's body. Danny's cold, clammy hand squeezed mine as I glanced outside, checking on Ginny. She was squatted down, kitten-like, scrunched up between two big root gnarls, on a pile of acorns.

"It wouldn't take much to walk right by her an' not know she was even there, wadded small as she is," I whispered to Danny, nodding at the tree. Mama, mostly entranced, noticed my soft-spoken breaths and nodded for me to shut up.

"You didn't know I was watchin' ya, did you? I saw it all, clear as day. You out there swayin' ya hips an' wavin' that f---ing handkerchief, signalin' that man from the dry cleaners to stop an' pick ya up. Jus' like the whore ya are."

A fat fist crunched her cheek again. Sick stomached, from the smashing sound of flesh-on-flesh, I tried to help her once more. He slammed me.

"I watched the whole thing go down." Daddy was cussing God and some man we'd never heard of. He had tried to get her off the curb. Daddy stormed on, an accusing middle finger ramming in her face, then it thudded the rumpled paper on the wooden table. His finger, whacking holes into the sheet, sounded like a rubber hammer. His cartoony finger, like an enormous club, seemingly covered the tabletop. I snickered.

Glazed eyes spiked. "What the f--- are you laughing at? Ya Mama's little bitch." Seething, he sniggered through clenched teeth.

"That inside finger was all," I whimpered, wetting myself, looking downward at my shoes. My urine gathered with Danny's, binding us together forever.

"How the f--- do you know about this finger?" His voice challenged me, the digit now ramming the air.

Mama's beleaguered eyes traveled warily between us. Distress peered out as she shushed me again without communication.

"Some kids at school said it meant for me to go straight to h---. You know what I mean. I can't be sayin' it," I mumbled. His eyes left me and went back to the worthless woman on trial. Her eyes hollowed out, receded, and lingered blank once again.

"Look at me, bitch." Her slow, clunky eyes moved toward his face, settling still. "Do you think you can hide from me? Answer me. You think ain't no lawyer is smart enough that I can't beat 'em in court. Huh?" He threw his mortar-covered work boot at her face, forcing her attention. Sandy grit clinked to the floor. Her battered head tottered like an apple bobbing on water.

Steely-eyed, he jabbered, "Ya better say something or I'll cut your damn throat right here in front of them kids. Cut ya damn head off clear to the backbone. Ain't nobody on earth or in hell can stop me. Ya damn well better speak or you and them both are gonna be sorrier than hell." He pointed to us. "Them first, then you."

Her voice pleaded, "Ain't nobody smart as you are, James."

"Damn right, ain't nobody smart as me," he snarled doggishly. "All I gotta do to take these kids from ya is get me somebody to say you been whoring—both black an' white men—laying up all over the place. All I gotta do is pay them some money, little darling. You gonna be dead as a doornail as soon as you come against me. I done told ya what I'm gonna do to y'all. You better tell me everything right now. You got thirty seconds to write them names down."

He pushed the shaved pencil into her hands, imposing marks on the paper using his fingers to guide hers.

"I don't know what ya want me to write. I ain't been seeing nobody."

He cussed God, repeating the "f" word. "You write them names you done whored yourself out with. That's what you gonna write."

She took hold the wrinkled paper and scribbled, dragging the pencil shaft with her sore, twisted fingers, with one now broken, swollen double, crooked and blue.

He grabbed the ragged sheet, scanned it, and shoved it back into her hands, unsatisfied. "Now the women."

She added more names. He jerked the list from her hands, cussing harder and louder. "That ain't all. Ya better write down them names, ever last one, before I kill ya. I ain't playing 'round with ya bitch."

Expressionless, she wrote in slow jags. He jerked her up by hair wads and pulled her across the floor like a rag doll. "Ginny, get ya ass in here," he hollered outside, through the open screen door, the porch light drawing mosquitos and anything with wings inside.

Ginny crawled cat-like toward us, whimpering, "Okay, I will Daddy."

"Now if y'all wanna see ya your sorry-ass mama come back alive, y'all get down on ya knees by this here couch and pray like hell."

Like London Bridges we collapsed. Heart-throated, choked, united, we folded on our knees and prayed aloud to Jesus, steeple-handed. We heard a loud bang. Together we lifted to watch him drag Mama head first to the car. A small handgun sprayed bullets from his clamped hand over Mama's head. Aggravated, furious over her tripping and not walking upright, he shoved her into the car, ramming her bruised head against the panel. Her face cringed sideways.

The passenger door slammed. Tires squalled, and then rocks sailed out like barbs. Leaving her scratched-up brown penny loafers behind in the gravel drive—a grave reminder of our Mama's impending death. The only Mama we had, rode away to be murdered.

We screamed, cried, prayed, begged, looked, wept, and pissed ourselves some more. We moaned, held hands, and begged Jesus to not let him kill our Mama. After what seemed to be hours, the breeze blew the creased, smudged, ecru list tumbling by my eyes.

I smoothed its crumpled wrinkles to read the un-chewed words, the unknown jerky letters scraped across the page. John Smith, Joe Doe, Nancy Doe, Doris Day, and a few others I'd never heard of. My mind not recalling sensibly—trying my best to know them, but couldn't with my engorged mind cloudy, way beyond comprehension, full of apathy and confusion.

A part of me wondered if Mama was a whore. Not knowing much about whores, except for Aunt Fanny. Even then, not knowing all there was, just parts and pieces. But thinking the names Mama had scrawled were nasty boyfriends and girlfriends. I'd never before believed she was a whore, but maybe she was, from the names she had written.

It seemed so unlikely, her being the opposite of my bad aunt. But names don't lie, I reasoned. My mind obsessed over the written people as doubt plucked at my heart. Thick, relentless night crowded us, pushing our feverish worried souls into despondency.

Darkness tramped sluggishly into the house like a monster. We stayed withered, crouched by the couch's altar edge, with me clutching the ragged paper tight to my chest, like Mama did; praying for Daddy not to kill her.

Long later, we heard the distant familiar engine's whine of Daddy's car. Gravels crunched as the vehicle braked. In unison, our eyes pried and probed through the windowpane, with mouths still murmuring and stammering worn-out prayers.

I spied a wormy shadow beside of Daddy. I moaned, "There's a person in the car with him."

Ginny groaned a relief, saddled with exhaustion. Danny hovered closer to me as I held him lop-sided on my hip to see her. His heart beat on mine as his body tremored with snubs. "Jesus heard us pray, like he did for your toy guns, Danny," I said.

Two people of the night, our parents, struggled toward the house. Almost gentlemanly, Daddy stopped for a second, allowing Mama to retrieve her upturned shoes while balancing on his strong arm, to shake some rocks out. I could tell by Daddy's untwisted face that his badness was spent. He opened the cantankerous front door with a sheepish grin. His unclenched jaw chewed nonchalantly on a squishy dead cigar end.

Mama came inside and swept up some broken glass pieces, the splintered mop handle and ladder-back chair slats, and the frying pans and coffee cups, while Daddy rested, chewing the tobacco stub that cradled his lower lip, his eyes ogling.

"Y'all kids go get ready for school for the morning, an' sleep a spell," she said. We bedded down, listening to easy whispers and squeaky bedsprings coming from their bedroom. Train rails rattled solemnly behind our house, and cracked dishes clinked and clattered as the long horn blew and our shattered lives went on.

Morning came quickly. Mama washed herself up as best as she could, readying herself for work at some dry cleaner place. But it was only a matter of time before Daddy would ruin that job too. Like every time she'd find work—he'd destroy it. She pulled on her blue and black tweed pencil skirt, clipped the blue rhinestone earrings to her lobes, and painfully straightened her soft blue sweater, gently covering scratches, welts, and swellings. Facing the dresser mirror, with me looking behind her, she dabbed makeup on her swollen bruises, flinching, and then we all acted like nothing bad ever happened as we readied for school.

27

Uncle Rudy's Boy

Strange sneaky things went on in my uncle's home, not being as they appeared. But I still liked visiting on occasions. Their bleach-smelling house interested me. They had lots of good stuff to eat, and the king boy lived there. I especially liked watching Jimmy, their odd son.

Really, I didn't give much thought to Uncle Rudy's boy, never speaking to him much. I liked him for the most part. Mostly, I just studied on him, watching his fingers twitch and jerk.

Aunt Fanny had given my uncle a retarded son, named after my own Daddy, Granny Isabelle said. Uncle Rudy babied and cooed over him way too much. He loved Jimmy, and sweetness oozed from my uncle's weary eyes when he stroked the boy's head. Aunt Lizzie said, "That boy sure has took a toll on Uncle Rudy, keeping him awful tired most times."

I remembered no such coddling for my own self from anyone except Granny Isabelle. Likely, I never got none and never would. Deep down, I'd wished for Uncle Rudy to be my daddy, or for me to be retarded like Jimmy, so Uncle Rudy would love and dote on me a while.

The odd boy always looked nice and clean dressed up in jeans, tennis shoes, and crisp ironed shirts. He sat propped up in a chair that my uncle had made just for him, posed like a king, looking down on everyone. I, myself, didn't like it. Not one whit.

He'd look at me sideways and giggle over nothing in the air, as if he was listening to sky voices. He'd point, wiggling his crooked fingers upward toward nothing, as if something was telling him a funny joke for his ears alone. I'd look out yonder where his points went, and never once did I see or hear a thing.

I think he acted up for attention, as if he didn't get enough. I decided he was afraid we might get his love portion when we visited. Even after we'd leave their home, I'd think on him, about what was wrong with the king boy. It was a secret.

One particular visit didn't go well for me. I'd had about all I could take, especially them petting Jimmy and not me. His continuous giggling, peering sideways slit-eyed at me, and the crooked-up finger-pointing at invisible sky people bothered me.

Like ducks in a row, the family went off toward the kitchen. Daddy paraded behind the rest, with his glazed eyes hooked on Aunt Fanny's wide, bouncing tail. Her dress was made of a silky fabric with falling pleats that swayed with her gait, as she led the way toward her lattice-top cherry pie and perked Luzianne coffee.

I didn't care for cherry pie much, wanting chocolate instead, and so I stayed behind with the king boy to get something off my chest. I sat down beside him, pondering some seconds over Daddy's fixed glossy eyes. I'd seen him a few times like that before with Red Cheeks. And other places, but not remembering where exactly. I'm a kid, but I see things. I see more than most adults, who don't have inklings of what's before them.

Time had come to deal with the king boy, my jealousy seething. The present seemed to be my only chance, as far as I could tell. I told it like it was. That's what I liked to do. I just spit the bothering out, so worry didn't fester inside of me.

That's what Granny Isabelle always told me to do when at times I'd mope, following after her through the house. "For God's sake, just say it, chile," she'd say.

I stared strong and hateful at the king boy sitting above me. "You think ya somethin', don't ya. With all that stuff you do. Well, I tell ya jus' stop it cause I got it all figured out. You already get all the 'tention. You just like Ginny. By the time ya get what you want it ain't none for nobody else. Not one speck." My tongue started racing louder, more annoyed over his increased pointing and foolish laughing. He stared off to the side and grunted goofy-like. I stared back goofy too, my fingers doing just like his.

"We ain't 'bout to get no 'tention unless we do something bad, an' you sure don't want none of that kind. So, you can just stop with actin' up an' with your stupid little sky people, an' fingers wigglin'. For goodness sake, stop that dumb giggly mess. By the way, don't worry your little selfish self 'bout gettin' all them hugs, love smiles, or head pettings. I don't want none."

120

By then, I'd worked myself up into a lather. Standing up, hands on hips, moving my top body side to side, intending myself to be heard by him. "It ain't never, ever, gonna happen unless you just die, and go on up there with your good ghost friends; you know, the ones ya keep wavin' to in the air."

Slowly, I sat down on the warm soft couch where my butt was before. I thought for sure he'd stop and listen to me, and act like he had a little sense. He just giggled, grinning more, smiling worse, finger-poking the air harder, and grunting louder than I was talking. Some blubbery words came rolling out at me.

So then I screamed louder, "Go on to your little yonder people. Jus' maybe someone else can get a little pettin' 'round here." His giggles and wiggles made me angrier. I jumped to my feet and faced him off. Yells and foot stomps, bigger than myself, came from somewhere afar.

I looked off to find who did the yells and stomps, but not a soul was nearby. Just us two, all alone. My feet and mouth were doing something awful, without my go-ahead. What took over was Daddy in me. I couldn't stop. My mouth was racing before my mind. Drawn back was my hand, stiff and ready to deliver a whop on his ridiculous midget-like face.

Together, like a ball of snakes rolling, the pie-eating people reached us just in time with cherry juice on their faces. Right before my slap got hold of his cheek, Granny Isabelle grabbed me. Ashamed, shaking inside, I was caught. I would've done it though. I would've hit him and hit him hard.

Jimmy, the king boy, just sat there with happy smeared all over his silly face, as if we were best friends, like he'd never heard a word I had said. On the inside, I almost hated his guts from envy. Nobody knowing the hate but me and Jesus cause I it covered up in niceness, acting as if I was sorry on the outside, but not really on the inside.

Yet something horrible clicked in my mind that moment. Maybe I was like Daddy. If a rage took over, perhaps it might go on for hours, depending upon the situation, just like him. But that hadn't happened yet.

Granny Isabelle wasn't one to let things go, especially concerning me. She stood up like God, staring right through me. She bent down and whispered in my ear. "We gonna have a Jesus talk when we get back

121

home." Some fear bubbled up in my stomach for a while, but it soon passed cause she hadn't never hit me or nothing.

Granny Isabelle had preached that if I started to be bad in myself like Daddy, I could fix it if I had a mind. You don't have to be like your sorry-ass daddy, she used to say when fretted. The first step, she said, is I had to decide what I didn't wanna be. Good would take root. She sure could preach good.

28

Aunt Fanny's Cherry Pie

I pushed the Jimmy squabble out of my mind and set off to have some pie, even though it wasn't my favorite. I ate it, cooked red cherries sliding off my spoon, as a slick lump of vanilla ice cream slithered and steamy swirls twirled off the pastry top, when cold met hot.

Daddy bragged a hundred thousand times over her homemade dessert.

"Now, Fanny, that's about the best thing I ever tasted in my whole life. And that coffee, so black and steaming hot, just like I like it."

I rolled my eyeballs to God, wishing for spiders to fall on his head. Daddy tore a paper match from a frayed Sky Motel matchbook, struck it, cupped a hand over a Lucky Strike tip, and lit phosphorous into red hot.

His mouth slurped some twirling smoke, savoring its pleasure, as his eyes shined like a thousand stars. A far-off look was pasted to his sly eyes. Nothing ever tasted that good. Not Aunt Fanny's pie, not even ice cream.

Granny Isabelle, Mama, and me knew he didn't care for cherry pie, never had and never would. All he cared about was Aunt Fanny's hindend as she skittled about, swishing her skirt in his face. That's what Granny Isabelle had said to Aunt Lizzie about her. And I could see it with my own eyes.

Auntie's spell pulled on Daddy. He followed her every move—up and down, side to side—repeatedly from the oiled, red-checkered tablecloth, to the sink, and then back.

She'd faintly snuggle up to him, gathering spoons, bowls, and cups. Touching this and that on my daddy's hairy arms when Mama and Uncle Rudy wasn't looking, which was most of the time, their eyes far, far away.

Then, auntie scooted to the other table side, bending, raking and scraping, her copious breasts flopping on the table top, unfolding from her scooped-out flowery dress. Daddy would choke, and then she'd giggle, wiggling back to the sink. I saw it happening before my very eyes, and I sure didn't need anybody to tell me anything.

"Why, James, sweet dear, I made it cause it's your favorite, and the coffee ain't nothing special," she cooed. I thought to myself, ain't nothing sweet about Daddy that I know of, cause he's mean as a snake unless he gets saved again.

Aunt Fanny seemed to be a woman on a mission. I couldn't figure what her mission was cause she'd already perked the coffee and baked the pie and scraped everything off of the table and then some. But she seemed to be in a tizzy.

"What's wrong with Aunt Fanny? All that swishing, squatting, and sashaying, full of titters to and fro?" I queried Granny Isabelle. Mama couldn't talk.

Granny Isabelle looked strange, shook her head and acted like I hadn't spoken. I yanked on her arm sleeve in need of a better answer and her head repeated no; so I quit yanking.

Daddy squashed his half-smoked cigarette onto the plate's edge, put his elbows on the table, praying. "Dear God, Dear God," he said repeatedly. I had never heard Daddy pray before. So I was thinking he might be getting saved again. Yet his praying didn't feel right. So I pulled Granny Isabelle's sleeve. She shook her head no. I let it go.

Daddy piled his curly head into his hands, clenched his hair, and groaned some more prayer words. I glanced down and saw a spit puddle on my auntie's pretty tablecloth under Daddy's chin. She giggled and wiped the drool with a small single rag swoop, then she swatted him on his left shoulder with it. Whoosh-pop-snap went into my ear.

I thought to myself, "Probably a lot of men drool over my Aunt Fanny's pie."

I whispered this to Granny Isabelle. "That pie was good, but it sure made Daddy sick, cause he sure is in a fix." Granny Isabelle seemed more upset with me bothering her than Daddy's fit. She jerked my hand off her arm, flinging it. I chewed my fingernails and tangled hair edges as I pondered, watching for something better to happen.

Daddy moaned some soft words to my snaking, shaking auntie. I strained to hear. Mama peered further off, over the checkered table, around the large family Bible, then over the sink through the sparkly window. Her gaze landed and stuck onto a stubby pink camellia bush.

Mama acted like nothing was happening. I started doubting myself. Was I imagining electricity stir the air? Did no drools exist? Nor did the towel zap?

Aunt Lizzie once said, "Aunt Fanny's house ain't nothin' but the devil's playground." I thought to myself she may be onto something, by the magic spell she'd done put onto Daddy.

Back to the table she went again, wiping crumbs and then trotting to the sink. Even when no crumbs were to be gotten she got them. She'd come swinging that wet rag, rubbing spots on the table that hardly needed rubbing.

Daddy's blue eyeballs varnished, turning gray and then a fiery red. His tongue searched between his teeth, making sucking sounds. He couldn't take it no more. Granny Isabelle had already told me about Daddy's weak flesh, when she explained the birds and bees to me; it making no sense at all, until now. Daddy jerked upwards in a huff as if to go home.

But both auntie and him headed to the basement to look over preserves and canned jellies she had put up for the winter. I pushed my chair back, it squawking like a hen laying eggs, as I rushed toward the cellar door behind them. A hand with polished red fingernails shoved me backwards into the kitchen, leaving her wet kitchen towel for me to hold.

Almost tripping, I hollered, "I wanna see them 'serves an' jellies an' get a can or two for Mama. How come you the only one to see all the cannins', Daddy?" I whined. It didn't seem right. Why didn't anyone else want to see her canned goods? I couldn't figure why the left-behind faces looked disgusted; Granny Isabelle worst of all.

"Somethin' awful strange's going on," I told Uncle Rudy. He sat rubbing king boy's head and looked at the flower bush with Mama, like nothing. We sat wordless after they went down to the basement to check on her jellies and jams.

I pried and squeezed my brain parts until a memory came. Clean out of the air. Old Smokey had had that same look on his face one time during his easier and younger dog days. That same look Daddy now had. I had asked Granny Isabelle about Smokey's fixed eyes back then. He wouldn't fetch a stick or nothing for me. Instead he chased after the neighbor's old mangy hound dog. Smokey's eyes got all glued to the bitch dog's tail, like Daddy's was to Aunt Fanny's. Smokey was sniffing on that nasty dog's rear. I pondered the similar looks and what it all meant.

Remembering Smokey and the bitch dog, I pulled on Granny Isabelle's shirt sleeve.

"What made Smokey get hooked up on that dog from down the holler way back?" Faces looked at me like I'd done fell off the turnip truck. "What?" I replied to the faces.

Granny Isabelle said, "Hush, chile, you asked the silliest questions. And 'sides, some things younguns' ain't 'pose to know. Forget it."

I wasn't one for letting go of things 'til I got it all worked out in my head. That's what was wrong with me, I couldn't let things go. If I knew it wasn't right or somebody was trying to get me off track, I pressed on.

Anyway, I said to my Uncle Rudy, while we waited on auntie and Daddy to come back to us, "Somethin' mighty strange is goin' on, right under our noses." I spoke as if I had one up on the basement situation just like that crippled Perry Mason on television.

Time passed stiff and dull, then some clunking shoe sounds hit the stair treads. A squeaky door opened shyly. Mama's and Uncle Rudy's eyes unglued from the bush. Two happy heads poked out of the door, then bodies, then legs and feet. Daddy and auntie scrambled, untangling up over one another, goofy like the king boy.

Daddy rubbed his mouth for a while, as if something was on it. Then he rubbed his own shirt front like his hand was a flat iron. Like he did when he ate all that pie, full and satisfied.

He said, "Guess we better get these little ones off to bed. Sure has been a good visit, brother Rudy. Thank you, Fanny, for that wonderful sweet dish." She chuckled as we hustled our belongings together, poking this and that into a brown paper sacks, without a speck of pickles to jelly or jam. I moaned and pouted up over the lack of something sweet for us.

We huddled together at the front door like a gaggle of chickens, anxious to shake the weird tension off, and ready for the ride back to Granny Isabelle's house to drop her off. I decided I wanted to spend the night with her. Daddy stood behind my Uncle Rudy's chair, his friendly fingers rubbing and squishing his brother's shoulders.

Saying teasingly, "Them's the prettiest pickles, preserves, an' jellies I ever did see," sneaking a wink at auntie over the back of uncle's head. Me not missing nothing.

Clearing his throat, he lit another cigarette and gave Aunt Fanny a drag. Uncle Rudy's eyes just studied the floor, fiddling some more with the silly boy's britches leg. Like it was wadded up, but there weren't no wads. We swelled out of the front door in a great boisterous throng. And we left out like nothing ever happened.

29

Granny, Jesus, and Me

When we returned home, Granny Isabelle forced scripture down my throat as we readied for bed. Something about doing to others like we want done to us. She churned words out while turning her back to button up her shriveled breast without no bra. She didn't know it, but I had done seen them a million times and they weren't nothing to brag about.

"Granny Isabelle, don't worry. I don't even look no more. Besides, nobody has nothing like Aunt Fanny does. When she was all bent over dish-ragging, it looked just like two Pilot Knob Mountains," I said. She twisted her head like a hen, glaring at me.

"Granny Isabelle, what does an apple tree have to do with nothin'?" Me listening in on Aunt Lizzie's conversation earlier when she visited had peaked my interest. She threw another strange look my way. "Aunt Lizzie says 'apples don't fall too far from the tree.'"

"It means a person can be as devilish as the parents they're born from."

Then I realized Aunt Lizzie's remark was about me. "Granny Isabelle, she'd better watch it, she fell outta Papa Harkus's tree that is rotten to the core. So she ain't got nothin' to brag 'bout."

I meddled further. "Why does Aunt Lizzie think she knows everything an' puts her nose in our business all the time?"

"Beats me, chile. It is what it is. Just let things be," she quipped.

"But Granny Isabelle, some things you can't just let be," I persisted.

"Why ya bringing that up this minute?"

"Cause we ain't talked about it." What I really wanted was to distract her from me and king boy.

Granny Isabelle had Aunt Lizzie's number alright, just like I did. Once, I saw it on Granny Isabelle's face when Aunt Lizzie had brought that coconut pie with green coconut on its top. I'd tasted a finger full of sweetness before it was grabbed from my hands. She said Aunt Lizzie might have "pisoned" it. As soon as the door shut tight behind Lizzie's back, that pie flew into the yard. The whole pie, pan and all, was pitched out to Smokey, Granny not tasting a speck.

"While we're at it, let's get somethin' straight," she said. My heart lunged. "Don't never let me hear of you stomping, yelling, an' slapping on no helpless, precious retarded child. What in the holy world done got into you, chile?" Her words punished me.

"But I—"

Not giving me a chance to explain, she repeated, "What in the name of goodness has gotten into you, chile? That poor chile can't do nothin' for his own self, an' you standin' there with your hand all reared back, ready to slap his tender face. What in the world is happenin' to you? All that scripture readin' ain't helpin' ya a bit."

Preaching, she pointed a swiveled-up finger at my face. "You better watch for the line. You will be steppin' over it in a heartbeat an' you gonna end up like your good-for-nothin' daddy. God knows where you'll be after that. You can't just go crossin' line after line, little by little, afore long you'll be a lost an' undone in pure darkness. Do you think you gonna come back to the Lord cause He forgives ya trespasses? I don't think so. No sirree."

I shook my head, unsure about trespasses. Didn't know about no lines neither. I just held my tongue cause she wasn't in no mood for me or Daddy.

She huffed around, pulling covers off and on the bed, forgetting what she already did and didn't do. Tucked, pulled, and stretched this and that. I had set her nerves on edge. She even brought up my dead Uncle John's goodness and shoved it in my face, making red shame crawl on my neck. I bellowed with tears and begged her for forgiveness and mercy.

She pointed another gnarly finger right at the tip of my nose. "I ain't the one who's to forgive you. You need to be askin' that poor helpless child an' his daddy. No, not me."

A second of quietness hovered like a blanket. I thought she'd settled down. Then out of the blue she ranted under her breath. "I tell you what. In the 'morrow you an' me is gonna go over an' make this thing right. You jus' wait an' see." Her small craggy face and hooked nose stared down at me. "For the love of God, you ain't gonna turn out like your sorry-ass daddy. I ain't gonna have it. No sirree. It'll be over my pitiful dead body."

"But I, I—" I tried to speak again, but couldn't.

"We gonna go sure as hell, even if we have to walk an' I have to tote you all the way. You just wait an' see. First thing in the morning. Soon as daylight hits the window pane," she planned.

"What?" I asked, flinching from her piercing eyes and hawkish face.

She continued as if more needed to be said. "If it was anythin' to your daddy, you shoulda done it there an' then. Apologize, I mean. But he don't care none for nobody but his own self. No grandbaby of mine is gonna be like him."

Seconds passed. "I, I," trying to speak again, not getting a word in edgewise.

"I'll die an' go straight to hell first. After I done half raised ya an' taught ya right from wrong. And ya go do something low down like this to a helpless little thing. Done read to you night after night from the good book an' you go off an' act like some kind of pagan heathen with no learnin' at all," she fumed. "Done did everything I could to keep you out of hell fire." Squawking, "You understand. You listenin' to me, chile? Better be, an' you better not sass me for nothin'."

Her tail feathers was ruffled worse than any hen I'd ever seen. I knew she meant business and no arguing was gonna help me. Sometimes it's just best to keep your mouth shut and do what you gotta do and get the bad over with. She pulled her icy feet under the covers and turned far away from me and faced the other side. I laid facing the opposite, figuring on an escape, but finding none.

She kept her promise. At the break of day she rustled me, dragged me out of bed, yanked on my ear, and tussled my hair, long before I was wide awake enough to move. No breakfast, not nothing, not even a cold biscuit she would give me. We left. I considered I should have spent the night with my sorry-ass daddy and pitiful mama.

Off to Uncle Rudy's we walked forever, her half dragging me behind, cause I was so tired and smaller than her, but not by much. Uncle Rudy forgave me for the stomps, the yells, and almost slapping his poor boy's face, as he smiled back a little with weariness in his eyes.

A week later, Uncle Rudy's boy died. He was only twelve years old. I guess he just left on out to the other side and went hunting the sky people he had poked at all the time. When he left, Uncle Rudy's smiles went away too. That's when I really felt bad about the yells, stomps, and the almost slapping Jimmy. I wondered about sky people and fairies and thought maybe they were real after all.

After the boy died, life turned bad in Uncle Rudy's house. Granny Isabelle said the boy, like glue, was the only thing that held that home together. I don't know what she meant, cause little Jimmy wasn't big as a minute and didn't have one muscle. How could that child hold much of anything together? Much less a whole house.

Uncle Rudy's religion waned, and his family Bible was burned. Aunt Lizzie said he went off the deep end. Uncle Rudy tried to hide his rotten self from me and just show the one I was use to. I wondered if I'd helped cause Uncle Rudy to fall off a deep end from my fussing and stomps. Granny Isabelle said no.

"Do you think the sky people took the boy?" I asked her after they had put him in a tank and dropped it into the ground and covered him up, making him all dirty for the first time.

She said, "Maybe they was angels. You can feel 'em in the room sometimes."

I looked at her quizzically. "Can you see 'em?"

"Nope, never seen none, but I sure feel 'em, 'specially when things don't make no sense an' life hurts your heart to the quick, like the time when my John got killed. You have to be still long enough to let 'em come to you an' help out. That's when Jesus sends 'em. In your darkest hour of need."

30

Uncle Rudy and Changes

Aunt Fanny stopped going to church and playing the piano and started frolicking like a whore. Uncle Rudy caught her more than once, my family said, sometimes in his own bed. Long before the boy left to the other side, others said.

I heard Granny Isabelle whisper to Aunt Lizzie, "She ain't nothin' but a big fat whore."

I ain't knowing exactly what a whore is, still yet, but it sounds bad by the tones they murmured. I'm thinking maybe it had something nasty to do with men, women, and dogs. Like Smokey with that hound dog and Daddy with Red Cheeks and Aunt Fanny. I'm just hoping I wasn't taking after my Aunt Fanny cause it doesn't sound worthwhile.

Eventually, Uncle Rudy lost everything he'd worked for. Things just changed after little Jimmy died and Aunt Fanny left him. Granny Isabelle said he'd about lost his mind. His job, the long shiny black car, and his big red tractor disappeared. Their big white clean-smelling house and fine furniture fizzled down to nothing. Their prized shiny horses, three calico cats, two red dogs, and a yellow-green parakeet that said "hello" went away soon thereafter, too.

"God knows where she took off to," Aunt Lizzie spat, shaking her head in disgust.

Granny Isabelle joined in. "She's always been a wild horse of a woman. She rouses 'em up an' takes all she can get from a man, any man, and then she heads off after another one. She ain't got no shame in her."

Aunt Lizzie smarted her mouth sarcastically. "She's always been that way, even when she played the church piano. It was just Uncle Rudy could never see her straight. His eyes were all crooked up with the eyeglasses of love, I guess."

Not long after, Papa Harkus finally died from stomach cancer. Anyway, it wasn't no big loss, some said. He just laid around all the time in bed, moaning a lot over nothing I could tell. Not a tear did I shed. I was glad not to have to listen to his devilish whoops down in the woods when he was drunk. Smokey was messed up bad. I had to listen to his constant whining. Him wanting Papa Harkus and Papa not being there to take him to the woods.

After Papa Harkus died and went to live with little Jimmy, or to hell, Uncle Rudy piled up on Granny Isabelle and me in her house without a hope and nowhere else to go. He brought nothing except his razor, a shaving brush, a pair of scuffed-up shoes, and two sets of worn-out clothes.

Most times us kids were dropped off at Granny's or picked up there by our parents. Sometimes I'd be the only one left behind, mostly from begging to be. I didn't mind being there with Uncle Rudy and Granny Isabelle, even if I did miss the others sometimes. Sure enough, though, my siblings would come back before I knew it and take some attention away from me and I'd have to supervise them.

31

Pieces of My Daddy

Daddy showed up here and there, especially if he wanted something from Granny Isabelle. Sometimes Mama was with him, other times she wasn't nowhere to be found. When he arrived at night, us kids would find a Baby Ruth candy bar hid up under our pillows in the morning. We'd get happy for a short spell, warming up to him, in hopes of some more sweets but not much else.

The family talked of how he had brains and of what he could be if he would try. They said he was smart enough to be a lawyer and how we could be rich someday if he'd just put his mind to it. But when he wasn't around, they didn't mention his name, as if he was dead as a doornail.

He puffed up bigger than a bullfrog when they bragged on him in ear's distance. However, he was the cleverest of all men when it came to taking what other folks had. He hated folks for what they had and what he didn't, even though he never worked for it. So he wasn't above taking what was theirs.

He mostly disliked people with different eyes and skin color. He despised lots of people, but especially black and brown ones and Russians, Chinese, and Japs. Plus doctors, lawyers, contractors, and other bricklayers were on his list, and those who had big houses, shiny shoes, and fancy cars.

He didn't have much use for his own folks either, his blood and bones. He never stopped hating Uncle Ed and Rudy because of the Cadillacs they had owned. Just because of that I guess. He even stole from them, his own blood and bones, if he got a chance. He wasn't above nothing much.

Daddy bragged on how the Ku Klux Klan refused him as a member cause he was meaner than hell. He did tote a gun around everywhere he went, to kill or hurt some people if he took a notion, I suppose. He'd spray bullets all over the place in a hot minute, plus he wasn't above using it on us neither as he had threatened.

Granny Isabelle said he didn't have as much sense as a hill of beans. She said he blew a lot of smoke in all directions. I didn't know much about smoke blowing, except the cigarettes he sucked on and spewed out all hours of the day and half the night, but that wasn't worth much either.

Almost everything associated with Daddy was illegal, even the car he rode in. He had a way of making things work against the law and appear legal. He stole inspection stickers and tags off of other cars. They didn't cost him a dime. He crowed a lot about his lawlessness and then threatened to kill us if we said a word. So we kept our mouths shut.

One day, Uncle Ed, the rich one from Nashville, came visiting us but was tired out from the long drive. He rested his back a while beneath the tall pine trees. His shiny car sat underneath the tall black pines, gleaming, while he snoozed a nap slumped beside a tree base. Daddy took off from us in the house and was sneaking like a shadow. I followed him.

I trailed close behind, hiding behind trees and broken-down cars and such other things, thinking I might get some more of them good candy bars. At least one perhaps. He looked intense as his whole attention attached to Uncle Ed's car sticker; his eyes roamed like a hen's eye on a bug. I decided to coddle up to him and watch what was happening.

"What ya doing, Daddy?" I asked.

Prideful, he responded, "Helpin' the family out. Ain't nothin' wrong taking what ya need, long as it ain't hurtin' nobody. He probably won't even notice it's gone."

To get some candy, I decided to work alongside him. I held on to the sticker's end, like it was a sow's ear. Assisting him by loosening it, realizing he wasn't thinking on us getting some more candy bars at the moment. Maybe later I'd go after him from another direction.

I said, "If it don't matter none, then why don't they jus' not have none? A sticker I mean."

He looked extra annoyed, pushing me off with a shrug. He wiped a jagged wet blotch from his forehead onto his grimy shirtsleeve. His jaw clenched as his teeth began to grind and scratch.

"If it don't matter none, then why do they have one to start with?" I could tell he wanted me gone by the way he sucked air between his

135

front teeth, phissing. I edged on, knowing it didn't make sense. "Why don't we jus' get our own sticker like other folks for once?" I had an urge, of late, to make better sense of things in life.

He cringed, slid his lips sideways, and spat tobacco juice at my feet. I jumped back. "But I don't see how it don't matter none for other people who have to pay for their stickers. Somehow, it don't seem none too fair to me." Getting older, I had begun to ask more questions, not understanding how right was wrong, and wrong was right.

Holding the razor blade outward in my direction, he gnashed his teeth and blew a stream of slimy stuff to the left of my feet. I stared down. The sticker ripped into two pieces cause I looked off at my feet at the wrong time.

He glared, wanting me gone and dead, I supposed. "I'm telling you kid, ya so stupid ya can't pour shit outta a boot." Now he was mad. I'd done ripped his wealthy brother's sticker. I wondered how shit ever got in a boot to start with. It made no sense. Like a lot of his sayings.

He yelled, "Go on and get the hell outta here or I'm gonna make ya wish you had. An' keep ya damn mouth shut or I'm gonna break both of those scrawny legs on ya."

He jerked his head, goring like a bull, and then he raised his hand for a slap. Instead, his fingers closed a nostril, and green snot wadded onto my shoe top. I held my not-yet-hit cheek, moving backward, wiping the nasty glob off of my shoes onto a stranded grass clump, and went on without answers. Moving off to tell Granny Isabelle in a heartbeat what he was doing, I ran. Going as far from him as I could, myself hating that candy bar I already ate, cause it never meant nothing from the get-go.

"Nobody tells me what to do," he yelled at my back, like it had eyes and ears. "Not nobody." Uncle Ed jarred from his nap, with me wishing he'd take hold and beat Daddy's tail end. But then I took it back, cause after all, he was my daddy.

To people like us, for the most part, abnormal things seem right and feel normal. There doesn't seem to be any other way in life but the one that was unlike the lives others lived. Family has all the answers, even if they are nonsensical. It was just the way it was supposed to be, more so if you were poor, without learning. Like us.

32

Uncle Rudy and Me

Uncle Rudy filled the little house up and breathed too much air. If he stood upright, his head scraped the ceiling, so he hunched and ducked, walking through doorways. He said damn when the head scrapes happened. I just knew one day he'd knock his head slam off, as I waited to see it.

"Uncle Rudy fell over a whole pile of them cats. Then the bad side of him jus' cussed and cussed. I jus' hooted 'til the cows came home; seeing his long legs all twisted up in the air, tangled in a giant knot. I peed my britches from laughin' so hard," I croaked, telling the story to Granny Isabelle through my hoarse voice. "He said ya ought to let him take them sons-of-bitches down to the creek an' drown 'em all. But you won't have it will ya?" Partly, I told her the tale to see if she would or wouldn't let him drown her cats.

She riled up, "He ain't drowning nary a thing of mine." Her eyes blackened like pitch and I felt relieved.

I knew she was worn out from cat piss and stepping over them and shoving them everywhere outta her way and cussing all time. But deep down she loved them bitches and would fight anybody who dared to harm a hair on one of 'em's head. Uncle Rudy knew she meant business without me telling him over and over again.

Uncle Rudy knocked his head hard when he stooped through the door cause he was so tall, stumbling and tripping his fool clumsy self over all them cats underfoot. I thought about me laughing loud, like a goat, over his head pain so hard that I went rolling on the floor.

My daddy was awful good looking, but Uncle Rudy he wasn't bad off. He probably could have done a lot better than Aunt Fanny, but he didn't know it. He was tall like Abe Lincoln without a big beard. He had terribly long legs that could reach halfway up a poplar tree. And his arms hung down to his kneecaps. He had all of his teeth, but sometimes snuff sat in his jowl cracks.

I talked to Granny Isabelle about him. She said, "It's a real plus in the world of men and women for a man to have all his teeth at forty years of age."

His dark blue eyes bowed down a lot, studying the ground for something or another, maybe dimes. His head was full of wavy, thick black curls, but they didn't bob none. At least not 'til Aunt Fanny came a calling. Then his hair would bob all over the place. Like I said, he could have done better, but he didn't know no better.

I asked Granny Isabelle, "Why does Uncle Rudy jerk on her arms so much?"

She replied, "Cause he ain't much beyond stupid, pullin' on that whore's arms."

"I don't think on him as stupid," I responded. "He can dance like I ain't never seen. Even sideways."

"What I mean is, he ain't got one drap of common sense," she retorted insufferably. Probably thinking on him and Aunt Fanny and them arm pulls I had mentioned.

For the fifth or sixth time, I told her about the shaving spells he had. Uncle Rudy shaved from an old dented porcelain wash-dish pan with a chipped red ring along the circle edge. We used it for most anything, so it was hard to give it a name. Biscuit-making, foot-soaking, vegetable-holding, face-washing, water-catching from the roof leak, and finally Uncle Rudy's shaving.

I watched him shave nearly every time. He reminded me of the black-headed puppet I saw dangling from strings at the schoolhouse library. He swished the razor's edge into the gray water. It made sloppy wet gurgling sounds like fish. I saw little black beard flakes and soap bubbles surface the gray water, like a fish blows sometimes.

Stubby dark bits circled as water drops splattered the smudged, scummy mirror. He lathered his face with a short, stubby bristle brush from a slimy Ivory bar, and then he razored smooth streaks sideways across his jowls.

"Uncle Rudy," I said innocently, cause Granny Isabelle weren't one to be sensible lately, "Granny Isabelle says ya ain't got no common sense pullin' on Aunt Fanny's arms all time."

He said without getting mad, "She did, huh?"

"What I can't figure is, why do ya yank on her an' why she giggles so much?"

138

He didn't answer nothing. cause there was air between us and no words. I moved on to something else. "Why don't Granny Isabelle and me have to shave?"

He splashed the wet razor again and peered at me from the mirror, as if in deep thought.

"Cause y'all ain't men." Stretching his neck skin tighter underneath, fingering some skin taut, and making another track through the soapy bed.

"But that don't make no sense at all. Aunt Lizzie could do with a shave, an' my cousin told me he saw her do it once. Just like you doin' now."

He noticed my confused look, then, stopping for a second, he turned and said, "Maybe she ain't all woman or something."

Wordless, I thought for a few seconds but didn't get too far with that idea.

"I pray I won't look like Aunt Lizzie when I get old," I pouted.

Then he got back to his own self, as if I weren't there.

The small scratched-up radio sat on the table and played Patsy Cline songs. I hummed to them for a while, pulled my skirt out, and twirled to a few dance steps of my own.

He smiled, put the razor down, face white coated with bubbles, took my hands into his, and spun me under his arm, then I rested my feet on top of his shoes and we danced together for some more minutes.

I smiled up at him, content inside to let go. Then I stood alone again, with my forefinger crooked onto my bottom left tooth, to watch him some more. Patsy Cline stopped crooning "I Go Out Walkin' After Midnight," an' Porter Wagner's voice whined out louder than hers was. I chewed my soppy hair ends some, with nothing better to do.

Uncle Rudy studied himself with a funny, faraway look in his eyes. He smiled and mumbled amusing, low self-whispers into the broken reflecting piece as it sat propped on the windowpane. I watched the mirror wink himself back, talking, "You a good-looking son of a gun."

I thought about how a body could be coming from a gun, but I didn't ask this time, cause they would always say I was worrisome with my questions. I fretted over his jigging and jagging on the rubbery weak floor and hoped to myself it wouldn't cave in or, worse, cause the broken mirror to fall and cut him in half. It didn't. He jigged on.

"Uncle Rudy, you splashin' water all over the floor," I admonished him, pointing at puddles. He looked down and then pushed his chin upward to scrape more beards away with the sharp instrument as I wiped the floor water with a rag for him, grinning up at him happily.

"Uncle Rudy, what's to keep you from cuttin' your throat wide open?"

"I just ain't," he said.

"You know I can't be savin' nobody with bleeding an' all," I told him warily. But he didn't seem to worry as I did. He kept shaving and jigging.

The music hit a beat, he backed off, laid his big hand stretched out against his skinny belly, and did some hip wiggles. I giggled. He looked at me, winked a few times and chuckled.

"Uncle Rudy, will ya teach me to dance a little more sometime?"

"Maybe, when I get a little time." He grinned, turned around ruffling my hair like he used to do the retarded boy's curls. I felt loved for a moment. The music box sang some more songs. Happier tunes brought lively dance steps from Uncle Rudy. His long legs jigged two and three-steps in a pattern. Periodically he did a quirky jerk, or a down-low dip with swift turnarounds. He bowed his arms, smiled oddly, and talked low and smooth to somebody invisible. It was like I wasn't there. I thought to myself, he's probably wishing for that no-count Fanny again.

Even though Uncle Rudy was sort of gangly and goofy, he was half-good and my favorite uncle. Then a pining squeaked out from somewhere deep within me. It came pricking my heart space for want of a good daddy, me wanting Uncle Rudy to be my daddy in the worst way. He wasn't half bad after a shave, and I would have been proud to have him meet my teachers. I would have told everyone at school about him loving me so much and how he danced with me and unsettled my hair.

I spied for a while longer, 'til he brushed his teeth with his shabby toothbrush loaded with baking soda and salt. He spit, splattering white stuff all over the fractured mirror. More bored than ever, no longer wanting to watch anymore, I left to play with the baby kittens packed in a box on the porch. Anyway, a person couldn't take but so much spitting, smiling, mumbling, whispering, and jigging and jagging.

By that time, Uncle Rudy, Granny Isabelle, Papa's old dog Smokey, who didn't die with Papa Harkus, and nineteen stray cats lived underfoot with me most times, in Granny's three-room house. Granny

Isabelle was a saint, people said, but even she got to her wit's end with them cats pissing on her floor. She would vex up about no cussing in her house, but she wasn't above it herself. She could bad-mouth when piss puddles settled over everything she had worked hard to clean.

She called them cats sons of bitches, even if she was a church woman. I told her it was okay to say the "s" and the "b" word sometimes and how I was becoming more like her every day. I didn't feel so awful about saying the "s" word and moving more on to the "b" word. Being just like Granny Isabelle was what I wanted. But she said not in that way.

I can't help it, I told her. Granny Isabelle said it was my flesh pulling against me. Well, my flesh won most times with dirty words slipping out. She didn't mention nothing about her own flesh coming out over them cats and Aunt Fanny's visits. The "b'" word just came out easier every time we saw too many starving cats or Smokey eating all the cat food. Especially stupid fat Smokey gorging his ugly self just like Aunt Fanny does when she comes to the table.

"You too little to be cussin'," Granny said, guiding me on the right path.

"But bad words come out when I see Smokey's ugly face cause he reminds me of Papa Harkus. I 'pose it's cause he was Papa's lazy flea-bitten hound, always up to no good. Jus' like Papa was. An' ya know how I hated Papa Harkus so bad," I explained.

"That old dog is jus' a dog. He ain't never harmed ya. So ya jus' let him be. He ain't got long left in 'im anyway," she said pitifully. "'Cides, ya need to do what I can't sometimes. Sayin' cuss words ain't doin' us no good at all but sendin' us on down to hellfire. We'd better be straightenin' up afore the Lord comes. We both better."

She peered at me strong from the slits of her eyes to make sure I was taking it in, like I stared at Smokey when I preached to him.

"I'm listening," I said indignantly. Not wanting to be hard-of-hearing, like that mite-infested, deaf-eared hound.

"If'n we don't get ourselves ready and sanctified, then we gonna be left behind to deal with them pagans an' whoremongers. Its gonna be hell on earth an' I won't be able to sell one single onion without some kinda mark on my forehead. Tribulation'll be on us afore we can turn 'round." She started evangelizing. My guts quivered as my forehead sweated where the mark might stick. I sneaked gradually away outta earshot.

141

I thought on onions and Granny Isabelle's fear until a revelation came. We might not be able to sell no onions, but there wasn't one word in the Bible that said we couldn't trade. I planned to mention it to her as soon as I could get a word in edgewise. I deliberately changed my head thoughts from mark-of-the-beast, hell and damnation, cause now we had a way out.

Instead of trying to sell what we couldn't because of the beast's spell on things, I reckoned we could trade. I'd done been through hell once when the black funnel sucked everything into the air. I was marked for the devil's work when that useless, good-for-nothing angel, Gabriel, came tormenting my soul. I was spared only by the grace of God, surely for some better purpose. I intentionally turned my thoughts to the baby kittens and moved on to join them.

The cats were scrawny, always meowing for food, such as spare bits of cornbread or biscuits. Sometimes, if Granny Isabelle was in a good mood, she poured a dab of milk on top of the bowl of scraps. And they all hissed, licked, and clamored and clawed over one another.

I was thinking that was how all of us gonna be acting in the end times for a scrap to eat when that black horse comes galloping through the land. Granny Isabelle had done said me and her would kill ourselves first, cause we weren't taking that mark, come hell or high water.

I liked to study on them cats and not the mark, while they scrounged to see who was the strongest. I hid pieces for the runt to eat later cause he never got any, plus he hadn't got but three legs. I figured on how some animals were less fortunate than others, and found no understanding on the matter. My uncle knew a lot about things in life. So I asked him during one of his shaving fits.

"Uncle Rudy, what happened to the cat's other leg?" I inquired.

"Probably some animal chewed it off," he told me nonchalantly. I gasped. He heard and saw.

He corrected his statement. "No, probably that cat was just born that way. Sometimes animals come into the world without everything, like my boy did."

I saw pain come in his eyes and it spread onto his face, gouging lines into his forehead like cornrows, and made a hollow, sad shadow creep across it. I thought of his boy sitting high up on the pedestal chair, grinning and pointing at people in the air. Sky people nowhere to be seen by the rest of us.

"I'm sorry, Uncle Rudy. Truly I am. I never meant to harm ya boy. It jus' come out from nowhere. Probably it was my daddy in me actin' out. I'm sorry Jimmy had to go with the sky people."

Big tears ran a pathway to his trembling upper lip. He nodded while looking down at the floor, and then he grunted a little understanding back toward me.

Heavy tears started coming into my eyes, wrenching from my heart, squeezing inside my chest, a weighty pain. I lifted a finger and wiped the water trails from his face and expressed to him, "It'll be okay Uncle Rudy, cause Granny Isabelle says the sky people was angels an' that's who took him back to Jesus."

He choked on some throat spittle, sniffed his nose, and hugged my thin shoulders. And then we went on standing and staring with nothing more to be said or done.

Later, I told Granny Isabelle about my broken heart for the bad thing I'd brought on Uncle Rudy. And for the cat without a leg and all the sons-of-bitches hungry cats on the porch we couldn't feed.

She looked into my eyes half-heartedly. "I know. But ya didn't have nothin' to do with his boy dyin'. It was his time, chile. It ain't for us to decide these things. Its all writ on God's calendar, not ours."

"I feel terrible for them good-for-nothing cats. They never get a speck of meat. We eat all the salty fried fatback, even the rinds." Knowing how bad I would feel without rinds, I whimpered over their loss.

"Chile, them cats is starvin' to death, an' we're half-starvin'. So we gotta come first. Don't ya feel bad like you slightin' them out of nothin'. cause you got no power over what ya can't change. See, we gotta learn what we can and can't make a difference in. Some things jus' ain't up to us, and we hafta let it go and move forward like them rows I hoe every day."

"Why we got so many cats, anyway?" I queried.

"God knows, it's like they go out an' find more to bring. Like they can talk or somethin'. Don't asked me questions like that, chile. They jus' show up by the numbers, out of nowheres," she chattered impatiently. "They just keep bringin' more and more with 'em. Like they run off an' find cousins, sisters an' brothers. Then, here they come, meowin' all over the place an' fightin' over empty bowls. Afore long it won't be nowhere to step. It'll be jus' like this or worse during tribulation. Everybody coming here to grab bread scraps outta our very mouths. We'll be fighting for food, you just watch and see what I tell you."

"Oh, I meant to tell you what thought came to me about the mark," I said. "We don't have to worry about it no more. We don't have to sell onions and such. We can trade. It says sell in the Bible, not trade."

Her toothless mouth dropped open as wide as a toothless mouth could. "Lord Jesus, chile. That thought only came on ya through the Holy Spirit. It's right as rain. We can barter. We don't need that awful mark no more. Praise God and Jesus."

It was good to see the relief spread across Granny Isabelle's face, like sweet jam on a biscuit. I was happy. And I was even more happy to know none of us got carried off in those awful winds that blew in on us that some folks called Hurricane Hazel. And that Jesus never took one of us away and left us to be with one another through our awful trials on earth like Granny preached about.

33

Aunt Fanny and Me

The goodest part left out of Uncle Rudy when Aunt Fanny came to visit. He laughed, pulled on her arms and stuff. Like he wanted to know her better. I did wonder about the foolish arm pulling, and I didn't understand it one bit.

Granny Isabelle said, "Jus' shut up. I can't take no more'n what's been throwed off onto my shoulders." So I quieted down after questioning her about it.

Now, I didn't know much about love, cause I wasn't but a kid still. But I did know Uncle Rudy and his useless wife claimed rights to Granny Isabelle's and my twin bed when Fanny came around. Leaving us to sleep on top of a quilt pallet on the hard floor with only one feather pillow betwixt us. She filled Granny Isabelle's bed up with her ample tail and barrel legs that flowed dimpled plump thighs and everything else fat over the mattress edges. Lively and with heavy feet she came, bringing shrieks of female laughter that overpowered Granny Isabelle's whole house, far too small for her kind.

Her high-pitched shrills were for no good reason that I could understand. Squeals and shrieks just filled up the rooms, pushing me, the cats, and everything else with legs on it outside. Into the dusty red clay yard I went to play with sticks, stones, cats, Smokey, fleas, and anything else. I didn't know what was worse, her shrills or the senseless outdoor playtime when lots more was to be seen and heard on the inside.

Aunt Fanny was half pretty in a comical sort of way. Heavy set, big boned, and always bouncing a curly head of fiery hair into the air when she walked. She pampered her round, chunky clownish face with cheeky circles of red rouge. Outrageous bright red lipstick marked her pouty, thick, heart-shaped lips that she puckered and pouted repetitively at the drop of a hat.

Ogling in the old dresser mirror, I'd sit beside her, coating my lips like hers, pooching them and blotting shapes on some torn cardboard

145

piece, perfecting my own splotches of red. She'd laugh at me in short snorts. Puffs of great, white talcum clouds ballooned into the room as she dusted, with a soft pink round pad, swatting seriously all under and over her enormous round breasts.

The mornings after Aunt Fanny romped on Granny Isabelle's bed were such big deals for both of us. I wasn't above taking her tube of red lipstick. I had needs too, I reasoned. Plus, she had all kinds. More than enough for any one woman. I twisted it up in my bloomers' elastic, while she was puffing and dusting everything between her legs and buttocks. I acted way innocent when she went to searching for the red tube with all her might, flipping pillows and tearing shoes from underneath the tiny bed. But she never even got close to finding it.

After she finished hunting for what was lost but not really lost, I patted some powdery specks on my own chest with her now moistened talcum pink puffer. It was then I showed her my sore kernel. I sheepishly displayed the aching pone and explained it as a "risin'" on my chest.

"I need to be seeing me a doc-tor for some help," stretching the word doctor like I always had since I was three. Sheepishly, I showed her. "I ain't been feeling so good since I got this chest pone. My belly hurts all time. I get feelings worked up inside for some reason or another. I get high strung and out of shape, ornery over nothing much. I ain't much above slapping somebody sideways if I get a chance. Granny Isabelle says it's nature coming to call. She talks of birds and bees but she don't make no sense, cause I ain't neither a bird nor a bee."

Aunt Fanny about keeled over grabbing her chest, slamming chunky fist, beating it like a drum, laughing loud honks as she fell backwards onto the bed, dangling her cow legs helplessly. She then was thrusting them as high up as she could get them toward the ceiling. While they stuck out like tree trunks thrown into the air, she pulled her stockings clear up to her roly-poly thigh tops, attaching nylon with some fancy gadgets that slid in any which way but loose. Things I'd never seen before. Laughing louder than any dock worker's fishwife, she kept on blasting noisy words, looking straight at me.

So I said to her, "What's so funny?" Then, just because, for all her laughing at me, I hid my body puffer along with my lipstick, both to be had another time when I needed them.

She said, "Chile, you growin' up and you gonna get breasts like my very own."

I stared back in disbelief at her, while I gently fingered, circling my aching kernel. "So ya mean I'm gonna have two Pilot Knob mountains like yours?" She reared back on the bed some more. Her legs kicked out like a wide "V" as she laughed louder then hell's demons, 'til she peed all over herself. I know'd for sure I was headed off to be a whore just like her, from the looks of things. cause I was howling alongside her, my legs "veed" up, wetting my own britches. Me and her were like two peas in a pod. I was doomed to be just like her.

She had a devilish look in her eyes that twinkled at men when they came around. Maybe all whores have twinkles in their eyes. I wondered if I was one, cause I could twinkle when I wanted to. Especially when Aunt Fanny came around and her sorry self rubbed off on me. I could act just like her if I had a mind too.

"She comes mingling in Uncle Rudy's life long enough to fill her black patent-leather pocketbook," Aunt Lizzie said many times. With a sharp snap, Aunt Fanny, now spelling it "Fannie," with an "ie" and not a "y," would close the golden clasp on her wealthier handbag, then with a few huffs and short breaths, she'd leave us all behind, alone with nothing more than her lavender scents and cardboard red lip prints.

It felt similar, the uneasy heartache did, like when my parents left me behind and took the rest. Except I was sick with spent, excited feelings, as the dusty lavender scents had me missing her. Wanting her shrills and shrieks and bouncing fiery curls to be in the next room nearby. And a certain empty place she left inside of me took a while to wash away and refill. Not forgetting her easily and craving her with me some more added an odd dimension to my small life. Wanting her to come back another time for whatever she had left with us before.

It appeared that after Uncle Rudy's love died for Fanny now with an "ie" and she had hit the road for good, things seemed better somehow. He changed some when Aunt Fanny really left for sure. He was sad for the longest time, saying he wasn't changing nothing to "ie," not now or never. But the good parts of Uncle Rudy far outweighed the bad. Like the way he patted my head, danced with me, and made me laugh and feel so safe.

Granny Isabelle said, "You don't ever know what's in a man's heart when it comes to a woman. They might love one 'til the day they die."

I had heard once that when love dies inside, just a dark black hole lives, with a soul blotch. And a few old moth-eaten memories are scattered in breaths, like cobwebs tucked into corners here and there, waiting to be pulled loose or just left to hang and gather dust in the mind's storehouse of pain.

I felt sorry for my uncle. I remembered him before and after Aunt Fanny. Aunt Fanny had scattered little bits of him behind her, just like she did me. Just leaving us with nothing much but crumbs of memories and empty pockets in our hearts. But we got by and made our own sunshine during dark times. Things like trips to town made us both happy. He'd shave and get all brushed up and off we'd go to sell Granny Isabelle's onions.

34

The Family Trip

Going places made us all grin and smile. I'd feel happy to have my family together, even with my bad Daddy. I didn't know where to call home most times. I never knew how it hurt Uncle Rudy and Granny Isabelle when I had to leave 'em. It musta been a lot like when Aunt Fanny hurt us when she would come and go. I stayed with Granny Isabelle every chance I got. I'd pretend Uncle Rudy was my real Daddy then, and I'd hold his hand tight when we went to town and crossed streets. Sometimes, even though I was growing up, I'd hold his hand if it wasn't no streets to cross. But people have a way of hiding their true natures. That's what Granny Isabelle said. Uncle Rudy hid his pieced-up self from me for the longest time, 'til we all went to town one day.

Excitement brewed as we piled and squeezed into Daddy's rusty green '52 Chevrolet. Uncles Rudy, being the last one to crawl in, cause he was so long and got tangled up easily, waited last. He bent down grinning like a cat at us through the dirty window glass. We'd grin back like cats at him. Packed in the back seat with Granny Isabelle, we sat like sardines, lapped upon one another, to make a good spot for him.

First one-half of a leg poked into the rear door, toward the back, with a foot on it, and then half of his curved butt followed. A long boned arm stretched clear to the other side of the car door. A giant hand with hair on it reached over all of us kids, Granny Isabelle, onions, and things, and grasped a handle opposite himself to pull on.

At last the rest of his gaunt frame pushed into a sitting space. Baking soda and Old Spice followed him into the back seat as familiar odors wrapped around us like a coat. He smiled broadly at us, which furthered our childish excitement.

The car was packed tighter than a tick. Virginia's July was unforgiving. Wet heat clung shamelessly onto our clothes, even with the vehicle's windows wound down to the rubbery rim. Sweat produced more sweat; we were arm to arm, thigh to thigh, with little space left between us. Our clothes manifested our own personal underarm whiff marks and odors.

Granny Isabelle had brought all of her rinsed and skinned green onions with pearly bulbs overflowing the boxes' edges to sell at Franklin's Food Store. I wasn't happy to hold the stinky cardboard cartons; residual red dirt crumbled out of the crates' edges onto my clothes. But I was the oldest and I had to do what others didn't. So I just did it.

We all reeked of onions and sweat, from helping her fix them the night before, but not Daddy. He said, "Hauling her ass 'round to God knows where is enough for any man." We rinsed them clean, handling them with care so as not to bruise them. Then we banded the rooted plants in batches of five with red rubber bands, but not too tight. I worked for Granny Isabelle to buy my first new school dress. Others had their own reasons for helping.

I think maybe toilet water would have helped, but Granny Isabelle said onion juice stays 'til it is good and ready to leave of its own accord. She said people are like that too. I just took what she said for what it was and let it be. I still wished not to smell like sweat and onions, but it didn't help none.

Daddy's old green car groaned under its burden as it made its way forward and upward on the red clay road. Four angry bald tires squatted down and lugged along like Smokey dragging his butt on the ground sometimes in front of God and everybody. The distressed vehicle gargled, snorted, belched loudly, and then sluggishly rolled on, spewing muddy clots behind and sideways at anything in its path.

Our eyes settled on the half-glued car inspection sticker as it flicked and flapped in the wind against the front windowpane, like a stuck, smashed gray moth, or a flibbie as we called them. We all knew why the sticker wasn't flat and smooth on the glass like other people's stickers but never spoke a word about it.

Daddy hocked and spit out a wad of dark phlegm through the open window. Thickened brown tobacco juice flew back and smacked square clean onto Uncle Rudy's face. But Uncle Rudy didn't seem to care none much, cause he just wiped the slimy goop off with the back of his hand and kept grinning in the breeze like a goon with his hair blowing, flapping wild and free.

Granny Isabelle whispered to me, "He's 'bout as stupid as a mooncalf." I didn't know what a mooncalf was, but I giggled because it

150

sounded funny. She continued, "I'm happy ya gettin' a little education, honey. Ya jus' keep on learnin' all ya kin. No matter who don't want you to have none."

Granny Isabelle said, "Odors mark and brand us with reminders of who we are and where we come from." I guessed it was true. From the inside looking out, poverty looked pretty normal. Folks like us didn't recognize how different we were from others in the world during the good moments of time; but, on the outside looking in, it was so obvious to those who had more and did better. In the clutches of poverty, the abnormal things just seemed right and felt normal and like there was no other way in life. Family members held all the answers to life in that moment of time.

The cramped drive to town seemed to last a long time. Finally, the Mockersville sign stared at us over Daddy's filth-laden, litter-packed dashboard that had "JAMES" scrawled through the dust. It was covered with dirty used envelopes, crushed Camel cigarette packs, chewed tobac-co shards, and a few dried wads of used snuff balls. For one brief mo-ment I felt shame crawl up my neck as I read Daddy's name written where nobody in their right mind would ever claim such a filthy spot on the dashboard. Then I had to ask him which was he gonna end up smoking, Camels or Lucky Strikes? And he just spit again at Uncle Rudy's face through the wind but missed cause my uncle dodged.

In waves, the stores danced and motioned like fingers, taunting us from the horizon. Glowing window shops with large lady manikins dressed in flowered hats and lovely matching dresses and red high heel shoes created more wants inside of me.

Long food stores tempted and waited with lined-up canned vegeta-bles, Bunker Hill Beef chunks, Spam, and Baby Ruth candy bars. We all piled out. I rushed off in search of my dress; Danny ran to find candy counters and to linger and loaf at storefronts. Ginny hung on to Mama's dress, scared from too much newness. Granny Isabelle took off to the grocery store to sell her onions, and Uncle Rudy went his own way.

All by myself I found a sweet pink, silky dress with long-sleeved lacy cuffs. A trail of pink pearl buttons made a path from the mid-waist to the throat. I could not believe this was happening to me. Not much good ever did come my way, but just maybe this was a new beginning. An excited good feeling came into me and covered me up to the point I wanted to share it, speak it out to others all around.

And so I did. I jibbered, jabbered, twirled, and whirled with the beautiful dress pressed up against my marked wet armpits, while other shoppers stopped and gawked cold and hard at me. I just kept talking to myself and the lovely dress and the mirror that reflected myself as I wanted to be seen. It was the prettiest dress I'd ever seen and I couldn't wait to show it to Granny Isabelle and Uncle Rudy.

A little girl with a big yellow hair ribbon stared behind me in the long mirror and pinched her nose and stuck her little pink tongue out as her mama pulled her away. I didn't let it hurt. Dreamily, I fantasized about the jealous looks I'd receive from the school kids as I caressed the tiny buttons and lace.

I thought of my Uncle Rudy, about his shaving jigs, and suddenly I knew how he felt all happy inside, because I felt the same. I filled up with some pleasure, expectation, and soul-longing like my uncle. Hurriedly I paid for my treasure with my onion money, as I protectively clung to my fantasy in the brown paper bag. I headed slowly toward Daddy's dirty cramped vehicle. I wondered how in the world Uncle Rudy could stand sitting in Daddy's car since he once had driven that wonderful big shiny Cadillac.

I rounded the corner of two side-by-side department store buildings. I heard familiar giggles and whispers as some shadows talked in the alley. A slight sunlight blinked through the tunnel. There stood Uncle Rudy, pulling on a strange woman's arms, just like he used to do Aunt Fanny's.

I heard Uncle Rudy say, "Come on, little baby darling. You and me can be so good together." Kind of like I'd heard him silly talk to the cracked smudged mirror before. I halted. My feet would not move. The hag tittered a little, acting like Aunt Fanny. I urged my shoes onward, scratching gravel on the ground. Between whispers, the nasty woman looked in my direction. Snakish, she eyed my shocked, pale face. She was skinny, knocked-kneed, and, worse yet, all of her front teeth were missing. Her tangled hair was rolled up in strips torn from a brown paper bag. What a sickening sight to behold.

For the life of me, I couldn't imagine why my uncle was pulling on that thing. Him pushing up her face trying to kiss her. His large hands rubbing her rolled-up gnarly hair and his fingers probing other dark places. My legs jammed. Clinching my bag, I shoved my hands to my mouth to hold what was inside from coming out, but I couldn't help it.

I gagged, puking, splotching the worn-out asphalt path. Uncle Rudy stalled briefly, cranked his head, and stared through me. Returning his attention to the woman instantly, he was frantically fumbling her blouse buttons open until a wounded breast fell out. My face burned, my chest hurt. Horrified, ashamed and tearful, I ran in a fog.

Returning to the car, I couldn't find my dress or the bag. Shocked. Wounded. I lost something beautiful that day more than my hard earned dress and pleasurable giddiness. From then on, my respect for Uncle Rudy disappeared. Never again would I watch him shave, do a jig, or brush his teeth.

He'd never be the same to me after the town trip, the talking alley full of kissing shadows. I felt sorry for him but sadder for myself. Because I wanted to have my good uncle back. The good man I knew before his pitiful boy and his piano-playing wife disappeared. Through the eyeglasses of love, I'd seen him. I groaned, grieved, and grew up some more, not wanting to hurt *anymore*.

Sometime later, I told Granny Isabelle about the alley situation and what I'd seen. I told her about my beautiful lost dress and why I never found it and how I had to lie to her about the loss of it. Uncle Rudy was becoming like his brothers, Granny Isabelle said. She said that was why she never named him from the Bible to start with. But I believed Uncle Rudy's heart had lost all hope, and his spirit just wasted away like my Granny Isabelle's old breast. Now, like his father and brothers, he was choosing the familiar well-trod path and taking on his ancient family legacy. Maybe it was too hard to rise above the way things are, I thought to myself, much less to claim a different life.

It was as if my family were chained together in secret bondage. Set up by some systematic formula to fail, waste away. If Uncle Rudy couldn't do it, then how could I? He knew what it was like to have it all. He had had a grand life. Granny Isabelle said, "The Bible says, 'A dog always returns to its vomit.'"

As adolescence crept up on me, I wondered why my good uncle couldn't win over the bad. And more so, how would I? Would my life ever be different, or was it carved out for me by my family?

I was morphing into a teen slower than most kids. A boy down the road wanted to come and see me at Granny Isabelle's house. I'd spent endless hours fixing myself up, questioning myself and my ability to carry on any decent discussion with anyone much but Granny Isabelle and Uncle Rudy.

I sat on the thick hairy sofa in Granny Isabelle's little sitting room, full of jitters and excitement, waiting for him to arrive. Uncle Rudy had stolen his chance to explain some things to me that day. After the alley confrontation, he'd started drinking whiskey. He hid it from Granny Isabelle, but I knew.

He slinked slyly into the room and sat beside me on the sofa as I waited for the schoolboy. A glazed look entered his eyes and an eerie smile plastered his face as he whispered surreptitiously to me through waves of alcohol, "Once the boy gets the tongue, it's all over an' there is no going back."

He then slithered away like a snake. I had no idea what he meant, except what I'd seen him do with that alley-cat woman. I had never held a boy's hand, nor kissed one. Even more so, my heart broke because the boy never showed up. Perhaps it was just as well. But it added to my feelings of not being good enough or pretty enough. I felt repulsed, sticky-icky, dirty after that, much like when I'd witnessed those horrid shadows, and Uncle Rudy unbuttoning the woman's blouse and fumbling with her wrinkled breast.

A child-like disappointment had spread through my heart that day in the alley, and I ached for my real uncle to return. Uncle Rudy grew more disgusting after that awful alley encounter. When he offered me his loutish encouragement that day, it made me wonder what was wrong with me, that he would talk vulgar like that. I had no one to talk to, and no place to weep, except the inside pit of my lonely self. Granny Isabelle would never understand, and I feared she might have chased my forsaken uncle off.

Later, on several occasions I had witnessed Uncle Rudy passed out drunk on Papa Harkus's old bed. Unclothed, he laid sprawled out with his private parts hanging for the world to see. Horrified, I'd cover him and walk away and go help Granny Isabelle garden. I had never wondered much about male body parts before seeing him. Granny Isabelle was getting angrier and angrier at him. Now, she realized he was drinking from a bottle like Daddy and Uncle Ed.

Yet I felt sorry for him, for his lapse of good judgment, but sadder for myself mostly, as another brutal truth came. Slowly, I began to put him into proper perspective, and later I placed him into my curio of non-pretenses and didn't want him near.

One morning, after Daddy and Mama left us kids with Granny Isabelle again, I went outside with the kids to play with them. I found dead chickens lying in the even deader dry, red-brick clay yard. Shocked, I ran inside to tell Granny Isabelle of her hens. She followed, with me leading, to see the poor lifeless creatures. Aunt Lizzie came and they checked Granny Isabelle's pet pullets. Forbidden to stay with them, I was sent away; but I snooped quietly, listening to their dialogue.

Some murmurs floated around about dogs or other wild animals. How could such a thing happen? Their egg holes had been pulled inside out, they said. They whispered that Uncle Rudy might be the culprit. I wondered why he would want our chickens dead since he loved them as much as we did.

I didn't know what they had meant, but he'd crossed some sort of a unspoken line in Granny Isabelle's way of thinking.

Uncle Rudy disappeared one night soon after, without a goodbye, taking only a few belongings.

Days later, I was cleaning the dingy kitchen of cobwebs, the smudged cracked mirror, and the porcelain shaving pan when I came across Uncle Rudy's cleaned, well-used razor. I smiled, feeling warmth inside as I washed it off and wrapped it carefully in a delicate handkerchief he'd given me one Christmas. I'd keep it forever, I thought, as I tucked it away.

Most folks would say my memories of Uncle Rudy should remain about alleys paved with asphalt vomit, drunken, with private parts showing, my lost beautiful dress, a toothless woman in paper curls, dead chickens, and a man who deserted me like most everybody else.

But rather, I choose to remember him as my favorite uncle—my Uncle Rudy with his stretched-out dancing legs, his brushed white teeth beaming at me like a 'possum, with a broad smile breaking out whenever I came into the room and his hair blowing in the wind like a goon riding in Daddy's beat-up car, and him reeking of Old Spice and baking soda, all full of happy acting like a mooncalf. And him tussling my head as if he loved me as much as his retarded boy, and me dancing on his shoe tops, and especially him being the only good real daddy I ever knew.

35

Another House on Barto Place

Barto Place weren't no good place to move to. Not much different from the other places we'd lived. I knew all about this horrid road. We'd lived there before, just in a different shack. I didn't look for nothing better. Not mattering none no how. We never lasted long, coming and going. Coming and going and going and coming, in and out and out and in.

Somebody called them row or shotgun houses, stacked one against the other pointed the same direction. Walking directly from one room to the other, then another, straight like a gun barrel. Some houses, a tad better off, yet the same, lined the road sparingly. Cotton lint flitted into the air, falling like gray snow, clogging our nostrils and clotting our hair in textile dots. We snorted and coughed a lot. Daddy said it was all about textiles being everywhere. Without textiles, people would starve, he told us.

Most people nearby and from all around us worked the mills, because tobacco farming was harder with less money gained. So folks, young and old, worked long days, fourteen or more hours sometimes, and weeks of seven days. They did what they had to so their families wouldn't starve. That's what Daddy said, but he wasn't about to.

Haggard-looking younger people sat high up, pedestaled, sewing from large factory sewing machines, threading pretty sheets through metal guiding cones, furiously hemming bedspreads and fancy thick towels. The hemmed cotton or terry cloth fell off the mammoth machine edges, almost as fast and loud as river water rolling over a dam. The worked fabric met ancient-looking, hump-shouldered people beneath who had repetitiously labored their lives away, grabbing and folding, grabbing and folding, grabbing and folding, all the while yearning for nothing more than smoke breaks.

"I ain't 'bout to work in 'em. People dying fast as flies with that brown lung," Daddy said, laughing. I looked at him oddly, thinking maybe my lungs were already gray or brown. And maybe I'd probably soon drop dead like a squashed fly, smelling all that lint that lingered outdoors and sifted through the cracks in the walls of our rented shack.

"I ain't studying on no lung disease." He grinned and took a deep drag off another Camel cigarette stub. Sucking it way down to get the last bit for his money, scrunching the leftover tobacco morsel into the saucer with two amber-tinged fingernails.

I glanced at the tobacco remnant. The jam-packed cigarette dish stunk stale and strong, especially on damp mornings. I'd hold my nose, pick up the plate, and shake the moist, fetid heap into a paper bag. The whole house reeked of different odors. But nothing that smelled good.

Sometimes Daddy appeared smart as a whip. He knew a lot about brown coughing lungs and textiles, without ever stepping foot into a building. And about dropping flies and sucking cigarettes deep to save money. But he didn't know nothing about taking care of us kids. For the most part we were on our own. I desperately wished to be with Granny Isabelle and not there with them. But of late, Daddy had wanted me right there. Not from love, just to babysit what wasn't mine to sit with.

The bathroom, shabby-nothing-to-brag-about, had a useless rusty sink and tub. The rickety commode worked occasionally, depending on whether number one or two was flushed. We'd plunge the thing often to unstop the drain for number two, prodding blackish-brown wads down the loose, stinking, stained pipe.

Most times, I plunged not just my own poop but everybody else's mess down the sorry commode, them half-forgetting or whole forgetting most times. When they'd walk out of the room, I automatically went behind them, poking and plopping and slopping shit everywhere. I longed for cleanliness in the worst way. I would never bring anyone here to this dump, I thought every day, at the same time knowing nobody would ever want to come visit me. Thinking Granny Isabelle's outdoor toilet with the big hole and granddaddy long-legs seemed much better than this. Me chasing everybody's left-behind shit.

The dingy kitchen had a chipped porcelain sink that constantly dripped rusty water, leaving a crooked path of embedded orange, rusty metal where the trickles went. Daddy said the carroty water might turn my hair orange by the time I turned another year older. I prayed every night for Jesus not to let it happen. I couldn't handle nothing else wrong in my life.

The rotten sink cabinet was slumped on one end, but Daddy propped it up to almost level with a two-by-four piece he'd found in the neighbor's backyard. He was good to figure out things that needed fixing. That was things he didn't break.

Underneath the cabinet, spiders lived, tucked into webbed nests with gobs of egg sacs. I'd shine matches, looking through their thick pouches, filled like pockets full of nasty coins. Daddy, the spider expert as well, said one pod held hundreds of baby spiders just waiting to come out and eat our brains.

Studying on baby spiders breaking free from their bags, I'd check on them repeatedly, waiting for them to hatch, so I hated the place even more. I'd wait for spiders' nightly crawls through the house, looking like soldiers; marching quiet and sneaky with legs as long as a dog's tail, they'd come, I imagined. I feared they'd cocoon us, like in the television program called *Twilight Zone* that we'd watch sometimes, and then nobody would find our bodies until our innards were melted and sucked dry, like slush through straws.

I was told by Mama not to whine about the ugly sink, and about how I outta be grateful to not be carrying spring water. But I despised her words because I wasn't grateful for nothing.

A gray frayed cord hung from beaded-board ceilings with dangling bulbs in each room, at least the ones that had a bulb. They wiggled, casting shadows over the walls, when wind touched them from opened and slamming doors. Their light charmed flibbies and mosquitos inside, and hence, the blood-sucking critters entered to gnaw and bite welts over our bodies during the hot nights.

The critters clamored toward the light to be scorched and charred. I'd watch their burning and recall the anguish of my own scar-burned leg. I'd think on how smart I must've been, being so young, to unstick myself from the stove's red belly without help. At least I knew enough to release myself when nobody reached a hand to help. Now I'd rub lard on my pitiful scar and often pray for God to do a miracle and heal it, but it stayed the same. I hid it with my dress hem, praying no one would see it.

Flibbies had wings, and I none, yet they couldn't free themselves from anything. I declared flibbies to be the stupidest of all breathing things, returning for more pain, not learning a bit from sizzling. Why God made such ignorant beings, I knew not.

"Damn flibbies," I'd say, entranced. Sometimes I'd use a broom straw to feed cooked flibbies to the cabinet spiders, hoping to keep them where they belonged.

At night noisy, nosy mice scooted about, scratching and scurrying throughout the house doing God knows what. I couldn't half sleep with all the squeaking and scrabbling about my head. Then too, I worried over earwigs crawling inside my head and about spiders eating on my brains. Daddy said they did that to people. Said they could eat people's brains out overnight. Said people never knew it was happening until it was too late—with me plugging my ears up with mattress cotton that didn't help, because I'd pull it out in my sleep. Insects, rodents, and that God-awful dripping sink didn't help my worsening wrecked nerves. Dinky-dink-dink all night long. Day dinking didn't bother me, but night dinks were unbearable.

I'd re-stick the mattress wads back into my ears, wondering if my brain was gray, pink, or rusty, since I'd drunk so much water trying to keep my belly full of less food. I dreamed of the ugly pink pig brains plated, like thick ropey worms, as Daddy sopped them with a piece of loaf bread, alongside of two or three runny eggs. He said we could eat 'em or go without food, so we went without. We didn't get eggs without brains. It was his rule.

I'd lay awake sweating, gagging my guts out—retching and dry heaving and pondering on how a person of any count could eat something else's brains. I'd try to go back to sleep, but seeing his chin smeared with pink brains and yellow yokes gored my guts.

Mama said, "You ought not be thinking on pig brains and such things. Count sheep instead." She spoke like it wasn't no big thing to worry over pig brains, breathing factory lint, growing orange hair, or hiding my scarred leg.

I replied, "What does it matter if I count sheep or listen to dinky-dink-dinks all night? They the same to me and one is as good as the other—your words are plain worthless to me. Let's just let it go."

She seemed always to take Daddy's side, smoothing out everything he said and did. She shook her head like I didn't have a grain of sense. I thought to myself, she didn't have none neither; but I didn't say it. I smeared some lard onto my leg scar and secretly prayed some more, wanting one leg to look like the other. And both to look pretty like those of other girls my age.

159

I said, "I never know if a mouse is going to chew my nose or ear off, or if I'll wake up with no brains or tied up in a spider web." She turned away, shaking her head like I was too stupid to look at.

Mice left tiny, hard, black, egg-shaped droppings all over the place. I tried to break them in half with my fingernails, or squash them between my thumbnails, like I did raw tomato seeds, but I couldn't. I cleaned them out from the sink with the dishrag, rinsing them loose into the dishwater, but more showed up by the morning.

So I just let their eggs pile up, knowing they'd probably turn into endless babies, like the spiders, no way of stopping it. Mouse eggs, pig brains, dumb fried flibbies, spiders and sacs, rusty water, drips, and stopped-up shit holes. What a life. Things couldn't get much worse, except orange hair.

Everything was messed up in our lives: rotten, rusted, wired-up, broken, and propped-up. Furniture got knocked down or thrown against the wall. Ugly, mismatched broken dishes stayed stacked on the table for lack of cabinets, not lasting long anyway when Daddy got to knocking stuff around. Lopsided bent forks gouged my gums when eating gravy and biscuits, if we had gravy and biscuits. Daddy would even get mad over the crooked forks and then he would cuss God and blame us for the things he did, like bending forks.

"Can't even have a decent damn fork to eat with," he'd say.

If he was drinking hard, the forks would get thrown against the wall or at one of us. He didn't seem to know he was the one who had twisted them in the first place. What did it matter? No different from anything else.

The wringer washer jumped all over the kitchen, when it worked at all. Sometimes sparks would shoot out from the plug, but I'd just dance away fearless.

Mama yelled at me, "Ya gotta make sure no water gets in the floor or you be 'lectrocuted." I was thinking, so be it.

The aluminum washtub didn't fit close to the washer, so when I'd wring clothes through the white crackled wringer, water poured straight to the floor. Danny and Ginny would stop fussing long enough to watch it flood. Shushed they'd get when sparks flew, then they restarted their quarrel when the fire slivers quit dancing. I wondered how good it might feel to tingle all over myself. I talked to everyone who would listen for a while about how electrocution might feel if an accident happened.

Then, I looked it up in the big school dictionary, with old, half-bald-headed Miss Jordan's help. After reading big words called defecation and urination, and looking up the meaning thereof, I decided against the whole thing, not wanting to mess my britches and land in such a predicament, thinking there might be a better way to die.

Getting older and just not caring about electric sparks no more, I'd shrug the maladjusted machine's and my own behavior off, saying, "Damn it to hell," as I carried heavy pans of clothes, raggedy bloomers and all, to hang on the old rusty barb-wire fence in the backyard.

Needing no clothespins, cause the clothes would catch on the barbs and stay stuck for weeks, even months, with no hard north wind coming. During the winter they'd freeze frigid, like stiff people standing still, before I even got them hooked onto the wire. Sometimes, they wouldn't dry until spring if nobody cared. If the time of need came, inside I'd throw the washed clothes over chairs, on the television antenna that was wrapped in Reynolds wrap, or on the table, hoping to dry them out for school, with some woodstove heat that helped to make it happen before the morning came.

36

Rusty

More things were rusty than not, even us. I never heard of ear rust 'til Susie pointed mine out to the whole class. She was pretty and prissy with long ponytails, touting a new bow every day. I hated her bright bows and her spiffy clothes, along with her too. My teacher pulled me aside one day, close by under her armpit, when Susie had made fun of me. It helped some with her armpit warm, up next to me.

"Come on and wash off my blackboard for me, would you, Jessie?" Mrs. Brewster said kindly, pity showing in her eyes. She helped get my mind off that girl's hatefulness. From that day forward, I was my teacher's eraser duster and board washer, without even begging.

I'd stretch my arms as high as I could, rag dripping, to please her because it showed how earnest I was. At least it was what I thought. For the high places, I pulled her chair up and stood. She'd brag. But I was still simmering over hair bow girl and planned to get the little witch's pretty ribbon somehow.

"What's rust?" I asked Mrs. Brewster as I wiped the words and numbers into oblivion and rubbed away all plus and take-away signs, rinsing and squeezing the rag into the little red water bucket, slopping the chalky liquid about meaningfully.

She hesitated. "It's where dirt builds up from not getting things clean enough."

"Like a dam's dirty mound?" I said.

"No, more like a smidgen of dirt," she explained. "We can't see behind our ears and necks so it's hard to know it's there. We call it rust because it starts to look like reddish brown splotches."

"It plumb shamed me when Susie called it out to the whole class laughin' an' pointin'," I pouted.

"I know. It'll be okay. It'll come off with soapy water and a good scrub," she said, hugging my shoulders.

I finished the board and headed home with Danny and Ginny by my side. Halfway, on the path, we filled up on juicy dark red mulberries from the olden tree. We returned home, pink-toothed and happy over getting some sweet fruit.

I rushed into the house, grabbed a rag, soaped it up from the slimy Ivory bar, and scrubbed my ears and neck red raw. I took hold of Danny's cute elephant ears and did his as well.

He hopped, yelled and kicked, screaming, "What ya doin'? I ain't done nothin' wrong."

Ginny came in to check out the racket. She screamed like Danny when I caught hold of her. I taught them about rusty spots and what we had to do, so as not to be made fun of in the future. Then I taught them some grammar besides.

"We ain't 'pose to be sayin' ain't no more neither. And we are supposed to put a 'd' on and say supposed to, not 'pose to," I told them.

"Who says so?" Danny asked.

"Mrs. Brewster says so an' she knows everything 'bout words and teaching," I replied. "If y'all listen to me you just might be spared a lot of heartache in life."

Danny and Ginny said I was bossing and they could say ain't and 'pose to anytime they wanted. Ear wringing didn't help their grammar, nor mine much, but it was a start.

Our Barto Place house wobbled and squeaked. It wasn't big enough to hold so many people, but we made do like we did everything else in life. Slanted floors in the kitchen made us walk a little lopsided. I guess it might have caused the sorry washing machine to do its stupid dances.

Mama mopped the worn-out linoleums, mostly now spotted tar-paper, long ago being flowered. Daddy started pissing on floors, like Papa Harkus used to some years back, when he was too drunk to care. Why does every drunk piss on the floor? I couldn't help but wonder. Mama's work coming to nothing—the same as mine—in this rotten hellhole.

"Why does he piss in the floor and you hafta clean it?" I asked her. I was feeling hateful over the rust issue as well.

She stared back, shaking her head in a wearied way. "I don't know."

After her blank look set in, I said, "It seems to me he should clean up his own piss for a change."

She rubbed the floor some more with the rotted rag mop, now smelling more like piss and mildew than clean. Then she reluctantly squeezed the raunchy water into the dishpan barehanded.

Clearing my chest, I kept on. "I can't figure none for the livin' life of me why he's gotta be with us. His drinkin', pissin', an' tobacco spittin' all over the place is disgusting. I done had enough." I said this more forcefully than the first remark. Nothing came back, like she couldn't hear or wasn't even in the room. She'd left me and went inside her own head, dark and alone.

"I despise this place I tell ya. You said it'd get better. Well, I sure don't see nothing good," I said angrily.

"I thought maybe it might," she whimpered, mouse-like, making me feel like a heel.

"Another thing I can't figure is why Daddy has put us in this lopsided house on a steep hill full of crabgrass, rocks, and red clay. Ain't no place for them kids to play. Redbugs makes bumps and blisters on our legs and we itch to no end. Jus' look."

Scratching, I pulled my skirt up to show her my scabs. "I hate the yard as bad as the house. I hate the neighbors cause they're more stupid than us."

Mama just studied the water pan, still wiping and mopping more piss and brown tobacco spit puddles. She gazed toward the scabs and breathed out, "Scabies." She rushed, off leaving dirty water and mop behind in the middle of the floor. She scrambled through all Daddy's dirty pants, searching for dimes and nickels. I watched her go for the neighbor's yard, catching a ride as Granny Isabelle arrived to help us out once again. Without us kids ever being informed of anything before it happened.

Granny Isabelle and I stared out the window; Mama was heading off in somebody else's car. My teeth was on edge—same as when I'd eat unripened persimmons—my nerves were shredded and raw. I was getting closer to another birthday. I would grind my teeth until my jaw hurt. I still chewed on hair ends, although Cousin Deb had said I'd get belly worms if I didn't quit. I didn't want worms, but I couldn't help it. I just couldn't.

As I cleaned Mama's mop mess, I recalled to Granny Isabelle, "I saw one of my cousins with his mouth full of slobber, standing by that well with his belly all swolt. I thought he was jokin' me, acting goofy. Then a big glob of round long white worms came puking from his mouth, fallin' to the ground in a big heap. Him gaggin' 'em out right by my feet. I jumped from the worm pile. I've seen lots, but I'd never seen nothin' like it before. He wasn't jokin'."

Granny Isabelle looked sad. "No he weren't. And he ain't no cousin of yours. Jus' somebody's cousin down the line."

I noticed Granny looked sadder with each passing day. I guess she wanted to go back to her three-room house. But I wanted her with me. Some of the time she'd stay in a nearby rental house or our house, depending on what was available or affordable. Other times she'd come just to get a crisis settled and then go back to her own home. Always, chaos or a crisis brought her to us.

I said to Granny Isabelle, "Lots of things happened at that well we had at one house. In fact the only well we ever had. Do ya remember the time Papa Harkus pulled that big copperhead up in the bucket an' he went runnin' for a hoe to kill it? I just watched that viper slide away while Papa was off looking for what he never found."

Granny Isabelle said, "Your people's cousins are starvin' to death, Jessica. We oughta be thankful we ain't starvin'. Starving was where the worms came from."

I retorted, smarting, "Mama says some people are worse off than us. But I ain't thankful. We ain't got two pennies to rub together most times. Even when them cousins came begging us for food. I ain't thankful for nothing. Daddy has all the cigarettes, beer, pig brains, and eggs he can eat. I ain't got a dress or decent pair of shoes. I ain't even got a bra cause it cost a measly fifty cents. I begged Daddy but he says we ain't got money for one. Do you know what it's like changing into my gym suit, hiding from them laughing girls?"

"Ya Daddy ain't thinking right. Never has for that matter. He's selfish as the devil. Here's some change. Go on get one if ya can."

Desperately, I snatched the coins. "I took that ovary class with them girls," I said. "They started bleeding in their pants already. God help me. I never hoped to do such a thing. They are hateful as hell when they're like that. I'm sorry I say bad words sometimes. Now they're wearing Kotex pads between their legs to the gym class. They don't have to play ball or nothing when it comes on them. I heard them laughing and talking about it in P.E. class. About how they wear those thick pads without blood, jus' to keep from exercise or running track.

"If I do get blood between my legs, Mama says I have to wear rag strips. What if my bloody scrap falls on the floor when I walk down the hall or go into my classroom? I can just see it happening. I ain't about to bleed between my legs. No sirree. I ain't letting it come on."

Granny Isabelle stated matter-of-factly, "Nature comes whether we want it to or not. Ya gotta hook that rag on with safety pins to your bloomers somehow."

I fidgeted over my helplessness, taking a piece of hair to my mouth to chew, worrying more over bloody underwear than worms for once as I emptied the nasty piss-laden water basin. Pausing, my mind settled on mouse eggs and spider pouches and belly worms being puked out, while my lower belly throbbed and my privates prickled funny. Then Granny Isabelle took hold of my hand and led me into the back room.

"Go ahead and get me a pair of your bloomers and two safety pins."

I looked at her as if she was crazy.

"Go on, now."

I rummaged through some paper bags and found a scorched-looking pair.

"Now find one that ain't much better than some old rag."

I pulled one out. She tore off a large piece, folded it, halving it adeptly, and placed the clean rag just so onto the crotch with two safety pins, one on each end. I looked at it, not believing how much it resembled a Kotex, hidden in the panty. I hugged her close, not wanting to ever let her go from me.

"If the pad doesn't want to stay together, then sew a little stitch or two in it before you pin it. You might be growin' up, but ya still my little angel." Tears trolled her eyes and mine.

"What will I ever do without Granny Isabelle?"

"Ya ain't never gonna be without me. Love lives forever and ever an' it ain't nothin' in my heart but love for ya."

Then solitary, in that moment, I stood not wanting to grow up. As a solemn whip-poor-will sang out, and a dove cooed nearby, I sensed the worst loneliness ever. A great coveting turned on in the pit of my soul, for more than what my present life exuded. A small life now consumed with Daddy's rages, mouse eggs and spiders, rusty spots and broken dishes, praying tables and Mama's busted fish-lips. As a gruesome awareness invaded my thoughts, I feared that it might never be any better than right now. The reality of always living in this kind of mess slapped me square in the face, as I craved to be little again making mud pies in the dirt for me and Granny Isabelle to eat amongst the corn rows.

A yearning to be alone with Granny Isabelle morphed large, filling my chest cavity. I desired to hold her mitten-hand and have her preach at me for hours as she hoed the corn rows. To talk about peeling onions, and living room suits for a few dimes, and things being better somewhere way off. Us dreaming of an unknown, vague place that we saw together through the distant hillsides, even beyond the multitudinous stars while walking homeward.

Us both, looking through her small smudged kitchen window, sopping milk gravy from dinner plates with warmed-up, leftover biscuits. Sitting there in the quiet, after the day had worn us out—just the two of us united into oneness, listening to the whip-poor-will sing a song just for us, and the two of us whispering about tomorrow being better. I wanted to go back there with her and stay forever little.

37

Hat Revenge

At school, Susie's hairbows needled my insides to no end and dragged on my nerves. I couldn't do much thinking on my schoolwork cause the devil had put something in my heart to fix her. She, being in the "A" group and me in the "C" group, didn't give me much of chance to get her back for the rusty spells she had pulled on me the other day. The class was spaced out with the "B" group in between us. I had to sit way back and look at her ribbons all day long. It was more than a body could bear.

The "A" group got to go on special field trips for two dollars and a signed form. Mama wouldn't sign forms. She said Daddy wouldn't let no forms be signed cause the government would be coming after him. She said we ain't got two pennies to rub together, much less that kind of money. It wasn't easy being left behind all the time. It weren't one bit fair. So, I thought, what's the point for me to make A's or B's?

On the trip day, Susie wore the prettiest hat I ever had seen with a big pink bow and ribbons hanging down the back. All of the "A" girls stayed huddled by her side, rubbing on it as if it would bring good luck. The smart boys pulled on the ribbon tails too, giving her far more attention than usual, causing a big stir. Mrs. Brewster made Susie remove it until the bus loaded up.

My guts riled up when Susie took off to the bathroom with the happy ogling and giggling "A" girl gang behind her. Her hat shined up at me from the caged lower shelf of her wooden desk—tucked into the open space, looking like some eyes begging me to come and get it— much like a prisoner in a jail cell, I thought.

Quick as a wink I hatched an idea. Something bigger than my own self took over. My lightning eyes slid over the room to see who was and wasn't looking. My pencil flicked up close behind the girl's seat, plinking wood as it settled. I lifted my hand, shaking the air side to side, like a fan.

"Mrs. Brewster," I said. "I done dropped my pencil. May I get it please?"

She turned from the blackboard, smiled and nodded her head for me to go on and said, "It's 'I *have* dropped my pencil,' Jessie.'"

I replied, "Yeah, yeah. I know. I know." Really not getting the gist of why a word needed another one to lean on—words like has, had, and have. Plus, I couldn't figure why the ain't word was useless in school when I had heard it everywhere else. And why I had to put a "g" on the end of "ings." No way could I get hold of don't and doesn't, and was and were, and why they were not the same. Mrs. Brewster's list of do's and don'ts just kept enlarging while I felt dumber than ever.

Two of the "B" boys turned to see my face lie to Mrs Brewster about chucking the pencil. I crouched down behind the desk, and with a quick snatch I yanked on the hat's lacey edge. I puffed a loop in my skirt, scrunched the bonnet, and crammed the straw thing clean up to my navel.

Full of satisfaction, with Susie's hat underneath, I raised myself with the pencil clinched in the skirt cluster for all to see. I walked back to my desk, duck-like, with an air of nothing-going-on. The two "B" boys stared at my skirt clump and I glared hateful back, warning them. Their eyes slid off toward Mrs. Brewster as she raised her sweet voice for us to watch her draw some diagrams adding nouns, adjectives, and adverbs, them all looking the same to me while others shook their mousy heads, not objecting.

Susie and her "A" friends quieted down and came back to take their seats. I raised my hand and swiped the air for some more consideration, since I was the teacher's pitiful pet suffering from poverty.

"Mrs. Brewster," I said louder than usual, "may I please be excused to the toilet for a bit?"

Some ugly boys snickered, whispering with their elbows knocking one another. "She doesn't know we have restrooms." I gritted my teeth nasty, sneering at them like Daddy does. I knew I'd never go pee with the "A" girls. This awareness made me satisfied with my new trophy.

My teacher looked up from her desk and said, "Sure, just get on back quick because we have to get ready for the trip and get the rest of you children to the library. You'll stay with Mrs. Jenkins to learn the Dewey Decimal System until we return."

That witch, Mrs. Jenkins, and the other one, Miss Jordan, the school librarians, weren't nobody to be watching us. I despised the Dewey Decimal System anyway. I wouldn't ever figure it out. Especially with that hound dog Mrs. Jenkins breathing all down my neck, with breath as bad as Papa Harkus's used to be. When Mrs. Jenkins found me down the wrong rows looking for decimals without a clue, she huffed and puffed about, shoving books in and out of the shelves, following close behind me.

I visualized her screwed-up face with half-moon glasses sitting on her uppity nose tip and pondered on how to get back at her for the shushing of my hums so much. I hummed that promises song that Mama used to do, despising Dewey and his decimals and the woman's dog breath.

Just my teacher saying Susie's name made me madder and more grateful I took that hat. I took what was owed to me, was the way I looked at things. I took it for me and them other unlucky, left-behind "C" kids. I shuffled out the door, shutting it slow and easy, to not draw attention from the "B" boys. It closed and then I gasped relief, leaving the cold classroom doorknob behind with some sweat on it.

I had to pee in the worst way, going against what Granny Isabelle had taught me about right from wrong. On the other hand, Daddy had taught us to take what we needed as long as it didn't harm nobody, but even that reason could be outdone if need be.

Weighing it all out in my mind, I decided Daddy was on the right track. Mostly, I just wanted to make Susie get a taste of not having something she wanted so badly. But that hat was awful pretty. Terribly pretty. So I thought on how to at least take the bow off and wear it to school some days. But then I figured it mightn't be a good idea since Susie or the two "B" boys might pick up on it and tell on me.

After peeing, I studied on the hat as I tried it on in front of the mirror, then poked it down my underwear as best as I could. Hesitating no further, I took off back to the classroom, not wanting the good trip bus to be late. God forbid it be late. Then again, just a little late wouldn't hurt none of them, I thought jealously, stalling as I lugged myself slowly down the hall, checking out bulletin boards full of turkey hands, orange pumpkins, and haystacks, plucking loose thumbtacks onto the floor, hoping Susie might step on one or maybe two. What a hoot that would be.

Too many times I had watched Susie's father pick her up in his shiny new car to take her home and other places, while I walked home, soaked and shivering in cold rain and snow. Her father treated her like a queen. I'd catch myself wishing deep down that he was my daddy, toting me around and picking me up in a new car. Tears of want came on me sometimes when we all waited for time to leave school. I'd look away from my wants and grit my teeth sideways for a while, to make sadness leave my mind—knowing her daddy could never be mine.

Susie required his attention a lot. Like the time at the Maypole dance when she tripped over my shoe and skinned her knee all up. He came running, acting like a fool, lifting her up babying her, and carrying her off like she had been hurt bad. She doesn't know what hurt is, I thought smugly.

Reaching for the doorknob to return into Mrs. Brewster's class, I heard God-awful squalls pouring through the door's thick bottom crack. A thin rectangular light streaked out, like truth coming after my feet—desks scraping on wooden planks—what an awful racket of sliding and scraping, going on the other door side. I opened the entrance to see that not so pretty princess wailing and bawling, acting in the worst way a girl could in the seventh grade, and poor Mrs. Brewster trying to console the pitiful, hatless soul, but couldn't.

I heard the trip bus just outside the window, honking and blowing for the bright-headed kids to come on along. Mrs. Brewster's face was pinched ruby red, probably with dread to call Susie's daddy again for another reason. Seemed like poor Susie was always getting hurt or some odd thing.

Hatless Susie went on the trip, full of squalls, leaving us dumber ones to get sent to Mrs. Jenkins, feeling full of worthlessness. We all lined up like a row of quack-quacks. Me and my wad lagged at the line's end, moving snail-like down the hall toward the boxed-in, dark, dusty, book-laden room.

I stood at the library window, sniffing paper ink from old books, chewing on my hair ends, watching from the inside out as the great orange bus, full of better-than-us kids, puffed and pulled off. They rode away into the sunshine full of happiness, wheezing a trail of black smoke behind them. The only unhappy face was Susie's, squished to the window with her ratty eyes staring straight at mine. I shrugged as if saying, "What?"

It wasn't easy carrying what I'd stolen between my legs all day. And then to walk home with it tucked up in my underbritches. Sometimes the rim wiggled between my legs, scratching like the dickens. I finally made it back to the house and ran as fast as I could to the room I slept in, without speaking to anyone. I checked my scratched-up body parts and studied on my prize hat, then hunted for a hiding place.

Afterwards, nothing went right for me at school. Mrs. Brewster pulled away from me, letting Susie take over slapping the chalky erasers and doing the blackboard washes. And the closet door in my room stared at me every time I walked in, as if it was gonna talk to me like Granny Isabelle did with preaching sermons. At nighttime, when I got hold of my school clothes for the next day, the hat would come toppling out, loudly knocking on my head, striking fear into my heart that my family would find out I'd become a thief just like Daddy.

The stolen hat came to no good whatsoever; it just followed me like an old haunt in my mind, reminding me of all my sins and ugly wrongness inside. Maybe, for kids like me, I considered, there wasn't no hope at all. Maybe it couldn't be helped that we were to end up just like our wicked daddies and papas.

Sorry as hell and no good for nothing, like my Granny Isabelle said. Maybe that was why we lived in row houses, one following the other— all looking the same—plain rotten inside and out. I reasoned on these things to myself, wishing I'd never taken that worthless hat that I never could show anybody or even wear in the first place.

Finally, Mrs. Brewster looked over my shortcomings after I won the class spelling bee. She gave me the goldfish and bowl at the season's end. After the students emptied out of the room that day, she asked me to dust the erasers and wash the board. It was the happiest day of my life.

She hugged me tight and then stooped down smaller like me. With her hands on my face she said, "I expect good things from you, Jessie." I nodded her some understanding, not believing a word. "No, I expect great things, not just good things." Then she kissed my cheek.

My heart melted over my wrongs and, as my teacher looked into my eyes, I said, "I'm sorry about taking Susie's hat. I really am. I just threw it away, not daring to give back what was hers. It won't happen again. I promise."

I left the room and her kind arms, crying good sobs softly, with my gulping fish in hand and a half-box of fish food tucked safely in my worn-out jacket pocket. A warm feeling of love hovered over me as I sauntered home against the cold air, water sloshing, to spend a month of Christmas with family, not wanting to. Wishing I could live with Mrs. Brewster forever or at least never leave seventh grade.

38

Doctor Isabelle

We'd moved over onto another ridge in the cottony town, further away from Granny Isabelle and the park so we didn't have her around much anymore. She stayed on at the old rental house on Barto Place since Daddy had insisted she be close by. She was still close enough to call on and visit once in a blue moon. Everything seemed to change, yet it stayed the same in other ways. Granny Isabelle still wished for the three-room house of her own, and I kept wishing to God for a good daddy and lunch money for school; but none of it happened. Then the time came when Granny Isabelle once again moved closer and helped babysit us. I suspected someday she'd move back to her little house, but we needed her desperately and so she was there.

"It's the worst taste ever," I fretted, with a hand cupped protectively over my jaw.

"Go on an' wash it out with a little warm, salt water," Mama retorted.

"I done washed it out a hundred times or more. It ain't helping none," I said, tormented. "Can't nobody tell me what's wrong? Maybe it's a cancer like the one Papa Harkus died with, but in my mouth."

She shushed me for carrying on so much over nothing. "You gonna hafta quiet it down. Ya daddy's in there sleeping. He was out all night again. Ya know he'll be mad an' all if we wake him with a racket going on."

"Oh, I guess it's my fault cause he ain't had no sleep," I said, hating him. Almost hating her also, cause she said it like we were supposed to be always watching out for him.

"No, I ain't meaning it that way, jus' I'd rather he be asleep than awake. An' for me to hafta deal with him an' his God-awful temper." She tried to ease my mood, and to get my sympathy back on her and with what she had to put up with.

"Somehow I gotta ease this pain." I cringed, my sympathy for her hanging by a thread.

I recalled Danny's suffering through years of incredible ear infections and his withholding tears of pain because of Daddy's wrath. All the times I'd watched Mama and Granny Isabelle pouring sweet oil and warm piss into his ear canal. I knew he needed a doctor and would bring it to their attention to no avail. All because of Daddy.

Like the rest of us, Danny would writhe inside and be acting normal on the outside around Daddy. Many times we pretended. Accidents happen when growing up.

Like that time a stick caught up in my leg while I was walking through the field. I, myself, worked on it, trying to pry the foreign body loose with my fingernails. Yellow gunk oozed out from my shin bone for months. The twig never came out, curing itself, most likely by rotting away.

Then another time, I had fallen on a piece of sharp glass, ramming it clean to my arm bone. Blubbery, bubbly pink stuff rolled out of the jagged cut. Mama and Granny Isabelle went wild, pulling their hair, outta their minds over what Daddy would do. I shouldn't play Tarzan no more on the grapevines. They said someday I would kill my own self.

I replied, "I like swingin' on the vines. I didn't know that a broken bottle was in my path," thinking when this was over, I'd swing when I got a notion but check for glass first.

They worked on it a long time, poking pearly puffed-out stuff back into my arm . They prodded and pressed, wrapped and tied it all together with rags while murmuring, urging that I didn't act like anything was wrong in front of Daddy when he came in.

Another time, some neighborhood boys began bullying us as we played outside. They chased us with a pickle jar full of hornets. I faced them, ready to fight if need be. I wasn't scared of a few jarred-up bees. A lot bigger than that had come after me.

Ginny and Danny took off like a mighty rushing wind toward the house, yelling for Mama and Granny Isabelle. The big boys grabbed hold of my dress collar, holding me tight as they slammed the glass on top of a rock at my feet. Then they took off like dogs chasing cats. A winged cloud of black and yellow angry hornets whirled onto me, stinging and biting everything I had under my flared-out skirt.

The tough boys squealed with laughter, sounding like a near-butchered hog's head, as I flew homeward screaming to Jesus. I cussed those sorry-ass, good-for-nothing boys. Never mind, the day before I'd paid Billy a quarter to be mine forever and to kiss me on the lips some, rather than me kissing on some mirror. But now I wanted my quarter back, like nothing else.

Granny Isabelle went crazy cause I couldn't breathe right. It took about four or five slaps or so to bring me back to my senses. She scraped the stingers off with a pocketknife, sucking ones she could get to, except on my tail end. I couldn't blame her for that since I'd messed my britches, running from devil bees.

After I'd breathed and washed off, she rubbed vinegar and soda paste on the hateful red spots, dabbing, as I wailed out like a scratched-up wild cat, full of misery.

She studied, deep in thought, wishing she could give me a shot to ease my pain, but had none since she was no real doctor. She found Daddy's whiskey stash and filled half a teacup and added sugar and two teaspoons of kerosene. She forced it down me—dribbling a nasty smell over me like Papa Harkus—with me fighting, heaving, and gagging, not wanting to resemble him for a second. But after a while, I didn't mind if I was just like my good old dead Papa Harkus, wanting more of Granny Isabelle's potion.

Another time of acting like nothing hurt (when it did) was when I had stepped into a shed and my foot landed on Daddy's upside-down skill saw—the blade sliced to the bone on my foot, gashing it wide open. Granny Isabelle and Mama were crazy, out of their minds, figuring how to pull my foot together without sewing.

Then, in dire straits, Granny Isabelle appalled me. She took out a needle and blue cotton thread and sewed me up, after pouring Daddy's straight whiskey down my throat. I squalled while gulping and kicking with my good foot. Later I was walking normal when Daddy was around; then other times I walked heel-toe, when he was gone.

That's how it was. Don't hurt when you do. If you hurt, don't ever show it. Sometimes we forgot which end was up. Like me walking on the heel—walking on my toes—getting it all backwards for the most part.

Like Danny, not big as a mouse, not hurting as he laid brick, ear-ache or no earache. Carrying bricks, buttering trowels, hoeing mud, and lathering bricks was Danny's job. Him, with a cotton wad stuck deep down in his ear hole to keep the wind out and the pus in, it overflowing yellow pus for us to look at.

Danny was forced to help Daddy lay brick before school age. Daddy was always yelling at him when he didn't answer back. Saying, "What's the matter with ya boy. Can't ya hear nothing? I swear ya dumber than a stick. A sorry damn stick."

Danny had heard Daddy call him names with his good ear. Sometimes, Danny would lay bricks alone if Daddy got a wild hair and went to a beer joint. Daddy expected a wall to be up when he returned. Nobody could tell me it was right. God nor nobody could tell me it was right.

Danny's pain was written all over his face like my own. My mouth was killing me like his ear had, I imagined. Like a train was rumbling through it. I was throbbing and squirting agony in all directions from my chin. Mama kept putting hot rags on it and dissolving aspirins into the cavity without relief.

Night came. A large pone arose on my lower gum that sent aching, pounding into my eyeballs and head, as if the very devil was trying to get out of hell through it. It felt like the evil one's searing hot pitchfork was stabbing and jabbing it. My cheek—swollen and red as a hen's tail—was so sore I couldn't eat or spit salt water out if I tried.

Mama said, "I'm gonna walk on up the hill and get ya Granny Isabelle an' see what she can do to help ya." Looking doubtful over her shoulder, she put a finger to her lips. It meant for me not to make noise to awake Daddy. I was thinking, if it was his mouth he'd be screaming his big bad head off. Yet we walked around on eggshells, quiet—all nice—acting like nothing hurt. Something just wasn't right.

I stood at the door, my hand holding my tender jawbone to keep it steady, being careful not to even step. Any motion set it off, jarring, shooting pain clear through to my skull. I'd told Mama that my tooth hurt and had a big hole in it. I had told her a hundred times. Did it matter? Did Danny's earache matter?

Minutes, like hours, passed after Mama left. Eventually, they came tripping down the hill, Granny Isabelle huffing, leading the way with her kerosene jug and half a likker bottle that she now kept on hand for such emergencies. Mama was trailing close behind, not knowing what to do about what she didn't know.

177

Granny Isabelle stepped inside the door, pried open my mouth with her gnarled-up fingers—powerful fleshly tools for an old woman—screeching something about lockjaw. Then she took a spoon, covered my tongue, and moved it about as she shined a lit match into my mouth.

Not meaning to—but did it anyway—she hit a bottom molar and jolted my head bones and brain. Tears hit my eyes, soundless; Daddy needed some good sleep in the other room.

"Lord, chile. Ya done got ya'self a big old abscess. The pison's probably done gone to ya bloodstream." She spoke with eyes full of concern. I knew she felt my agony, like I did Danny's. "Lord, have mercy to Jesus. Help me help ya chile, Lord Jesus."

"Jus' pull it on out, Granny Isabelle. Jus' get it out. I can't bear it no more. My head is killing me and I done took a whole box of Anacin and aspirins. Nothing has helped me," I explained.

"Lordy, chile of God. I ain't no denis'," she yelped.

"I already done tried to pull it last night with the pliers. I jus' can't get hold of it good 'nough," I told her.

"Lordy, chile," Granny Isabelle repeated, emphasizing hopelessness.

"I don't care. Jus' please get it out. Here, use Daddy's pliers. I been in pain for four days or more. I can't go no more." I pulled the pliers from the kitchen drawer and laid them on the table, waiting for her response.

"Lordy, chile, if I pull that there tooth ya will have pison up to ya eyeballs afore nightfall. An' ya might end up with ya brain full of 'fection. We gonna hafta figure 'nother way somehow." She stood gazing. She turned to Mama.

"Ya got a big needle anywhere?"

"I think so, but it's off in the room where James is sleeping," she whispered.

Granny Isabelle's eye squinted sideways, meaning business; she wasn't gonna put up with letting this go. Mama slinked off barefoot, tiptoeing, eyes teared up. She slid her fingers over the doorknob gentle, as if rubbing a sweet baby's head. Squeaking, it opened. Snakishly, she slithered through the entry.

"It doesn't matter if I die as long as my head quits hurting," I slobbered. Granny Isabelle's tongue clucked like a chicken. She grabbed the kerosene jug and poured a dab in a glass, with half a teacup of emergency booze, and mixed a whole packet of white powder into it. The spoon clinked; metallic tinkling bounced hard and pried through my head.

"Go ahead," she urged, putting the tumbler onto my lips. I pushed it away, sputtering words.

"That stuff is for fleas. Ain't no fleas on me. What's that white stuff?"

She glared hatefully as if I had doubted her doctoring.

"It's a BC or maybe a Goody powder, I don't know which." Her mouth smarted as she went outside. She immediately returned with a yellow sticky glob on her fingertip and placed it on a dish nearby to use. Scowling, I gulped the rest of her concoction.

"Swish it all around ya mouth and swallow. Do the powder three times a day but without any likker. An' remember not to put no more heat on it. Any human being knows that. That rag needs to be as cold as possible."

Mama returned, holding the small spike instrument before us. The dark gray tip indicated it had already been scorched in the past, to dig a splinter maybe.

"Now ya got another match?" Granny Isabelle said, taking charge. Mama followed her lead like a sheep. A light snapped. Granny Isabelle held the needle's eye as the sharp metal end glowed red. My leg scar and the hot-bellied iron woman came to mind. I jerked from the point, then caught myself, leaning back to Granny Isabelle. Mama picked up the dropped spoon, wiping it on her skirt.

"Go ahead," Granny Isabelle screeched as if she had something against Mama but not saying what. "We ain't got all day. The chile could die an' go to Jesus afore we get to going. Get hold of that spoon and hold her tongue down. Not too hard or we'll tear it clean outta her mouth. There'll be blood all over the place. Ain't nothin' bleeds more than a tongue or a tore-up head. It'll flat scare the dickens outta a body. All that blood. Sometimes it's a lot of blood for nothing. They jus' bleeds easy is all.

"Now Jessie, ya jus' don't be floggin' all over the place, an' don't grab holda my hand for nothin'."

I looked into Granny Isabelle's eyes. She tugged my lower lip. Taking hold of a rag and the needle, she started poking holes, gouging, pressing the gum pone. Foul yellow gunk squirted into the air and made a vile taste come into my mouth. Momentarily, relief came.

"Now don't be puttin' nothin' hot or warm on it," she stated emphatically, glaring at Mama. "Cold is what's needed for gum boils. Ya gotta 'member what's what or ya can get into some awful messes. Folks can die with them pus pockets."

Death rose up in me. Then again, it didn't matter much, knowing all the times I had wanted to die and didn't. Death by gum boil would read in my obituary. What a way to go.

After my nerves and pain had settled, Granny Isabelle fingered the amber hunk of goo toward me.

"What's that stuff?" I asked.

"It's pine resin. Best thing God ever made for times like this. Now sit still an' let me work on it some more." Packing little bits into the cavity with a heavy broom straw, she filled the rotten tooth. She took my chin into her hands and looked me in the eyes as my tongue finagled the sticky gob.

She squinted, "Now when ya feel that big risin' come up on ya gum, ya jus' suck it out and spit. Suck an' spit. Thataway the pison leaves ya body an' won't go to ya brain for a worse abscess."

I nodded.

"If'n ya ain't better in the morning I'm gonna take ya to the doctor. If I have to tote ya all the way myself and use some of my own dab of money. That's what we gonna do. You and me. Dab-blame it all to hell. If all goes well I'll get that old tooth out in a few days."

Lifting my arms, I hugged her gently. She opened the door and pushed on her paper bag hat, snugging it onto her head. She looked steely-eyed at Mama, no words being said, and headed back to that old shack up the road apiece, to a spot in her yard to hoe and plant more onions.

Granny Isabelle would take good care of me. She would do what was best for me, even if I despised it. Like making me suck gum pones and drink whiskey and kerosene with BC or Goody powders, when a situation called for it.

39

Uncle Ed and the Jukebox

He was a big blustery hulk of a man dressed in pressed suits and fine spit-shined shoes. He barely fit into his long gleaming Cadillac. Bigger than life, his wealthy presence filled the room. It'd take two of Daddy to make a man like him. Uncle Ed walked straight-backed, cocky, bold, rooster-like, speaking strong dignified words beyond my understanding.

We'd heard stories about Uncle Ed playing the guitar and singing with some of Nashville's country singers. Daddy fumed over his brother's success, until he needed something. And hard times always came to us, and then off we'd go to live with Uncle Ed's family—or close by them, leeching on whatever they had after leaving Granny Isabelle behind to figure her own way outta things.

Sometimes, Daddy would take off and leave us to fend for ourselves for long periods. He'd go live with Uncle Ed, mostly to lay brick on one of his brother's many construction sites. At least it was what we were told.

Uncle Ed was rich and famous. He had everything. A big house, a fancy new car every year, his own beer joint, a construction company called "Big Ed's Construction," and oodles of money.

Great piles of quarters, dimes, and curled dollar bills laid atop the chest-of-drawers in his bedroom. So much currency laid about, but I never took a cent. I didn't want to be known as a thief like I was with Susie's hat. I felt proud being around them, even if I was on the outside looking in.

Once, we lived in Uncle Ed's camper. It was situated beside his big brick house and a beer joint he'd purchased after leaving Nashville.

I'd walk to school and back, behind my better-than-me cousins, feeling better about life, although I was always following. Daddy's rages had cooled down cause Uncle Ed was close by, I supposed.

Sometimes his daughter, my cousin Dorothy, the one who used to smile at me a lot when we were smaller, would take me by the ice cream shop after school and buy me a milkshake or a cone of vanilla cream. I'd pretend to be her sister as we slurped sweet stuff through straws or gnawed on crunchy cones.

Afterwards, I'd leave the ice cream shop and go to do what I did every day. I'd wash crusty, dried oatmeal bowls from our morning meal, sweep floors, and make beds with some raggedy quilts. My irritation often spilt onto Ginny, who did nothing helpful. My insides seethed over unfair responsibilities.

Uncle Ed's Bar and Grill was the first beer joint I had any respect for. Mama waitressed there, looking pretty in pencil skirts, soft sweaters sparkling with sequins, and rhinestone sapphire clip-on earrings. Aunt Sadie, Uncle Ed's wife, had given her two earring sets, pink and blue. It seemed working at Uncle Ed's made Mama come alive. She'd often disappeared into dark back rooms for days during our childhood, out of sight mostly, even when Daddy left, sort of an invisible presence. Her beauty became real to me as I slowly morphed into my teen years. As my body changed, I noticed her more.

Mama was the most beautiful woman in the world, I thought. Her dark auburn hair, freshly shampooed, curled downward. Dark brown eyes glistened as her lips sang along with jukebox tunes. Her long, shapely legs in heels made her look elegant. Other men watched her work, but she never noticed, it seemed. I did. I wondered about the way they gawked at her, much like Daddy did Aunt Fanny.

I'd watch her wire-brush the blackened grill and wipe stools and the counter with bleach, happily humming. She'd wipe the wood-grain counter sleek with Johnson's Paste Wax. So slick, filled beer glasses glided down by me without tipping over. The oak wood reflected light like glowing diamonds.

Beside of the bar sat eight bright, stainless-steel swivel stools with red vinyl seats. I'd twirl around on the cushiony stools uplifted, feeling grown up and special. Wanting to wear rhinestone earrings, pencil skirts, and seamed stockings, desiring to look like Mama and be close to her.

Mostly, frumpy men hovered over the bar stand, sipping and gulping beer in tall, icy glasses. Some would buy hot dogs all-the-way and scoff them down in seconds, leaving onion bits and mustard smears for me to rake up with the bleach-scented rag as I tasted onions through my nostrils.

Onion scents made me hungry for different food and for my poor Granny Isabelle. She had gone somewhere else to live, cause we'd left her behind again. But the fancy bar and grill made up for her absence in some ways.

Sometimes, a twinkly-eyed woman in red high heels and black-seamed stockings would come clicking along, leaving later with some mustard-lipped man. Mama had no use for her, I could tell. She had twinkled at Daddy more than once right in front of Mama.

As evening came, the jukebox revved up, tunes pummeling my ears and other body parts. I'd hang on to the jukebox as if it was a treasure box full of jewels, swaying, shifting my hips to some fine tunes, acting like older women did when they came around.

Typically, sad melodies arose from the bar. I loved to watch grown men snivel and cry over songs flowing from black vinyl records as they dropped, slipping into place, one after the other, the bright turquois jukebox glittering like gallium, gobbling coins, her sides juddering with delight.

Punched buttons released songs like "Red Roses for a Blue Lady," "Last Dance," "Someday," "I Wonder Who's Kissing Her Now," "Somebody Else Is Taking My Place," "Are you Lonesome Tonight," and "I'll Never Smile Again," repeatedly. I was the only one who wanted to hear "Sixteen Candles." I would push the moneyless controls in hopes the record might fall accidentally, but it never did.

I practiced every song, learned every word, until I sang them perfectly as notes hit the air. If I was alone in the evenings, cleaning the camper, I'd leave the windows open, keeping beat to the music with my hips swaying seductively. My hand spread like an iron on my belly like Uncle Rudy used to do. I'd daydream while purple and pink hues blossomed and bounced off of the flashing neon sign. Through the thin trailer curtains, Uncle Ed's Bar and Grill neon letters slid like silk over my face, arms, and hips.

Granny Isabelle used to say, "All good things come to an end." Suddenly, Daddy blew up at Uncle Ed, calling him a cheat behind his back. He packed up and hauled us off to find Granny Isabelle again. Knowing full well he'd be on back, working with Uncle Ed in a day or so, just without us. Free to be getting close to the twinkly woman like he did Red Cheeks.

40

The Invisible Man

Granny Isabelle gave Daddy a little piece of her land on the upper road-side to build a house on. We were happy to be so close to her. Off of the metal bus steps we hopped like happy rabbits. Just as if we were headed for the greatest place on earth at the day's end. Like we were going to some place for hot chocolate and snacks long before supper was ready. Trying to make them all jealous even if they looked the other way.

The Bletcher boys, J.B. and Wayne, were always tripping us up on the bus and laughing like hyenas when our heads lumped from a fall. And their sorry twin sisters, Dale and Gail, stuck middle fingers with nail-chewed nubs at the school bus window every time they saw us waiting by the mailbox when the bus pulled away. Their big cow tongues licked the grubby bus windows as the bus pooted black stench into our nostrils—it leaving us behind, wanting to sock their stupid foolish faces to smithereens.

Such surliness I'd never seen in human beings, except Daddy. I knew we'd lived in much worse places with worse people, yet I hated these people. Folks living off down the holler was a bad sign anyway. It's what I heard. And we sure had our share of living in hollers. God knows what kind of family the Bletchers had, Daddy said. Daddy hated their old man, and theirs hated mine.

My legs walked from the screeching yellow bus door toward home hesitantly. I would jerk the mailbox open, acting important with mail getting. Acting like we had received a lot of good stuff from tons of friends and family, like Uncle Ed. Pretending as if we were just waiting to hear from them, and them from us. With this daily mailbox spectacle I had invented, I was trying to impress the bobbing bus heads that licked the windows (and my buggers I'd put there the day before), showing them that we were as popular as anyone.

I made it obvious for them to see brown packages and big white envelopes with lots of stamps. I'd wave them into the air, acting significant. Never mind that U.S GOVERNMENT was all over it with "priority" stamped in the corners. I didn't care about words like "priority." Rather, I stared steady on the Bletcher eyes watching from wistful, tongue-smudged windows as my siblings and I grappled with letters.

At the end of the day, the twins and their no-good brothers were trapped inside the bus like sardines in a tin, while we were free. I pleasured myself with the thought that they still had miles to go. The long loaded vehicle puffed and pulled off as black smoke sopped my face and nose.

"What they don't know won't kill 'em," I choked to Ginny and Danny. Surely they thought of us as rich, from handling so many letters.

Yet I wondered if the Bletchers might be richer than us with so many spotted, tail-wagging dogs. The hounds would chase behind those wretched overgrown boys, who had failed three grades already. Every time Daddy rode by their driveway I saw it. When we passed by their road, their fingers went flying off at us. I loathed them and their sorry-ass dogs, maybe more than Daddy did. I'd not be taking much more leg tripping and head banging from them.

Daddy had become a brick contractor. Uncle Ed had taught him as much as he'd listen to about contracting. Folks said he owned his business like Uncle Ed and that we were getting richer by the day. He had built several houses, up to three with his own bare hands. We'd try them out before he sold them right out from under our noses. But some burned down for one or another reason. Usually he'd take a notion to sell one after Mama had nested us inside and we'd just begun to feel hopeful again. None of us wanted to leave the houses he built. Except him.

We'd already moved a hundred times, it seemed, since I was born, not counting times at Granny Isabelle's house. I'd been to lots of schools, not knowing the names of most. I knew we wouldn't be in one spot long enough to care or try much in school.

After school let out, going into the empty house wasn't fun. Nor was it when somebody was there, so it didn't matter either way to me. There was no hot chocolate or treats like I wanted the bus kids to believe, rather lots of dirty dishes and cleaning for me to do.

One day Ginny started acting crazy after we arrived home. She stormed around yelling, beating her fists on the walls and throwing shoes. She acted like death had come after her. I ran toward her howls. She stood pointing a finger at the closet door. Not talking, just stuttering in screams.

She finally settled down after I'd looked around, finding nothing. A man was squatting in dirty overalls and a brown hat in her closet, she had said. With a butcher knife pointed, staring mean, saying he was going to kill us all. I searched the house and looked over the yard, seeing nothing. We took off to Granny Isabelle's nearby house where the phone was.

Old lady Haden, a neighbor of Granny's, stayed on the party line gabbing, asking me a thousand times, "What's going on?"

"Nothing, but I'm needing the phone for an emergency," I yelled. Getting her and the other three party-liners to give it up, as I promised to tell her the matter later. Directly, I returned home as Daddy pulled in the driveway, fired up over some job thing. I'd already told the sheriff where to come, and he was on his way when I used Granny's phone.

Sirens squealed importantly as black automobiles with top lights twirled fascinating red rays, like arrows shooting. Gravel scooted from the tires, tearing into the drive. Angrily, Daddy looked at me. He despised all lawmen and the government.

He sweet-talked the lawmen to their faces, giving them the middle finger as they went off to speak to Ginny alone. Ginny cried, shook, and shivered as I watched through the keyhole. Then, some odd giggles came cause Deputy Hanks gave her a green sucker and a piece of wrapped pink Bazooka bubble gum, twisted on both ends.

"I ain't seen a soul in this house except us," I told Sheriff Jake. Then again, I was thinking Ginny might be making stuff up for candy cause it wasn't above her.

The lawman said, "Y'all watch out now. Maybe y'all got some enemies y'all don't know of."

"I'm thinking you got that right," I said. "My daddy's got his share and some more." I was thinking that the Hanks man might be cute if all his teeth was in. Daddy stood looking like he wanted to hit me, thinking I'd pulled a stunt. Everything bad was put on me, whether I did right or wrong.

Ginny settled down, getting extra oatmeal cookies for the night, and we just went on like before, getting nothing. Licking her mouth, thick white cream leaking to the sides, she grinned triumphantly. Mama toted her cups of hot coffee without cream as she watched *Lassie* on the television in peace. Danny and me ate reheated pintos and dried cornbread one more night with some onions. I kept thinking it wasn't one bit fair.

For one cookie, I'd scream over a closet ghost in bibbed overalls. Only thing, it wouldn't turn out easy for me. My hostility was growing for Ginny because I didn't want to watch over her anymore.

But the Bletchers were cats of a different color than Ginny. I thought on them and their sorry-ass speckled rabbit dogs. Maybe I came to hate them so much because they made fun of the stockings I had stuffed my bra with earlier that day. Mama's old nylons had slid clean through my blouse buttons for all to see. I'd used them like other girls had spoken of, but mine had to be the ones to show. Or maybe it was when I started my period sometime back without any warning and it showed up on the back of my wrap around skirt as I moved off the bus, leaving behind squeals, hoots, and jeers from the rotten-mouth Bletcher boys. I hated them more and more each hour.

41

Hounds, Fights, Fingers, and Feuds

Daddy had become somebody important around the area, having a company of his own and us in a real house. Folks said he was the best bricklayer for miles around. I thought maybe it was something to brag on. On the other hand, I knew how bad Daddy was to tear things down after he had built them up, especially if things went wrong. He wasn't above standing up for what he thought was right or wrong, whether it was or not. Me neither, for that matter.

The nasty big-mouth Bletcher boys had tripped me one time too many. I had a little something ready for payback. The next day, as the bus slowed down to a crawl, the stop sign arm flung out like a bat wing, I got up outta my seat. I salivated, ready and waiting for my opportunity to set things right in my world of being wronged too many times. But seeing the tail end of Daddy's car parked behind the house had me wondering what was happening.

The ugly cow-face J.B. stuck his leg out one last time. Anxious to get to the mailbox and see why Daddy's car was there, I raised up my foot and brought down my shoe heel as hard as hell on his shin bone, my ears hearing a crack. J.B. roared to high heaven, screaming I had killed him.

"She kicked my leg!" he thundered to the driver. Mr. Peavy, the bus driver, had seen it all go down. He had also seen me getting tripped too many times before. Mr. Peavy's grin—scooped out like a thumbnail moon—showed the delight crossing his shallow face in the rearview mirror, revealing a mouthful of brown, dingy teeth. I knew then that he was on my good side.

I said to the bewildered J.B., spreading my Southern drawl thicker, "Your leg was stuck out a little too far. I declare I was trying my derndest to step over it. I guess maybe my heel got caught up in that big hole ya got in ya pants leg at the knees. Or maybe ya leg was just got too high for my short-climbing legs. I'm awful sorry 'bout hurtin' ya so bad. See if ya can get to the doctor to take a good look at it."

I turned frontwards and trotted off, leaving his bellows of pain behind. Thinking how good it felt to fight back, like squashing yellow jackets underfoot. Feeling taller than ever before, I left as J.B. wallowed like a hog on the black rubbery aisle.

As I stepped down and off, Mr. Peavy winked at me. Then I grinned, lifting some IRS letters from the box, hiding my middle finger, poking it clear up into the Bletcher twins' window as they beat the glass, pounding and shoving fat fists into the air. Now, knowing exactly what finger-sticking meant, I felt good as Danny and Ginny trotted close behind.

Going inside the house, tired out from stomping that crow's leg, I saw Daddy splayed in the floor, in front of the picture window looking dazed. He did not even know we were there beside of him. His shotgun was loaded and pointed straight toward the road. He jabbered a language I couldn't understand—some mixed-up crazy words—as his eyes lit up.

Mama was off in the bedroom crying, sniffling over something. I took Danny and Ginny back to find her to get them away from Daddy and whatever might be happening.

"Who's he talking to? Why is he holding on to his shotgun?" I asked Mama.

She whispered, "Lordy, child, he's done run over old man Bletcher's hunting dog."

"That dog with the black and brown spots an' short dumpy legs who barks after our car all the time?" I asked.

"That's the one," she said, shuddering.

"I heard them Bletcher boys talking one day last week. It's their old man's favorite beagle," I said.

She sighed, her face paling more so.

Daddy's cussing started worse for no known reason. Cussing God, the neighbors, all the people he ever worked for, and then he cussed Granny Isabelle and our dead Papa Harkus. Plus, he didn't leave us out.

Sheriff Jakes and Deputy Hanks returned, driving furiously. With guns drawn, prune-faced, the men came hesitantly. Daddy was still lying on his belly, sweat blobbing his forehead, his forefinger gripped tight on the gun trigger.

I watched the big-hatted sheriff through the window as he habitually swiped his hat brim several times before speaking, nudging it into place on his head a bit at a time with each rub. Loudly, he spoke from the yard for Daddy to answer.

"Now, James, you need to listen close to what I'm gonna say. I ain't saying it but once. I know you got a loaded gun in there pointing it at them Bletcher men in the cornfield across the road. But I've done hauled one of 'em off to jail, and I come to get your side of the story before I take the others and maybe you. Now, are we gonna do this the easy or hard way?" His voice was more deep throated than usual, meaning business.

"Ya done carried his sorry ass off for sure, or ya jus' stringing me along?" Daddy said back in his most lawyer-like voice.

"They're closing the cell door as we speak," the sheriff replied.

Daddy's gun barrel sank downward, hesitating a little; yet the nose still posed on the windowsill on the brink of firing.

"Ya come to hear my story?" he asked.

"Yep. I sure did. Me an' my deputy here." He patted Deputy Hanks on the shoulder.

"I was minding my own business. Done laid brick all day. Fingers got blood blisters to the bones. Tired as hell. Had me one beer at Page's Diner up the road."

"One beer," Sheriff Jakes stated back to Daddy.

"Ya calling me a liar?" Daddy quarreled. "Jus' one. I swear on my kids' lives."

"Only one beer?" the sheriff repeated.

"Just two. Honest to God as my witness. May my wife be struck dead with lightning." Daddy groped sweaty fingers, steadying his gun better on the ledge.

"Just two?" Hanks took up again.

"Just two. I swear on my dear mama's life." He said this more convincingly, sounding more like Perry Mason than ever.

The sheriff must've believed him that time.

Becoming gentler, like Matt Dillon in *Gunsmoke*, "Well, if you had just two beers we oughta be able to sit down and talk a while. Open up this here door." He twisted the doorknob, rattling it some.

Daddy nodded his head toward me, and I turned the latch up, letting the man's big self in with that good-looking Hanks fellow following shyly.

Jake sat on the couch, squishing pillows down toward the floor with his heavy, sunk legs poking out. Hanks stood off to the side, picking his tooth holes with a frayed toothpick. I was liking him more than ever in that brown deputy uniform with patches on his shoulders. I began looking for his eyes, mine twinkling like Aunt Fanny's.

I studied his face, twisted my behind a little like my Aunt Fanny did when Daddy was near her. Thinking I might just marry that man someday, even if his front teeth were gone.

Then he sucked on some leftover food bits, made a clucking sound, eating some old foodstuff. Disgusted, my eyes left him and went to staring at his scuffed-up boots then to his nice, pressed clothes. Thinking nothing matched on him, my eyes traveled to his brass belt buckle shining like the sun. That scuffed and pressed just didn't go together. With that, I figured him not to be worth much at all.

Daddy propped the weapon against the window frame like a leaning broom, leaving it there after checking for steadiness. He sat on a ladder-back chair facing the officers, artillery an arm's length away, just in case.

"You done come to hear my side of the story?"

"Exactly." The sheriff spoke stiffly.

"Ya want me to go on?" Daddy said, unsure.

"Exactly." The officer removed his round hat, bald head emerging like a hen's egg coming out of a feathery tail. Me thinking, it's a good thing he at least has a mustache. A man needs a little hair.

"Go ahead," he urged.

Daddy explained, "Well this ain't jus' happened. It's been going on for years on end. Even when my mama built that little house down the hill and we only visited her for the most part. Even then if I was seen they'd come for me. Me having to slow down to a crawl to get down the road without killing them scrawny hellhounds. Nothing but rabbit dogs running every which way with no sort of training. Barking and chasing after my car down the road. Not listening none when I'd slow down an' holler."

"Yeah." The big one nodded for Daddy to go on.

Mama was still sniffling, nowhere to be seen, but heard. I wanted to be exactly where I was for the time being. Ginny was right with me, hinting for another sucker. I didn't care for no green one, my tongue wanting red or purple.

Officer Hanks stepped over and tussled Ginny's yellow curls, stooped down, and handed her some peppermint sticks. This time, he gave me the worst creeps; hairs went to crawling on my neck. I took hold of Ginny's hand and grabbed the candy sticks, shoving them back, warning him with my stare, stay away from my sister. His sleazy eyes looked eerily at me as I pushed the candy back into his face.

I wondered why I'd fallen in love with him to start with and why my neck hairs took so long to raise up to warn me. Ginny took off shrieking to Mama about not getting what she wanted. Mama shushed her, probably listening through the walls like I do most times. Ginny would get cookies when this was over, cause of me. Maybe more than cookies, if Daddy was hauled off to jail.

"I even spit tobacco juice in one's eyes an' it didn't make a blame bit of difference—still chasing an' yapping like beagles do," Daddy was saying. "That's when old man Bletcher got a hornet in his britches. We took to trading licks for half an hour or so the other day. Today, he hauled a rifle out in my face. Cussing like ya' ain't never heard."

Daddy considered the big man's reaction. I was thinking, ain't no way that geezer's mouth is worse than Daddy's, as I looked through my squished-up, lie-searching eye, checking Daddy out.

"Okay, I heard you," the sheriff assured him.

"I got to thinking on him pushing that rifle in my face. Him cussing me like I ain't worth nothing. Tired of them dogs coming after me." Daddy started letting too much outta the bag cause he was on a roll and couldn't stop, thinking him and them were friends by now.

"Yeah?" The bald head shimmied some. "So what did you do then?"

"Well, after them three or four beers, being so tired and wanting to get on home, I stopped and hollered for all the Bletcher men to stay outta my way. But the dogs kept coming, nipping on my legs and pissing on my britches. I just stopped in the middle of the road and kicked one against the head. Tough as hell, they are. I think it stunned him a little bit, though." Daddy cackled.

"Bletchers, all of 'em, come rolling down the hill after me like a barrel of snakes, so I got into my car not wanting no trouble. That dog, being hard-headed, took off to the front fender, yelping and snarling at my car bumper. Trying to tear the tires right off with his bare teeth. Me thinking, I ain't stopping this time to save his sorry hide. Old man Bletcher was spying from the hilltop at me with that rifle saddled up next to him, sighted to blow my head off."

"So you mean to tell me, he watched for you to come along every day just to torment you somehow?" the sheriff clarified.

"He's looking every time I go up an' down the road. Like he owns the highway. He don't own nothing 'cept a passel of rabbit hounds."

"So you had done had enough? Like most folks would have." The cop looked at Daddy square-eyed.

Daddy felt the man's sympathy, it seemed. "Yeah. I done had 'nough. Him standing there with that gun. Like he's gonna show me a thing or two. Ain't nobody gonna get by with that. Ain't nobody."

The sheriff adjusted the sunken pillow, shuffling his broad butt sideways into a big "W."

"I jus' let that dead dog stay where he was and took off toward home, figuring they had too many dogs as it was anyway."

"What did he do then?"

"He raised that rifle an' fired right through the windshield. Right by my head."

"Right by your head?"

"Sure did. Come on an' I'll show you the bullet hole."

We all took off outside to the car. Me behind Daddy, wanting to see it all and not miss one thing. The sheriff rubbed over the holed-out, crushed back glass.

"The bullet's over the other side laying in the seat." Daddy pointed. He went around, opened the door, and got hold of a flattened brass piece. The men followed. Sleazy stood gaping a crude grin, fingering the circle on the wrinkly glass, looking at Ginny and me.

"You say this has been going on for years?" Sheriff Jakes asked.

"Ever since I started building houses. He's been after me up an' down the roads," Daddy replied innocently. "I ain't done nothing 'cept 'tect myself an' my little family. That ain't no crime, is it sir?"

"No, it ain't no crime. But deliberately destroying a man's property is," Sheriff Jakes explained, recapping his head. "You want me to go see if he'll let you pay him for the animal, or do I need to carry you off to a cell too?"

Daddy got a mistreated look in his eye. Like he couldn't believe what was happening to him. He scanned the ground, thinking for a minute.

"Guess I'll pay him some money. But I ain't got much to give that son of a bitch. Them hounds don't come cheap, I've heard."

"I heard the same thing. They ain't cheap. You stay put until I call on you again. Don't leave this house. And don't touch that gun. In fact, I think I'll confiscate it for a while. Any more weapons inside?"

Daddy lied, "Naw. Jus' that one."

The big officer nodded for Toothless to get the shotgun and come on.

"You need to tell that bastard he better never point another gun in my direction or he's gonna get what's coming to him," Daddy spouted as his dignity filled him back up.

"I'll do just that," the sheriff yelled back sarcastically as the cars revved up and sped away with Daddy's shotgun in the fat cop's trunk. Daddy trudged up the steps, angry at us and Mama for the gun being taken and everything else that was against him. Mama quieted him by saying, "Honey, ya want me to scramble ya a plate of brains and eggs?" He nodded.

Turning more like Daddy every day, I was fired up, wondering how to get even with the Bletcher boys and how to get better at foot stomping on the bus. I knew I was gonna have to tramp harder before this thing was over and done with.

194

42

Daddy's Day

My daddy James, unready for work, squatted glassy-eyed, trembling at high noon. His tattered khaki work pants, with shredded knees, were splotched, soaking wet from crotch to upper thighs. Black belt unloosed, most of the worn-out leather strap caught up, twisted under his right buttock. Floored—clear slobber dripping from his nose and chin, stringy snot groping down to his leg, akin to a damp creek bed.

A man without work runs low on hope. No work, no money. Virginia's red clay held no forgiveness for brick masons. Winters were harsh. January most of all. The land's surface had frozen into crunchy layers of vertical ice towers that collapsed when stepped upon—the underneath being far worse.

Concrete footings couldn't be dug with mattocks and shovels. Brick mortar would freeze and crack as soon as it was slabbed on with a trowel. If a day got below 32 degrees, laborers whined about freezing to death for a measly few dollars, so they only halfway worked.

A pitiful sight to see. Our father, a puny, bare-chested man piled up, groveling, babbling foolishly. His body listing leftward, legs slid off sideways—each stacked, one atop the other. Bare feet crooked, strange, appearing club-footed. Beside of a wooden chair sat his dusty, crusty, mortar-covered boots with a pair of red-clay stained socks wadded together. A loaded rifle with its gunmetal barrel locked onto his bulging veined temple: cocked, ready and waiting.

"What's happening? What's he doing?" My eyes scanned the nearby rooms for damage and then settled on what lay before me. "What's going on?" I yelled over their heads, as if the family had no faces. Danny's beet-red expression swiftly traveled to me. His white-knuckled hands began to wring, fighting each other.

Different screams had come from Ginny, hunting me. A heaped-up Daddy was mind-boggling. Odd shrieks brought me to the room, dragging me to see his smallness—a thing I'd never witnessed before.

195

Mama's hair wasn't hooked onto his hands. His fists weren't drawn up to hit nobody neither. Chipped dishes sat stacked off-kilter on the kitchen table, much like a leaning chimney, ready for eating. Beside of the blue-iced cake Mama had made laid the newspaper wrapped packages tied with twine—a new brick hammer and trowel, replacing the nearly worn-out ones.

I had been alone in the far back bedroom. With nothing better to do, sitting on the striped mattress edge, picking at its grayish cotton stuffing, it peeking out at me like ears. I'd just tried on the sweet little pearls Granny Isabelle had given me for Christmas. The beads wound smooth, easy and gentle around my fingers—as if speaking out some comfort. I knew she'd worked hard for our small treasures. She had sold a lot of onions and corn.

A mixture of sadness and lovability filled me as my thoughts visited Granny Isabelle. Guilt, like dust particles from the air, floated into my thoughts. Sadness danced through my mind like a worrisome imp who had come to steal all shreds of joy. As much as she wanted, she couldn't do one thing to make our lives better. Relapses always came.

Then too, I was thinking on Daddy's day when Ginny's hollers came slapping me. I was wondering why he'd gotten a birthday cake and we never did; even when his company was making money, it was thrown away on whiskey and beer. Wondering why his day was so special and ours never was. My own special day had just passed without a cake or gift or barely a mention.

Being older should've been worth a little something, I reasoned. But Daddy had always said I was born at a bad time. I wondered why I was born at the wrong time and he wasn't, and us coming into the world a month apart. I was studying on this when Ginny's yells came to get me. My guts filling with gall and rumbling.

Ginny's panicked screams had come searching for me. I ran when her hysterical yells grabbed my ears. The room seemed empty except for the slumped-up man. There was no sense of cold or evil like most times when he was drunk. The gun barrel wiggled as his hands trembled. Then the shaft steadied, poking and pressing further into his skull. How could our daddy be in the middle of the floor, so pitiful?

Ginny cried, "Don't, Daddy. Please don't, Daddy. We'll be good. We will." Danny nodded his head, agreeing, supporting her. Her blond curls swung sideways as she bent down, searching Daddy's eyes with her big, blue-eyed promise.

Time stopped. Thoughts became motionless. Why was a gun at his head and not ours? I wondered blankly as my eyes traveled over his clean fingernails—now Daddy had been saved again for a month, longer than ever, the reason for his unsoiled nails.

Mama was crouched on the floor, leaning by her man's side. Tormented, squeezing her hands—like Danny—as if a string mop in need of emptying, twisting her fingers. He'd cleaned himself up—sanctified himself

"Please don't do this, James. Jus' listen to them kids. They don't want ya to kill yaself. I don't want it none neither," she whimpered. I had wondered at times if she had any feelings. Not even when he got saved all of them times, not once did she cry for joy.

Not once, when he had hit the altar begging forgiveness for all of his sins, did she weep like we did. Nor did I figure she had a voice, never humming or barely speaking. For us, she seemed not to have feelings or words. Now she declared her voice, for him, not for us.

We'd all begged Mama to take us and leave Daddy. She never would. We'd all spoke of wanting Daddy to get killed with a car wreck or something, at one time or other. Maybe to get shot or stabbed at some beer joint. We all wanted him dead, from what we'd said in the past in backroom whispers. In a mixed-up sort of way we talked of it—even Ginny, his favorite child.

I just wanted the pain to go away. To quit hurting. To be like other families. Not be afraid. But wanting it and seeing it happen were two different things. Not here. Not like this. Not while he was saved again. Just maybe an accident of some sort, when he got mean again.

Instinctively, I knew what to do. I squatted down and pulled the gun barrel from his head. The shaft waved about as I wheedled its position. My eyes fastened onto his Adam's apple. It bobbed midway with swallows as he garbled babyish sounds.

My hands pried the swaying weapon—mine stronger than his today. Tight, but not so tight at the same time—big, his hands were. My cheek touched his beardy scratchiness as my head squeezed between his and the sharp cold round point, scraping my scalp, shredding the top layer of skin. The closest I'd ever been to him in a lifetime.

"Ya gonna hafta kill me too," I said. "In fact, me first." He slobbered thick stringy gunk. I watched as it touched the floor worming. My eyes followed the slime trailing, as if a snail, reluctantly crawling onto the worn linoleum. My ears pierced painfully as my little Christmas pearls pinged, one at a time against the floor, stressed, bouncing broken. Granny Isabelle's gift to me.

Our lives were worthless, amounting to nothing. Especially mine didn't matter. I came to know it sometime back. My parents never wanted me. Strangely, the realization resurfaced, dissolving my fear, like water sucked up by soft, plowed earth. Absolute peace came. We sat, Daddy and me, sealed together by some unkind fate. Father-daughter, and family encircled about us.

Peculiarly, Doris Day's song journeyed through my mind like a soft woman floating in swirls. "Que será, será, whatever will be will be. The future's not ours to see. Que será, será." I tasted Doris's calmness as her song entered me, through some distant rhythm; time lingered, unmoving.

The bitter steel barrel drifted down. Slow and easy. Slimy dribbles ended. Daddy's throat knob stilled. Squirming hands became motionless. Screams died. Begging ceased. Whimpers and snubs came into the room like miniature air waifs. The space felt calm like it does after storms or beatings. Empty and timeless, we sat together, as a woman's hand wiped Daddy's chin drool with a rag.

"I can't do it. I jus' can't quit the old way. The drinkin' is bigger than me. I try an' try. I jus' can't keep goin' like this. It eats my guts up—the drinkin' does when I do it—an' it eats 'em up when I don't. I don't know how to fight it no more." Self-pitying, he moaned, wallowing. We were silent. Knowing full well what would soon happen again. Knowing we should've let him die when we had the chance but couldn't.

We lifted ourselves up from the floor, one at a time, circled the table, lit the forty-five candles, and sang happy birthday.

I stood, backed off from the rest, the circle now broken. I gathered and held on to my destroyed, broken beads, miming meaningless celebratory words. Had they seen the gun hooked onto my head? Was I invisible to them? Did anyone care?

Danny grimaced in confusion. His hand-covered, cotton-plugged ear guarded the infected well. Thick green pus beneath the earlobe had left a crusty trail. Mama's home remedies hadn't helped. In hopeless shock, I watched Danny's unspoken agony, matching mine to his.

Ginny pulled on Daddy's hand, saying, "Can I help ya open ya presents, Daddy?" Our plastic smiles stood stiff as Ginny was scissoring the twine. Sheepishly grinning, he opened his packages. She'd given him an oatmeal cookie. Danny and I had none to give him. He gobbled it up in front of us and we went on like nothing bad had happened.

After the birthday song was over, Mama's face returned voided, and her voice retreated within. We, the family, never spoke about how we wanted Daddy dead after that. Nor did we ever speak of the event, or that I had offered my life for his. But something reflexively changed inside of me that day.

I'd always lived in a lopsided world, a see-saw world. Daddy was always on the solid bottom—and myself, a nothing kid, always flailed about high on top, scared to death, just waiting to fall—like during that Pilot Knob trip. Waiting to be hurt. Waiting to be rescued by someone who cared. Waiting to die.

Oddly, I felt more powerful after I'd witnessed Daddy puddled up in his piss, groveling and whining like a baby. I fantasized that just maybe he did love me a little because he didn't pull that trigger to blow a bullet through my brains. I wrapped my precious broken pearls into a handkerchief, tied a knot, and stuffed them into my dresser drawer. I knew somehow that everything good, if there was any, would always be destroyed by Daddy. And I learned something even greater: I no longer had to stay on the teeter-totter waiting for him to drop me.

43

Lying Cheat

My beginning sense of self was squeezed, swallowed, and packed back into a place, revolving around Daddy. Tenth grade came trembling with stages of this realization. I sat agog, alone. Words stirred about and floated around ghostly-like. It seemed like Daddy had put me into an invisible box. He said I was getting too big for my britches. His hold was getting tighter and tighter.

This box or carton was a meaningless, space-less place to be. I was timeless in pain, needing to grow, but shouldn't, but couldn't, but wouldn't. His uncouth voice rubbed me like weak hands patting, and poking, and piercing my soul. Growing up small inside, gnat-like, I existed. Outside looking in was the way I lived. Wanting nothing was the way I lived. Lonely was the way I lived. Who was I? Where was I? Two months into grade ten—that's who I was, where I was.

Dennis sat grinning, his desk in front of mine. He didn't know my name. Nobody did. My leg was numb or maybe not. Granny Isabelle said it was all in my head because of the scar. The scarred leg rested underneath his seat. I'd wiggle life back into it throughout the school day, trying to bring my story to life, never forgetting about how it happened and about how Mama never came to help unhook me from the red-belly stove. The sorry tale of my scorched skin that mottled purple later and never healed right after using butter and with no doctor to be had.

The wounded leg needed to feel something. I shook my foot alive. A hand groped backward, rubbing my calf, making it feel alive outside of Daddy's box. The boy's head turned slightly backwards as he sneered triumphantly. A brown eye glided smartly at my cheek. I sat motionless. Numbness crept to the bone and I waited, mechanical, unfeeling. My eraser was chewed and swallowed; a bent metal end scrubbed my paper vigorously, scraping holes into e's and i's, f's and the little g's. I wrote, "I hate Dennis."

A gnawed number two yellow pencil—a tooth-marked wooden shaft—held my chin as I looked at Dennis's back, hating his guts and hating his unscarred legs, maybe wanting to stab him between his shoulder blades with my chewed number two.

An hour of geography with handsome Mr. Strader; he was my favorite teacher. What it would be like if he loved me for his own? If I was his girlfriend? If I was his one and only? I had tried harder to please him than the other teachers. And Mrs. Flannagan, the math teacher. She gave me B's sometimes. I tried to delight her some when I got outta Daddy's box for bits of time. I could do that whenever Daddy got saved.

"The project is due April 12th," Mr. Strader said energetically. I bit off some more fingernails, tried to tuck the nail pieces into the eraser shaft, nodded, and wrote the date down.

"Choose a country. Write three pages on it. Make sure I can read it or you will get an F. That's a promise." Shuffles scraped the floors, books slid, and murmurs warred across the room awkwardly. I squirmed. "Tell me everything about the economy, land, people, occupations, and animals." Chalk marked the board, squeaking. "I will give extra credit for anything other than the written work. And do not plagiarize."

"Like what kind of stuff for credit?" Dennis chimed without hand-raising. The redhead boy was rich. He didn't need to have permission for anything, not to speak and not even to go to the restroom. Without permission he would rise to leave the room because he could.

"Like posters, maps, pictures, and paintings. Be creative." Mr. Strader smiled through two pearly white rows as he ousted us from the room. He stood tall, clean, neatly dressed and smelling of Aqua Velva. How I wished to be good or pretty enough for him to notice me like he did Betty and Wanda, some other girls.

My mind whorled, worried over the project, but I was so grateful it wasn't a group task. I hated doing any and all kinds of group projects. How would I get pictures and such things without transportation or money? There was much to think about. Like supplies. I had no resources at home. No guidance. Maybe I'd just settle for my usual "D." The task was great but something jarred inside me. Will power surged, urging me forward. I heard Granny Isabelle say, "Do what you can with what you have. Put one step in front of the other and the rest will come."

I can get three pages from the library, I thought. First, I'll look up "plagiarize," hating new words but not asking just because. I scooted to the library during lunch period, half-concerned over my ineptness, half-excited over trying, and craving to please Mr. Strader. He was my beloved teacher and I wished that I could erase the board and wash it for him.

Memories of Mrs. Brewster in sixth and seventh grade flooded me. But I couldn't go back there. As Granny Isabelle used to say, "Keep moving one foot in front of the other. Don't stop with looking behind ya."

The assignment was due in ten days. I pondered, probing the library's world globe, continents heavy lined—twirling it softly as if seeking guidance from a higher power. My finger landed on Australia. Flames ignited. I could do this. Within two days my paper was complete, corner dog-eared and neatly written, unstained by coffee or food. Not having paper clips, it was the best I could do. Not feeling fully satisfied, my hands hungered for more information from Britannica Encyclopedia's pages.

I imagined Mr. Strader's face smiling at me, delighted with the work I'd done. He'd give me an A+. He'd use me as an example of excellence before the class. I'd feel bigger in my desk seat. My chest full. The instructor's face beaming. Dennis not touching my leg again. Not ever.

At home, I scavenger hunted. Partial empty paint cans with dabs of colored liquid residue. An old paintbrush, bristles twisted and stiff. Flour for paste. A bowl. I gathered clay from the creek bed, keeping it moistened in a plastic bag. After searching through rubbish of leftover boards, I found a flat piece of wood about two feet square.

Eagerly, with paint cans in a row, I removed the hard paint-encrusted lids, some rusty from rain. With brush and rags, I dipped and smeared colors together. First, the entire space was shaded with deep blue. I couldn't wait for it to dry. An hour or two passed.

My excitement blossomed into anticipation, as I expected an overt appreciation of my hard work. I sketched Australia perfectly from my library sketch, leaving no detail undone. Happy inside. Feelings alive. Fingers working. My mind racing and groaning to give birth to something of my own. Letting go of the hidden voice of, "I can't do it" and "you can't pour shit outta a boot cause ya just too stupid."

Hours passed. The clay was woven, patted, smudged and became as real as the encyclopedia's picture. Seas waved, reefs peeped, hills arose, and islands greened as my project came to life. Pride filled my breast as I watched colors mingle and Australia grow. My continent was ready to dry.

April 12th came too slowly for me. I lugged my treasure onto the bus. Protecting it from many harsh pushes, gangly elbows, and snickering shadows was difficult. My eagerness overwhelmed me as I pridefully placed it on the teacher's desk. He looked down at it. I looked up from it. Joy locked inside of my chest, dribbled out as I left it behind.

Days passed. Hours crawled as I awaited my grade. My desk became cagey. I wanted to mention, "What do you think, Mr. Strader?" A week passed. Then another.

Mr. Strader called out one day as the class dwindled to a few stragglers, "Jessica, would you stay for a second? I'd like to talk to you." Ecstasy surged through me. Of course I'll stay. I wanted to jump, to dance, to shout, "Of course I will." My words muted but real. The day was finally here.

Mr. Strader was going to tell me it was the best he had ever seen. He would tell me I had great possibilities and that I should reach for the stars. Maybe he'd say I was good enough to go to college someday. This would show my stinking typing teacher who called me a worthless thing or two. I couldn't contain my excitement. I wanted to tell him how good it felt to make something out of nothing and how hard it was to do so. I wanted to say how much I wanted an A and to go to college someday. But the words wouldn't come out of Daddy's box.

I stood at his desk alone, smiling lopsided, as his grim face studied mine.

"I don't know how to say this, so I'll just spit it out." He said this as he sat down behind his desk, pushed his squeaking chair back to give him additional space, and crossed his stretched-out legs. He played, bouncing his yellow pencil sideways, making it look rubbery. "Where did this work come from?"

"What do you mean?" I replied, stunned.

"I mean, where did you get it?" A deeper grimace covered his face. "Did someone else to do this?"

Dumbfounded, I stepped back from him. He was slapping me without hands. Sinking. Sinking. Sinking.

"No sir. I did it all. It took me the whole ten days. Nobody helped me."

More than disappointment clouded his face. "You're lying to me, aren't you?" A disgusted look, hoisted like spears and retched from hateful eyes as he pontificated.

I shook my head, ashamed—gut-retching shame flamed my neck. My head bent as if I'd done wrong. Tears threatened.

"I did it all, sir. I worked so hard on it. Nobody helped me one bit. I even dug clay from the creek." Hurt daggered and dug into my heart. But he'd never see it, I vowed. He'd never see it. I'd die first before I showed him my heart.

"This is the work of a student I had last year. You are a liar and a cheat. Your grade is F. Not another word is to be said." He pushed by me as he left the room.

I never thought to have him ask Mama. She wouldn't have come in or called anyway. To ask someone who would vouch for me never came to my mind. They would never be in my corner. I was on my own, like always. Except for Granny Isabelle, and she was too tired.

I walked away from Mr. Strader in humiliation, wounded. Speechless, feeling identical to Mama's blank face. Like a tail-tucked dog. How could I have been born so stupid? Why did I even try when there was no hope to start with?

Aching, I went on just like nothing bad had happened at Mr. Strader's desk. Like my spirit had not been damaged. The next day, Dennis reached backwards, rubbing my leg, and from then on most days. Me feeling nothing, but squished up a little more, packed inside of Daddy's box.

The bitter words of Mr. Strader and Mrs. Finch, my typing teacher, hurt me like salt on a sore. I worried on them constantly, feeling more hopeless and stupid. I could barely hold my head up because of it. I studied the floor most times like Uncle Rudy often had. It seemed most teachers never looked beyond my desperation to find something better in me. Was I too ignorant to learn anything from world globes and encyclopedias? I still couldn't pour shit outta a boot, like Daddy declared, but I didn't want to anymore.

Granny Isabelle fussed, saying I had to keep going. Not to let Mr. Strader or Mrs. Finch stop me from reaching for the stars. I was better than them anyway, she preached furiously, but that as sure as hell I could flip a few book pages, read them, and twirl a globe.

I began to put one foot in front of the other regardless of what laid ahead. I began to dream about going to college, maybe even getting a little apartment with my cousin Dorothy someday. I just kept my thoughts inside or wrote them in my little hidden book of letters to God.

Mrs. Finch had said I wasn't college material. Blades stabbed into me when she said it. She would give me looks as if I had no feelings. She had told us to practice typing one hour each night. I had no typewriter, but she didn't know that. I made myself a pretend keyboard on cardboard, and I practiced unceasingly.

When I didn't practice on the paper, I practiced in my head, pecking myself to sleep at night. I'd keep my fingers nice and steady on the make-believe keys, typing constantly. Pecking, pecking, pecking, and more pecking; all through the night and day, I typed. Maybe I would be a secretary someday.

I was so distressed over my inability to learn without a struggle. I told Granny Isabelle about my hurt and the way the teachers treated me as if I was fit for nothing. She advised, "Since you passed that typing class without no typewriter in sight, it showed you was smarter than all the other kids. And seeing as how you loved it so good, maybe you should take the next typing class and become somethin' in life." She said she was going to go to town and buy me a typewriter with her onion money one way or another. I figured it like Granny Isabelle explained and decided surely there was hope. She wanted to buy it for me, but she never made enough money. She'd worked so hard in life, but didn't have enough energy left to buy me a typewriter and ribbon.

I became determined in my head to keep on trying and not give up. Granny Isabelle said, "Ain't nobody ever had nothin' without some hard work behind it, and for some folks who want better, it might be a harder row to hoe, but it can be done."

44

The Morning After

It was another morning after. The wet black night seemed to be ending. It dragged into light, grinding into the misty morning, as we went on like nothing ever happened the night before. We were still alive. Beyond exhausted. The air's morning haze hung heavy, thick as if talcum powder had been sifted onto the earth from heaven. Sneaking through the wet poplar leaves, the sun came peeking in small splotches. Us outside, away from the danger of the house, watching it rise.

Mama sat slack—slumped up against a tall black pine trunk with the kids heaped on her. They were getting bigger, but it seemed to me they would never think themselves too big to be held by her. Danny was the baby. Ginny was the lost child. And me, I was the black sheep, destined to be the leader of our sad little flock. It was a role I didn't care for none. I wished Mama could hold me too. She looked lost and most pitiful that morning. My heart skipped beats, hurting as I considered her vacant eyes.

Her face was swollen and bruised. Her blood-stained blouse drooped, shredded loose at one shoulder. Little brown thread pieces poked out along the ripped fabric, like a shattered wooden swing bridge in need of fixing. Both straps on her work shoes were broken, and the soles looked like floppy black tongues, lapping to the sides. A crow spoke one loud caw and left. Quietly we waited, not talking, fearful Daddy might find us.

A harsher noiselessness came slinking down like a soft spell, as the sweet sun pushed the floury vapors away. Like a steamed-up mirror wiped clean, we could see. We wiggled restless, straining to hear more screams, cusses, and gunshots, but silence crawled into our ears like thunder.

Rustling leaves and crunching pine needles came creeping down through the hollow in small specks of time. My heart stopped as fear gurgled in my throat like gall. I knew the others' fear was identical to mine, because their faces were as white as paste. I'd seen and felt those looks a thousand times. I could read their minds and smell their fear a mile away. It's what happens when you are stuck together, inseparable in lives such as this. Agonies laid, one upon another, like a wall. Putting a finger to my lips gingerly, I shushed them without any sound. Danny's mouth quivered like a rabbit's nose does when it's trapped. Hands covered his eyes as his head turned into Mama's lap, hiding.

Twisted brambles were pulled, swatted apart by some fingers. Twigs snapped loudly like when a broom handle breaks in half. Jumpy, we pulled back to run some more. And then a ratty head stuck through the created nothing space, haloed by sunlight and dancing dust motes.

"Ya'll come on home. It's over. He can't do no more meanness, right now anyways. He's spent out for the most part." Granny Isabelle sighed guiltily, as if she'd brought hell on Mama and us kids by birthing Daddy into the world. The same look had crossed her face when she had told Aunt Lizzie she wished to God she'd never seen him take a breath.

We gawked at Granny Isabelle for a second, half-grinning, and goofy with smidgens of relief.

She said, "Y'all come on now. Ain't none of us had a speck of sleep."

Danny asked between grins, "How'd you find us, Granny Isabelle?"

Her back hunched over as she spoke wearily, "I just figured. I just figured it." Moving off toward home, she added, "Y'all best just get on off somewhere if ya can, 'til we make sure how it's gonna be. An' try to eat a little morsel if you can. I done got a pan of biscuits jus' out of the oven. They will be a waitin' on ya."

Our arms and legs were covered with deep, long, dried bloody scratches from the tall, wild blackberry briars and tangled razor grasses. They stung. We had sneaked out of the woods like thieves toward the house. Through the backyard slow and easy, we tiptoed, stopping spells, listening closely for trouble.

The unbearable quiet felt loud and way too thick to crawl through. Placing one foot in front of the other, we trudged doubtfully, unsteadily, and ungratefully. Getting through fear another night, with meaningless, soundless steps we went homeward, linked tight together, knotted one behind the other.

I opened the kitchen door. A long whiny squeak stopped us. Nothing was spoken. It opened a little further, then it stopped as I shuddered impulsively. I slipped inside, sneaking toward Daddy's room. He laid peacefully engulfed in snores as if nothing had happened. Like a baby, he slept on as I shuddered, even more filled with hate.

His mouth gaped open. Yet I felt torn with hate, pity, disgust, and a wistful love. I pulled the door together, thinking he had tried to be good. No women, cigarettes, sugar, or whiskey. Just hot coffee, the Bible, church, and focused on building this house for us.

I kept looking for Mama to lead the others inside. For her to make a plan. She never did and never would. We had begged her to leave him again. We stayed, doing the same thing. I was tired, weary, and edgy from this time of running and hiding, and all of the other piled-on times.

So many occasions we'd been through this, enough to learn. But we always got caught off-guard. We should have been used to it by now. I blamed myself sometimes. I should have known what to do before it happened. We all should have, but we didn't. It would never end. Our problem was believing it would end.

Why didn't I plan ahead to have a place for us to run and hide? Mama couldn't do it. I could feel the terror coming; yet when it did, I was stunned. It was like getting caught naked in the daylight, with nowhere to turn for cover.

Our eyes often were dark-circled from sleeplessness. We were spacey-eyed, with concentration near impossible. Today, like every day after, I was sick to my stomach. My guts felt like an animal was gnawing them. They were hot and jittery inside, maybe akin to naked electrical wires sparking against one another.

My fingers were numb and my lips were dry. My hands felt strangely useless, often shaking and dropping things. My legs wobbled in an odd weakness, neither balancing nor holding me upright properly. A throbbing headache banged my skull like a ram butting inside.

I looked at my shoes and said, "Shit." How would I ever wear them to school? One was covered in sticky shit, and the other looked almost as bad. I checked Danny's shoes. But he had run barefooted, so no concern there. I washed his feet in a pan of cold water and dried them real good. He was still small, not like other school boys near eight years of age. I worried over his littleness.

I felt sad and sorry for him. Hugging his narrow shoulders, I rushed him. I wanted to get him out of the house before any bad stuff happened again if Daddy awakened.

"Where's Ginny? The bus is due any time," I said. My voice shook, dry and screechy, similar to words spoken into a tin can. Danny shrugged. He looked as if he wanted to cry. I picked cockle burrs from his rusty curls, and beggar's lice and devil needles from his clothes as if it was what everybody did each morning. I assured him without petting on him much, because if I did he'd be bawling the whole school day. It didn't take much to set him off.

"Ya must be awful hungry," I told him, my voice cooing. "Stop by Granny Isabelle real quick and get a biscuit. Maybe she'll put you a little sugar in it. Don't you be pulling on her for that butter. She ain't got much to start with. And don't dilly-dally 'round. We can't miss no more school. People'll be comin' back to the house after y'all again."

His head twisted backwards, like a little chicken does; taking tiny steps, he hesitated. I pushed the air with my hands like a broom, shooing him off. Reluctantly, he went on, looking sad.

"I'll be okay, just get on. I'll be there in a few minutes. And don't be forgettin' 'bout them biscuits," I said.

Mama had already left for work at the dry cleaners. She rode with a neighbor, as always, never learning to drive for her own self. Daddy wouldn't have it. Somehow, she'd patted enough orangey makeup over her bruised eye to suit her. I flinched. She didn't. She went on tapping and patting.

She said to me, "It don't hurt that bad. Jus' go on and take care of them kids, Jessica."

Looking for Ginny, then forgetting her again, I quit hunting, not thinking clearly. I tossed a look over the kitchen sink through the window, thinking of Danny's lip trembling. Feeling old, I stared off at the lonely woods we'd hidden in during the night. I wondered if God would ever help us. I thought about the stack of letters I'd written to Him over the years. I wondered if He cared at all what went on with us.

The handle squeaked as I turned the sink faucet on. I filled the rusty, rickety-handled porcelain pot with water. It wobbled unsteadily. Frustrated with life, I said to the morning light as it peeked inside, "I hope I can get this here shoe shit off and wear them to school cause I sure can't go barefoot." I took the shoes outside to scrape the mess off with a stick. I thought of all the times I'd seen Papa Harkus scrape snot off the stove burners. Then, I just puked.

The new house had a kitchen sink and well water hooked to it. Granny Isabelle had given Daddy a lot right beside her three-room house. Our other house had burned to the ground, much like his rental houses he had built. Daddy had dug the well by hand with a bucket tied to a rope to pull dirt out. We still didn't have an inside bathroom yet, not even an outside one, but Daddy said we would soon. Two years had slipped by since he first said it, but he was building the house slowly between jobs. Mama just shrugged helplessly when I asked about the toilet again.

We all went to the woods to shit, wiping with some leaves and covering it up with more leaves, without even a spade to dig a hole for it. It seemed it was the only familiar place we knew to spend the night hiding away. Funny how in times of insecurity or fear, we ran to familiar places whether bad or good. Even bad places could feel safe in a moment of crisis.

I thought to myself, What in God's name am I living for? Do I even want to go on? I felt so drained. It just wasn't worth it. I kept fooling myself that we were gonna have a better life. But things kept staying bad. A piece of wet shit flicked onto my skirt. I cussed. Who cared if I went straight to hell? Seemed to me I was already there, it just wasn't hot like the Bible said.

I finished cleaning my shoes and went back inside, grabbed a rag, dampened it, and dabbed some baking soda on it. I rubbed it over my teeth and gums best as I could. I thought things'd be different this time. Since we'd have a real house and by the way Daddy had acted and worked so hard on it.

We'd helped him carry cinder blocks, mix mortar, and dig ditches for the foundation. None of us ever did a thing to suit him; even though he was saved, he still cussed at us some. Building the house didn't leave much time for school and homework. He wanted it finished before winter, but already it was October.

I looked at my arms, rubbing a squishy wet wash rag over them, getting the briars' crusty bloody streaks off. My mind drifted to school. How in the world could I hide these scratches from Mrs. Finch? What was I gonna tell her had happened? I guessed I'd think of something.

A stumbling noise bumped against the kitchen door, then thudded onto the floor, flop-plop, as I rinsed my soda rag out. Rancid cigarette stench reeked onto my backside as I faced the sink window. Glancing behind at the noise, I saw my sister's putrid green face gawking at me from the floor. Her blue eyes were rolled up into her head, only the whites showed, and her mouth flowed full of white, pink-tinged foam, rolling down her jaws like molten volcano lava. I knew she'd been sneaking smokes while hiding out in the woods like she usually did.

Ginny's hands twisted backwards, her fingers scissored like Uncle Rudy's boy did sometimes when he pointed at sky people. Her rigid legs, knock-kneed, drew up and down rhythmically. Falling to my knees, I screamed uncontrollably. Stale tobacco wafted into my nostrils as I held Ginny's head, protecting it.

"Dear God," I screamed. "Dear God, don't let her die. Please, dear God, don't let her die." I was frantic without a clue about what to do. She was choking to death. "She's dying. Dear God, she's dying." Wrapping my dress hem around my two fingers, I pushed and pried them into her mouth, between her clenched teeth, to keep her from choking. The pain was unbearable as she gnawed my fingers down to the bone. I didn't know what else to do. I was sure she was dying.

I shouted through the open kitchen door, "Somebody come and help me! Ginny's dying! I need help!" Granny Isabelle heard my terrified yells from her house, and then hers echoed the same as mine.

I had not given a thought to Daddy, but half-naked he came running, stumbling over broken chairs that had blocked his way. His eyes were dull, bloodshot, and bulging. Ginny thrashed about like a fish without water.

He hollered, "Ginny, my little baby, what's wrong? She's dying, I tell ya, she's dying." He was weeping. Sinking to the floor, he rubbed and patted her golden hair and babbled to the same God he had cussed without end the night before. Ginny's piss-soaked clothes, her fecal-coated panties protected her helpless, small, frail body.

I glared at him as she chomped on my fingers. I sneered, "Your baby. Your little baby. You are the one who's done killed her. You have done drove all of us crazy! You and your sorry-ass drinking and getting saved for nothing a hundred times."

An animal strength, like a lion, arose inside of me, engorging my hands, my legs, my mind. I was ready to fight him if I had too. In fact, I wanted to. I felt for a heavy object to grab hold of with my unchewed hand. I looked at the dropped butcher knife lying by my feet and grabbed the handle. I thought, Today I will fight back or die if need be. I will do it as God is my witness.

I glowered into his eyes and said, "Go on, I dare you raise your hand to me. I'll shove this knife right through your heart, you son of a bitch." He must have read the hatred in my eyes because he said not a word, nor raised a hand; he just melted down, crouching closer to Ginny's helplessness.

Granny Isabelle yelled from a distance, "I called an ambulance."

I kept going at Daddy. "Shooting the gun and wanting us all dead again. Remember last night. Remember all the times you've gotten drunk and beat the hell out of Mama and us too. Bet you don't recall the wonderful little family cookout in the backyard last night, you slobbering drunk. Poking raw chicken down your little baby Ginny's throat and her gagging to death on it. You don't, do you? Now ain't that jus' like you. You never know nothing you do, but we sure do." I kept raging like a shook-up soda pop bottle now unplugged.

"Well, just maybe your wishes are all coming true. Maybe we'll all just die for the hell of it. There sure ain't no damn reason in this sorry-ass world to live for anymore." I couldn't stop myself. "Here, let her chew on your fingers for a while. Maybe you need to see what it feels like since you care so much about your little baby girl."

He whimpered a weak sorry. A word for the moment.

"For God's sake," I said, "why didn't you go call an ambulance and get her to a doctor or was that too hard for ya? No, poor old Granny Isabelle had to. Not you. Now she's waiting up the road to show the ambulance where to come." I flat didn't care what he did. I was saying whatever came up in me. It poured out like water through a hole in a river's dam. I kept on, even as he headed out the door in his underwear toward Granny Isabelle's as if to get help. Now there I sat, mothering Ginny, a job I never signed up for since she was born. I was in charge of her, and if she lived or died it would have somehow been blamed on me because I was the oldest. Daddy never came back until the ambulance arrived, lights flashing warnings, and carried Ginny away.

45

Running for Our Lives

After Ginny went off to the hospital, I thought on the night before. I had screamed alarms that horrible night, the one before Ginny's seizure in the morning. Run. Run. Run. We fled to a known place. That's how we landed—squatted amongst stinking heaps of human shit—while rain poured down in gushes. Soaking us and the leaf-covered mounds of dung until the soppy mess was everywhere and all over everything. Danny's toes were packed full of shit, but I raked it off as best as I could with leaves and sticks. We would move from one site into another into more shit piles. Loads and piles of stinking shit. Our toilet in the woods.

Bullets zipped through the air above our heads as Daddy screamed foul names, hating us. Moist smoky trails followed our whispers. Danny's teeth chattered, but we all shivered more from fear than the cold.

I had prayed to Jesus, "Don't let us die in this shit." I tried not to look scared for my sister and brother's sake. Mama's face was stark, yet she pitied Daddy. It was as if her allegiance was always for him. It really showed in this circumstance. Or perhaps my eyes was opened.

She had stood in the yard, frozen statuesque. Daddy was yanking on one side of her as we pulled the other. He had fired the shotgun in my direction but missed. She appeared determined to assist him. Tiny sparks flew with each loud loading, the ratcheting of metal-on-metal sound squalling deadly warnings.

Immobile, Mama stood hooked to Daddy with a strange, plastered look. It seemed she pitied him more than us. Mama's conflict rang louder to me than the mighty gun blasts that evil night. Could my mother be so torn about her priorities? Did she not realize the danger we were in? Did she not see our terror? It was at that moment when Granny Isabelle's bird and crow tale came to me outta the blue. The story about how some parents couldn't get beyond their own selves enough to protect their children. It all began to make perfect sense that night. It was as if a veil had started to lift from my eyes.

213

In that instant, as those questions knifed through my mind, I noticed that Mama's paralyzed look matched her glued feet. She had legs, but they would not move. I knew without a doubt that she would have let him kill us all. That she couldn't help it. That's when I frantically pushed the kids toward the woods. I saw something in her eyes that I had never read before until that day.

He was her priority, not us. That was why, for years, we had lived with terror, poverty, and death. That was why we lived in Daddy-made boxes and why we all walked on eggshells. That was why we acted like our scars and wounds never hurt when they did. That was why I had to make the decision for us to live and for Mama to die if need be. It was up to her to choose her path.

"Run as fast as you can," I screamed, pointing the way. The kids looked back at me, doubtful and confused. "I'll be right behind you." Danny grabbed my hand like a snapping turtle that wasn't about to let go. Somehow, I shook it off.

"Run, Danny, run," I shouted. Whiteness circled his mouth as he took off with Ginny, both wailing fear. I grabbed Mama's arm, yanking harshly, and said, "Today, you choose life or death, Mama. You know he's insane. Don't you see he's gonna kill us all?" I tugged one last time and she followed.

"I'm gonna kill all of you," Daddy roared, cussing, shooting at us. He was too drunk to hit us from the distance. But the chance of us taking a stray bullet was strong.

Catching up to the kids, I heard Danny sob loudly, "Why does Daddy want to kill us?"

Mama couldn't talk or wouldn't, so I responded, "Wasn't nothing you did. He is always blaming somebody else for his problems."

Mama started pulling against me, wanting to go back to him and let us run alone. She kept looking back the whole time like the salty woman in the Bible.

"He might kill his own self," she whimpered.

"And he might kill you and us if you go back. Do ya not understand what I'm saying? Please Mama, get us out of this life. Dear God, please leave him. Someday, if not tonight, he will kill one or all of us. It's just a matter of time. I just know he will."

That's how we ended holed up together in the shit piles, waiting for death.

We waited for it but death never came. After trudging home the morning after, and after I had washed shit from our shoes and sent Danny, with trembling lips, to school, and after Mama covered her bruises, and after Ginny rode the ambulance, my realization about Mama's loyalty to Daddy never left me. The seed had been planted; the veil had been ripped.

Daddy returned home with Ginny by his side, acting as if nothing had ever happened. He told us that the doctor had said Ginny had bad nerves that had caused her fit. He marveled. It was as if he could not comprehend why Ginny had bad nerves. Not long after, Mama came home from work and scrambled eggs and pork brains for his meal while we cleaned up Daddy's broken mess.

46

Ginny
Trying to Cope

It just came outta nowhere the morning after the hospital trip, when Ginny had to go to the woods to pee. Without thinking. Without planning. She'd guessed things just happened without any kind of meaning. But it helped. Even if it didn't last long. The pain left momentarily from her broken heart into the cut.

No rhyme or reason to it. It just happened. Like an impulse. She was going to the woods anyway. Not mad over the cold weather. Not angry over nothing. Just tired and empty. Empty and tired. But she was full of the worst kind of loneliness known to the world. The deepest, darkest loneliness. She felt like she didn't belong anywhere. Not with her family. Not at the school. Nowhere.

In fact, she never had belonged. Except once or twice when she went on field trips to the hideaway with Jessie and Danny. She fit in, but only with them and only there. They were a threesome back then, but not now. Ginny recalled the stretched-out meadow full of plant life, scents of pine, and the bitter taste of early persimmons. She thought about how that bitterness tasted. If she could link her heart to a taste, it would be unripened persimmons.

Fat wooly worms came to mind, then the horrid memory of Jessie balled up. Jessie had sat cornered with piss puddles underneath her, after Daddy had beaten her so unmercifully that time. Like a snapshot it popped into view, Jessie in the corner all alone. They were smaller back then, but things remained the same. They still lived in piss puddles and shit.

Ginny was nearly twelve. Getting older hadn't help. Like last night. When Daddy decided to cook outside over a campfire. A makeshift grill from the oven rack was placed over some rocks and wood in the backyard. He'd never done that before.

"And then, outta the blue, the idea came to me," he had said. But that's how he was. He would come up with notions, espousing how much fun something might be; but then it never was fun. Or if any fun was in his grand ideas, he always ruined it. He ruined everything. But still she still loved him so much. Ginny loved him more than the rest and always came to his defense. She'd do nearly anything for him.

Her stomach shriveled as she recalled the cookout. Still, she felt the greasy, charred, raw chicken being pushed down her throat. Even now, with the memory, she gagged against what was being pushed and poked inside her cheeks, her mouth, and then down her throat. Her father was wild-eyed, frantic, forcing the unwanted on her.

She dry-heaved, retching the memories. Mama and the others had come running to help. But no one could help her. So she gagged on as her father cursed. His face was flushed red with determination. He would force her to eat. She would swallow that gooey, slimy, prickled skin and meat or he would be damned. Her face purpled. No one stopped him. No one.

Motionless, he stood with his determination fulfilled, as the blackened, remaining slimy flesh hung from her mouth. She laid limp, pale, unbreathing on the ground. At least, that was what Jessica told her the next day. Ginny would never touch another piece of meat, raw or cooked. Never.

She'd mastered the art of puking. She could puke anything, anytime. She'd take off to the side of the house and puke her guts out. That's what she called it. Stinking life guts. Hoping someday she'd just wither up and die from not eating. Maybe they would all be happy then.

She vowed death as she sucked the last drag from a stolen cigarette and squashed it dead indignantly. She reviewed the hospital details—the ambulance ride—the whole thing. She was pissed over what the doctor had said about her needing some mental attention. But then again, maybe she did. It was all about her not eating enough. About how thin and little she was. The doctor had blamed everything on her nerves and her need to have control.

"What kinda doctor was he, anyway?" Her daddy had shrieked on the ride back home. "Ain't no kid ever had bad nerves. 'Specially no kid of mine."

Mama replied, "He said she might need to talk to somebody or take some pills to help her. That's what you told me the doctor said anyhow."

"What in heaven's name does a fit have to do with a girl's nerves?" he railed. Mama's face was slapped for answering him wrong. She clammed up after that, not wanting to be hit.

Maybe that was why it started—the cutting. Now Ginny walked by the wash pan full of beard trimmings after another ambulance ride, some weeks later. Another fit had happened. She saw the double-edge razor blade, beside of her father's silver razor. A cracked coffee cup sat beside it, a shaving brush propped edgewise, sopping a sudsy Ivory bar. Soapy goo had jammed onto the sharp edge. She rubbed it off and stuck it into her sweater pocket.

A perfect place to go off by myself, Ginny thought. In the deep wooded shelter, away from it all. In the quiet circle of pines, where she could feel the pain better. Let the inside come oozing out. It started with little marks. Then bigger ones, more like slashes.

A good feeling of relief came from her gaping skin. A sweet warmth exuded from the slit. It was relief to watch blood-letting. This way she knew she was real. She alone, had control of her pain. Even if only for a little while, it was so meaningful and nobody could do a thing about it. She would eat what and when she wanted, and she would cut what and when she wanted.

After cutting, she would sit on the peat moss mounds leaning her head back onto a tree trunk, sucking cigarettes, sighing while peace engulfed her. Touching, loving, dabbing the carved lines she murmured. It was only the beginning of well-hidden slashes that would mark her scrawny thighs and upper arms. It was only the beginning.

In little streaks, the numbers and length increased as days went on; because tiny nicks began to give her less relief, size and width increased. The marks were hidden with long sleeves and pants. And Ginny went on cutting and puking as if she had no secrets to tell and nothing bad had ever happened.

47

Goodbye to Granny Isabelle

I'd quit school and married a boy named Johnnie. We were living about ten country miles away from my clan, near his family in a small apartment. I'd even gotten a job as a cashier at the food store where Granny Isabelle had bartered her onions. I'd tried to move on with my life, sorry as it was.

Then came the phone call from Daddy one day when I was working. "Your Granny Isabelle is dying," he screeched. "She's asking for you to come."

Gravel crunched, gathering grime beneath the tire treads of our car. I was reminded of the time Granny Isabelle had lifted a withered corn husk, crumpling it within her old hands back then, indicating that all things would die whether they wanted to or not. Life and death were mandated for all things.

Granny Isabelle was dying. How could she leave me now? I'd feared it so often when growing up. But had I not been the one who had left her? Had I walked away, leaving her? Never giving her so much as a thought, seemingly.

That dreaded day had come. My feet planted onto the bare dusty yard, spraying red, dirty puffs into air. Her familiar hoe stood cock-eyed against the front doorway. Off kilter. A string of crabgrass hung at its metal hub, and a moist clay clump lay beneath it, as if it had just dug the earth somewhere that very morning. Her dusty shoes sat stacked beside of the tatty implement. She was unwilling to track dirt inside. Always had been.

Dazed, I wondered, how could grass ever live in this barren red clay? Yet, Granny Isabelle had reaped crops from it. Amazingly, she had made something from nothing for as long as I could remember.

Alone, I slowly walked through the small house, fingering things. Splotchy images materialized: of Smokey, the nineteen cats, Uncle Rudy's shaving jigs, Aunt Fanny and me puffing powdery talc clouds and pissing ourselves senseless with laughter over my kernel, Aunt Lizzie's glassy frog eyes darting around searching for somebody to spy on.

Granny Isabelle's essence lingered everywhere. Visions clamored in and out of my head as I inhaled her. The old rocking chair creaking, the kerosene lamp flickering, her soft snores purring from her crinkled, toothless, musky-smelling mouth, the Bible sliding from her lap when Papa Harkus's farts blasted, angel biscuits, green onions and corn rows.

Images of her scrimmaging for cantaloupe slices and Dr. Pepper for my birthday celebration. And Jesus not coming to get her during the hurricane, as she stood shrieking with ripped stockings, wet dress, and paper hat plastered on her pitiful ancient body. And then her crying for days on end after the storm, being left behind by Jesus as I tried my best to comfort her, to no avail as we realized Jesus wasn't coming yet. Later, from neighbors' news and crackling telephone conversations, we learned it was Hurricane Hazel, showing her force.

Granny Isabelle was everywhere, in every nook and cranny. I felt, smelled, and tasted her. Her sermons invaded my thoughts, and I thanked her for each one at that moment. Those times I had learned by watching her take care of my wounds and then her caring for animals and other things bloomed into my thoughts.

Like the time she had urged me to hold Smokey's tail tight while she lathered his mange in kerosene, and her holding me still while she pulled bee stingers from my flesh, and her popping my gum abscess and pouring whiskey concoctions down my throat to keep my pain at bay.

The many times she had doctored my wounds and sewed me up— my wounds, whether physical, spiritual, or emotional, or all three mingled together—she did her level best to help me go through some imaginary needle's eye. She would patch me up and send me out again to face the world, however cruel my world was.

She taught me right from wrong, when wrong was all I saw for most parts of my growing-up days. Like the time she trotted me down to Uncle Rudy's house to beg forgiveness and start over again with a new slate. Preaching and preaching to get stuff through my thick head before she had to leave me alone. Not wanting me to let one person "tread on my back" for even a solitary second. She had found that saying in the Bible also, I supposed. She wanted me to have something better in life, and she believed in me when I didn't have a chance or an ounce of faith in myself.

Her worn paper bag hats and hoed gardens were enough to grow me up and help me become determined to go as far as life would let me. That was her hope. She'd fought Daddy's demons with appetizing food, hiding spaces for us, and common sense about protecting us during storms. Now she laid helpless, child-like, smaller, with some tatted covers pulled snug over her ribbed chest and my pillow close to her head.

Her hands closed over on top of Uncle John's little Bible. It was full of tear-smudged, crackled, dog-eared pages. A silver chain with a cross wound between her feeble fingers, and a pretty but ancient handkerchief laid tucked underneath it all, upon her breast. I wondered why she had pulled that old book out again. To be close to her beloved son, I thought.

Aunt Lizzie and I sat huddled near her bed. I held Granny Isabelle's delicate hand in mine now, mine being the larger one. Hers had securely and safely snuggled mine like a mitten on many occasions. Now it was reversed, mine being the glove. It seemed to be enough for the moment as her face relaxed in my unseen company. The semblance of a smile floated by her parched, puckered lips.

"Is that you, Jessie? It's ok, Jessie. My little angel. Get me a drop of water. I thirst so bad." She was unable to drink from the glass, so I dribbled her dehydrated mouth with drops of well water from a twisted rag. I recalled the many squabbles we'd had over sparing the water that I had so laboriously carried by myself with much grumbling; too many times she had retorted, "Life just isn't fair sometimes, Jessie, but ya have to still carry the water."

Mama was arriving as Aunt Lizzie departed. Granny Isabelle wiggled my hand as they switched sitting times. Granny and me were finally all alone for the moment.

"Jessie," she muttered.

"What, Granny Isabelle?"

"Promise me if ya forget how to peel the onions, that ya will call on me. I'll come like John came to me in my darkest hour. Jus' 'member, hold to it with both hands to pull the skin, but after the other steps are done. Then, slide the outside skin on down. It's jus' like life, my sweet lil' Jessie. It's jus' like life. Make sure ya believe in who ya are, even if nobody else ever does. And don't never let nobody ever 'tread on ya back, chile. Promise me that, Jessie."

"I promise, Granny Isabelle. I promise ya with my whole heart." I kissed her hands and forehead lightly.

"Ya special, chile. Ya favored by the Lord. Take this little bit of things I got on my chest to 'member me by. I gotta go see John soon. He's waiting on the other side. I see him clear as day. My John died on some railroad tracks way back. Just like you being my favorite grand-baby, he was my favored child. He always tried to do right and trusted Jesus. I guess sometimes God takes those outta this evil world sooner than later, to get 'em into heaven, elsewise they might not make it. I couldn't talk of him cause it hurt me all my years. But I see him now and I'm going to him on the other side. I want you to promise me you will come to me there. Always do the right thing, even when nobody's watching."

I nodded through my tears.

"I love ya, chile. Take that hoe too and use it in some gardens. The earth is close to God. It's where a body can find out who they really are."

My tears dropped onto her sheets.

"Now I need another promise from ya."

I nodded again, still sobbing.

"Ya gotta 'member everything I said about swine and pearls, and goin' through the tiny needle's eye. Ya gotta go through it, chile, and it ain't gonna be easy. It ain't even gonna be hard, but more so. It's gonna be the worse pain ever, cause ya gotta leave the family behind to go through the needle's eye. They ain't never gonna understand. They ain't never."

"How will I know about the needle's eye, Granny Isabelle?" I whispered into her ear with my head laying beside her pillow, like I had often done when we talked into the wee night about life things and stars in the sky.

"Ya will jus' know like ya ain't never knowed before. It'll be brought to yer 'tention by the Holy Spirit. But chile, nobody hardly can ever get through that needle's eye. It's nigh impossible. It'll take all the gumption ya can muster in ya weary soul. But I know with everythin' in me ya kin and will do it. Ya will go through the needle's eye. It's written in the stars by the finger of God. With Him all things is possible. I love ya, chile. Ya my precious angel. Hug the young'uns I'm leaving in ya care. Lil Danny and Ginny. God be with 'em."

I squeezed her hand. "I will. I love ya so much. More than words."

"I gotta go now, sweet thing. I'm awful tired. Awful tired. My little..." Her eyes closed to rest as her words trailed to nothing.

Mama came in and we sat together. An eerie sound came from Granny Isabelle's bed. A rustling stirred, as if huge bird wings were flapping. We ran to her side. She had not moved an inch. Great bird wings? Where did those sounds come from? It wasn't kicked covers. But she was gone now and peace filled her face.

And although she had departed, in an uncanny way, she was right there holding my hand in hers, warmed and mittened in that room. And in that moment when time stood still, a dove tapped the windowpane just beyond the ledge. Night had fallen. The dove cooed relentlessly. A song flowed into that room as if all was well, when it should not have been well. I knew doves didn't coo at night, but Granny Isabelle had told me of a different story.

Later, after Granny died, I walked down the hill toward Mama's house, having no idea about how to feel, fumbling over feelings. I had lost the most important person in my life. Granny Isabelle was gone. The sulking house was full of dead talk as some words met us at the door. My chest ached.

Chatter spurted from uncles and aunts, nephews and cousins. No tears though. Dull, emotionless air hung, gathering in pockets of cigarette smoke. A few fusses fretted here and there. Someone wanted the broken candy dish with legs. Someone wondered how it ever got broken in the first place. Clutter and trash gathered and was packed into paper bags. Free food and covered dishes from neighbors. Someone else talked of moving away somewhere else. Murmurs sniffled, then cornered somewhere quietly. Arrogance floated through the air, sounding like Daddy's cold voice.

Granny Isabelle was not mentioned much. A stone for her grave? Why not? But a man said, "Ain't no need."

And then we all went on like nothing bad had ever happened. Never to speak nor hurt nor cry over our pain with one another. We just let our feelings stay crammed down, forgetting she'd lived or left. Like it never hurt and never would.

It's what we did with the pain. Felt nothing. And never would. But I had her small book and silver chain wrapped in her tear-stained handkerchief, tucked safely underneath my pillow, where it would stay until she would come and help me put it away somewhere else. She would be with me forever because love never dies.

48

My Snake House

Though married now, Johnnie and me were both so young. Daddy offered us to stay in Granny Isabelle's house for free, so we moved back closer to my family.

"Ya in the family way?" Daddy asked, his voice holding a foreign tenderness, which was unnerving in itself. His face glanced downward as if I had no eyes to meet. My eyes dropped too, feeling shame for no known reason. Feeling small again, like that time at school when Mr. Strader accused me for what I never did.

I could tell Daddy wasn't mad at me from the tone he had used. My shoulders shrugged back like they didn't know. I had no clue what he meant as I wiped the morning's vomit from my mouth with the back of my hand. My stomach churned less as the sickness settled. I clutched the porch rail and rubbed the putrid juices from my lips on my shirtsleeve.

I turned away, feeling awkward, returning to the kitchen with nothing more to say. My gaze searched the scratched floor surface, not near finished. Convoluted, dark and light sandy sylvan splotches peered up at me in grooves. So much work to be done, I thought, feeling restless. Plans simmered in my head about how pretty I'd make the house. I smiled, thinking about my hope chest, just a single cardboard box full of trinkets and things I'd bought at the discount basement store.

Gingham curtains hung with little turquois and brown teapots on them. Olive green what-knots sat about. A little red and white checked oil tablecloth covered the repaired table Mama had given Johnnie and me—that old praying table from way back—I'd disguised it with turquois paint. Regardless of its past, it gave us a place to eat. I had thought I could cover up the soiled memories with a little paint. Granny Isabelle's kerosene lamp would center it. Like it used to sit on her table.

I couldn't shake the spooky dream. Granny Isabelle had taught me that when a dream wouldn't let you alone, take it as a caution. This dream

225

brought serpents. Snakes everywhere—all over and under the floors of the quaint house. I couldn't put my foot down safely. Poisonous vipers slithered in all directions, squirming in piles, skulking up walls. There was no escape. I hugged onto myself, tiptoeing on tiny vacant spots as I made my way through the room in terror.

The awful dream must have been because we were fixing floors. We had wanted to make them pretty and shiny. Granny Isabelle would have liked them, I reasoned.

The nightmare was foreboding. I wasn't able to rid the omen from my spirit. It haunted me as I unpacked my treasures, loving on our what-nots through my fingertips with notions of how things would be for Johnnie and me. We would be together forever, joined as one, man and wife.

I was only fifteen years old when Daddy had called me outside one morning before the school bus arrived.

Secretively, he said, "Jessica, things ain't going so good for me now. Ain't no work much, an' ya gonna have to go get a job somewhere. Ya can save a little money an' buy some things for your own self, too. I done talked to the neighbors and they said ya can ride with 'em to an' from work."

Feeling disoriented and somewhat stirred by his humble speech and our hush-hush talk, his strange closeness overpowered me. I stayed home that day and went with him to find a job. He eagerly drove me to various spots, only the two of us. I was filled suddenly with desire to please him—not realizing he was out to take every dime I earned for "the family." He would spend it for beer and cigarettes.

At that point I realized it would never be possible for me to attain my dreams of an education. Later, after working for nothing, I decided I would find some way out of the hell hole. It seemed marriage was the only option I had. College was out and Johnnie was in. I was in love from Johnnie's kisses and soft words. My mind was made up. Within the year I was a married woman. We were wedded by a JP (Justice-of-the-Peace), and we took off to start a new life.

Although Mama had never signed forms for me before, for free lunches and such, she gladly signed legal papers to let me go. Daddy stayed home, refusing to hear our vows because it was too hard on him. I barely heard his mutters, shrugging them off, thinking his words meant nothing. Yet I ached from the lack of Daddy's caring for me; but whatever was to be would be.

49

Return to Vomit

Johnnie and I had settled into Granny Isabelle's house, back to living next to my family. The one I'd left behind. The one I couldn't wait to get away from. We came back because the house was free and my family was better. At least it was what we were led to believe. It's what I told myself as well—such a small kernel of truth—but mostly Daddy had changed, from what Mama alleged. Finally, I now had some good, decent kin people.

Daddy said, "Ya Granny Isabelle's old three-room house is now yours, cause I built it with my own hands a long time back." It's true, he did build it with his own hands with help from Granny's onion money, but not without an underlying motive. I'd come to know him pretty well through my hellish years of being manipulated by him. He'd keep that house of Granny Isabelle's some way. He would. Even though her produce money had paid for it. He would still get it.

"I know that, but it ain't just your house to give away, Daddy. Its part Aunt Lizzie's too." Yet his offer sounded good—a little too good— and considering our scant earnings, we barely could pay for food. We had tried for a year to make a go of it without any outside help. I had worked long hours at the food store, while Johnnie helped Daddy for a pittance.

However, most of Johnnie's earnings was returned to Daddy on payday—frequently, charges were dreamed up by Daddy. It was his way of doing business. He said he was teaching Johnnie to be a brick mason, but Johnnie labored mostly, carrying and stacking bricks and mixing mortar in a trough with a hoe. His hands stayed full of scraped skin and blood blisters. Johnnie had taken Danny's place helping Daddy.

Daddy had figured it all out. He'd give us a place to stay rent free, and Johnnie would work for him. He came up with ways to get our money. We had to pay the whole electric bill, but Daddy had rigged his own power cord from Granny Isabelle's house to his. Johnnie's lunch would be on him, and then he'd double the price at the end of the week, taking Johnnie's paycheck.

Daddy hadn't changed at all, I reasoned. I pondered his words earlier that day when he had queried me about being in the family way. I didn't have a clue what he meant at that moment. It was as if he had rubbed my head with loving fingers—my hair roots still tingled from imagined concern and the way I wanted it to be.

We'd always moved here and there and then again back to places we'd left behind, like nomads in a desert. Granny Isabelle's house sat beside of Daddy's brick house: the same one we'd all labored so hard over when I was younger. The one where we'd run to the woods to hide from him while sitting in shit piles, with the gun blazing bullets overhead. That one.

I came back to where I had said I never would. Unbelievable. Being on the outside made things look different somehow. In a weird sense, from a distance, the family looked more normal. It seemed, since I was out of the way, Daddy's rages had calmed down. But I didn't have the whole story. Secrets still loomed at my family's core.

Detached and distracted, I didn't see Mama's bruises or hear Daddy cussing anymore. Nobody talked about his factious behavior and I didn't ask. It was as if I'd been wrong all along, that the things I had seen and heard were not nearly as bad as I'd made them out to be— maybe I had been the problem after all. Danny and Ginny were missing me. I had left them behind to fend for themselves with Mama and Daddy, and I was saddened as if my arms had been torn off. I just wanted out.

After I had married, I figured the only way to have the material things I wanted was to get educated. To go against what everybody else in the family thought was right and wanted me to do. But all systems were against me. The high school wanted no part of me because "you know too much about things," they said vaguely as I entered eleventh grade. I was very pregnant and they didn't want other children exposed to a girl their age in such a condition.

The more shunned I was by the school, the more strong-willed I became—as Granny Isabelle's words rang into my ears. She urged me to make something out of nothing. I was not to lead a feckless life like others before me. She had anticipated better of me. I pushed onward after I got married, taking high school subjects and working half days regardless of their disdain.

Granny Isabelle had expected me to believe that fabricated fable about her blind mother leaving some worn-out, coal-mining town. Her mother had left with nothing but the clothes on her back—and with nothing more than a weary mule pulling a rickety, pieced-together wagon, leading her in some supernatural way. The woman proceeded through the wilderness and forded rivers to a safe place to raise her unborn child. She determined to rear her youngster all alone without some strong arm to hold on to. She would plant and grow her own gardens. She would do something.

Granny Isabelle estimated that I would believe that her sightless mother had gone through some mystic needle's eye and reached for some luminous stars. That's what she wanted me to do as well. She said her mother had done it, and that she herself had done it somewhat. She said she had intended that I would go far beyond her. Way beyond onions and cornfields, and cold biscuits and gravy. Way beyond getting my back tramped on by some heavy feet, and way beyond throwing my precious pearls to some sorry swine who didn't believe in me in the first place. Beyond those who had called me a liar and a cheat, desiring nothing better than to trample my pearls to pieces.

And that I was not to believe every sweet-talking fellow that came along, rubbing my head, because not everybody could be trusted. I must rely on my own gut like nothing else mattered in the world.

And when everybody else, especially family, especially Mama and Daddy, turned their backs on me, I was to turn mine away and shake the very dust off my shoes and garments, just like the Good Book said to do. By God and high water, Granny swore, and she meant every word. Until breath left her body, she determined to do everything in her power to push me through that needle's eye. God Himself was going to do something great and mighty with my sorry lot in life that man had given me; and He was going to change my ashes and rags into beautiful riches. Granny was sure of it.

In my tenth grade year of high school, when my teachers belittled me, she gave me encouragement. "Ya done got to be a fine, growed-up girl now," she'd say. "Do ya think maybe it might be time to try an' go through that needle's eye?"

I giggled back then. "Like that camel did in the Bible you used to tell us about? Right, Granny Isabelle. I'm gonna just glide right through that little naked spot and reach for some few stars," I replied facetiously.

She wanted me to be more than the cards I was given and have better than I was raised in. My two big thumbs, once a source of shame, now reminded me of how similar Granny Isabelle and I were. If I had to raise onions to get a bedroom suite, then so be it. I would do it. I would put one foot in front of the other until it became a path; though somewhat dim at times, I would keep walking.

Now Daddy was treating Johnnie as he had treated me when I quit school to go to work, nickeling and diming Johnnie to death. I thought on it as I swept sawdust specks into a pile on the floor, hurrying to get ready and leave for work and for high school, which I'd pushed to get into as a student once again—the school Daddy had talked me into leaving when I was fifteen. Now I was seventeen going on eighteen. It seemed I was always cleaning floors somewhere, trying to shine the unshineable.

Knocks hit the door.

"Who is it?" I asked.

"Ya Mama," she answered faintly. She'd come to check on the floors as I was dressing to go to school. I'd go to my lonesome classes, lonely because I knew too much. And then I'd go work cashiering at the store until nine o'clock. My grades went from D's to C's, then C's to B's, proving I wasn't as dumb as a stick. Grammar was the most difficult, still messing me up at times, especially the word "ain't." It was difficult undoing what was drilled in.

That's when Aunt Lizzie drove up into the yard, raising hell with me and Mama. I couldn't believe what I saw and heard. She came inside filled with fury.

"Y'all done stole Mama's house and everything else," she rattled off, knocking some of my glassy what-nots from the table, shattering them.

"It was all empty when we came," I said in my easy voice, not to fret her worse.

"Ain't so. Who took it all then? Jus' tell me that." She had a big stick in her hand, waving and whacking the air. She started to come for me with the pole but stopped herself, with it pausing in midair. Then she went back outside.

230

She threw the stick into her car and, with the window rolled down, she left in a huff, howling, "We'll see who wins this war."

"What's she saying?" I asked Mama.

Mama stood with her mouth gaped wide because Aunt Lizzie had always liked us. "Maybe she's jus' grievin' over ya Granny Isabelle," she said.

"She's coming back to cause trouble. I have felt something bad was going to happen the whole time I've been here," I said. "That snake dream came for a reason."

"I don't think so. Dreams don't mean nothin'," Mama assured me.

"I have seen her act up before. She's like Daddy. They come from the same briar patch. Just that she's a woman," I retorted.

Mama's shoulders sagged as she drifted back to her house down the hill, wordless.

I had made a few friends at work, mostly adults. They'd look me in the eyes and brag on how smart I was to go back to school with all things against me. Daddy had gotten wind that I had an adult female friend, and he came by my job with a warning. For some odd unexplainable reason, I never had expected him to come there. I had two different worlds, demarcated by an invisible line.

Daddy didn't exist in my work world. It was a place where I forgot all about where I came from and where I'd been. I forgot my family too when at work.

Family and work were completely separated. This man, my father, wasn't supposed to be at my job. He seemed so stroppy, out of place. I wanted no part of him or Aunt Lizzie. Nothing that reminded me of my connection to pain or shame.

"Ya better watch older women like her," he said, shifty-eyed, nodding his dark curly head toward my friend. Women like her might want to get you to herself." His face flushed red. He reeked of whiskey.

My stomach knotted the way it used to when I was a child. Fear gripped me. If he acted up, I would not be able to face my friends again. My repressed hatred surfaced with a vengeance.

"She's my friend. She taught me to be a cashier, how to fix the peanuts with salt and oil at the snack bar, and how do work orders at the lipstick department," I whispered through gritted teeth. I wasn't sure of what he was insinuating.

Then, doubting myself some in the old way, I wondered if maybe something was wrong with my friend because she did invite me to her home for lunch someday. Shame cringed inside of me. I hoped no one knew who he was. Work was my respite, and now he'd come to mess it up.

Later, I arrived home dejected. I told Johnnie about Aunt Lizzie's behavior and Daddy coming to the store. We jumped into his old Chevrolet, hunting another place to live. Not knowing what else to do, burning gas, feeling desperate and used again, we drove for hours searching in the dark. I felt thankful that Johnnie's family was large and loving. His father worked hard in a factory, sometimes sixteen hours a day. He was kind to his family, a caring father—not something I could comprehend. I felt lucky to have found Johnnie, to have him attracted to me.

"We'll find something," I said.

"We're just plain stuck," he said.

I thought of the snake dream, Aunt Lizzie's anger, and Daddy's meanness.

Determined, I said, "We will find something."

Feeling sad over the unfinished floors, the fixed praying table, and the left-over, broken what-knots, but letting go at the same time, I resolved to leave. I wanted out and saw no good coming from staying stuck with my family any longer. My mouth was watering for dill pickles, salty potato chips, oatmeal cookies, and chocolate ice cream. Johnnie would see to it that I got them somehow. Johnnie would do that.

50

Ashes to Ashes

Mama, Daddy, and the rest of them took off to Mama's parents—the ones we hardly knew because Daddy had rarely allowed us to visit them. There were way too many secrets that could be told. Isolation was a strong characterization of our family. The more isolated we were, the less secrets got exposed.

Johnnie and I had stayed in the snake house until we could move. Country darkness crept in, covering everything up with a gut-wrenching loneliness. A strange loneliness comes when nothing much goes on—a disturbing quietness—after way too much bad has gone on.

Curiously, I missed Daddy, as mean as he was. How could I miss a family as messed up and bad as mine? I couldn't understand myself. Wanting them with me and wanting them gone at the same time was tugging me into pieces. A different life than the one I was reared in was paramount in my thinking. I would have to let go of Danny and Ginny. That was the hardest thing to do, leaving them behind.

An eerie weariness came on me. Not expecting anything bad. Not a pressing forewarning, just a different knowing and not knowing. Like air floating between my head and shoulders. Too thin to see, but heavy enough to consider. Nothing there, but there too. An edgy waiting for something to happen.

I took care in case a snake was hid up somewhere in the bed covers, under the dresser or elsewhere. Searching for something, maybe a snake, maybe not. A weird unsettling needled me. Bedtime didn't help my peculiar sense of nervousness. A murkiness hovered over me as I dozed, tossed, turned, and dozed again in spurts.

At midnight, another recurring dream came. My body fell headlong into a pitch-black pit, an endless falling. Mine and other screams mingled; helpless engulfment ensued. Startled and perplexed I jerked awake. I didn't die.

I never died with the falls, but the terrible reliving was powerful. Was it daytime? I wondered as my eyes open to an enormous light. It morphed about the walls, pushing every shadow away as a jittery sensation filled my stomach.

Such a short rest, I thought. Arising, I went toward the rays pouring through the window like glowing waves. My hands fumbled the thin rope cord and gathered the shade upward, like a pulled-up skirt.

I glanced through the wavy windowpanes as my husband's snores floated gently upward, cuffing my ears. My next project will be to clean these windows, I thought. My fingertips rubbed some smoke-smudged lines clear.

How could anyone not be bewitched by this great moon? I took a breath of delicious wonderment.

"Great ruler of the night, brilliant and full of shining," I whispered poetically. "Incredulous, icy white lamp of pockets, full of secrets." I'd spoken from some higher source. The words emptied from my lips as if dipped in wisdom. The moonish gleam melted me and, like a cup, I filled. My face, shoulders, arms, legs, naked feet, and belly mingled as her majesty illumined me. I prickled with a sense of destiny.

An omen came: "Something is going to happen, Jessica. Get ready. Be prepared. Remember the dreams." Taken aback, I wished for Granny Isabelle to help me understand the moon gift.

Befuddled, tired-out, and cold-footed, I padded back to bed in need of rest. Hungry for sleep.

"She knew my name," I whispered into my pillow, as if speaking into Granny Isabelle's ear. I dozed again uneasily. Granny Isabelle had always said if the moon spoke to a person, they'd be able to tell the future or prophesy some vision.

Soon, it seemed, an urgent voice awakened me. I peeped out of the window, thinking maybe another dream or vision had come. Bangs came to the door like boards jamming against it. Loud and deadly raps and rams, earsplitting like the kind I was used to from Daddy's rages; but these raps were not accusing us.

"Y'all gotta get outta there," a neighbor man screamed with the pounding.

I thought about my snake dream and the moon bath. My eyes looked off to the yard corners, sadly searching. The yard must be full of snakes, my thoughts confused. Scared to open the door, I did it anyway.

The mousy man's shadow was way too big for his shriveled-up self under the moon's glow. It laid on the porch like a flat gray ghost, as my husband and I stepped onto its chest. I became afraid for myself and Johnnie. Afraid for the possible life kicking inside of me as Daddy's words became plainer about me being in the family way.

"What's going on?" Our words vomited out in unison. Streaks of yellow and gold painted the man's old cheeks as he chattered and spattered through a toothless mouth.

"Ya daddy's house is on fire." Saliva sprayed onto my cheek as he waved a finger toward the fiery house.

Together, in disbelief and panic, we peered off. Everything was red, orange, and yellow, like a garden full of huge, bright flower blossoms. Flames littered like lightning strikes, hoops and roaring balls enlivening the land. Romping smoke rolled from the roof, licked and slurped at the tops of poplar leaves, melting them like ice cream.

Car motors sounded in the distance as fidgety flames gyrated around the brick house, like Indians doing a war dance. Crackles, pops, and shattering glass howled, while sounds much like shotguns blasts pounded the air—blam, blam, blamity, blam, blam. The house was too far gone for the small unit of volunteer firemen to begin to fight.

"Is anybody in the house?" an immense, freckle-faced man asked me.

I shook my head. "They all took off to Mama's parents' for a while." I stood, shivered and shook as my stomach searched for vomit, knowing something felt wrong. Daddy hardly ever went to visit Mama's people without wanting something. We toughed the night out, watched and waited as the fire died down.

The next day Daddy, Mama, and the kids came riding up in the car. Later, aunts and uncles clamored into Granny Isabelle's little house that Johnnie and I were fixing up. They talked big, discussing how cruel life could be, leaving Mama and Daddy helpless without offering an arm or a penny for them to lean on. That's what we were told. My parents spent the night with us in Granny Isabelle's diminutive house. I wondered how one's own kin could talk about others not helping them, as they didn't help us either. But I didn't know how much Uncle Ed had done for Daddy when the situation occurred. It was another secret.

The next day, Daddy, seemingly unworried, left to find a place to live until things worked out. Questions crisscrossed my mind as I wondered about what "things needed to be worked out." I was hurting for all of us, my siblings the most, and Mama of course.

We'd all worked hard on that house. It was the best one we'd ever had as children. Now it was a pile of smoking rubble, still belching flames from the ground. But Mama never cried a tear over the loss. She stood around empty as if it was as any other day.

That house had been more than a building, more than a home. It was all about us working and making something out of nothing, making a family. Roots, stability, security. A better life. No more moving from shack to shack.

It had real kitchen cabinets and a sink to wash dishes with clean well water. Occasionally, a new linoleum replaced the older one, after Johnson's Paste Wax quit working a shine. No more potbelly stoves. (How I despised them.) Daddy had built a central vent system to heat the entire house, stemming from a basement woodstove.

Saneness came for short intervals when Daddy would quit drinking. He had planted beautiful rose gardens all over the place, bragging to all about his green thumb.

From the exterior of the house, things looked pretty good, while the inside was deficient. No inside bathroom existed yet. Crusty paint buckets served as piss cans, and the woods served as a toilet, with papery leaves for butt-wiping. Clothes remained raggedy hand-me-downs. Furniture was fragile, stitched together. Dishes stayed cracked. Mama stayed beaten.

Still yet, Daddy would go away in the coldest winters, leaving Mama and us behind to salvage ice-laden stumps, broken tree limbs, or whatever to stay warm, with little more than a few pinto beans, Irish potatoes, and cornmeal for food.

That house wasn't perfect by any means. It was where my body had changed from girl to woman. I had my first period, grew breasts, had my first kiss, and came to know my first love, Johnnie, in that house. It was where I stood up to Daddy as Ginny gnawed my fingers to the bone, and the last time I hated her for not helping me do housework. That house held the beginning of my real self, and it was the last time I pissed my britches from fear under Daddy's despotic regime; because my eyes had been unveiled and I had grown up enough to fight back, or so I thought.

51

Fork in the Road

Mama and Daddy, along with the others, moved further into the mountains. Johnnie and I stayed behind, dwelling in Granny's small snake house. My family's charred home sat flattened and heaped in places like begrimed graves filled with dead men's bones.

Blackened two-by-fours stuck from the ground like twisted crosses, as smaller ones crisscrossed and daggered skyward and sideways. We knew not which way to turn, nor where to go from that point in our lives. A baby kicked inside of me, as I looked on at what was left of my burnt, tattered past.

I was checked out by a nearby family doctor, who had delivered me when I was born, to be evaluated for persistent nausea.

"We don't know what's goin' on, exactly. But Daddy says I'm in the family way."

The doctor snickered.

"I came on here to make sure."

"Well, far as I can tell you gonna have a baby," he replied.

"How could such a thing happen?" I questioned.

"Let's just say if you keep your legs crossed, it won't," he joked. I looked at him, puzzled. No one ever told me anything. I had only learned of ovaries and bloody underwear in the high school physical education class—not about sperm, sex, and babies. Finding out I really was pregnant made me miss my family.

I was jealous that my parents left Johnnie and me behind and purchased a big, beautiful home with nice furniture. We'd never had new furniture growing up. I was envious of my siblings, who appeared to have a better life than I'd ever known.

My family had purchased the big white house on a farm with the burned home's insurance money. Daddy had also bought a red tractor similar to the one Uncle Rudy had at one time. He had added a huge creek-fed pond and planted gardens that were filled with enormous red tomatoes, silver queen corn, long snap beans, and tons of yellow squash and cucumbers. Roses occupied outside flower gardens, flooding the lawn with beauty.

He and Mama would pack the harvested vegetables into cardboard boxes. He'd go sell the garden produce downtown, in store parking lots. He'd leave Mama behind with his much-admired brown Chihuahua pooch to care for, along with Danny and Ginny. Sometimes he made Danny go with him. Danny never wanted to go. He had no choice.

But some things remained unchanged. Mama alone worked, slaving in the large, cold, somber white house, as well as in acres of vegetable fields, hoeing and picking and gathering things that mostly ended up rotting. Daddy was still drinking long and strong. He was happier than ever. Mama was sadder than ever. Emaciated now, her beautiful front teeth had decayed, and her eyes had hollowed out like someone who endured a concentration camp.

Half lit from alcohol, Daddy often rallied fistfights with anyone who looked at him wrong. Especially, he fought other farmers hawking their wares close to his new truck, which was another thing he had purchased out of the insurance money. After tangling with the law for a while, and after the fights would end, he'd shut up and calm down until he got home. Then Mama received his leftover rage.

52

Johnnie and Me

Johnnie and I left Granny Isabelle's little home, the floors and our dreams undone because of Aunt Lizze's previous behavior and because we'd been left behind. Johnnie had found a house nearby, for twenty-five dollars a month, with an outside toilet. I kept our little home spick-an-span, even the toilet. Everything was scoured, bleach scented, like Aunt Fanny's house used to be. I'd scrub on it for hours, set on making it a nice place for us.

I nested, wanting things to stay the same forever. The nursery, a tiny space, was ready with recycled clean baby hand-me-downs. I was tickled over the life wrestling inside me, ready and waiting for it to be born. I longed to see its smile and touch its tiny hand. Joy bubbled in me as I could hardly wait.

But Johnnie had started to grow restless and preoccupied. It seemed I wasn't enough for him anymore; even though it hadn't seemed like a long time to me, almost two years had passed. He'd come home from his gas-pumping job sometimes smelling of beer, and other times he'd just stay away for days. Yet to me, he was my one and only true love and would always be.

Our precious little girl, Lisa, was born with the six-month colic. She cried day and night. So did I, as I felt scared, intimidated, and helpless—a terrible mother. Even the prescribed paregoric didn't help her pain. Carnation milk wasn't cheap, and I'd stretch it, sometimes adding Pablum. I didn't know one iota what the heck I was doing but did as best I could regardless.

I turned to my neighbor, Peggy, for help. I had walked the floors day and night, crying with Lisa. Precious Lisa survived my ignorance, and, as she turned eighteen months, our lively baby boy, Tommy, was being weighed on the same old doctor's scales.

By then, Johnnie had had enough parenting. He was never physically abusive. Just very young and self-centered. Often he left the three of us for long stretches of time. I'd plead with him to stay for the children's sake, but to no avail. With no one to call on except my messed-up family, I felt resolved when Daddy showed up to move us in with him. I packed what I could, my heart piercing with pain over being abandoned by Johnnie. My numb mind was rattled by a familiar fear as Daddy's beer-laden breath wafted into my nostrils and we headed toward the farm.

My little ones and I stayed in a cold bedroom on the north side of Mama and Daddy's mammoth white house. Meagerly fed fireplaces lent dabs of warmth at scarce times. I felt as if ghosts lived there with us. I guess in many ways they did. The winter was punitive and desolate, as hateful and empty as the heart inside of my chest seemed.

All I wanted was for Johnnie to come back and do right by us. I longed for him day and night. Working third shift at the textile cotton mill, and staying with my parents, twisted gutted knots into my stomach as continuous worry fraught my sorry life. Zombie-like, I became. I existed dog-tired, watching the babies when Mama didn't, going to and from work. Drained, barely managing, I did the best I could to hold on to a textile weaving job and watch my children the other hours. Just barely managing as the weeks dragged by. I felt I was a horrible mother, doing nothing right.

Three months later, Johnnie showed up, driving a sparkling two-tone, blue and white '57 Chevrolet, smiling like a goffer, acting like nothing bad had ever happened. He stood out like a sore thumb, decked in a teal green bell-bottom polyester suit, with a hippy, self-permed, afro-looking hairdo. He showered me with words of love, adoration, and insignificant tokens; and he was looking so good to my weary eyes.

Parcel in hand, he presented me with a big white leather family Bible, etched in real gold. He knew I held Granny Isabelle's beliefs about God and the Bible.

"I won it through a drawing raffle," he said. "We can write all our names in here and keep it to pass on."

I took him at his word, but with some reservation lurking. Good thing, because later on, I realized he'd gotten it on credit and had lied to me. We barely had baby milk and cloth diapers. The last thing we needed was an extravagant Bible. If only I had listened to what Granny Isabelle had taught me about not letting people walk on my back. But Johnnie could walk on my back any time.

Months later, one Friday evening, he drove up the driveway with a fake inspection sticker pasted on the car's front windshield, just like my father. Earlier, we had asked Daddy for a little piece of land, for us to build a house on. Daddy, not wanting to give nothing to nobody, not even us, got drunk instead and raised hell that day.

As nighttime was approaching, Daddy had pinned Johnnie to the ground. My husband was on his bent knees in the yard with a loaded shotgun pointed at his head. Johnnie was crying and begging Daddy for his life. Daddy was angry over him leaving me all alone with two babies, but he had never said that to me before. How ironic, I thought. I knew he had done the same thing with us a hundred times as we grew up. I ran to the phone and called the sheriff's department to save Johnnie. I knew time had run out for Johnnie possibly, but maybe I could save our kids.

With baby Lisa on one hip, and baby Tommy on the other, we took off running for our lives. I screamed for Mama and Ginny and Danny as we scampered across the hardtop road. Mama lagged behind, worrying over Daddy, not caring for Johnnie's welfare, nor ours, it seemed. I forced one baby into her arms, while yanking on her to help carry my load, and led her toward the woods into the darkness of some tangled path beyond, as the sun lowered downward.

Glancing behind us, I saw Daddy's red rose garden darkening, ebbing away as night overpowered us. The big house was lit up like a shrine. I thought it was just that. A reliquary, honoring ghosts of our past long gone by. I marveled at how that large, kept house looked like a perfect home, yet it harbored death and ghosts. It contained no inside valuables. It housed evil and not much else. I hoped to never see it again, nor Daddy.

We ran haphazardly through the blackberry briars and brambles, tripping over rotten limbs, falling into the darkness—just like old times—we knotted together like a linked chain. Gunshots rang after us repeatedly, but we kept going, hoping to find shelter somewhere. I prayed to the Lord Jesus, and He helped us in our darkest hour. And He did just like Granny Isabelle said He would. We were not murdered. All the while I wondered would Johnnie survive.

53

Mama Talked

Johnnie did live, unharmed physically. The sheriff had made it in the nick of time. He found us at a neighbor's house and brought Johnnie to me, holding our family Bible. Mama had escaped with us by her side, as she resolved to make things right while Daddy was locked up in jail. Mama left Daddy, and we grew closer in time. Welcomed by Mama's parents, we settled in temporarily, and one day she shared a horrible secret with me.

"Jessie, I think ya need to know what really happened that night the house burned to the ground. Plus, I wanna get it off of my chest so I don't hafta carry it no more. It was cold 'nough for a fire that night that it burned. Ya Daddy's drinking was bad. Real bad. I kept it hid for the most parts. The beatings too. You was fixin' Isabelle's little house so pretty, working good an' going to school with a lot on ya mind, a baby was probably coming an' all. Not minding much of what was going on down to the hill. An' I didn't wanna spoil things for ya.

"Your Daddy was in such a fit that time. It was no reasoning with him. Sometimes I could get through an' get him back on track. But his mind was set. 'Ya gonna do exactly as I say,' he yelled.

"'I can't do what ya asking me to James,' I screamed back. I'd seen him act crazy many a time, but this was worse than ever.

"'I ain't asking ya to do nothing,' he exploded. 'I'm telling ya 'xactly what ya gonna do.'

"'Ya can kill me if ya want. I ain't never gonna do it,' I said back. Never speakin' this way before to him. 'I don't care none if I die anymore. Jus' let things be what it is. Even if you kill me. It won't matter none,' I told him."

"What'd he do then?" I asked.

"So he leaves on out an' walks on off to the other room. I was thinking maybe he might let things go. But he didn't. He comes back as I'm up making some biscuits an' fried apples for his supper. The pressure he put on me was unbearable. Standing over me. Hounding me. Cussing. Later he knocked me down the basement steps, stomping me with his heavy shoes, biscuit dough still sticking on my hands," she said, drawing a familiar picture for me.

"'Ya coming with me,' he said with the shotgun in his hand. He had ripped my blouse off and slapped on my face a few times, flat-handed, not his fist, trying not to make bad marks. Wanting to take off to my mama's house later on. Then he dragged me down into the basement by my hair next to the wood heater.

"'Ball up them pieces of paper an' set that kindling around like I told ya to do last night,' he said, motioning around the stove with the gun barrel.

"'I ain't doing it,' I told him, rubbing, rolling dough off my fingers like little white worms onto the floor.

"'Ya' ain't doing what?' he mocked.

"'If ya want it to be done, ya can do it ya'self,' I said, but was scared to death. Not much caring if I lived no more but knowing the need to go on for them kids' sake.

"'Let me tell ya how this is gonna go down,' he said. 'You an' them kids upstairs are gonna burn to hell, if I have to do it. Ain't nobody gonna get out of this but me. So ya decide how ya want it to end. Ya biggity bitch.'

"'It's craziness,' I told him.

"'Ya calling me crazy,' he screamed.

"'I didn't say ya was crazy. Setting the house on fire is crazy. We done worked hard on this place. Now ya want to destroy what we tried to build.' I did what I could to soothe him. His eyes glazed over so I knew it weren't much use gettin' through him.

"'Don't ya 'member nothin' I told ya last night. We gonna take the money and get away from here. Ya gonna get some new furniture an' me a tractor to farm with. Are ya so dumb ya can't see what I got planned? Maybe even get us a Cadillac,' he said.

"I'd heard it all before. His grand ideas. The words meant nothing to me.

"'Don't ya know ya can go to prison? 'Sides, ya done moved John-nie and Jessie off down here to help you. Who ya gonna use when he ain't around to?' I said to help him see what might happen.

"'I ain't gonna go to no prison. Them firemen ain't gonna know nothin'. They gonna think this here stove got out of control,' he said, having an answer for everything.

"'Don't ya know they can figure things out. They got their ways,' I reminded him.

"'Ya gonna do what I tell ya or ya gonna watch them kids die,' he exclaimed.

"'But them kids ain't done nothing wrong,' I said to him."

Talking to me, she asked, "Don't ya see there weren't no way out for me. He'd kill 'em an' me. I knew he would."

"I think you are right, Mama. He would have," I assured her.

"I shoulda smothered all of y'all to death when you was babies. You'd been better off than the life we gave ya." With a guilty look, she shook her head.

"Did ya know I almost did you? I almost smothered you. Ya Daddy pulled ya arm outta it's socket grabbin' and getting' ya from my arms, said he was gonna take ya riding in the car with him drunk. I weren't thinking right. My mind was half-gone from him beatin' on me all the time," she confessed.

I looked at her, stunned.

"I thought maybe he'd change when a little child came into the world, but he just got worse. That night, your little arm hurt in the worse way. I couldn't help the pain. The bed was soaked, cause all your raggedy old diapers were wet and dirty an' me no way to wash 'em. So, I picked ya up and put ya in my dry spot while I laid in the wetness. You was a crying so hard for want of milk and that arm hurtin' so bad. You'd say, 'Dadley bring the bilk on.' Ya couldn't say Daddy or milk.

"The thought came on me to jus' smother ya easy when ya dozed off. I wanted to get ya outta the mess. I couldn't see no hope with James crazy. He was mad from the crying, an' the sheets being pissed on, an' him wanting sex, all at once. I don't know what kept me from it. But ya still here." She smiled half-heartedly as if she'd done me a favor or some good had come out of it all.

"So what happened in the basement?" I asked Mama. "Go on," I said, moving on, not wanting to think of my own mama wanting me dead for my own welfare.

"He cocked the shotgun and laid it on my head just like he did Johnnie back there. I knew he wouldn't back down. He never had and

244

never would. Visions of the kids' dead bodies kept coming to me. So, I did what I had to.

"I twisted the papers an' strewed kindling an' lit the fire with that dried flour on my hands." She wiped her hands on her dress as if flour still covered them as she told the story and said, "Then we rushed to my folks while things happened. Ya know what the hardest part was?"

"No, what?" I asked. Thinking maybe it was worry over me being left behind to see the house burn.

"Pretending everything was okay with my folks while everything we had was being destroyed by fire. All that hard work for nothing."

The thought came to me. It should have been the easiest thing to do. She'd been doing that ever since I could remember. Us too. We'd learned how to keep secrets. How to look okay on the outside while a rotten stench lived on the inside of our home. We had learned that jealousy was a good thing. That if a man was jealous, he really loved you.

I said, "I can't say I'm totally shocked by what you shared, Mama. I knew something was off kilter when the house burned. Daddy had not been upset but was high on life for some reason. I just didn't know what. The following weeks the puzzle pieces didn't seem to fit. The night of the fire was horrifying, but mostly I'd suffered a broken heart over your loss. Y'all had nothing. That was the worst. I'd already learned to live with the terror."

After the fire, Mama had carried on like things were normal for them again. But they weren't. They never were. I figured Daddy had burned the other houses he had built for money. That it wasn't his first. And that was the real reason none of the relatives had lent him a hand. Perhaps they had sensed what he had done. But from that point forward I never understood Mama's reasons for staying with him. They never calculated. She had wasted her own precious life and ours.

Across the railroad tracks, on the other side, where nobody else wanted to live. That's where Mama and the others ended up, after running for their dear lives that night at the farm. Mama, Ginny, and Danny. Johnnie and I had found a small house near them. This time Mama left Daddy to stay gone for good, she declared. But most likely it was too late for us to have a normal life.

Perhaps way too late. Daddy had made his mark on all our hearts when we were growing up. His heavy thumb had held us captive and pressed his hopelessness into our minds.

All of Mama's kids were now high school dropouts. No reason to keep going. Too hard to fight what was against us. Even after Mama had left him, enormous fear of Daddy loomed in our minds. The horror had been imprinted.

Mama was hired at a veneer plant near the railroad tracks, making paneling boards. Ginny worked at a little café down Market Street, walking to and fro to get there. Danny, in Daddy's shoes, laid brick as he got older—the only thing he was raised to do. Danny laid brick, his back crooked up, hands and feet curled cramping, his lungs filling up with mortar dust. Each of us were shackled to our own demons that Daddy left behind. Shackled to his familial legacy. When you grow up with demons, they follow you everywhere, sticking hard and fast, nearly impossible to get rid of. There was no way to have a relationship with Daddy. He offered nothing but pain and turmoil. Mama vowed to never go back to him. But Ginny determined a different way to loosen the devil's grip during her adolescence.

54

What Ginny Did

A pretty little thing, Ginny was. A pretty girl she grew to be. A beautiful woman. A head of blond curls and a face full of blue eyes. Empty blue eyes. Small hands and feet. Frail feet that had a hard time moving forward, mostly stuck; stuck in futility.

It was a mess from the start. Her life was. Just like mine. She left a trail of scratched scars and brokenness, toddling behind other people unwittingly as she tried to make a go of her life. For a while she determined to go in a different direction from the family unit. It never worked out for her, even doing her best; it never worked.

Everything went against her. As if the walls were way too high to climb over and far too wide to go around. Ginny wanted better. She'd stretch herself outward and then spring right back to her beginnings, as if hooked onto a rubber band.

But she clung to difficult things. Glued to glitches, like lichen on a tree. In hard times, hard places, Ginny thrived, but forever wavering between things indecisively. Taking for the most part, without much left over to give to anyone else. Then, when nothing worked, she settled for life's crumbs, not asking for much more.

"Just a good meal once in a while's 'nough to keep me happy, as happy as I'll ever be. Jus' a good meal," she'd say. I had heard her say it a thousand times, and thought it was probably all she would ever have. So often Granny Isabelle had told us, people speak things into being, and it made sense to me.

But Ginny, a girl in her teens, thought life was worthless. Proof being over the countless times she had tried to cut her wrists or take pills; she had tried to leave the pain behind, but it followed her like it did the rest of us. Then again, used razors never would cut deep enough to take her breath away. And a few pills at a time only did the job halfway.

She drew lots of attention the times she tried to end her life, though. Especially empathy from Mama. Mama's true feelings emoted

247

then. Fear brought Mama's feelings out for Ginny, I guess, when nothing else could. Fear in its purest form, over losing her prized child, Ginny. It brought out her maternal side.

Special, to Ginny, had another meaning. It meant not having responsibility. It meant being waited on hand and foot by Mama. "Ginny was sickly," Mama would say. Doing only what she wanted, not much more was exactly what Ginny wanted, and Mama was so predictable to rescue.

Ginny also had a difficult time problem-solving. We all did. But Ginny didn't have to solve her problems, cause Mama always liberated her. Ginny's world was stark black or white—no shades of gray. She saw things just like Daddy did.

Insecure, unsure, she groped Mama's dress hem, holding fast, never ranging far from the breast. She never knew that she could walk alone or have friends. She never knew those things.

That raw chicken Daddy had shoved down her throat choked her life forever. She never ate a piece of meat again, of no kind. But Ginny never connected the dots. What Daddy did to her, she blanked it out. Childhood trauma left her emaciated and pitiful. She grew older, unwilling to face the truth about things becoming more infantile, waiting to be coaxed to eat by someone else, usually Mama.

Walking to and from work every day was a new thing for Ginny. It seemed to the rest of us that she was trying to better her life. Then things came to light when she was carried off to the hospital by Mama in awful belly pain. All of us were afraid for her life again, but not from razor blades or pills.

Mama called me at our house from the hospital, whispering. I could hardly make the whispered words out. Then her shame came through the phone.

"Jessica, Ginny done had a baby. A baby girl."

"What?" I said, perplexed.

"She had a baby girl."

Silence cracked through the phone line like static. I stood full of shock, speechless. Mama couldn't speak either.

"She can't have a baby. Her belly isn't big," I told her.

"Well, she did. She's done hid it from us all. She wore a girdle to keep the swellin' down. That's how come we didn't know nothin'."

"What are y'all gonna do with a baby? You can't feed your own selves, much less a baby. Where's she gonna keep it?" I asked, bewildered. Things started to make sense. Ginny's sudden interest in work and her trying to save some money but couldn't.

Mama whispered some more, "It might not live. Its head's too little. Teacup size and she don't weigh much over one and half pounds. I guess we'll figure somehow what to do. I can't be puttin' it all on my own mom and pop. They done had 'nough to deal with from helping us get away from your daddy."

Mama added, "I shoulda' knowed when I didn't see no bloody Kotex laying around. But I jus' didn't give things no thought." The shock turned to reason. "We gonna hafta figure things out somehow." She sighed as a new heavy weariness sunk into her bones.

"Have you seen Daddy or heard from him any?" I asked.

"I seen him ride by the tracks a few times with some redheaded woman. I swear it looked jus' like ya Aunt Fanny. But it ain't botherin' me none. He always was a mighty fine-looking man. Always has been. Guess he's better off with somebody else." I could hear her missing him through the phone. I wondered when she would go back to him, like I'd gone back to Johnnie time and again.

55

Ginny
The Abyss

After the birth of her child, Ginny withdrew more than ever. It was another cold night, the coldest of times this season. Ginny poked another stick of wood into the stove, stoking it quietly. Sparks flew out, telling her the fire was alive, although the room had cooled down considerably. Too cool for a small baby. The train's whistle squealed louder than the yelps of her hungry infant. Ginny walked over to her, exhausted from months of worry over her premature infant, a fatherless being, touching her gently.

How would she ever raise her? Where would she get the money for diapers, milk, and doctor bills? Much less all the rest. Already her breast milk had been dried up purposefully. Nurses had poked pills into her mouth when she was too tired or drugged to resist. Pills "to take care of it," the doctor said, without even asking what her plans were. Besides, it was frowned on to use anything other than canned milk. It was progress, the new age.

Her bare feet padded off to the kitchen to search for the last can of Carnation. She watched steam lift off the boiling water pot, added milk, and poured it into the bottle with a spoonful of amber Karo syrup as she had seen Jessie do with her babies. Karo was to help the little thing's persistent jaundice. The nurse had assured her it would help. It made the baby poop a lot of yellow slime. The more poop, the more diapers. The more diapers, the more detergent and water.

And it went on like that, expenses adding up without a supply of money. The kind nurse had slipped some extra bottles of formula from the office supply into the paper bag on the way out; but that was three months ago. She needed bigger bottles, more nipples, and more milk. More strength. More money. More something or another. Granny Isabelle would have told her to ask for help from the Lord. But she was

250

through with all that. This last heartache, being abandoned by the baby's father, had unraveled her faith, if she'd had any to start with (never mind her father's abandonment).

The realization that this was one problem no one could solve hit home like a bomb in her chest as she reviewed her priority list. Should she take her darling to an orphanage or adopt her out? How would she take care of someone else? Ginny could hardly take care of her own self.

The panic attacks had increased. The cutting had as well. She could hardly go outside of the house without losing her breath, her heart pounding clear out of her chest, her legs not holding her up well. People would be talking when they found out. Family more so. She had already heard the whispers behind her back.

She went back to the dresser drawer the child was sleeping in, rolled the tiny pinkish blanket down, and lifted her up, nuzzling her close. She looks just like her father, Ginny thought as she rubbed the feathery black hair and chipmunk cheeks. A baby would love her forever. That's what she wanted—to be loved.

Just to be loved. She wanted the baby's daddy, too. But he was long gone. God, how she missed him. He had told her he was leaving his wife. Why would he tell her such lies? She thought they would be married soon. But it seemed he couldn't get away from her fast enough after she told him she'd missed her period. He was gone like a light. So gone. He never loved her. Not for a second. Maybe that was what Granny Isabelle meant about casting your pearls before swine. Her heart sure felt trampled on.

She fed the extra-diluted milk to the infant and burped her—no doubt—as it was, she had stretched the formula again. Softly she tucked the baby back into the drawer, on her side. A tiny smile crossed her face, then her eyes shut. Or was it gas or a real smile? It seemed to be a smile of relief.

She bent over, fetched her socks and shoes from the corner, and took hold of her mama's heavy work coat. Mama would give the baby a good name—one she'd be proud of, she reasoned. After she pulled the big coat over her thin shoulders, she steadied herself. Her strength was depleted. Peeking through the door, she checked on her mother and Danny as she tucked her Lucky Strikes and matchbook into the coat pocket. It looked like all was well. They were sound asleep.

The doorknob squeaked as usual, mouse-like as it turned. It probably needed oiling, she assumed, but there was no oil. There was no oil and no milk, but misery abounded. Misery grew and lived, robust with its filthy tentacles strangulating everything good in sight. The train had passed by thirty minutes prior and the midnight one was due. The tracks rattled noisily further down the roadside as its whistle sounded shrill. She'd been told, by her mama, that it was the very same tracks her Uncle John, many years ago, had been killed on. Funny how things come around full circle, she mused. She had it all figured out. The baby wouldn't wake any time soon, being full and familiarized to the train noise by now. She should sleep a good while. At least two hours or so.

As Ginny left the door, she whispered, "I love ya, little girl. Sorry, I jus' couldn't give ya a name."

Outside, she sucked on a few cigarettes, inhaling down to the nub, and then squashed some tobacco remains into the small gravels underneath the toe of her right shoe. The moon glowed down the way, staring hard and fast at her; sticking her feet heavy to the ground, she walked unwavering. I have to do this for my baby, she whispered to the wind, the moon, and herself.

Pulling the heavy jacket off, she felt to see if the note was still pocketed. She folded the garment neatly into a square by the outside rail, about two feet away. Tremors channeled under her feet, jiggling the colossal bulk of rails.

She shook her shoulders from shivering, as if to free herself from some abysmal secret bondage, and breathed the night's icy air deep into her lungs. Giggles spewed from her dry tobacco-stained mouth as she stepped into the moon's path, headlighting the tracks. And Ginny went away, cut into pieces, never to worry again. She was gone.

That night Ginny's baby died from the coldness. That was everyone's guess. The embers even went out long before daylight. Some said maybe even at midnight she died. Ginny's mother called Jessie at her house to come help. She'd whispered into the phone.

"Little Ginny's gone. She's done been kilt by the train. Jessie, come help me. I can't do this by myself. Her baby's just froze to death, too, I believe."

Jessie called for the hearse. Together, with Danny, they buried the nameless baby with Ginny's scarce remains in an old cemetery lot near Granny Isabelle's, that grave also left without a headstone.

They tried to go on like nothing horrible had ever happened. The left-behind family did try. As if it had not hurt and never would hurt. But it did. It just did, and all was not well. It was a pain of such gravity that it could not be identified nor verbalized. The night after the burial, as Jessie tried to sleep, years of tears doused her face unceasingly. It was as if a dam had burst. There was no solace to be found.

A strange phenomenon occurred; the pillow beside of hers had indented, forming a head shape without a body. Little familiar musky puffs exuded like breaths into her face. Urgent window taps resonated and then a dove cooed, and a whip-poor-will came to call. Jessie's pain was unendurable, and there were no words available. But kind words were spoken as she pulled Granny's little book from the pillow's underside. Through a supernatural urging, she quietly released some damaged lettered pages to the very end. Not the written page, but the page that held the binding.

Scribbled in childish handwriting was, "In ya darkes' hour He will come help you thru it." It was Granny Isabelle's lettering. Then something gathered Jessie's hand, cupping it ever so softly, gently, as an almost indiscernible murmur said, "I'll never leave you, love lives forever." A comfort and peace filled all her empty spaces up, like a cup fills with water, and Jessie slept. The next day, a strength came over her and urged her through the emotional brambles Ginny had left behind.

56

My Abyss

I was alone. Loneliness clutched at my heart. It seemed everyone I loved had abandoned me. I was so afraid. Fear squeezed heartbeats into my ears. Thumping, thumping, and thumping.

I wondered, "Will it just stop beating?" The aloneness was heavy and real. I waited, still and quiet. Eerily soundless. Distant voices mumbled, somewhere in the vast unknown. My toes inched back from the rocky edge. An unseen force dragged them back toward the rocky cliff, ungluing my feet. My eyes squinted, searching for the other side, a far-reaching place beyond.

"It's at least a mile," I whispered as if someone somewhere was listening. "Where is everybody?" I was alone. So very alone, unmoving, entrenched on the edge.

A distanced trumpet blew the ending of something, a journey, perhaps. I realized its meaning. Instinctively, I was aware that this road had been traveled before I set foot on it. Everyone I'd left behind would come here too. I just knew it.

"Is this a test? Is it a dream?" I whispered, muddled. "Where did I come from? Where am I to go from here?" Ruefully, I spoke.

"This is the true unknown."

My soul blinked. Something had indeed spoken.

The edge, opposite of my feet, screamed sheer impossibility. Unreachable! There was no help. I looked for an out.

"I must go back. I must go home," I begged loudly, feeling like Dorothy in Oz's poppy patch.

An odd awareness permeated my being. The problem was, this was the end of the line! There would be no turning back. I would leap, like everyone else did and would.

Perhaps I could bargain or come back later, I articulated in my mind. My foggy thoughts had shades of realization. Everyone passes over the gulf or falls into the abyss.

We, meaning all humans, must stand alone, on this very precipice, toes inched onto the edge, looking behind, straining forward, and peering down into the throat of hell. The black abyss, where past decisions and consequences are displayed in motions and shadows of what was.

The chasm was unyielding, uncompromising. I stood toe-gripping, listening and waiting for my fate. Phantom beings fought to free themselves from the dark pit's invisible grip. Explosive, verbal haunts of fallen veterans reached my hypersensitive ears. My nostrils filled with rancid smells of never-ending death.

Shrills, lamenting wails, pierced my eardrums, begging for mercy. Abandoned, exploding utter terror, pain seeping from the endless pit, agonies beyond my comprehension. Creatures called to me from the dark canyon, as tumbling and falling eternally they twirled helpless. Some faint beings whispered weakly, thirsting for a drop of water. Just one drop, they whimpered, chanting. Others recited evil repulsive praise, peering beyond their corner-less world. Stronger ones howled like lonely animals, as starving beasts.

The tangible yearning, inconsolable, shrouded grotesque beasts. Depths were submergible, gripping, and powerful. Between the gulf's edges was pitch darkness, such that human eyes had never seen.

The thick, smoky color fell downward weeping, interminable. I sensed the need to gather blackness into my hands, cup it and hold it. Rather, it was illusive, changing constantly, misty, clinging, and cloud-like, draping itself.

My face was uplifted. Whiteness beckoned me come to Him. Tentatively, my hand drifted toward His. His fiery eyes rested solidly on me. Then, telepathically, he encouraged me. He was the man who had pushed me on the swing and loved on me in that long-ago dream.

"Come on, you can do this. You can make it. One must know that one can. Only faith can bridge this gulf. You can't do it on your own. You need my help."

"But it is too wide," I replied with great hesitation. "I can't do this by myself." I pointed downward, doubting. "The chasm is too wide. It is too deep, too wide, too dark, too terrifying. Impossible."

He gently fixed my eyes directly onto His. I felt His awesome love beat into my chest. He said, "Nothing, no, not anything can separate you from Me. Not height, depth, width, nor darkness can separate us.

Not now, not ever. I am your true friend and guide." He reached for my hands and I leapt. Faith crossed me to the other side.

Faith was the key to crossing the abyss. One must know who one's friend is before going to the other side. I awakened, feeling troubled.

Johnnie had disappeared again. Finding lodging for myself and two kids had been difficult. Making rent was hard. Eating welfare food was worse, degrading. Seeing Mama and Danny in their miseries was difficult. "Somehow, I will get by," I declared. "I will provide for my children. I will survive without Johnnie."

There were times, while standing in my vegetable garden, I would feel delight as my children's small hands slipped into mine, snug like gloves. We'd stand in the tall straw grass looking over the horizon as the big orange sun would melt down and pull a quilt of muted purples, reds, and yellows over its head at day's end.

I'd mimic Granny Isabelle to them. "Y'all can do whatever you want to with your lives if you got the gumption to reach for the stars and go through the needle's eye." Their little heads, covered with molded paper bag hats, would nod yes, weary of my preaching, like I did with Granny Isabelle.

I knew I would have some awful hard rows to hoe. But Granny Isabelle had told me many years ago that I might not have to dig hard in life, that she'd done softened up the earth for me.

Squinting my eye sideways, like Granny Isabelle had done to me, I'd rattle on, urging them when a life-point was being made. I'd check to see if they had taken my wisdom in. They would draw in the dirt with sticks, moving rocks around, looking at my face, saying yes with nodding heads just like I had way back when. I had hoped to soften the rows for them a little more than Granny Isabelle had done before me, wanting better for them in the worst way.

I said, "I love you babies as far as the rainbow stretches from one end of the earth to the other. As big as a sun full of gold. I will always be with you, even when I'm not around. I will always love you. My darlings. My sweet darlings. Don't ever forget it. Like my Granny Isabelle loved me, I love you more than you will ever know. And love never dies; it lasts forever."

Regardless, I knew life was going to be tougher for them to stay the course than to choose the easier one. Granny Isabelle said back years ago, "No matter how hard Jesus pushes to get us through bad times in life, all the pushing in the world won't make a speck of difference if we don't do our part."

57

Plastic Smiles, Plastic Faces

As I grew older, I found I could easily and instinctively spy people's plastic smiles. They were everywhere. Because of my childhood and eventually the psychology background I acquired at college in spite of many hardships, I could detect powerhouses of hidden emotions underneath protected exterior fronts of other people. I knew fake when I saw it, even my own fakeness that revealed itself periodically.

People carried pseudo-smiles in their pockets, pulling them out in necessary times. Their smiles said all was well, even wonderful if stretched a bit. Did pictures show truth? Or some other thing?

I'd found an old black and white photo and decided the pose said what someone wanted others to see. A voice behind the camera sweetly said, "Say cheese or smile." The character behind the lens produced a replica. One Easter, when my siblings and I first had new clothes, Mama's mother—the other grandmother we never knew or very rarely knew—had lovingly coaxed us to smile. Responsively and obediently, we did. Click, click, click went her camera.

My smiles always looked fake and plastered on my school photos—with lower teeth slid sideways—and always askew. Teeth not knowing which way to go. Not knowing if it was safe to smile. Not knowing why my face felt lopsided, why I felt lopsided, inside-out and upside-down. Pain with curved lips painted on it was what a smile really was.

I studied the faded, graying, crinkled photograph and pondered the surfaces of those people back then—my siblings and my lonely self—my eyes searching beneath the sheepish grins. Not many, if any, photographs were taken of us before that day, except a few school pictures. Smiles were foreign, worn awkwardly at best. We feared that beatings might occur if a grin was taken the wrong way, misinterpreted. Was there any happiness at all? I strained to find a shred. I recalled how dreamily the holiday had begun, much like normal families I had fantasized about.

I studied my first new dress and recalled the filmy lavender layers. It was pretty, though not as frilly as Ginny's. Excitedly, I'd unwrapped white tissue paper and pulled it out of the large Globeman's box, in utter disbelief. I thought I had died and gone to heaven.

It was so beautiful. Confused and fearful, I didn't know how to accept the dress—so out of the ordinary. Uncomfortable good feelings were concealed by a vague uneasiness. I stood waiting for the net to trap me, for the shoe to fall.

Like statues we'd posed on green, freshly mowed grass as the picture was taken. A lawn manicured by a rotary push mower, an arduous job recently done by our maternal grandfather. Tall pecan trees waved green leaves above our heads, like fingers.

I was the oldest, never as pretty as Ginny. My straight hair was pulled backwards into a ponytail, and I stood between the other two, holding their hands. Always mothering them. I recalled how I'd just found a fresh dandelion puff and blown it into the air, minutes before the camera snapped. An unrestricted feeling had come upon me as the fluffy, air-driven seeds scattered gently from the stem.

I felt a deep ache as I looked at the image of my sister, Ginny, so beautiful with her curly, golden locks of hair topped with a pretty yellow bow. Her fluffy see-through, buttery-layered dress made her blossom much like a spring daffodil. Almost like the ones blooming in succinct rows alongside the lawn. Her sweet blue eyes peered into the camera hesitantly. And to think that under that lovely surface, her heartache was the worst of all. I could hardly bear to think of her.

My eyes moved to Danny's image. I had adored my little brother from the beginning. Though the picture was black and white, I could still see his red hair, fair skin, and the sweetest freckles sprinkled across his stubby little nose. In the snapshot, his adorable face was turned upward, looking at me. Perhaps he was uncertain about the smile and needed my reassurance. Maybe he just looked up to me as his big sister, like a mother to him.

He had little blue shorts, a little pink and black plaid coat, and a white shirt. A tiny bowtie matched his coat. A plastic black knife pointed down from his right hand. My heart lunged as the memory began pressuring my chest. I realized how much my baby brother had suffered at the hands of our father.

A cotton ball was stuffed into his right ear canal. Years of untreated infection had finally penetrated the bone. Osteomyelitis, a bone infection, had developed, and could have been deadly. A brain infection or abscess could have occurred. But he was left with "only" deafness. A cruel, devastating deafness.

I cringed and seethed inside, seeing him so tiny and innocent. So humble and sweet-looking in the photograph. I remembered the horrible pain he had suffered that Easter with his awful infection, though he grinned sheepishly for the camera.

Danny had been forced to work like a man at a tender child's age. I had always grieved over the loss of his and Ginny's childhoods, more than my own. I would never stop questioning how loving parents could allow a little child like sweet Danny to suffer with such pain and not address it.

A memory of Daddy's humorless joke came to me. Before the picture was taken, he had babbled a joke to our maternal grandparents in the kitchen, where we'd gathered for an Easter meal. I had sensed palpable tension. Everyone's lips had curled upward when Daddy told the joke. Every person chuckled with fabricated laughs and puzzled looks.

"What's funny?" I had said. Even as a child, I had picked up on a weird, tinny mirth. No one else had gotten his jokes either. Their amusement was phony, like the photographic image.

The ride home from our false Easter celebration ended in rotten reality. The show was over. Our grandmother's delicious fried chicken, mashed potatoes, and hot biscuits were gone. Ended were the Easter egg hunts, hugs, and safe feelings. It was all an act. It always was.

On the ride home, Daddy taunted Danny with promises of a pony. Daddy knew he loved animals, especially ponies. Daddy would point and say, "There's a pony. If I could jus' see it, I'd stop and get it for ya." He'd hee-haw his head off as Danny struggled to turn Daddy's head from the back seat, an effort to show him the pony. None of the rest of us thought it was funny.

The car finally slowed down, but not for Danny's sake. Other cars were lined up by the beer joint, neon lights glowing like signals. I knew what was coming. I could still hear the dreaded gravel crunch under the tires as the vehicle slowed, then stopped. Daddy's footsteps drudged rocks, headed for the door.

Not again, I thought.

"I thought today would be different. How long will he be this time?" I asked Mama.

"Not long," Mama replied. I sat back, stroking Danny's hair as he laid in my lap in the back seat, weeping, snubbing nonstop from ear pain, and no pony again.

"But what about Danny's ear? Can't we please take him to the doctor?" I asked Mama, again.

"We'll see," she responded. But I knew they wouldn't. He'd just suffer. Green and yellow puss had been draining from it for weeks. What would it take to make my parents see that he needed help?

We had sat there huddled for hours before Daddy stumbled back to the car, starting the pony story all over again.

I studied the long-ago black-and-white, my mind sadly wandering into my childhood's painful quagmire as I puddled through unanswered questions. So many questions surfaced from this one portrayal, and I was thankful not to have more pictures taken for that very reason.

Why would our parents conjointly buy new clothes for us when we had never had any before? Why would they spend money for clothes instead of a doctor's visit for poor Danny?

Why was alcohol more important than anything else? Why would Mama say, "We'll see," and never see? Why did we wear false expressions and pretend all was well when all was hell? Why did our parents destroy their own children's lives? Those were the questions the Easter print brought to me. And although the images were imprinted forever in my mind, time had at least healed some wounds. We had lost our beautiful Ginny, but Danny was still trying.

He had been left to fend for himself but chose to stay by Mama's side, working as a brick mason, slaving his life away for wages that never met his needs. Hard, harsh labor that humped his back and crippled his knees and hands with pain. Pain that required the relief of a beer once in a while, then more. Then more. Then more. But he did stay by Mama's side, helping her survive. They continued to live on the wrong side of the tracks, the same tracks that took the lives of Ginny and Uncle John.

58

Illiterate

As Granny Isabelle would have said, "Life is a hard row to hoe." Most people would have quit trying a long time ago. Why I didn't fall into the abyss, or stay on the wrong side of the tracks with my family, was beyond comprehension. A force kept pushing me forward, one foot in front of the other.

Who would walk through the halls of high school kids, pregnant as a cow, for nothing more than a diploma? Who would cram classes and work hours together, grabbing for some invisible stars? Who would work for eight years on a piecemeal bachelor's degree in psychology?

What woman could raise two little kids without any child support, and little family support, self-determined against the odds?

Finally, I settled comfortably in a grand old university setting of 10,000 students. Inadequate feelings lessened as I wrote essays, paper after paper, doing my best and getting straight A's.

Only once did a composition come back scrawled with a large word, "illiterate," raked across the top in red. A word I had pursued endlessly to erase from my life. "Illiterate." The cruel letters probed my core. I had delved into all available resources, determined to do a good research paper, and yet it came back cursed in red.

It wasn't quite the same as being called a lying cheat, but it hit the same vulnerable spot. I wallowed about in self-pity for days, thinking maybe it was true, that there was no use trying. That I really was hopeless. Then I became indignant, realizing I didn't have to allow someone to rub my legs behind the desk anymore or trod on my back.

I determined that I would speak out. I wrote a letter to the dean, including a copy of my research paper. The professor was gone within a few weeks. I knew I would never be a victim again. I had a voice and, by golly, I would use it. I would defend myself when the need arose and others as well if presented the task.

I gained assertiveness and culture in the nation's capital. Experiencing culture was delicious to my depleted soul.

The Kennedy Center drew me to endless social events. What utter delight danced in my soul with each play I saw and each musical I heard. It was a generous gift often given to me by a dear friend who hosted at the magnificent center of arts.

It was then that I was admitted to another prestigious university while working a full-time nursing job. Continuing work, I also acquired a master's degree. Determining to overcome all obstacles, I participated in personal counseling sessions and devoured rows of self-help books and, somehow, learned to love myself. My confidence increased.

I had learned that I wasn't illiterate and I wasn't worthless and, yes, that I could peel an onion and hoe a garden, and if I wanted I could pour crap out of a boot. But I would leave that boot thing up to the abusers. My life was filled with miracles: against all odds I grew into a vocal, visible entity—a real woman with a voice.

Against all odds, I crossed the deep, dark abyss and stepped over nightmarish screams and wails of familial opposition. Through faith I made it through the needle's eye, leaving pain behind like shredded rags. Much more good was gained as a new hope and joy and peace lay ahead.

My legacy was now filled with truth and hope. Yes, divorce from Johnnie caused horrendous pain not recommended for anyone, but I moved forward as family cried out for me to stay the same. "What are ya tryin' to prove?" some said. But my soul screamed to learn from books, from musicals and play, and from places I'd never been.

Not knowing or having an answer back then, I didn't respond or try to prove anything. I only knew it would take an education to get my head above the murky waters and raise two children. That was all I knew.

I was a small woman who had set out to prove that I could be anything I was born to be if I tried and never gave up. Folks like me had bad hands dealt to them in life and had to go the long way around to get to where they had belonged in the first place. That's what Granny Isabelle would have said.

Years later I sat in the warm summer's night, watching stars shoot towards me, knowing Granny Isabelle would have been so proud. Nestled, enfolded within my gentle husband's arms, my heart blissful, I looked up at the navy, blackened sky and watched fireflies dance to the singing of whip-poor-wills and bobwhites. Me and my soulmate sitting happily, blanketed on a Blue Ridge hillside full of rhododendron and mountain laurel with scents of honeysuckle in full bloom. A great meadow of buttercups littering the land, with winding creeks and cold-water springs running through it. It seemed like the hand of God had poured a handful of stars downward just for us to see as a dove cooed in the darkness.

Stars lit the heavens and sprinkled down on our little part of the earth, bringing unfathomable delight. Fireflies darted, males attracting females, in front of the navy-black canopy of trees below and beyond us as the water gurgled in distant creeks. It was as if our toes could touch the water's edge in our mind's eye.

59

Princess, Granny, and Me

Granny Isabelle would have been so proud of me. She would have thrown that paper bag hat into the hallelujah air and danced a gleeful jig. Country church bells would toll every day in celebration over my victories large and small. I threaded the needle.

Uninhibited, reclaiming my lost adolescence, I happily drove Princess, my white convertible, all over the place. Ray Bans perched upon the bridge of my nose, some wild blond, perfumed curls flung about my face as half a ponytail protruded through my Carolina blue cap; I drove on, traveling numerous miles with the top down. Princess was a looker. Like a Christmas tree, she gleamed and sparkled in the capitol's night lights when I went to purchase her.

Topless, Princess voyaged during the cold winter days, heater blasting wide open, over the winding bridges that covered the Potomac and in the capitol's square. We circled DuPont Circle a hundred times, doing 65 mph just because.

I loved the feel of wind as it blew wild puffs through my hair while the radio thumped Motown tunes deep into my chest like drums. Sometimes, I held a lit slim menthol Capri cigarette between my daintily painted fingertips, mostly to signal to the world that I could do it if I wanted to. I guess it was one way I proved that I could crawl out from under a rock. We do things like that when we've been beaten down and held hostage by fate's cruelty.

I grinned and gloried in stares from people who didn't understand this newfound freedom I felt in my soul with Princess—basking in her soft leather bucket seats. They cradled my behind through some uncertain years as I learned to crawl and then walk and run into womanhood.

From a young age, I had determined to have a different life from my family, and I became resolute to get out of the bad situation I was born into. I would heal myself. I struggled through pages of learned books for degrees, magic self-help books, social groups, therapist chairs, and stacks of long-hand journals—yet there was more to it than that. Life could be more.

I returned to Virginia with a case of the jitters. Emotionally, I wobbled in indecision over moving back. But I knew how to make lots of decisions all by myself. Things like how to get an education, to marry and divorce, to play the stock market a little, to buy and sell houses and cars, and to reject and take great job positions.

However, the choice to return home was the hardest of all. No doubt, I would have to let go of my new world. Would I drown? Would I lose myself? Would I find myself again if I did?

So what would possess me to return to a pus-pocket, pain-filled place? Why did I need to search through ancient relics and torn, shady pages of dusty memories? Why was I willing to risk my good life to find a light speck somewhere in the shadows and darkness?

It was as if an invisible force, like a predestined hook in my jaw, drew me back home, like a spell or die had been cast. The strong need to belong with family pulled me back to where my embryonic self originated. Whether I wanted to or not, I couldn't help it.

Granny Isabelle's grave called me. I never really knew her. But didn't I? I did not beg to know her great secrets of life, her heartbreaks, who she was or where she had come from. But as a child I read lots about her from her tired eyes, her withered face, her wounded soul, and her hunched-over shoulders. Some folks say kids don't see and know a lot about what goes on around them, but they do. They know bunches.

She had died when I was sixteen. I sat in the living room as she took her leave. The sound of large wings fluttering turned my face toward hers at 8:35 pm. Her body laid the same. Not a finger had changed positions. I knew then that angels existed. They had taken her away to rest. Numb, I went on like nothing had ever happened.

Not many weeks later, still newly married to Johnnie, I was lost and alone without Granny Isabelle, without a clue about life. My adolescent husband was headed to find himself not long after the vows were pledged at the JP's office and our two children were born. He had died an early death from alcoholism and bad decisions. Looking back, I didn't blame him; we were just kids. From day one, the writing was on the wall.

With regret, I wished I had really known my sagacious grandmother, Granny Isabelle, better than I did. I wished I had hungered for her wisdom, her preaching, rather than shrugging it off so childishly. Yet I was nothing but a child. Now, I just filled in pieces like a puzzle and added my own historical condiments, so to speak. I guess I came to take back what had been stolen from my life. A discarded shameful identity I had purposefully let go of.

I had to see her. I scrunched the brake and stopped Princess. With one foot still in the car, the other crunched on gravel as I looked down the grassy knoll; with a hand I shaded my eyes from the sun as I had seen her do many times over our years together among the corn rows.

Down rows of sunken graves at the Spring Garden cemetery, my eyes scanned. Most were decorated with ugly, scattered, faded fake flowers. Some had unstuck from the ground and bobbed and floated about on tuffs of wind as my eyes searched for Granny Isabelle.

Like a troubled inspector, my mind tallied through the graves. I had no idea where her chalky bones lay. I didn't know how to find her as hundreds of dead people's stones poked up from the earth like hats and stared blankly back at my face.

Then something surreal occurred. My family name came into view from way down the hill. It was impossible to see the name with the naked eye. As if magnetized, my feet took off running toward the patch of gray stonework. I hunted through various large monuments, lambs, angels, and markers. Unprepared, I stumbled upon the tragic grave of Ginny and her baby. Memories of my beautiful, golden-headed sister poured over me, and I wept as pain seeped from my heart for her lost life and for the tiny infant who had barely lived at all.

When I felt spent, I stood up and looked around. I knew Granny was close by, but I couldn't find her no matter how hard I looked. I was ready to give up when my toe stubbed on an insignificant brass plaque. I lifted my troubled foot and read aloud, "Isabelle."

"There you are, Granny Isabelle," I whispered. On my knees I sighed, sank down, and scratched crabgrass off the edges of her head. Rubbing gingerly, I patted my hands over her earthy bones. "You should have had a monument, but this is all you get for your life, Granny." For the first time, I wept over her sad life, posterity, and because she had left me behind.

I pleaded, "Help me peel the onions of my life, Granny Isabelle."

"Sometimes life is like an onion," she'd say. "You can take a layer off here and there, and look what's underneath, but it is still just an onion, no matter what caused it to be a shape or how it grew to be what it is."

Many thunderstorms had come into Granny Isabelle's life from the time of her conception until she drew her final breath. She was an illegitimate child, raised by her poor blind mother. That's what others had told me.

Only one hope could have saved her from the poverty-stricken life. She had fallen in love with a rich man, and he loved her. I was told this by her relatives years after I had left home. Granny Isabelle's mother believed her daughter should not marry above her raising. Obeying her parent, she didn't.

Later, Papa Harkus brought his impotent life and mingled it with hers. They married and left her sightless mama, and with little else left behind they went on to live in a string of worthless shanties throughout Virginia's mountains until Granny Isabelle built the three-room house with Daddy's help and her onion money.

So I came back home to search haggard and dead faces of those I had left behind, because I had to. They mirrored myself. I scrutinized remnants of houses and schools that grew me up and the overgrown dirt yards I'd once rode stick horses upon, where I had picked fleas off of pets and made mud pies with my pitiful siblings. Worn-out garden spots had replaced my haven of tall green corn rows where I had watched silver threads sew the sky together. Sadness covered me like waves.

Wounded, caved in, I wept again, as would any broken child, while scanning the present uncontaminated, wooded area. Woodlands that once served as a haven from screaming bullets and as a backyard family toilet, which bred maggots and green flies by the hordes in piles of human dung. The same forest obliged as a tenuous girl's hideaway for Ginny's cutting and smoking, momentarily releasing her vicious pains. This same area had functioned as a make-believe sanctuary where fairies lived amongst corn rows. The once tormented land now stood as a clean, worthwhile community sport's center.

I hunted for pieces of my life's story through old things like left-behind wrinkled faces, dusty Bibles, scraps of sepia and black and white photographs, obituaries, grave headstones, and cheapened epitaphs. Oh, where was the comfort in these sad stories? Like ghosts with stinky trinkets, they taunted me. I thrashed about for justification in a cesspool of doing and undoing, trying to make sense of it all.

268

Like a spy I pried, poked, and prodded into minds of unsuspecting old neighbors and relatives who knew our family secrets. I begged them to open lockboxes with proffered keys and clues of forbidden bits and pieces, but the ancient onlookers held their stories tight with clenched hands and just wanted to "let sleeping dogs lie."

Dementia feigned as their eyes and ears went far away from me and my questions. They clutched and snuggled memories close to their bosoms as if they were important heirlooms never to be parted with. Ashen faces focused blank stares at cobwebs on the wall or dirt grains on the floor, speechless.

I watched old bony legs squirm like worms on hot coals and hands tremble. Fidgety fingers pulled at threads on the frayed edges of crocheted doilies or handmade throw pillows as treason twisted their insides out. It was a sin to speak. So I learned to let it be and ask nothing more.

I had returned to this place. Once illiterate, but not now. Once ignorant, but not anymore. I had groomed myself through universities; yet I hungered for something deep inside the caverns of my soul. I never wanted to come back to this land of poverty, strife, and odd spiritual stench. I said as much, time and again. "Oh dear God, where am I? Why am I here?"

Often, I had longed to beat square pegs into round holes and make us fit into one big happy family, but people can't be forced. I had to choose my real self repeatedly. I don't think we ever let go of the roots of our lives, our history. They are sensitive and specific. Maybe that's what Granny Isabelle meant. Without them, we'd blow away in the winds of time like a vapor.

Granny Isabelle's words breathed on me periodically, and those wonderful memories illumined beyond her world of onions. I knew of Uncle John's love through her, although he had died long before I was born. Granny Isabelle etched her son's love story into my mind like written pages as she showed me his love of Christ without speaking of his death. She told me about him as we sat together at the end of the days, by the flickers of her smoked-up kerosene lamp. I only had bits and pieces of her beloved son's death through hearsay. Perhaps her pain over John would have come alive and tormented her if she had talked about how he died. I don't know. It was just the way it was.

She imparted to me what she felt was most important: that no matter what darkness you go through, love will help you. That evil does live in a world of good, but we are responsible to help protect others, and ourselves, as much as possible and let God do the rest.

She taught me that if we listen, love and enlightenment will come in a variety of forms. Perhaps through a love note, or a touch, or the voice of a lonesome dove, or the hoot of a wise, ancient hoot owl. Or the flapping of angel wings when a loved one goes to the other side. If we heed it, the supernatural is all around to help us thread the needle.

Maybe Uncle John's light would have helped me. I don't know. For the life of me, I don't think he had a chance, not with the father and brothers he had. Maybe it was better, after all, for him to go on across the abyss. Who could know? Like Granny Isabelle said, "Play the cards you're given and play them well." And so I did.

Acknowledgments

I especially want to acknowledge Thomas Crowe. Thomas, a beautiful human being, took the time to read my work, latching on to it like a bulldog as he urged me onward. There are no words to relate how valuable Thomas has been in facilitating this book into the public arena. Without Thomas, there may not have been a book called *Through the Needle's Eye*.

My precious friend: Shirley Sparr, earth mother, who has always believed I could move mountains; Connie, Eileen, Phyllis, Debbie, Anne, and Jennifer who have waited patiently for "the book" to be birthed; Tom, George, and Mary, true friends who have encouraged me to be true to myself.

The dedicated staff of Mercer University Press, for giving my work a chance and hanging with me, challenging me toward a work of art.

My loved ones who have laughed and cried with me over the hard years and have listened to seemingly endless chapters as I droned on and on.

Aubrey, my dear husband, for his brave support through each chapter that was rendered with tears. His great faith in me was never-ending.

My daughter, Melissa Faye, who proofed, typed, and re-typed each word, and came to know me through the chapters that passed before her, always saying, "It'll be okay, Mom." Her joy at my accomplishment has been contagious.

Chad, my son-in-law, who whooped for joy when this work won the Mercer University Press Ferrol Sams Award for Fiction and never doubted that *Through the Needle's Eye* would be published.

Timothy James, my son, who has had pride in me and is so happy over this book. Another chapter of our lives together has unfolded. Your remarkable creative spirit amazes me.

Christy, Aaron, Eric, Lacey, and Cameron, who have delighted in this venture.

To my parents because without them there would be an untold story.

All of my grandchildren: Joshua Cameron, Zachary Taylor, T.J., Brandie Leigh, Matthew Ryan, Hannah Elizabeth, Owen Connor, Andrew Barrett, as bits and pieces of each of their personalities can be seen woven throughout the pages.

My great-grandchildren, Mason Jacob, A.J., and Levi.

To all friends, especially Jana and Barbara who have woven their wonderful personalities with mine in the past. Thank you partners of a life's story.